D0205007

Louisiana BRIDES

Three Young Women's Hearts Are Rooted in the Bayou

KATHLEEN Y'BARBO

BARBOUR
PUBLISHING

Bayou Fever © 2004 by Kathleen Y'Barbo
Bayou Beginnings © 2005 by Kathleen Y'Barbo
Bayou Secrets © 2006 by Kathleen Y'Barbo

ISBN 978-1-59789-628-3

All rights reserved. No part of this publication may be reproduced or transmitted in any form or by any means without written permission of the publisher.

Scripture quotations are taken from the King James Version of the Bible.

This book is a work of fiction. Names, characters, places, and incidents are either products of the author's imagination or used fictitiously. Any similarity to actual people, organizations, and/or events is purely coincidental.

Cover image © James Randklev/Getty Images

Published by Barbour Publishing, Inc., P.O. Box 719, Uhrichsville, Ohio 44683, www.barbourbooks.com

Our mission is to publish and distribute inspirational products offering exceptional value and biblical encouragement to the masses.

Printed in the United States of America.

Bonsior Mes Amis,

I didn't grow up in Louisiana, but you could just about see it from where I lived. In fact, there were so many transplanted Acadians in our area that the city of Port Neches, Texas, held a Crawfish Festival every spring for many years. I counted among my friends and neighbors people with last names such as Delcambre, Gallier, Champagne, Hebert, and Thibodeaux, among others, and my mother made shrimp gumbo more often that other folks made fried chicken or meatloaf.

Later, as newlywed, I spent four years in Broussard, Louisiana—the heart of Cajun Country—so the soft cadence of "Cajun-speak" is as familiar to me as my own Texas twang. When it came time to "hear" the voices of the Trahans and the Breauxs I did not have to guess how they would sound. I'd not only "heard" them, but I felt I already knew them. During those years, I learned that the Acadian people are warm and fun-loving, always ready with a smile or a quick *"Comment ça va?"* They value family, faith, and a good bowl of shrimp gumbo on Sunday or a cast-iron pot of red beans and rice left to simmer all day on Monday. To be Cajun is to know a deep connection to the bayou, to a shared history, and to a people who thrive in the face of adversity.

As with any book, there are so many people involved besides the one named on the cover. First and foremost, without the direction of *Le Bon Dieu*, the heavenly Father, my words would be worth nothing. Second, I'd like to acknowledge my earthly father, Farris Miller, who did not live to see me write a book but believed in me all the same. There is much of him in Theo Breaux, and much of him in me. Thank you to my mother, Bonnie Miller, for making the weekly drive to the Gates Memorial Library that began my lifelong love of books. To Bubba, Robin, and Sue—the inspiration for the Breaux siblings—and to my Simpson and Aycock grandparents who showed me that family ties are forged not only with blood but also with permanently knotted strings of unconditional love.

Finally, the writers, aka the cheerleaders:

To the precious ladies of *Seared Hearts*, past and present; to Sharen Watson, Linda Kozar, and the wonderful *Words for the Journey-ers*; to Cathy and Kelly Hake; to Tracie Peterson; to Kim O'Brien; and to every sweet soul who lifted me in prayer during the writing of these stories I give you thanks! This book is proof that God listens.

It is my hope that you will enjoy your journey through the pages of this book, and that you will grow to love the stories and people of South Louisiana as much as I do. *Les le bon temps rouler!*

Kathleen Y'Barbo

Author's Note

Wherever possible, I have inserted a bit of the native language of the Louisiana Acadians. A spoken language rather than a written one, Cajun French—as the language is known—is a blend of proper French, African influences, Indian words, and local dialect. The language has been passed down by word of mouth over generations and thus can vary slightly from one community to the next among the bayou people. A dictionary of common Cajun French phrases has been provided below. Any mistake is mine alone.

Guide to Conversational Cajun French

Allons – Let's go
Arête – Stop
Bonjour – Good morning
Bonsoir – Good evening
Ça va bien, merci – I am fine, thank you
C'est moi – It's me
C'est tout – That's all
Cher – Dear or darling
Comment ça va? – How's it going?
Dieu te beni – God bless you
Je t'aime – I love you
Le bon Dieu – The good Lord
Les le bon temps rouler – Let the good times roll!
Madame – A married woman
Mademoiselle – An unmarried woman or girl
Merci – Thank you
Merci beaucoup – Thank you very much
Mes ami(s) – My friend(s)
Monsieur – A man
Pas du tout – Not at all
Quoi y'a – What's wrong?
Sa fini pas – It never ends
Sa te regard pas – It doesn't concern you
Vien ici – Come here

BAYOU BEGINNINGS

Dedication

To Mimi.
I know you would have loved a houseful of little ones just like Mama.
Well, maybe not *exactly* like Mama. . .
To Dana. Research diva and real live Trahan.
You are such a special gift from God.
Merci bien et Dieu te beni. Celebrate the beginnings. . . .
And to Janice Thompson, aka Janice the Magnificent,
who critiqued this manuscript faster than I wrote it. Long may you rule!
Finally, to my children, Josh and Andrew, who are Cajuns by birth,
and Jacob and Hannah, who are Texans for the same reason.
Like Cleo and Tante Flo, I *do* love my babies! You are *my* heroes!

Chapter 1

Latagnier, Louisiana, March 1904

Most days, the effort not to eavesdrop proved too much for Clothilde Trahan, especially when the pastor came to call. It was a sin, and she knew it, but the Lord *had* made her curious. Knowing the difference between inquisitive and nosy, however, was an ongoing project.

Then there was the problem of speaking her mind when good sense and proper raising told her she ought not. It did keep her busy, this effort to keep her ears and her mouth from causing her grief.

Just about the only time she stayed out of trouble was when she had her nose in one of Uncle Joe's or Tante Flo's books. Fortunately, her adopted parents—the childless brother and sister-in-law of her late father—valued a good book over almost anything except *the* Good Book. Quick to catch on, Cleo soon found books became the friends she would otherwise not have in this isolated area of the Bayou Nouvelle.

Funny thing. This time books just might be the cause of the problem.

"I declare, *mon ami*, it's a crying shame," she heard her uncle say. "There ought to be something we can do about it."

Cleo leaned closer to the parlor doors, keeping the dust rag moving along the cypress wainscoting in case Tante Flo might quietly wander down from her afternoon nap. For her uncle to close the parlor doors on a Tuesday afternoon meant something big was afoot. It also meant he didn't want her listening.

But to what?

"I agree with you, Joe. I can't tell you how many letters I've written, and nothing seems to come of it. The powers that be up in New Orleans, well, they got bigger fish to fry."

The reverend used his Sunday voice, the loud, insistent one that called for action rather than the softer thank-you-for-the-dinner-invitation version she generally heard outside the churchyard. Another reason for concern.

"Even if we could manage a way around the *how* of it, we'd still have to find a place to hold the classes. And then there's the problem of the teacher. Have you had any luck?"

"I sent a few letters," Uncle Joe said, "but so far there's been no one willing to quit a sure job teaching to come take a chance on a town with no schoolhouse and no money to pay a teacher."

Cleo let the rag hang limp in her hand. Realization dawned. The school. They were talking about it again.

For all the folks who called Latagnier home, there was much to recommend the little place. Good food and good friends, that's what bayou folks made. But for all the common sense the people of her adopted home held, few had the book learning to go along with it.

To be sure, Uncle Joe had been educated over in New Orleans, but he was one of the rare few. He'd met and married Tante Flo there and taken her from the schoolroom where she presided to the home where they still lived today.

No doubt in the beginning Tante had expected she would fill the rooms of this place with babies to make up for the children she'd turned over to another teacher at the end of the term. Instead, the cradles were never filled. Not once. At least not until Cleo came to live with them at the age of three.

But that was a story unto itself, fifteen years in the past and not worthy of consideration when an event such as the one going on behind the parlor doors was occurring.

Through the tiny crack in the sliding doors, Cleo could barely make out the shape of the pastor sitting beside the fireplace in the stiff horsehair chair. Gesturing while leaning forward, he reminded Cleo of the funny little praying mantis she had caught on the screen just yesterday.

Although she could not see him, she knew Uncle Joe would be across from him, probably perching his wiry self on the edge of the rosewood divan. Between them would be the remains of a plate of cookies alongside two of Tante Flo's teacups, a wedding gift from the New Orleans side of the family and brought out only on special occasions: Christmas, anniversaries, birthdays, and visits from Pastor Broussard. With Uncle Joe being an elder, the pastor's visits were the most common.

Cleo let the pretense and the rag drop. "Of course. The teacups." She smiled and bustled toward the summer kitchen to put water on to boil. Where were her manners?

An eternity later, the big pot had boiled, and she wrapped a thick towel around its handle and headed for the parlor. "More tea," she said as she pushed the doors aside and barged in. Avoiding Uncle Joe's gaze, she centered her efforts on acting like the hostess Tante Flo had trained her to be. "Bonjour, Pastor Broussard. Sugar?" she asked as she set the tray aside and poured steaming water into the pot.

"Bonjour, Mademoiselle Trahan."

"Clothilde," Uncle Joe said.

One word. Many meanings. None good. She braved a look. Did she detect a smile?

"I wondered when you'd find a way in here. I'm sure the wall outside the door shines like a new penny."

Cleo felt the color rise in her cheeks. "Why, Uncle Joe, whatever are you talking about? I'm just doing my chores like Tante Flo asked."

"The Lord loves a busy body," the reverend said. "And that's two words, not one."

"Yes, sir," she said softly.

Uncle Joe settled back on the divan and grinned. "Remind me to tell Flo there's more to dusting the hallway than just that little section beside the parlor door she told you to concentrate on." He winked at Cleo. "Now along with you, *cher.* The reverend and I have business to conduct."

"Oui," she said under her breath, all the while wishing she had the gall to plop down on the divan beside her uncle and tell them exactly how they could solve the problem of finding a place for the local schoolhouse.

She took her time collecting the items to take back to the kitchen. Just when she thought the men would never resume their conversation, the pastor set down his teacup. "I declare, Joe, we're in the business of saving souls, but we ought to do something for them while they're waiting for Glory, don't you think?"

Cleo gathered up the tray and pretended to study the door. She walked as slowly as she could, but still she traversed the distance far too quickly.

"I agree," Uncle Joe said. "But even if we could find a place to hold classes until we raise the money for a decent schoolhouse, who in the world would we get to teach the children?"

The old building in the corner of the property, she longed to say. *Fix it and fill it with children, and I'll teach them.* Instead, she clamped down on her tongue, tucked the tray under her arm, and shoved open the parlor doors.

"Clothilde Trahan, *vien ici.* Where have you got off to?" Tante Flo's voice coiled through the room and made Cleo cringe. Her aunt would have her hide for sure if she found her bothering the menfolk.

"Coming." Cleo failed to reach the hallway before Tante Flo barged through, nearly upsetting the pot of hot water. Tiny in stature but with a smile that radiated larger-than-life love, Cleo's aunt now wore just the opposite—an uncharacteristic frown. "What have you been up to, child?"

"Flo, come on in here and say hello to Pastor!" Uncle Joe called. Tante Flo turned to offer Uncle Joe and the reverend a greeting, then cast a glance back at Cleo. Her smile had nearly returned. Nearly, but not quite. "You get along with yourself now and leave the men be."

Cleo looked past her aunt to the men who watched the exchange with amused faces. "Pleasure to see you again, sir," she said to the pastor.

"Flo, you were a teacher once," Cleo heard the reverend say as she stepped into the hall. "Joe and I were just discussing the problem we're having finding someone to take on the teaching of the children once we get ourselves a building."

Carefully setting the pan of water on the sideboard, Cleo tiptoed back to the hallway. She'd been giving the problem of the local school much thought on her morning walks to the bayou, and just last week she'd come upon what she thought might be the perfect solution. If only she could find a way of telling Uncle Joe besides just barging in and stating her case.

"Oh, I just couldn't." Cleo leaned out of her hiding place to see Tante Flo sitting next to Uncle Joe on the divan.

"It's just not done, Joe. *Pas du tout,*" Tante Flo said, shaking her head. "I'm a married woman, and I haven't seen the inside of a schoolhouse in nigh on twenty years. I can't teach those children. Besides, we don't even have money for a place yet."

"Oh, we've got a little bit saved. Enough to get things started," the pastor said. "The rest'll come. I just know it will."

Uncle Joe clutched his wife's hand. "The reverend and I are believing the Lord for both a teacher and a place to teach. The need is so great, what with all these young'uns coming up. I just know He will bring someone forward who has the answers."

"I have the answers." Cleo pressed her fingers to her mouth and felt the heat rise in her cheeks. Had she actually spoken the words aloud?

"Clothilde Trahan," Tante Flo said. "Are you eavesdropping again?"

Cleo stood stock-still. What to say?

"Vien ici, young lady."

Come here? Uh-oh. Uncle Joe's firm voice. Cleo tried to convince her feet to either flee or obey but found them as stuck as if she were up to her knees in bayou mud.

Her gaze first met Tante Flo's, then locked with her uncle's. Neither looked pleased.

"I'm sorry," she mumbled. "I'll just go on back to the kitchen."

"Come here, child," the reverend said. She shifted her attention to him. At least he wore a smile. "I would like to hear what Clothilde has to say. What plan have you brought us? Will you be telling us how to build our schoolhouse or where to find a teacher?"

Rather than attempt to move, Cleo lowered her eyes and studied the roses on the carpet. "Actually, sir, I may have the solution to both."

She watched their faces as she let the long-pent-up words spill forth. When she'd finished detailing all the fine attributes of the run-down cottage at the edge of her uncle's property, she said a little prayer and plunged forward with the finest idea of all.

"And I will be the teacher."

Cleo clamped her mouth shut, then paused to offer a weak smile. The silence in the room roared louder than last summer's Fourth of July tornado. Did they sit in stunned silence at the audacity of the plan, or had her idea been such a good one that they needed a moment to wrap their minds around it?

The pastor leaned forward to rest bony elbows on bonier knees. Neither Tante Flo nor Uncle Joe moved a muscle.

Outside the parlor window, a crow cackled, then swooped toward Tante Flo's vegetable garden. The bird had become the first to laugh at her plan but obviously would not be the last.

"You know, Joe," the reverend said, "Clothilde just might have something there."

Cleo let out the breath she'd been holding. She shifted her gaze to her aunt and uncle.

"You think so, Reverend?" Uncle Joe cast a sideways glance at Tante Flo. "We always said we'd fix that old place up or let it be torn down, one or the other, but I never got to it."

Tante Flo nodded. "Nothing but a home for mice and the occasional cottonmouth. Do you think it's worth fixing, Joe? I mean, we don't want the children in a building that's going to fall down around their precious heads."

"The old place is as sound as it gets. My granddaddy's daddy built it to last. Not even old General Sherman could tear it down. It wouldn't take half the money we've set aside to turn it into a proper schoolhouse." Uncle Joe hit his knees with his fists. "You know, Pastor, I think my girl just might have something here."

He rested his head in his hands as if in prayer, then lifted his gaze to smile at Uncle Joe. "I do believe she might."

A moment later, the men were embroiled in animated conversation, each topping the other on the improvements that could be made to the modest cottage, until Uncle Joe shook his head. "You know, the only thing is, the men of the church, we're farmers and trappers. We've got the know-how to make this place shine, but we just don't have the time. It'll take an eternity to get all of this work done unless we hire the biggest part of it out."

"You're right, Joe," the reverend said. "And I believe I just might have the man for the job."

Chapter 2

Theophile Breaux leaned back against the porch rail and studied the moss-covered trees dotting the horizon. A chill wind blew across the porch and settled in his soul. All the while, birds chirped a rhythm old as the water flowing silently past the eastern edge of the Breaux property. Somewhere beyond the cypress and pines and the Bayou Nouvelle lay that big old world Theo loved so much.

Ever since he could remember, he'd been on a path leading out of town. He'd been knee high to a grasshopper when he first saw how hard his papa worked and how little he got for the hides he took to town. Way back then, Theo had made a promise to himself and the Lord.

Well, actually, it was more of a deal.

If Theo obeyed his mama and papa and did all the things the Good Book said, the Lord would give him a life free from toil and trials. So far, so good. He'd all but made good his escape, having been gone from the old home place the better part of three years before Papa slipped and fell on a patch of late-season ice.

Mama'd tracked Theo down through the big network of family spread across Louisiana and Texas. A telegram arrived on the doorstep of his rooming house in Houston just about the time Theo was thinking of saying good-bye to his Texas kin and heading north to Oklahoma or maybe up to Canada.

He smiled. Perhaps someday his travels would lead him to Grand Pre in Nova Scotia, the place his kin, the original Acadians, once called home.

Now wouldn't that be something? This old Cajun sitting pretty in the place where his great-great-great-granddaddy wasn't welcome.

His smile deepened and turned to a chuckle. Funny how he thought of himself as old. While he was the eldest of the bunch, he still had a few years to go before he would see thirty.

Off in the distance, the younger children played a game of some sort, and across the way, his sisters washed clothes in the bayou's rolling waters. Bessie beat one of Mama's white aprons on a rock, while Addie worked a pair of Papa's trousers across the rub board. Somewhere along the bayou, Alphonse and Pete checked the traps, and in the house, Lucy and Kate helped Mama strip the beds. In the summer kitchen, Alouise and Jeannine would be starting the gumbo that would simmer until suppertime.

Closing his eyes, he could see it all. The faces of his brothers and sisters eventually replaced by their children and their children's children, just as it had been in the centuries since government orders sent the Acadians spilling down the Mississippi into south Louisiana. Nothing had changed in the bayou, and it never would.

Sa fini pas. It never ends.

"By your age I'd been married to your mama for a coon's age and was raising a houseful of young'uns," Papa had told him over coffee just this morning. "Your time's a-comin', son.The Lord's about to let you meet your match."

"Must be your broke bone you feel it in," he'd joked. But standing here with the sounds of the bayou swirling around him, the joke fell flat. If he didn't get out of here soon, he just might fall into the same trap that bound Papa to the muddy land. Then what?

Theo turned up the collar of his heavy shirt and shifted from the shadows into the warmth of the sunshine. Foolishness, this idea he might get hung up here indefinitely. He and the Lord had a deal. The road had detoured for just a bit, but he'd soon be back on it. Daddy's broken leg was healing nicely, and Mama said he'd be back to trapping in no time.

The faster the better, to Theo's way of thinking, because he had plans. He loved his mama and daddy, but nothing set his teeth on edge worse than being stuck in a small place with a big number of relatives.

With one kinfolk shy of a dozen, the old house overflowed.

"Theo, you'll be back in time for supper?"

He turned to grin at his mother. Careworn yet wearing a smile, she stood in the doorway with a set of bed linens draped over one arm.

"Oui, Mama," he said. "I aim to see that place the reverend told me about, and then I'll head on back home. Don't 'spect it'll take more'n a few hours unless I get a mind to catch a fish or two."

She shook her head and clutched the bleached white sheets to her chest. "Fishing, that's a man's excuse for sittin' still. You tell the reverend he's overdue for a gumbo supper, and I aim to set an extra place this evenin'. If he's a mind t' join us, he knows he don't need no engraved invitation."

"I will." Mama wouldn't know an engraved invitation if it slapped her upside the head, but she sure liked to use that term. "Theophile, you know you can come home anytime you want. You don't need no engraved invitation." He'd asked her once if she had any idea what she was talking about. She'd responded with a comment about how sassy he'd become since he no longer lived under her roof, then stormed off.

He'd hoped to talk her and Papa into visiting him in Houston, but it never happened. There was always something that kept them stuck here. Well, when he got himself a little place up in Canada, he'd send them all train tickets.

Theo watched Mama climb the wooden steps leading from the front porch up into the attic space where the boys slept. Years ago, he'd offered to build an inside staircase. The old tax laws that forced the Acadians to get creative with their living spaces were no longer in force, making the outside stairway unnecessary. Still, Mama and Papa refused the change, preferring instead to go out on the porch in order to reach the upper half of the house.

One more example of how things never seemed to change on the bayou.

He turned east toward the Trahan place. Whatever the reverend had to show him, it ought to be more interesting than what went on around here.

Tromping through the marsh, he fell into his habit of conversing with the Lord. Generally a one-sided conversation with him doing all the talking and God doing all the listening, the prayer this afternoon involved Theo merely asking a single question—when his time in Latagnier would be done—and then waiting in silence for an answer.

"This is your home. It will never be done" came the soft reply.

Stopping short, Theo looked up toward the cornflower blue sky and squinted. "Lord, did I hear You right? I'm *never* leaving Latagnier? Well, I just don't think I'm gonna believe that."

He stomped his boots to shake off the remains of yesterday's walk through the muddy bayou's edge, then shielded his eyes from the sun. If only he could shield them from the Son, as well. That, Theo knew, was useless. The Lord saw everything; He just acted like He didn't sometimes.

Like now. Couldn't God see he wanted to be free of the life that broke his daddy's spirit and sent him to carrying an old man's load at a young man's age?

"What if the load is not a burden?"

Again the Father's voice teased his ears and pierced his heart. He'd never considered Papa might actually *like* the lot he'd been cast.

"What if I mean for you to carry the same load?"

"I won't do it, I tell You," he muttered. "I just can't."

"That you, Theo?" Rev. Broussard stood a hundred yards away, waving his arms.

"Oui, *c'est moi.*" Theo returned the greeting and stomped toward him. Where did a man go for an appeal when the Creator of the universe handed down a verdict he didn't like? Even the reverend wouldn't have an answer to that one.

He shook off the thought and plowed forward through the mucky ground until he hit the hard-packed earth. By that time, the reverend stood only a few yards away. "*Bonjour,* Reverend," he said as he closed the distance between them. *"Comment ça va?"*

"Things are going well, son. Thank you for asking." The reverend adjusted his hat, then shook Theo's hand. "Pleasure seeing you on a day besides Sunday. I'm glad you've chosen to stay here in Latagnier for a while."

This parson, different from others Theo had come across, had calluses that signaled a workingman's life. Like the rest of the men in Latagnier, he worked hard for his living, saving souls on Sunday and tilling the land the rest of the week.

"Well, not me," Theo said softly as he shoved his fists into his pockets and looked away.

"Excuse me?" the reverend asked.

Theo shook his head. "Nothing," he said as he turned his attention to the ramshackle pile of boards and windows gathering leaves—and most likely snakes—beside the little cabin. Many years ago, the structure had been someone's home, but now it sat empty and forgotten. "So this is the place you're thinking of turning into a schoolhouse, eh?"

The preacher nodded. "What do you think?"

His carpenter's eye told him there was hope in the little structure. His heart, however, said there was much more to life than staying as long as fixing up this place would take.

Chapter 3

Now don't you go bothering the menfolk, Clothilde Trahan. You hear?" Tante Flo stood at the back door, tiny hands on narrow hips. Her frown spoke more than her warning. "I want you to promise me."

"I promise." *I won't bother them. They'll never know I'm around.*

"Some folks, they can't help the way God made 'em. They just go on about their business without thinking what they're doing might be their downfall." Tante Flo shook her head. "Honey, I know you're curious, but you're also a lady, and a lady knows when to make herself scarce."

"I don't know what you're talking about." As Cleo said the words, she knew she could offer no proof. On the other hand, Tante Flo had caught her spying too many times to count.

Tante Flo placed her hand over Cleo's. "Someday you're gonna have a house full of young'uns, and at least one of 'em's gonna be just like you. More and more every day, you're becoming like your mama, God rest her precious soul."

Cleo looked into the eyes of the dear woman who'd raised her. "I am?"

"You are. Look just like her, too. If the fever hadn't taken her and your papa, well. . ." Tante Flo looked away. For a moment she seemed lost in memories. Then she straightened her shoulders and clapped her hands. "Enough of this foolishness. You and me, we got work to do. Allons! Get me plenty of eggs, then, chile. I've got to make pies enough for tomorrow's church social and Sunday dinner, too."

"Yes, ma'am." Cleo slipped her arm through the handle of the egg basket and turned in the direction of the henhouse. Uncle Joe hadn't exactly forbidden her to go out to the site where the men were meeting, and neither had Tante Flo. Her only promise had been the one she had just made, and to the best of her ability, she meant to keep her pledge.

Buster, Uncle Joe's ancient Catahoula cur dog, trotted over to wag his tail and sniff at the basket. "Nothing in here for you, Buster," she said. "But I could use some company. *Allons!* Come on, and let's go get Tante Flo some eggs for her pies."

Feeling her aunt's watchful eyes boring into her back, Cleo headed for the chicken house with the dog on her heels. The basket swung from her elbow and slapped against her side as she traveled the short distance to reach the henhouse door. Casting a glance over her shoulder, she saw Tante Flo still standing in the doorway.

"Well, I suppose I'm going to have to go inside," she said under her breath. The hound, nose to the ground, headed off in pursuit of some unknown quarry.

Cleo stepped inside the dank warmth of the henhouse and blinked to adjust her eyes to the dimness. The birds began to fuss and cluck as she went about the business of collecting the day's eggs as slowly as she could manage.

When she'd gathered the last egg, she cautiously pushed the door open and peered outside. No one stood nearby. Even the dog had disappeared.

She craned her neck to get a better look at the back door and the open windows along the back of the house. No sight of Tante Flo.

Cleo set the egg basket on the floor of the henhouse and darted toward the stand of trees shielding the bayou from sight. Once she slipped into the shadows of the thicket, it was a simple matter to stroll casually along the bank. If anyone saw her, she'd easily make the excuse that she'd followed the bayou where the bayou led, taking the fresh air on her daily stroll.

Funny how the bayou seemed to be leading right toward the prospective schoolhouse.

"I don't know, Reverend. It looks like we can save most of that wood if we. . ." The voice faded and disappeared as Cleo neared the site. The reverend and his carpenter friend must have gone inside the cabin to check things out.

No matter. She could wait. But first, perhaps she should make sure they truly were inside.

Cleo crept toward the cabin, being careful to keep out of sight of the lone window on the easternmost corner of the building. She moved slowly, a difficult thing for her, until she reached the side of the cabin. From that point, she began to make her way around the edge of the house, hoping to reach the front in time to see the men exit.

"I see what you mean," the reverend said from somewhere nearby. "What do you think, Joe?"

The window. Cleo looked up to see she stood directly beneath it. She cowered against the side of the house and tried not to breathe, all the while willing the men to move so she could do the same.

"Theo, if we were to take out that wall, would it hurt the integrity of the structure?"

The carpenter's rumbling voice answered in the affirmative. "But, Joe, if you'll look over here, I think it can be done this way. See what you think, eh?"

"You know," the reverend said, "I think Theo might just be on the right track."

All three voices moved away from the window and faded into silence. Leaning against the rough wood, Cleo expelled a long breath to still her racing heart.

She'd been spared the humiliation of being caught listening, but with the sounds of the men's voices drawing near once more, her reprieve was only a temporary solution. If she stayed in the clearing, she'd be found out for sure.

"Let me show the window casing on the back of the house," Uncle Joe said, his voice too near for comfort. "Vien ici."

Casting a glance over her shoulder, she realized the only way to leave was to go the same way she came. Saying a quick prayer, Cleo darted toward the thicket and dove into the stand of pines. She landed with a thud in a pile of pine needles, then rolled over and lay facedown. Peering up, she held her breath while three sets of male legs filed past just a few yards away.

A mosquito buzzed past her ears, and no matter how hard she tried, Cleo couldn't get rid of the pesky thing. Swatting it was out of the question—too loud—and enduring it for five more minutes was more than she could consider. Thankfully, none of the other bayou creatures had joined her—yet.

As she watched the backs of the men, heads bent in conversation over a paper the reverend held, Cleo's mind began to conjure up all the possibilities for animal and reptile companions. Behind her, the pine straw rustled, while overhead a black crow screeched, seemingly determined to give away her hiding space.

She had to do something.

Cleo inched closer to the clearing, where the reverend stood side by side with the stranger. He was a tall man, this Acadian whom the reverend had chosen to do the cabin repairs. Dark arms emerged from beneath rolled-up shirtsleeves, proclaiming him a man who'd spent time in the sun.

Uncle Joe said he was a Breaux, the oldest of the bunch and the only one who no longer lived on the bayou. Cleo closed her eyes, trying to remember him, then opened them quickly when the mosquito struck again.

From her hiding place in the thicket, she could barely make out the top of the fellow's dark head as he disappeared behind the structure with the pastor on his heels.

"Hey there, Joe," she heard the reverend call. A muted response drifted her way. So did a familiar bark.

Oh no.

Suppressing a groan, Cleo gathered her skirts around her legs and crouched lower. She tried to force herself to breathe slowly, but the effort made her dizzy. If Uncle Joe caught her eavesdropping again, she'd surely end up riling him. The last thing she needed in her campaign to be chosen as the first teacher of the new school was to upset one of the men who would be doing the choosing.

Another bark, this one closer.

Buster.

Cleo suppressed a groan and gathered her skirt and apron close beneath her. Wouldn't you know the dog with the greatest tracking sense in the parish would show up now?

Uncle Joe called the hound by name, then knelt as the Catahoula cur bounded into the clearing. Unfortunately, Buster did not head toward Uncle Joe but rather stopped abruptly a few yards away, then turned in her direction.

Nose to the ground, he made short work of crossing the distance to where Cleo cowered in the thicket. "Go away," she whispered. "Allons! Get out of here."

"What you got there, Buster?" Uncle Joe called, his voice coming closer. "You got a rabbit?"

"A nosy rabbit. Now go on," she said under her breath as she slid farther back into her hiding place and laid her head on the blanket of pine needles. Again the mosquito buzzed past her ear, but she dared not swat it.

The dog continued to press his way through the thick branches to bury his wet nose in the top of Cleo's head. His whimper turned into a full-fledged bark.

"Here now, Buster!" Uncle Joe called. "Vien ici. Leave that little rabbit alone."

Buster hesitated and barked once more. Cleo lifted her head and swatted his nose, sending him running. She inched forward a bit to watch him launch himself at Uncle Joe.

"Did it get you, boy?" Uncle Joe knelt to ruffle the dog's ears. "You want me to go catch him and put him in the stew pot?"

Cleo sucked in a deep breath and held it until Uncle Joe stood and turned away. In one quick motion, she let out her breath and swatted the mosquito.

Uncle Joe stopped in his tracks and whirled around. He peered in the direction of Cleo's hiding place, then shook his head and motioned to Buster. "Allons, hound dog. You and me got some work to do back at the house. You coming, men?"

The reverend nodded and joined Uncle Joe, but the Breaux fellow motioned them away. "I believe I'll stay here a bit longer if you don't mind."

Uncle Joe smiled. "All right, but before we go, I need to know if you'll change your mind about taking payment for this, Theo. It's not right you doing all that work for nothing."

The Breaux fellow stepped into Cleo's view. *Oh my. He* did *turn out to be quite handsome. And tall, too.* When he looked over in the direction of the thicket, her heart skipped, only in part from fear of being discovered.

The carpenter said something, then turned and headed back toward the cabin, disappearing inside. Cleo plucked a piece of pine straw from her hair and wished for a comb. "What am I thinking? I won't be meeting him today. He can't know I've been spying."

Did she say spying? Well, actually, she'd been. . .the truth was, she'd actually wanted to. . .see, she just needed to know. . .

Cleo sighed. She'd been spying, all right. The reverend was right. God loved a busy body but not a busybody.

She sat back in her hiding space and tucked her knees beneath her chin, wrapping her arms around her legs. A big ugly water bug skittered past and disappeared into the straw, and she kicked at it with the toe of her shoe. Right at that moment, Cleo felt like that ugly bug.

Stretching out her legs, she leaned back against the rough bark of the nearby pine. She closed her eyes, her heart heavy.

I'm sorry, Lord. Please forgive me for snooping again. Teach me to keep my nose in my own business. I'm ready to accept the consequences, but be gentle while I learn.

Before she could say "amen," she felt something cool and heavy slither across her legs. The operative word was *slither*. When she opened her eyes, a big old cottonmouth lay across her ankles.

The snake looked almost as unhappy to see her as she was to see him.

Chapter 4

Theo climbed onto an abandoned kitchen chair and studied the old building's rafters. Joe was right when he said the place stood as sturdy as the day it was built. Planed smooth and straight by hands long stilled in death, the wood held true and plumb. A job well done. Only the cobwebs that hung like Spanish moss in the corners gave away its age.

He stretched to reach the nearest cypress beam, then ran his hand over the aged timber. Nothing felt more permanent than a piece of wood well crafted.

"Help! Snake!"

The chair tumbled from beneath him as Theo tried to right himself. He landed with a *crash* and hit the ground running. As he careened off the porch, he grabbed the shovel off the top of the lumber pile.

"Where are you?"

"Over here!"

Following the sound, Theo crossed the clearing and bounded into the thicket, only to stop short when he saw the woman—and the woman's predicament. A rather small-sized female had attracted a big old snake. It sat on the hem of her skirt, mad as a hornet and perched to strike.

Theo smacked the ground with the shovel, and the black monster turned his attention away from the young lady. As soon as the snake moved, so did the woman. Using the tip of the shovel, Theo made short work of the cottonmouth. With a flick of his wrist, he sent the head flying into the thicket and watched it land, then bounce into the black water of the bayou.

When he glanced back at the terrified woman, he had to suppress a groan. She stared down at the twitching body of the snake as if she'd never seen one. The only thing worse than a riled-up cottonmouth was a riled-up woman.

And this one looked ready to strike.

Mouth covered by shaking hands, the woman began to cry. "I asked Him to be gentle, and He sent a snake." She swiped at her tears with the hem of her apron, then thrust her hand toward him with a weak smile. "I'm sorry. My name is Clothilde, Clothilde Trahan. How do you do?"

"Theophile Breaux." He handed her his handkerchief. "You must be Joe's girl."

"Oui," she said as she dabbed at her cheeks. "I'm his niece."

He shook her hand. She sure was a pretty little thing. No bigger than a minute and covered in pine straw, yet he couldn't recall when he'd seen anyone more appealing. He frowned. Last thing he needed was a distraction, and this brown-eyed beauty sure looked to be one. With little encouragement, he just might fall in love, and then where would he be?

Just like his papa, that's where.

Focus, Breaux. Think of something besides her broad smile and that upturned nose.

What had she said about the snake? That someone sent it? Was she loony? Joe had mentioned his niece was a bit of a challenge, but he'd never stated specifically what he meant.

"What are you talking about? Who sent a snake?"

"God, I think." She spared another quick look at the twitching remains before meeting his gaze. Her lower lip quivered a bit, but at least her tears had stopped. "You see, I know God corrects us when we do wrong, and I was. . ."

Theo jammed the point of the shovel into the soft earth, then leaned on the handle. They were heading for dangerous territory. She'd been watching him from the thicket, and now he couldn't take his eyes off her. A gentleman, especially one in a hurry to get on down the road, would walk away right now and leave the lady to her concerns.

Well, he'd rarely been accused of doing what he ought. What was the harm in just a little more conversation while he watched the sun glint off her blue-black hair?

"You were *what*?" he asked with a mind to tease just a bit before he sent her home to her uncle.

"I was. . ." Her face colored the prettiest shade of pink. "Well, never mind what I was doing."

"You were eavesdropping."

She had the decency to appear ashamed. "Oui," she said slowly, "I was."

"You were hiding in the thicket, listening to everything we said." He gave her the look he generally reserved for his younger brothers and sisters. "I should tell your uncle."

Brown eyes opened wide. "I wish you wouldn't."

Rather than respond, he decided to say nothing and watch her squirm.

She offered a weak smile. "I have a good reason."

"A good reason to do something wrong?" He leaned down to look her in the eyes. "Is that what you're trying to tell me?"

"Yes. I mean no." She worried the hem of her apron. "You see, I thought maybe I. . . Oh, goodness."

"Goodness has got nothing to do with it, girl." He tilted forward slightly and noted with satisfaction that the Trahan girl took a step back. "Was what you heard worth nearly getting snakebit?"

She shook her head.

"Was it worth whatever your uncle's going to do when he hears about this?"

Again she shook her head. "No, but you don't understand. If you tell him, it will ruin everything."

There went the tears. Theo groaned. This girl shed more liquid than a rowboat with a plank missing.

Be strong, Breaux. Just walk away.

Of course, he ignored his own advice. "If I don't tell your uncle, you'll probably keep sticking your nose where it doesn't belong until you run into something—or someone—worse than that snake there."

"I think I already have."

Theo grasped the end of the shovel and yanked hard to pull it out of the dirt. Slinging it over his shoulder, he turned and walked away.

~

Why didn't she keep her big mouth shut?

Cleo stepped over the carcass of the snake and headed after the Breaux fellow. If only she could make him see his way clear to keep quiet about her little indiscretion. Indiscretion? Who was she kidding? She'd blatantly ignored both her aunt and her uncle and hidden in a thicket like a common criminal, all in the hopes of learning whether or not a teacher had been chosen for the school.

She'd tried asking Tante Flo outright and Uncle Joe indirectly, but neither offered an answer as to who would be offered the task of teaching the children. Both knew she wanted the position, so repeating her wish would serve no purpose. It certainly hadn't kept Uncle Joe from sending a letter to New Orleans to the teachers' college to inquire about qualified applicants for the job.

Going to the reverend was out of the question, because he would just inform Uncle Joe. If only she'd learned to take to heart some of the scriptures on patience she'd memorized through the years.

Cleo watched the broad back of the man who could single-handedly ruin her plans for the future. *Stop him, Lord. Please.*

Abruptly the man halted and whirled around to face her. "Get on home, little girl."

Little girl? When would people see her as a full-grown woman of almost nineteen? Her uncle and aunt certainly didn't, or they wouldn't be ignoring her requests to hire on as a teacher for the bayou school. And this man. . .

Well, she would show them all.

She drew herself up to her full height and stalked toward Theophile Breaux. "Little girl?" she called as she closed the distance between them. "You think I am a little girl, Monsieur Breaux?"

By the time she asked the question, she stood inches away from him. He leaned toward her as if to study her a moment, then crossed his arms over his chest. A broad grin split his handsome face, and he broke out into laughter.

Laughter.

Cleo felt the heat flood her face. How *dare* he laugh at her? If she hadn't been brought up to be a lady, she would certainly wipe the smile off his face with a choice word or two. Instead, she merely stood her ground and endured the humiliation until the Breaux fellow finally tired of his fun.

"Are you quite finished?" she asked as properly as she could.

The Breaux fellow's face sobered, but traces of the grin remained. "I suppose I am."

"Then may I ask you a question?"

He looked stunned. "I suppose so."

"What will you accomplish by telling my uncle you found me out here?"

"Accomplish?" The Acadian seemed to consider the question a moment. "I don't rightly know. You got the answer to that, eh?"

"Then don't tell him." She made an attempt to smile. "I have such plans, and all you will do is ruin them."

"Well, of all the. . ." He shook his head. "You mean to try and tell me that even though you are in the wrong, I'm the one who'll cause trouble by telling the truth? Little girl, you are something. Did you know that?" With those words, he turned and stormed away, crossing the distance to the cabin's front porch with angry steps that raised little clouds of dust on the dry ground.

"I was just trying to figure out if they'd hired a teacher," she called. "And you can believe that or not."

"Why would you care about a teacher?" he asked without breaking his stride or looking her way. "You might be little bitty, but I know you're past school age." He glanced over his shoulder as he stomped up the porch steps. "At least I think you are, but then, now that I—"

His leg disappeared into the porch step up to his knee. Catching the rail, he narrowly missed falling forward onto the porch. The big man leaned precariously against the rail, unable to lift his leg out of the crumbled wood that held it imprisoned.

"Are you all right?" Cleo picked up her skirts and raced toward the struggling man, climbing past him to stand on the porch. She offered her outstretched hand. "Here. Let me help."

Gratitude was *not* written on his face as he looked up at her. "What in the world can a little thing like you do to help me, eh?"

"You never can tell." She tried not to laugh at the bits of rotten wood and dead leaves decorating his dark curls. "Uncle Joe says I'm stronger than I look. I'll pull, and you try to lift your foot over those boards."

She grasped his hand and tugged. A moment later, he caught his balance. Unfortunately, she lost hers, tangled her feet in her skirts, and landed with a *thud* on her posterior.

The Breaux fellow completed his climb out of the rotten stairs, then pulled himself up on the porch beside her. He shook his head, and leaves and wood chips fell like the snowflakes in Tante Flo's snow globe all around him, some decorating the hem of her skirt.

For a moment she thought he might see some humor in the situation. The wind kicked up, sending another shower of debris her way. She offered a smile in anticipation of the return of his good humor.

Return? When did she actually see any of it? A glance up at the frown on his face told her it would not be today.

What a shame that such a handsome man had such a sour disposition.

The object of her thoughts lumbered to his feet and reached for her hand, practically sending her airborne as he pulled her to a standing position. To his credit, he held her steady until she could regain her footing.

"Get on home now," he said as he released his grip.

Cleo hesitated a moment before pressing past him to carefully make her way across the rickety porch. Head held high, she stepped onto solid ground and walked away from the most irritating man she'd ever met.

Chapter 5

"You go tell your uncle what you've been up to, little girl, or I will!" Theo called after her. "Hurry on, now, or I just might get there before you. You wouldn't want that, now, would you, eh?"

Clothilde Trahan just kept on walking at the same leisurely pace, back straight and head up like she was counting the clouds. If he hadn't seen the high color in her cheeks as she walked away, he would have thought she was out for a Sunday stroll.

Despite the fact she now wore sawdust on her skirt and pine needles in her hair, she was a lady, that one, and according to his mama, raised up to be a godly woman by good people. His only memories of Clothilde Trahan were as a quiet girl forever carrying a book under her arm or hiding in some remote corner at church picnics, reading while everyone else went about their foolishness. He had to admit he hadn't expected back then that she'd grow up to be quite so pretty.

Or spunky.

What was it about the Trahan girl that set his teeth on edge and his heart pumping all at the same time? Joe and his wife were the salt of the earth, and he knew they'd loved and raised that girl like she was their own.

If she'd turned out anything like her tante Flo, she would make somebody a fine wife someday—once she let go of that nasty habit of sticking her pretty nose where it didn't belong.

Maybe she ought to go back to carrying a book around. At least then she'd have a place to stick her nose where it wouldn't get her into trouble.

He watched her disappear into the thicket and gave passing thought to whether she actually went home or stood there spying. From the look on her face when he told her he'd go to Joe, she probably hightailed it back to the house to head him off.

Scared to death, she most likely intended to give her uncle her side of the story before Theo could tell him otherwise. A fat lot of good that would do. The truth of the situation spoke for itself.

A twinge of guilt hit him hard. He shouldn't have been so rough with her. No, he decided. Served her right. A body ought not hide out like a common criminal and watch people. What in the world was she thinking?

Theo pondered on that a moment. She did have the book learning, and she knew more words than just about anybody he'd ever spoken with—and he'd talked to some very smart people in his day.

Her tante Flo worked as a teacher way back, so the feisty gal probably got her hankering for it through her kinfolk. Yes, he could see her as a schoolteacher, at least until the little bitty thing ran across a big old bayou boy who didn't want to learn.

That last thought gave him pause. *She already has, you big fool, and she did just fine.*

Theo went back to work, taking his aggravation out on the porch steps. In short order, the rotten boards were gone, replaced by salvaged wood from the pile behind the cabin. If only he could pound away his irritation—and his thoughts of Clothilde Trahan—as easily.

~

The following morning, Theo arrived on Joe's doorstep to discuss his ideas for the renovations. Flo welcomed him warmly. In short order, she'd hustled him into the kitchen to offer him a plate of eggs, biscuits, and bacon, which he tried and failed to turn down.

"A man's got to eat well if he's going to work well," Flo said.

"Well, I can't find an argument for that," he replied.

Joe seconded his statement with a wave of his napkin, then bowed his head to offer a blessing over the food. Fork in hand, Theo added his "amen" to Joe's and Flo's, then reached for the Tabasco sauce and doused everything on his plate. Satisfied he'd upped the temperature with his favorite pepper sauce, he stabbed at the bright yellow eggs and looked beyond the kitchen to the empty parlor.

Funny, here he sat at a family breakfast, and Joe's niece was nowhere to be found. He chewed on the thought—and the fiery eggs. Both burned as they went down, but only the eggs caused him to shed a tear.

Must be prettying herself up or sleeping late. No, she's probably hiding somewhere, spying.

He finished the meal and sipped good strong chicory coffee at the big round kitchen table while Flo cleared the table and then made herself scarce.

"Let's get down to business." Joe fetched a thick file off the sideboard and began to spread papers out on the table. "Tell me what you've decided we need to do."

Theo explained his ideas, all the while watching for Clothilde. He finally left, wondering where in the world the irritating woman could be.

The next morning and the one after that passed in similar fashion until the habit of starting the day with Joe and his wife fell into a routine. Theo arrived early, discussed the previous day's progress with Joe, and partook of the best coffee and eggs outside of the ones he had at his mama's house. Never had he eaten so well or sat so long at one spell.

Each time when he left, he wondered where Clothilde Trahan could be. He also promised himself each night that tomorrow he'd go straight to the building site and forgo the lollygagging at Joe's table.

Funny how he'd forget his promise every single morning. Funnier still how he figured each day would be the one when Clothilde Trahan finally stopped hiding from him.

~

Nearly two weeks had passed, and Cleo was getting tired of missing breakfast. She stood in the henhouse with the basket hanging from her elbow. Good thing the hens were laying well.

Surely the Breaux fellow would end this annoying habit of showing up at Tante Flo's table in time to eat a half dozen eggs and drink a gallon of coffee before finally leaving. How he could hold so much food and still maintain a lean frame baffled her further.

Must be all that work he did out at the cabin.

Still, why one man sat so long at a breakfast table was beyond her understanding. Uncle Joe did, of course, but he was old—well nigh to forty. One might expect old folks to sit and sip their coffee as if they had nothing better to do all day.

Her thoughts returned to Theophile Breaux. As far as she could tell, he hadn't informed Uncle Joe about the incident at the cabin. If he knew, Uncle Joe hadn't let on, and he certainly hadn't told Tante Flo. Perhaps the rogue had no intention of telling on her after all.

Well, wouldn't *that* be an answer to prayer?

Cleo patted her apron pocket where the letter she had written the night before lay hidden. Writing to Uncle Joe's friend at the teachers' college in New Orleans had been a risk.

She thought long and hard before resorting to the drastic move of pleading her case to a man whom she barely knew. Surely he would see her side of things when he read her letter. A man fit to run a teachers' college would obviously recognize a qualified teacher when he read a letter from one. If he wouldn't let her into the college, maybe he would recommend her to Uncle Joe as capable of teaching the children of Latagnier.

The sound of voices across the yard caught her attention. She watched Theophile Breaux emerge from the shadows and take the front porch steps two at a time. Uncle Joe followed him out onto the porch, shouted a good-bye, and then disappeared back inside.

From experience, she knew her uncle would return to the kitchen table to work on his figuring a bit more, then take the big folder over to the church to show the reverend. After all, it *was* Friday.

Time to implement the plan she'd been working on all week. Patience was not her strong suit, but then, the Lord must have known when He made her that she'd have trouble with waiting. Why He chose to give her that peculiarity was something she planned to ask when she met Him someday. In the meantime, she prayed much and failed some.

This week, however, she'd managed to stick to her plan and keep her peace while she ticked off the days on the calendar. Around about Wednesday afternoon, she hadn't thought Friday would ever come, but it had.

And somehow she'd made it through the week.

Cleo plucked the last egg from the straw and settled it atop the basket. With care, she made her way out of the henhouse and up the back steps to the kitchen.

Uncle Joe sat at the table, his spectacles perched on the end of his nose and the ledger before him just as she expected. He looked up from his scribbling when the door closed.

"You been working hard this morning, cher?" he asked before returning his attention to his figures.

She slipped behind him to leave the egg basket on the sideboard. "Yes, sir."

He stopped writing and began tapping the tabletop with his fingers. A sure sign something was on his mind. "Seems like all that work would make a body hungry."

Cleo cringed. Enduring scrutiny from Uncle Joe hadn't been part of her expectations. "I suppose."

Had he somehow discovered that she planned to visit the postmaster on her trip to deliver eggs this morning? She cast a glance from beneath lowered lashes and found he'd gone back to his numbers.

"You want some breakfast?" he asked as he tallied a column and wrote a figure beneath it.

In truth, she did, but sitting across the table from Uncle Joe and enduring his cross-examination did not set well. An empty stomach suited her much better.

Her uncle whirled around to face her. "Any particular reason you're avoiding that young man?"

The swift change of subject startled Cleo and sent her thoughts spinning. "No, sir." She stuffed her hands into her apron pockets, then felt a pang of guilt when her fingers came into contact with her letter.

"You're not going to forget my penny candy, are you?"

Her uncle's sweet tooth was a secret to no one, but every week he felt the need to remind Cleo to fetch his favorite treat. Cleo smiled despite the worry gnawing in her gut. How she loved the familiar routine of life in Latagnier.

He stood and reached into his pocket. "Bring your aunt back one of those fancy magazines, will you?"

"Yes, sir." She accepted the coins he held out, then dropped them in her pocket alongside the letter.

Uncle Joe returned to his seat and continued to stare, all the while drumming a furious rhythm on the table. Another moment under his scrutiny and she'd spill her plan for sure.

"That you, honey?" Tante Flo called from the parlor.

Cleo suppressed a sigh of relief. "Yes, ma'am. It's me."

Tante Flo met her in the hallway, a dish towel in her hand. "You going to fetch eggs to folks?" she asked as she smoothed back iron gray hair.

"Yes'm." Cleo looked away. "Did you need something in town?"

Tossing the dish towel onto her shoulder, Tante Flo peered into Cleo's face, then pulled a letter from her apron pocket. "Mail this one with yours."

For a second Cleo could only stare at her aunt. When the words came, they emerged as more of a string of sounds rather than an actual statement of some sort. Finally, she gathered her wits enough to construct an entire sentence and speak it aloud. "How did you know?"

Tante Flo smiled. "I didn't." She took Cleo by the elbow and led her outside. "Now don't you set your cap to worrying. I was young once, too, and I know a natural-born teacher when I see one. I just thought I ought to let that fellow at the teachers' college know, too."

Cleo opened her mouth to say thanks but once again found the words had escaped. She wrapped Tante Flo in a tight hug and held on until the tears ceased.

"Hush now and dry your eyes, or your uncle's going to wonder what we hens are cackling about." She lifted the hem of her apron to dab at Cleo's tears. "Now here's how we are going to handle this. I'll talk to your uncle, eventually, and until I do, you will keep your peace on the subject. Oh, and it wouldn't hurt to pray, too."

"I will, and I promise." Cleo kissed and hugged her aunt one more time before fairly floating to town to post not one letter to the teachers' college but two. After filling her pocket with penny candy for Uncle Joe and tucking a *Godey's Lady's Book* under her arm, she headed for home on the path that wound beside the black bayou water.

Anyone who didn't know better would think the bayou looked like a good place to spend a warm spring afternoon. Cleo knew differently, though, especially after the snake episode of last week.

She shuddered at the reminder of the black monster. While growing up on the bayou meant dealing with the ever-present snake population, she'd never seen one as large as that one.

Thoughts of the snake brought forth thoughts of the man who had dispatched it to its doom. Theophile Breaux. Now there was a man who. . .

Who what?

Before she could complete the thought, the sound of hammering echoed across the quiet of the bayou. Cleo stopped short and looked around. Had she strayed so close to the cabin that she could hear the sound of the Breaux fellow as he went about making repairs?

The familiar landmarks told her she had. Strange, but she hadn't intended to go this direction.

"Well, as long as I'm nearby, perhaps it would be a good time to see what sort of progress is being made on my school."

My school. She rolled the thought across her brain. Yes, that did sound good. And with Tante Flo's endorsement, she all but had the job sewed up.

Smiling as she headed toward the school, she toyed with the idea of letting the big Cajun know that she was the one for whom the repairs were being made. Wouldn't that just irritate him to no end?

As she reached the clearing, she cast a quick glance down at the spot where Theophile Breaux had saved her from the giant cottonmouth. Instantly she felt ashamed of herself. He really wasn't such a bad sort, just a bit grumpy and rough around the edges.

Of course, the last time she'd seen him, he'd just pulled his foot out of the steps. She looked up to see him perched atop a ladder, hammering a nail into the eaves of the cabin.

Perhaps she'd best alert him to her presence so she wouldn't startle him. A shout of greeting would probably take him by surprise, so she decided to whistle.

Chapter 6

Where in the world was that infernal whistling coming from?

Theo continued to pound nails into the roof, patching places where the rain had once too often entered the little building. He'd been at it most of the morning and intended to keep going until he finished. Once the roof was in place, he could begin work inside the building.

Reaching for another nail from the pouch at his waist, Theo soon let his hands work at the task while his mind roamed. The Lord had been good to heal his papa right quick. Already he hobbled around with his leg bound up, and just yesterday he told Mama he was ready to see to his traps again.

Mama'd had a fit, of course, but soon she'd not be able to keep Papa sitting on the porch when he wanted to be out working. "A man has to work, Nellie," Theo had heard his papa say that morning. "You take a man's livelihood away, and he's got nothing."

As the screen door closed behind him, Theo heard his mama's reply: "A man's always got his family, Gaspard, and don't you ever forget that, you hear?"

Theo smiled. Nellie and Gaspard Breaux bantered like children in a schoolyard sometimes, but no one who knew them doubted their love. Thirty years of marriage come this fall, and they still held hands.

Thirty years of daily routine, of too little money and too many mouths to feed, and yet they acted like theirs had been the easiest life imaginable. He shook his head.

Papa had come back from the war with a bright future. He'd made his plans to go east to the agricultural and mechanical college in Texas. He meant to build great things that would advance civilization.

Instead, he'd come home to the bayou to say good-bye to his mama and papa and ended up falling for Nellie Boudreaux, the pastor's daughter who'd unaccountably blossomed into womanhood during his absence.

Nellie's people were here, family with roots dug down so deep that uprooting them—and Nellie—would be unthinkable.

What in the world did a man have to do to find a woman worth giving up everything he held dear? He once asked his father that very question. His response had been characteristically vague: "I looked at Texas, I looked at Nellie, and I'll tell you, son, Nellie looked a whole lot better. And. . ." He paused as if to draw out the moment. Theo remembered watching Papa's smile broaden, then narrow as he pressed his lips into a thin line. Surely the next words out of Papa's mouth would be words of wisdom.

"And?" Theo had asked, impatient as ever.

"And besides, signs pointed to a cold winter, and it was nigh on the fall."

Mama had walked up during the middle of that statement and threatened to go after Papa with a rolling pin. Instead, the moment they thought Theo was out of sight, the pair had locked lips like newlyweds.

Theo banged another nail into the roof, then leaned back slightly on the old ladder to admire his handiwork. A neat row of shingles covered the place where a hole the size of a full-grown coon had been.

He thought about his own plans, important things to do that had been set aside for this trip to Latagnier. If he had his way, he planned to do just what he promised his papa all those years ago.

Canada. Yes, wouldn't that be something? If the pastor hadn't roped him into this repair job, he'd practically be packing his bags. Instead, he'd bought another month or so in Latagnier, paid for with good intention and plenty of persuasion on the part of the pastor and the elders, chief among them, Joe Trahan.

Again the whistling teased his ears. No bird sang like that, at least none he'd heard in Latagnier. Leaning over, he slammed the hammer atop a nail that hadn't gone in to his liking.

There, that's better.

If a man couldn't be known for the quality of his work, well, what was the purpose of doing a job at all? It got all over him when he was called in to fix something that hadn't been done right the first time. At least that was not the case here.

"Hello? Monsieur Breaux?"

What in the world? Theo dropped his hammer onto the roof, then managed to grab it before it slid out of his reach. He turned in time to see a woman in a yellow dress emerge from the thicket. As he moved, his feet slipped, and he reached for the roof. Failing to get a grip, he settled for holding on to the only solid thing he could latch onto—the ladder.

With his heart pumping furiously, he took a deep breath and let it out slowly as he returned his attention to the work he needed to do on the roof. Releasing the ladder with a shaking left hand, he wiped the perspiration from his brow.

He'd narrowly escaped disaster this time, and he still bore the bruises from their last encounter. What was it about the Trahan woman that invited disaster each time they met? If he ignored her, maybe she'd go away, and he could leave at the end of the day without doing himself—mind or body—further damage.

"Do be careful!" she called.

Several choice responses came to mind, but Mama had raised him better than to say any of them. Instead, he settled for a brisk nod and a quick, "Sure will."

Once again the crooked nail caught his attention. Somehow it didn't look right anymore. He palmed the hammer and adjusted his position on the ladder. If he gave the troublesome nail a few more hits, it would lie flat against the shingles like the others.

"That doesn't look safe, sir."

Theo jammed the hammer into his belt and cast a glance over his shoulder. She'd almost closed the distance between them, and she strolled along with a basket hanging from her elbow. The sight of her caused his mouth to go dry. If he didn't find her so irritating, he just might find her. . .what?

Attractive? Noonday sun glinted off blue-black hair that hung in a thick braid reaching nearly to her waist. Yes, he did find her quite pretty.

So what?

Pretty girls were a dime a dozen. He'd seen his share and would most likely see a good number more before Jesus called him home. Canada probably had a whole slew of them just waiting for his arrival.

So what if a girl in yellow caught his eye?

He'd be gone in no time, and she'd be just a memory. Whether she was to be a good memory or a bad one remained to be seen.

Clothilde Trahan stood at the bottom of the ladder now, and he had to lean down to see her face. "How about I do my job and you go do yours, whatever that may be, eh?"

"I *am* doing my job." She shaded her eyes and squinted up at him. "I'm going to be the teacher here, and this will be my school. As such, I felt I should come see how you were getting along."

"Your uncle and the pastor agreed to this? To you being the new teacher, that is."

She dropped her hand and looked away. "They will."

Theo chuckled. "That's what I thought. You're no more the teacher here than I am."

He whirled back around, using his left hand to steady himself as he stretched to reach the crooked nail once more. Realizing too late that he'd wiped his brow only moments before, he scrambled to keep his damp fingers wrapped around the wooden bar.

In a valiant effort to keep from sliding down the ladder, he dove for the safety of the roof. Had he been a smaller man, this might have been a good move. Unfortunately, he took after his papa's side of the family.

His last thought before crashing through the roof was that whatever happened, it would all be the Trahan woman's fault.

~

Cleo dropped the egg basket and picked up her skirts, hurdling over the fallen ladder to reach the newly repaired porch steps. Throwing open the door, she stepped inside the semidarkness. The room smelled old and musty, and dust threatened to choke her. Obviously the carpenter's work inside had not yet commenced.

"Monsieur Breaux?"

No answer.

The cabin had been laid out in a rabbit warren of rooms, and she now stood in what remained of the largest of them. Several odd pieces of furniture—a chair here, a small table there—had been stacked into a corner, remnants of her grandmother's years, living in the building.

Ahead she could see threads of light spilling around a door not quite plumb on its hinges. From memory, she knew the area where the carpenter had fallen through would be the small front room on her right. Long ago, the space had served as a formal parlor. In more recent years, it had been the sickroom for Grandmother Trahan.

Making her way carefully around the corner and into the hallway, she stopped short at the scene unfolding before her. A brilliant shaft of light illuminated the shadowed room as if heaven itself had opened up in just one small spot. At the center of the spotlight, surrounded by a fine mist of dust, sat Theophile Breaux.

Chapter 7

The Breaux fellow had landed intact, it seemed, and unharmed and currently sat upright atop her grandmother's ancient feather bed. Pieces of shingles and lumber littered the bare mattress and spilled onto the old wood floor.

Covered in dust, the carpenter's dark curly hair resembled the powdered wigs she'd seen in history books. His dark clothing appeared as white as an angel's robes.

This man, she reminded herself, was no angel. She gave him a long look.

While he appeared unharmed, he held his eyes shut tight, his head slightly bowed. He seemed as if he were caught in prayer rather than as the lone survivor of a recent fall through the roof.

Cleo inched nearer, sidestepping the debris to stand at the end of the iron bed. The ornate metal felt cold beneath her fingers.

"Monsieur Breaux?"

He neither spoke nor moved. If she could move closer, she might be able to see if he still breathed.

"Sir? Are you harmed?"

Silence. Gripping the cold metal of the bed, she leaned a notch forward to nudge his oversized booted foot. Nothing.

Cleo's heart sunk, and tears stung her eyes. She'd really done it this time.

As a young girl, she'd watched a baby bird fall from its nest and land, seemingly unharmed, outside the parlor window. When she rushed to its aid, she found the tiny creature sitting as if it hadn't a care in the world. Only when she picked it up to return it to its nest did she realize the precious baby sparrow was dead.

Theophile Breaux could have suffered the same fate. She suppressed a groan. Why hadn't she gone straight home?

If the carpenter did not survive the fall, it would be her fault. After all, if she hadn't allowed her curiosity to get the better of her, she would have gone straight home and not stopped at the cabin. Had she not stopped, she and the carpenter wouldn't have exchanged words, and he wouldn't have fallen through the roof.

It all seemed so. . .preventable. If only she could tame her persistent curiosity.

What a can of worms she'd opened by asking the Lord to help take care of the problem. First the giant snake and now this. While she fully expected to bear the cost of her improvement, she never expected someone else might be hurt along the way.

Cleo moved to the side of the bed, kicking a rather large piece of the roof out of her way. Slowly she knelt, then peered up at the Breaux fellow's face. Traces of blood glistened from a tiny cut just beneath the fringe of dark lashes on his right eye, but he seemed otherwise unharmed.

"If you can hear me, sir, please say something." Still no sign of life.

Taking a deep breath, she bowed her head and began to pray. "Father, I really did it this time. I killed a man, or at least I hurt him badly. Lord, he didn't deserve this. He was helping us to build a school and doing a good work so the children could learn, and well, You know my part in things. I probably don't have the right to ask, but—"

The mattress shuddered slightly. She paused to open her eyes and stare up at the carpenter once more. Still no sign that either Theophile Breaux or the Lord had heard her prayers.

Dropping her chin again, she continued her plea. "If You are listening, please forgive me and heal Monsieur Breaux. He might be a bit cranky, but he is one of Your children and should have a long and happy life instead of having it end just because I fooled around and got in the way. I'm the one who should pay the price for my curious nature, not he."

"Amen!"

The carpenter's chuckle seemed to shake the very floor Cleo knelt on. She jumped and nearly fell backward. As she caught herself with her elbows, she looked up to see the smiling face of Theophile Breaux.

"Well, of all the nerve." Cleo scrambled to her feet, her heart racing, and shook off as much of the dust as her trembling hands would allow.

"I'm sorry, but I am still very much alive." He dabbed gingerly at the cut beneath his eye. "Although I must say, if ever I need someone to write my eulogy, it will be you."

Realization dawned, and her eyes narrowed. "You were fine all along."

He shrugged and, for a moment, had the decency to look almost contrite. "I'm afraid so. Other than a little dust in my mouth and a few bruises in places I can't show you, I think I'll live. You look disappointed."

She opened her mouth to speak but coughed on some of that very same dust herself. When she recovered, she found the words had gone. All she could do was stand and stare at the spectacle before her.

The most irritating man on the planet had just made a total and complete fool of her. Worse, she had helped him to do it by being so. . .what? Naive? Maybe. Nosy. She groaned. Yes.

Still, he should have been a gentleman and spoken up before she bared her heart before the Lord. Even a heathen would have done that, and she knew Theophile Breaux to be a churchgoing man. Why, his granddaddy had been a preacher and his mama a preacher's daughter.

Oh, how he seemed to be enjoying her discomfort. He'd twisted that mouth of his into a grin that would have made him awfully handsome had he not been behaving just plain awfully.

"I'm just sorry I had to go and laugh so soon." He shifted positions, and the old mattress creaked in protest. "I could have listened to your prayers all day."

"Heathen." There, she'd said it.

"Makes a man feel appreciated when a woman praises him to the Lord like that." He punctuated the statement with a wink. "I had no idea you held me in such high regard. You keep your secrets well, little girl."

How dare the man actually pull such a prank at her expense? She climbed to her feet and kicked a shingle out of her way. "You, sir, are the most despicable, dastardly man I have ever met. I do not care to linger in your presence."

He swung his long legs over the side and shook his head. Fine particles of debris rained down around him, dancing in the sunlight as they swirled and landed. "My, how your tone has changed. Am I a better man in death than in life, Mademoiselle Trahan? If so, I'd gladly die to hear you sing my praises again."

Hands on her hips, she fought her rising temper. "If I weren't a lady, Monsieur Breaux, why, I just might answer that question."

Leaning his elbows on his knees, the carpenter rested his head in his hands. "Seeing as how I've got a roof to repair, why don't we just skip the part about you being a lady and get right to it? Speak your mind. Answer the question. How *do* you feel about me? Tell me."

Oh, how she wanted to. She opened her mouth and tried. Unfortunately, all of Tante Flo's words about proper behavior came flooding back at once. The only thing she could do was turn and walk away.

"It's been a real joy, Mademoiselle Trahan." The mattress creaked once more. "Do come and see me again soon, eh?"

She paused in the doorway to turn and face him. To her surprise, he stood mere inches away, looming over her with a broad grin.

"Change your mind about running off?"

She tilted her head to stare into his eyes. "It was the schoolhouse I came to see, sir, not you, so don't flatter yourself by thinking otherwise."

This time when she made the decision to turn and flee, she did not look back or pause. Pressing past the shadows, she emerged into the bright sunshine of the porch without slowing down to allow her eyes to adjust. In the process, she ran into the porch post. A sharp jab of pain radiated up from her elbow, but thankfully, the Breaux fellow hadn't emerged from the cabin to see her near humiliation.

"You'll be back!" he called from near the door. "You've already proven that you can't stay away from me."

"Humph" was the most proper answer she dared give as she stormed across the porch, heedless of the delicate condition of the boards. "Just see how I can stay away. I won't miss you a bit, that's for sure."

"Oh yes, you will!" he called. "You'll miss me so bad you won't be able to stand it."

"If I do, I'll go visit the neighbor's donkey."

Oh, she'd have to apologize to the Lord for that comment. *And maybe to the carpenter, as well.*

Never.

Head held high, she forced herself not to pick up her skirts and run. His laughter chased her across the clearing.

As she stepped into the thicket, she took one last quick look over her shoulder. There stood Theophile Breaux on the porch, covered in dust and leaning against the rail with something brown hanging from the crook of his arm.

He raised a hand to wave, shaking the object as he stepped toward the edge of the porch. She ignored him and picked up her pace.

Cleo had almost reached home when she realized what the carpenter held. Her egg basket.

~

Theo watched the Trahan woman storm off and tried to muster up some measure of irritation. After all, she'd practically caused him to kill himself and ruined three days of backbreaking work in the process.

Somehow as the swirl of yellow skirts disappeared into the thicket, he knew that trying to work up anger at Clothilde Trahan was a wasted effort. She still vexed him greatly, but the thought of making her so mad that he never saw her again didn't sit well.

He placed the egg basket on the porch rail and stared at it. The new copy of *Godey's Lady's Book* it held was probably meant for Flo. He'd seen her reading a dog-eared copy just the day before yesterday and thought to buy her a new one the next time he went to town. The penny candy had to belong to Joe. As long as he'd known the man, Joe Trahan had always had a sweet of some sort in his pocket.

Returning these items along with the basket would be the neighborly thing to do. Making Clothilde Trahan eat her words and come back for the thing, however, would be the more satisfying choice.

Knowing better than to make the decision in his current state of mind, Theo left the basket on the rail and stepped off the porch, limping slowly toward the ladder. He might be a few years shy of thirty, but his bones were going to think he'd hit the century mark by bedtime.

As he hefted the ladder back into place and reached for his hammer, he felt his muscles complain. Surely he'd go home with bruises he hadn't come to work with. Those things happened in his line of work but rarely due to female intervention.

Again he chuckled. The Trahan girl had left her mark and not just in the toll on his body. His mind protested, as well.

He picked up his hammer and hefted the bag of nails onto his shoulder, then reached for the nearest rung on the ladder. The bruises would heal. Thoughts of Clothilde Trahan, however, promised to stay with him much longer.

Chapter 8

As the sun sank toward the tree line, Theo's conscience began to bother him more than the ache in his bones. Clothilde Trahan had most likely arrived home and been asked to explain how she came to return without the items she went to town for.

He should put the girl out of her misery and just take the basket to her. Joe had probably run out of candy by now, and Flo surely had nothing new to read. There was no sense in the two of them paying the price for their niece's silliness.

Yes, that's what he ought to do. Just a quick trip to the Trahan place, and he'd be on his way. Leaning against the porch rail, he tried to come up with a good reason why he shouldn't.

In short order, he decided there was any number of reasons for going straight home now that the dinner hour was coming soon, not the least of which that his mama had promised a big mess of shrimp *étouffée* and hush puppies for supper. He did love fresh-caught shrimp cooked up over rice, and his mama's cornmeal, green onion, and spice concoction made for the best hush puppies in south Louisiana.

His stomach growled at the thought. Yes, indeed, forgetting all about today and heading for a meal made for a hardworking bayou man was just the thing to end the day better than it started.

Still, there was the matter of the basket.

Scanning the horizon, he almost hoped he might see a flash of yellow that would tell him the girl was at her games again—spying from the thicket until he left so she could sneak up and fetch the lost basket. That would certainly get him off the hook, and he could go home with an empty stomach and a clear conscience. Unfortunately, no sign of anyone, male or female, greeted him.

Theo sighed and shoved the hammer into his belt as he turned his attention back to the work at hand. He'd done a fair job of patching the Breaux-sized hole in the roof and weathering it in. Tomorrow he'd begin the tedious process of lining up the shingles and hammering them in place—again.

This time he would use twice the number of nails to make the roof stronger, not that he planned to take another dive through the thing. Of course, with Clothilde Trahan on the loose, a man never knew.

Anything could happen.

Theo wiped his brow and looked off toward the west. Dark clouds had been gathering all afternoon and now rode in great gray clumps along the horizon. Their fat bodies stretched as far as the eye could see, covering the sun and leaving the earthy scent of rain in the air.

Unless he missed his guess, the night would be a stormy one. At least the cabin's front room would stay dry.

He thought of the abandoned iron bed and the feather mattress upon which he'd landed. *Someday if I marry up with that girl, I'll have to have that bedstead for our home.*

Theo nearly fell off the ladder. Where in the world had that come from?

Climbing down with care, he decided he must have hit his head on his way through the roof earlier. Nothing could be further from possible than for him to marry up with *any* bayou girl, least of all that one.

He'd wed himself to that donkey she'd told him about before he'd shackle himself to her.

For just a moment, he put aside his plans and allowed himself to wonder what it would be like to wake up next to the fiery beauty every morning until the Lord took him home. On first consideration, the idea did have some appeal, at least in the abstract.

He chuckled. Life would be entertaining, certainly never boring. With his luck, they'd end up with a dozen daughters just like her. Now *that* was a sobering thought.

No, surely the Lord had better things for him than a trip down the aisle with a certain hardheaded busybody, even if she was the prettiest thing he'd ever laid eyes on. Mama told him God only held the best for each of His children, and in Theo's estimation, the best had to be something other than a life spent never knowing when he'd fall through the next roof.

Besides, he still had roads to travel and adventures to live. There was plenty of time for him to settle down someday.

Life as a married man could start after he'd seen the world—starting with Canada. He'd get there before the first snow fell and stay through the spring. After that, who knew? Alaska maybe, or perhaps he'd just hop a ship to parts unknown.

He'd always wanted to see the world. No better time than the present.

But first he had a mess of shrimp and hush puppies to eat, and if he didn't get home on time, there'd be nothing left but the crumbs.

That decided, Theo left the basket on the porch rail and headed for home. If she wanted it, she'd find it.

He got close enough to the home place to smell the shrimp frying before he turned around and headed back to the cabin to fetch the basket off the porch rail. The Lord might be willing to let Theo see the world, but it seemed as though He was telling him he needed to clear up a bit of business with Clothilde Trahan first.

Stomping his way to the Trahan place under protest, Theo clutched the basket in his hand. As he neared Joe's home, the first fat drops of rain hit him square on the head.

"Great," he grumbled as he stopped to pull the magazine from the basket and slide it beneath his shirt.

The candy fit easily into his pants pocket. Basket empty and Trahan treasures secured, Theo set back on his way as the rain began to come down in earnest.

He arrived at the Trahans' front door, soaked to the skin and starved. As he knocked, he smelled the unmistakable scent of shrimp étouffée. His stomach groaned, and so did he.

Why the Lord seemed to be picking on him today was beyond understanding.

A thought occurred. He could leave the basket right here and take off for home without any member of the Trahan family knowing he stood on their porch. He removed the slightly damp *Godey's Lady's Book* from beneath his shirt and placed it in the basket, then dumped the penny candies in after it.

Now to find a place to leave the basket where it wouldn't get wet. The porch rail was out of the question as the rain poured down upon it. A swing sat at the far end of the porch, but it might be days before someone thought to look all the way down there.

"Come on in here out of the weather."

Theo jumped and nearly sent the basket and its contents flying across the porch. He gathered his wits and turned to see Flo standing at the door, an apron tied around her waist and a dish towel thrown over one shoulder.

"Well, actually, I just brought—"

"Is that Theo Breaux?" Joe Trahan pressed past his wife to shake Theo's hand. "How's it going, boy? You come by to share supper with us?"

He thrust the basket in Joe's direction. Rather than take it, Joe stared at the item as if he'd never seen it, then turned his gaze on Theo.

"Did my niece know you'd be visiting tonight?"

"No, I don't think so," he said, although it was just a guess.

Flo looped her hand around the basket's handle and smiled. "Well, thank you for bringing this by, Theo. Especially in this weather. I'm so pleased to have something new to read. And, Joe, isn't it nice that Theo would go to all this trouble to bring your penny candy by tonight?"

Relief flooded Theo's aching bones. "It was no trouble, really."

Joe took a step toward Theo and grasped him by the elbow. "Flo, set another place at the table. Theo and I'll be in just as soon as we talk some business."

Theo made a weak attempt to protest, but Flo had already disappeared inside. He turned his attention to Joe. Maybe he could talk his way out of staying. Surely Joe Trahan wouldn't hold a man to a dinner invitation he didn't want to accept.

"I appreciate the offer," Theo said, "but I really ought to get on home."

Joe tightened his grip on Theo's elbow past the point where it felt neighborly. Theo looked down into the older Cajun's eyes and saw something that surprised him.

The man looked positively angry.

"I'm glad you stopped by, young man." He motioned to the swing on the far end of the porch. "Go sit down. I was speaking the truth when I told Flo you and I had some business to discuss. If you hadn't had the decency to show up at my front door tonight, I would have been at yours before bedtime."

From the look on Joe's face and the urgency in his words, something big was going on down at the schoolhouse. The last thing Theo needed was to try to make sense of another set of building plans.

It was hard enough to make out the chicken scratching Joe wrote on the pages he regularly gave Theo. Generally Theo would smile and do the best he could, then take the papers home for his brother Alphonse to decipher. Tonight of all nights, he just didn't have the strength to deal with it.

"Honestly, sir, it's been a long day," he said with the best smile he could muster. "How about I come a little early for coffee in the morning? We can talk all you want then, eh?"

Joe leveled a hard stare in Theo's direction. "After I finish with you, I'm not sure you and I will be having coffee in the mornings anymore."

Chapter 9

Cleo drew back from the window and sucked in a deep breath. Whatever happened between Uncle Joe and the Breaux fellow, neither seemed to be happy about it. She could certainly sympathize. His arrival on their doorstep hadn't exactly filled her with joy, either.

At least he'd returned the basket.

"Clothilde Trahan, are you spying again?" Tante Flo stood at the parlor door with a frown and a dish towel. She held the basket in the crook of her elbow. "I thought you learned your lesson when that boy out there fell through the roof this afternoon."

Cleo had told her aunt the whole story when she arrived home earlier that afternoon, even backtracking to describe the previous incident with the snake. Of course, telling Tante Flo had been easy compared to worrying about delivering the news to Uncle Joe that her snooping had almost ended in disaster—twice.

"I saw the lightning and wondered if we had a storm coming." Cleo released the hem of the starched cotton curtain. "I didn't know we had company."

Her aunt set the basket on the sideboard. "So you weren't expecting him?"

"No."

But *had* she expected him? Cleo wasn't sure how to answer.

A gentleman would have saved her the trip and the explanations. A man like she figured Theophile Breaux to be would have waited to gloat when she finally returned to the cabin to claim it.

"I thought I might find Uncle Joe alone and speak to him about what happened this afternoon before we sat down to supper. Do you think he spied me coming up the road this afternoon?"

"All I know's if he did, he never said anything to me." Tante Flo shrugged. "But then, he's been busy all day doing this and that. Until he came in to wash up for supper, I hadn't seen hide nor hair of him since lunchtime."

"I just hope he was too busy to notice." Cleo looked away. "If he saw me before I had a chance to brush the dust out of my hair, he probably thought the same thing you did."

Tante Flo's frown tilted into a smile as her fingers worried the end of the dish towel. "What else is a mother to think when her girl comes home from town covered in dust and her hair all in a mess? And the basket, well, I asked myself, *Why isn't it with her?*"

"Yes, I know," she said softly. "I'm sorry."

"I'm not your real mama, but I sure feel like it, and I don't keep my mouth shut at times like that."

Stepping away from the window, Cleo embraced her aunt. "I'm so glad you feel that way. I wonder if you guessed what a trouble I'd be."

"Trouble? Nonsense. Why, this old house has become a home since you came to live in it."

Cleo shook her head. "That's very kind, but I doubt you expected you would end up with someone so. . .well. . . curious."

"Oh, child, you're so like your mama at her age. So full of life and smart. Why, that girl could outthink just about anybody, then charm them into not caring. And curious? Well, you've not seen curiosity until you've seen Marie." Tante Flo held Cleo at arm's length and shook her head. "I miss her so, but it's like a little bit of Marie still lives on in you. You've been a blessing."

Cleo gave her a sideways look. "Even when I'm a busybody?"

Her aunt pretended to study the question with great concern. She chuckled. "When you put it that way, well. . ."

A movement outside the window reflected in the pier glass over the sideboard caught Cleo's attention. It was Uncle Joe, and he seemed to be pacing. The murmur of his deep voice rattled the windowpane, but the words were undecipherable. The tone, however, sounded decidedly angry.

"Oh dear," Tante Flo said softly. Her gaze met Cleo's. "I think we ought to walk ourselves to the other side of the house and see to supper. You stir the étouffée, and I'll mix up the hush puppies."

Cleo snatched the basket and followed her aunt out of the parlor. An ache had begun in the pit of her stomach. No matter how good Tante Flo's cooking was, she doubted she'd be partaking tonight.

~

"Monsieur Trahan, if you'll just calm down, I'm sure we—"

"Calm down?" Joe stopped his pacing and stood at the far end of the porch, hands on hips. "Calm down?"

Planting his feet firmly on the porch boards, Theo stood. "Sir, I think there's been some misunderstanding here. I'm not sure what I've done to set you off, but—"

"Sit down!"

Although he was the bigger of the pair and younger than Joe by a decade and a half, Theo did as he was told.

Joe began to make a path across the porch again, passing the window where Theo had spied Clothilde standing moments ago. She was gone now, or at least she had the good sense to observe from a less visible spot.

Theo turned his attention away from the house and off toward the horizon. The rain seemed to be coming in fits and starts, blowing hard, then tapering off. Right now, there was nothing but a light drizzle falling from the eaves—a good time to make a run for home.

Except that his respect for Joe Trahan wouldn't let him move from the porch until he'd heard what Joe had to say. Judging from the way the man had taken up his pacing once more, he might be there awhile.

While he had no idea what had set Joe off, he knew better than to try to say anything to further aggravate him. One thing he knew for sure: Bringing the basket back had been a mistake.

Theo leaned back and heard the chains protest and clank. His stomach growled, joining the chorus of noises. Off in the distance, a flash of lightning zigzagged through the evening sky. The fresh smell of rain teased his nose and warned him that the lull in the weather soon would end.

He'd most likely be going home tonight hungry and wet.

Finally, Joe stopped short and grabbed a straight-backed chair and shoved it near the swing. He turned the chair backward and settled on the seat, resting his arms on the back. Eyes narrowed, he stared at Theo as if he expected Theo to know what had brought on his fit of anger.

"Anything you want to tell me, boy?" He shifted positions slightly but never broke his stare. "Because in my experience, a man owns up to his misdeeds up front. Now am I mistaken about judging you as a man?"

What in the world is Joe Trahan talking about?

"Sir, I'm not sure how to answer that. Is there something in particular we're talking about? Something I've done that's got you riled up?" A thought dawned, and along with it a possible explanation for Joe's anger. "Have you been talking to Alphonse?"

The older man looked puzzled. "What does your brother have to do with this?"

"Well, I just thought that maybe he. . .that is, considering I am supposed to be able to. . ." As Joe's confusion became more apparent, Theo stopped talking altogether. "Never mind."

Perhaps that secret was still safe. If so, then what was the trouble?

Joe made a slashing motion through the damp air with his hand. "Let's get right to it, young man. You got a problem with plain talk?"

Theo sat up a little straighter and squared his shoulders. "No, sir. In fact, I prefer it."

"Good." Joe grabbed the back of the chair with both hands, turning his knuckles white. He lowered his gaze and seemed to be studying the floor. "This isn't a conversation I ever hoped to have."

Theo's stomach complained again, and a gust of wind blew cold raindrops down his back. "Whatever it is, I'd appreciate if you'd get on with that plain talk."

Joe nodded and looked up. "That I will." He let out a long breath. "This is in regard to my niece, Clothilde."

Good. Finally a topic he could warm to.

Joe must have heard his pesky niece was snooping around the cabin today. *Serves her right to suffer her uncle's ire.* The only puzzle was why Joe seemed to be taking out a share of that irritation on him.

He pointed his finger at Theo. "Unless you can give me a good reason why my niece came home this afternoon with her clothes in a mess and her hair full of dust and pine needles, the next man you'll be talking plain with is going to be the reverend."

Theo opened his mouth to say something—anything—in his defense. Instead of allowing him to speak the words that would get him out of this mess, his mouth went dry and refused to work.

"Say something, Theophile Breaux, before I get my shotgun and loosen your jaw."

"Go ahead and tell him, young man."

He looked past Joe to where Clothilde's aunt stood at the front door. Again he failed to force words of innocence from his mouth.

She strolled across the porch to rest her hand on her husband's shoulder. "Joe, the funniest thing happened today out at the cabin." Meeting Theo's gaze, she nodded. "Don't be afraid to tell him about that hole in the roof my niece caused you to make. I got a good laugh out of the story when Cleo told me this afternoon."

Theo nodded. "Yes, well, you see, I was patching the roof over on the north side."

"That weak spot over the parlor?" Joe asked.

"Oui." Theo paused to swallow hard, praying the words wouldn't leave him again. "I was leaning over to make sure those nails were in straight when I spied a flash of yellow over to the east in the thicket."

"Clothilde," Joe said under his breath.

"Yes, sir, it was. I figured her for just hiding out and watching a spell, but she surprised me."

"I whistled." Clothilde stood at the door, leaning against the frame. "Well, I *did*," she said when her aunt and uncle turned to face her.

"So you didn't know she was underfoot?" Joe asked.

"No, sir. Before I knew what happened, there she stood at the bottom of the ladder, talking to me as if I'd seen her walk up." He continued to stare past the Trahans to their niece, eyes narrowed. "Which I *didn't*."

"I made plenty of noise. I didn't want him to think I was spying." She stared right back at him. "I thought you heard me."

"I was hammering." While he *had* heard whistling, he had no recollection of thinking it might be the Trahan girl.

Clothilde toyed with the end of her braid. "Not constantly."

"Enough for any normal person to know a man was working." Theo felt his blood begin to boil. "Last thing I expected was for you to change your mind about never seeing me again and pay me a visit while you were out on your stroll."

"I wasn't out for a stroll. I went to town on an errand."

"Which you failed to complete until I brought the basket back." Theo stood. "For all the grief it's caused me, I should have waited for you to come and get the stupid basket."

Joe rose and pushed the chair away. "I believe I've heard enough." He took his wife by the hand. "Why I thought there were shenanigans between these two is beyond me. I don't think I've ever met a more mismatched pair."

Flo offered a smile before she headed for the door. Joe disappeared inside, leaving Theo alone with Clothilde Trahan. At that moment, he decided taking his chances with the storm brewing on the other side of the porch rail was preferable to staying and risking another five minutes with the female tornado.

"Theo," Joe called. "Come on in here and get yourself some supper. I can hear your stomach growling from here."

Theo looked up at Clothilde. The object of his thoughts stood arrow straight with her arms crossed and her eyes narrowed. He felt about as welcome as that big cottonmouth.

"*Merci beaucoup*, sir, but I believe I'll just go on home."

Joe appeared in the doorway and pointed at Clothilde. "Get on in there and set this young man a plate. It's the least you can do, considering you nearly killed him this afternoon." As Cleo pressed past to disappear inside, Joe turned his attention to Theo. "Good thing my mother's bed never got moved out of the parlor after she passed on."

"You knew I fell through the roof?"

"Boy, that much was obvious." Joe shook his head. "What I *didn't* know was what part my niece played in the whole mess and where she was when you landed on the mattress." He paused. "Or where she ended up afterward."

Theo let out a pent-up breath and smiled. "I'm sure you can see you have nothing to worry about when it comes to your niece and me."

The older man gave him a level stare. "I see nothing of the sort. Watch yourself with that girl, or next time your fall won't be off a ladder."

~

Only later, across the kitchen table from Clothilde Trahan, after spending several hours sharing a meal and conversation, did Theo realize what her uncle had meant. By then, it was too late.

He'd fallen hard for Clothilde Trahan—and this time it had nothing to do with a hole in the roof.

The realization hit him somewhere between the shrimp étouffée and hush puppies and the sweet cake *gateau de sirop*. He'd been minding his own business, sipping chicory coffee and listening to Joe and his wife finish each other's sentences and laugh at each other's silly jokes, when he felt the wall around his heart begin to crack.

I want what they have. He suppressed a groan as he snuck a peek across the table at Clothilde Trahan. *And I want it with her.*

She smiled, first at her aunt and uncle and then at him. He tried and failed to return the gesture.

Lord, please take this feeling away. You and I have a deal, and it doesn't include Clothilde Trahan.

Until He did, Theo knew he'd just have to stay out of her way.

Chapter 10

Cleo swiped at the bottom of Uncle Joe's coffee cup with the dish towel, then set it on the drain board to dry. Once again, Cleo had only one cup to wash. Nearly a week had passed since Uncle Joe had had company in the morning for coffee.

And by company, she meant Theophile Breaux.

No sight of the Breaux fellow graced the front porch, nor did he come around on Sunday after church to talk to Uncle Joe. The only time Cleo had seen Theophile Breaux had been Sunday morning during services and then only from a distance. Rather than sit with his family in their usual third pew from the front, the carpenter chose to slip in the side door as the opening hymn began and sneak out the same way when the last strains of the hymn of invitation ended.

His behavior seemed even stranger since they'd spent such a lovely evening with her aunt and uncle—after the incident on the porch, that is. Cleo had actually begun to think that Theophile Breaux just might be a nice man.

The ruffled curtain swayed in the stiff north wind, winter's last dance before spring dawned on the bayou. Cleo suppressed a chill and inhaled the sweet scent of Easter lilies. She and Tante Flo spent hours babying the beautiful blossoms and had been rewarded with a bountiful crop.

They'd bloomed early, and as long as a freeze didn't come along before Easter Sunday, there would be plenty of fragrant white blossoms to decorate the altar at church. Before spring ended and the heat of summer set in, she would have to think about separating them out and creating a new bed with what they didn't give to neighbors and friends. Come winter, the process of growing the lilies would begin all over again.

Cleo wiped her hands, then tossed the dish towel over the drying rack. One chore down. What to do next?

She could polish the silver, but her aunt usually shared that job with her. Good conversation and frequent laughter often took place over the shiny pile of forks and spoons.

Tante Flo had gone to take a mess of freshly fried chicken to the Landry family down the bayou a ways. They had a new baby, born just last Wednesday.

Although Tante Flo claimed dropping off a meal was the neighborly thing to do, she always seemed to be most eager to visit the new mothers. Cleo suspected it might have something to do with the babies her aunt loved so much.

"She should have been a mama many times over. Too bad all she got was nosy old me." Cleo chuckled and reached for the broom. "I hope I do better than that."

As she swept the cobwebs out of the corners, she allowed her mind to drift to a time and place far in the future where she had a home of her own and a passel of children. In her mind, a brown-eyed son smiled up at her while a daughter with dark curls crawled at her feet. She pressed forward in time until she could imagine children of various sizes running and playing on the green lawn. Finally, a pair of twin boys chased butterflies past thick patches of Easter lilies.

"The first will be named Joseph. The second will have dark hair like his mama. I'll call him John."

She closed her eyes and smiled. The broom became her partner in an imaginary dance watched by the children she'd have someday.

Swaying to music only she could hear, she pictured her groom.

And saw Theophile Breaux.

Cleo's eyes flew open, and she dropped the broom. "Oh my," she said under her breath. "That's odd."

As she reached for the broom, a clanging sound made her jump. The mail boat.

Dropping the broom in the middle of the kitchen floor, she raced out the back door and headed for the little dock on the bayou. The arrival of a mail boat was rare—only once a month if that often—so the warning bell only had to be sounded once. Before the boat could dock, Cleo stood waiting for whatever the postman brought.

"Mademoiselle Trahan?"

"Oui. C'est moi."

As the portly, gray-haired gentleman dug down into a seemingly bottomless leather pouch marked UNITED STATES MAIL, Cleo tried not to fidget. Several times he examined letters or parcels through his thick spectacles, only to drop them back into the pouch. She found her patience nearly at an end when the fellow triumphantly pulled out a fistful of letters and thrust them toward her.

"Merci beaucoup, monsieur." She gathered the letters in her apron and raced toward the house.

"You're welcome," he called as he stepped back into the mail boat.

Waiting until she reached the kitchen to look at the letters was near to impossible, but somehow Cleo managed. When she finally reached the kitchen, she lifted the hem of her apron and let the papers spill onto the table.

Two notes from relatives and a postcard from her friend Margie covered a third envelope with a familiar return address: New Orleans.

Cleo lifted the letter from the pile and stared at the writing. Beneath the name of the college was the unmistakable handwriting—and name—of Uncle Joe's friend.

She dropped the letter onto the stack and took a step back. What to do? Waiting until Uncle Joe returned from his meeting with the reverend occurred to her, but only for a moment. Those meetings could take half the afternoon. And wait for Tante Flo? Well, that could mean she might not see the contents of the letter until after supper.

Inching forward, Cleo picked up the letter with her thumb and forefinger and held it to the stream of sunlight spilling through the kitchen window. Only the slightest outline of decidedly male handwriting appeared.

She sighed. In order to read the letter, she must open it.

Cleo dropped the letter into her pocket and made a neat stack of the remaining mail. Rather than read the letter immediately, she decided to wait in hopes that Uncle Joe might cut his visit short and return soon.

Actually, she hoped he didn't cut his visit short, but somehow delaying her plan to open the letter seemed better than doing it immediately. Retrieving the broom, she finished the job of sweeping out the kitchen, then patted her apron pocket. The letter felt stiff beneath the soft fabric.

With another glance out the kitchen window to ensure neither her aunt nor her uncle approached, Cleo slipped upstairs to her bedroom. She made short order of opening the letter. Actually reading it, however, took a bit longer.

First she had to close her eyes, and then she decided to pray. When she opened her eyes, she grasped the envelope and wedged it open. Barely breathing, she pulled the letter out and unfolded it.

Her eyes scanned the opening lines:

Dearest Joe,

It is with great pleasure that I received your letter of 4 March. For that reason, I felt a quick response was in order. Thus, I held the postman in waiting until I could write a brief note of. . .

The lines of handwriting on the page began to shake. When she realized it was her hands that quivered, she released the paper and let it fall to the coverlet.

"Maybe I don't want to know this." Cleo held her breath, then let it out slowly. "It might be bad news."

She stared down at the letter. *Just one more sentence, maybe two. If the news is bad, I'll reseal the letter and return it to the stack.*

Taking care to lift the letter by the corner, she leaned back against the wall and tucked her feet beneath her. Another deep breath, and she began to read again:

. . .a brief note of delight that you are committed to the education of the children in Latagnier. You and I have long believed local schools are sorely needed in remote areas of Louisiana, and I am most interested in helping you to fill the position of teacher that the new school will require.

Cleo smiled. "Well, nothing terrible yet. He's happy we're going to have a school, but who wouldn't be? And of course he's interested in filling the position. He works at a teachers' college."

With renewed hope, she went back to her reading:

And thus, in the spirit of friendship, I will be more than happy to come to your assistance by providing you with the name of a suitable candidate. In fact, I have taken the liberty of speaking to a colleague of mine who happened to be in my office at the time your letter was delivered. This colleague, a learned woman by the name of Ellen Granville, would be most pleased to take on the education of the local children, and she is. . .

"No," Cleo whispered. "It can't be."

Once again she let the paper fall. This time it sailed past the coverlet and lodged between the washbasin and the wall. She fell back against the pillows and tried not to cry. Failing that, she let the tears flow and closed her eyes.

When she opened her eyes once more, the sun slanted through her windows, waking Cleo from what was a brief but fitful sleep. She blinked hard, then shook her head to dislodge the cobwebs from her brain. Was it morning?

She looked out the window at the position of the sun. Hardly morning, it seemed more like midafternoon. Cleo rose and washed her face in the basin, then patted it dry. As she returned the towel to its place, she noticed the slip of paper at her feet.

The letter.

Bending to retrieve it, she allowed the page to fall open. As she reread the words her uncle's friend had penned, she noticed she hadn't read the entire text of the letter.

. . .and she is pleased to state that pending your favorable response, she will arrive in Latagnier at summer's end.

"At summer's end." Cleo whispered the words, then repeated them, rolling the sounds over on her tongue as she enunciated each syllable with care.

What lovely words they were. Words that bought her an entire summer's worth of time to convince Uncle Joe that she should be the teacher, not some woman named Ellen Granville whose only credentials were a college education and a letter of recommendation from Uncle Joe's friend.

Cleo giggled. So much could happen between now and summer's end. After all, March was on its way out, and April dawned in two days. In five months' time, Cleo fully expected to have the children of Latagnier on their way to a well-rounded education and to have her uncle convinced that another teacher was unnecessary.

Folding the page back into its original shape and inserting it in the envelope, she tucked it into her pocket and pinched her cheeks to heighten the color. With five months until her deadline, she would definitely need a partner to see it to completion.

As she passed the kitchen table, she gave passing thought to replacing the letter in the pile of mail. Instead, she decided to own up to reading the letter in person rather than risk Uncle Joe or Tante Flo finding the evidence before she returned.

Crossing the lawn, she veered toward the path leading along the bayou, then struck out for the far end of the property where the little cabin—and her future—awaited. It wasn't until she neared the building site that she began to have second thoughts.

What if the carpenter went to her uncle with the news that she'd been meddling? Worse, what if she caught him by surprise again and caused him to. . . Well, she just wouldn't think on that. This time she'd call his name from the time she stepped out of the thicket until she neared the cabin. Until he responded, she'd just keep calling.

This decided, she picked up her pace, stepping carefully through the thicket lest the big cottonmouth left any friends or family behind. The thought of asking the carpenter for help made meeting a snake seem positively fun.

Signs of progress greeted her as she neared the cabin. The roof seemed to have been patched, and the porch no longer held rotten boards on its newly painted floor. Even the handrails seemed to stand straighter, although they did not yet wear a new coat of paint.

Cleo peered into the parlor window. The mess she'd encountered upon her last trip here had been replaced by a room swept clean of wood and dust. Grandma's bed still stood in the center of the room, but it had been stripped of its mattress, which now sat rolled up in the corner.

Was it her imagination or perhaps a trick of the light? Rather than wearing the signs of age, the old iron bed seemed to have been polished to a bright shine.

"Strange."

She walked to the front door and pushed on it, smiling when it gave way. "Monsieur Breaux!" she called.

No answer.

Cleo stepped inside and looked around. This part had also been cleared away, and the wall that formerly divided the space had been removed. Marks on another wall showed where the carpenter planned to create space for a new door.

To her right, an area perfect for rows of students to sit greeted her. On her left, she saw a place for the old desk from Uncle Joe's attic. The center had been left open, a grand space despite its tiny proportions.

Wrapping her arms around herself, Cleo tried to imagine what the room would be like once it had been filled with children. With the windows open to the breeze off the bayou and the cobwebs gone, this would be a fit schoolroom.

The carpenter had outdone himself.

"Merci beaucoup, Lord," she whispered as she made her way to the door and emerged into the bright sunshine.

She stepped carefully off the porch and called the Breaux fellow's name once more. Still no answer.

Rounding the corner, she spied Theophile Breaux standing beside a pile of lumber, a saw in one hand. When she waved, he seemed to ignore her. As she called his name, he shook his head.

"Go on home" came the gruff response.

"I'd like a word with you." She ignored his frown to offer a smile. "Please," she added. "I won't take up much time. I promise."

"You already have," he said as he pressed past her to head for the cabin, then disappeared around the corner.

Chapter 11

Theo tempered his anger as he stomped across the porch. His first inclination was to give the heavy front door a swift kick or, better yet, to send it swinging so hard it flew off the hinges.

But slamming the door and causing something he had repaired to break again wouldn't serve any good. Given his frustration level, it sure would feel dandy about now, however.

Still, he'd be the one who would have to fix it, and extra repairs meant extra time in Latagnier. The last thing he needed was more time in this town.

More time in close proximity to Clothilde Trahan.

"Last thing I need," he grumbled.

Theo stomped inside, leaving the front door standing open. He didn't dare touch it for fear he'd go against his good intentions and close the thing so hard he'd bust out the frame and half the front wall.

A swirl of blue caught his attention outside. He stopped short. Clothilde Trahan still stood beside the woodpile, her skirts swaying in the fresh breeze. While he watched, the wind picked up her waist-length braid, then let it drop once more. All the while, she seemed to be staring at a point opposite the house.

Theo stepped back when she directed her attention toward the cabin. What on earth was she doing here?

He'd certainly reminded himself and the Lord of his promise to keep his distance from her, and yet there the woman remained. From his vantage point, she seemed to be in no hurry to leave.

She pulled an envelope from her apron pocket, took out a piece of paper, and unfolded it, taking care to keep it from flying away as she turned her back to the wind. Head bowed, she studied the paper, then refolded the page, returned it to the envelope, and put it back in her pocket.

Maybe she'll understand I want nothing to do with her, and she'll go home. He stood there a moment longer in hopes of watching her disappear into the thicket, but she never moved.

Theo grumbled under his breath and set to work on the one chore that seemed appropriate to the moment—demolishing something.

With every swing of the sledgehammer, his muscles—and his heart—pulled and twisted. As each piece of wall crumbled and fell, so did his resolve, until he knew he could stand it no longer.

"Listen to her."

He let the heavy tool fall to the floor and swiped at his brow. What?

The words had come to him as plain as if someone stood beside him and had whispered in his ear. He looked behind him and to the right and the left. He was alone.

"Listen to her."

There. He heard it again. "Who's there?" he called.

No answer.

Then, in the depths of his heart, he realized whose voice he'd heard. Goose bumps rose on his arms.

"Just listen."

Theo leaned against what was left of the wall and shook his head. He was a churchgoing man and a believer in the ever-reaching power of God, but never had the Lord spoken to him in such a clear voice.

It figured that He'd be asking for the last thing Theo wanted to do.

Arguing with the Creator of the universe seemed pointless, but obedience felt even less logical. What could that silly girl have to tell him that he didn't already know?

"Plenty."

Theo straightened his back and set his jaw. If he must do as he was told, at least he could try to make one last deal.

All right, Lord, You win. If she's still out there, I'll hear her out. Remember though, You and I made a deal, and I'm supposed to be free to head out of here whenever I wish.

He paused, thinking the Lord might answer. He didn't.

All right, then. If I have a say in things, could You see to her not being there, and we'll just call this conversation between me and her over before it starts? I'd be much obliged. I promise I'll listen just like You said next time I see her.

Once again, God was silent on the subject.

Whichever way You want it, then, Father. I want what You want, or at least I'm trying to.

Adding a quick "amen" to his prayer, Theo set off toward the back of the cabin, where a glance out the window showed him the Lord had indeed answered his prayer.

She was gone.

No flowing blue skirts or dancing black braid greeted him. No big brown eyes or pretty face to charm him and scare the living daylights out of him all at the same time. Only the woodpile and a skinny orange cat with a bent tail and an ornery look were framed by the window.

"Well, how about that?"

Theo couldn't help it. Right there he threw back his head and laughed out loud. He chuckled like a fool, laughing so hard his side began to ache.

"Thank You, Jesus!" he shouted to the rafters. "Thank You, thank You, thank You!"

As he headed back to the front of the cabin with a spring in his step, he began to whistle the closing hymn from last week's church service. It was a peppy tune, one of those songs that seeps joy all the way down to the bone and causes the toes to tap. He made it all the way to the second stanza before he picked up the sledgehammer and aimed it once more at the remnants of the wall.

Wood crumbled beneath each blow until bits and pieces of shattered timber littered the floor and decorated his clothing. While he worked, he whistled, giving thanks to God with each stroke of the sledgehammer.

The job completed, Theo paused to shake the particles from his hair and wipe his brow.

"Finally. I couldn't say a thing for all that noise" came the sweet voice behind him.

Clothilde Trahan.

Theo whirled around to see the vision in blue sitting primly on the lone chair in the room. In his astonishment, he dropped the sledgehammer. It landed with a *thud* on his left foot, and he howled.

"Of all the—" Theo bit his lip and stared at the menace in blue.

He looked down at his foot, as much to check the damage as to keep his gaze from meeting hers. While there seemed to be no outward damage, it hurt something awful. No, it throbbed. He'd have a hard time sleeping tonight for sure.

And it would be a long walk—or rather hobble—home.

He risked a glance and saw the girl sitting peacefully on the edge of her chair. Something about her calm expression sparked his ire.

She seemed to be enjoying herself immensely. "I'm terribly sorry. I thought you knew I was sitting here."

"You know, Mademoiselle Trahan, I once had a pretty mare by the name of Stella," he said through gritted teeth. "Every time I came close to her, she would bite me." He moved a step closer to the smiling source of irritation. "When I put a saddle on her, she stomped my feet, and when I managed to ride her, she threw me every time."

Theo paused to gauge Cleo's reaction. She gave nothing of her feelings away. He closed the distance between them in three steps and stood towering over her.

"I finally figured out that every time she and I shared the same space, something bad happened to me."

He leaned down to get on eye level, being careful to favor the foot that did not ache. The Trahan woman sat very still and silent. Only her large eyes gave an indication he might be causing her some measure of upset.

"So," he said slowly, "the day came when I decided enough was enough. Do you know what I did with that mare?"

She leaned slightly back, putting some distance between them. "What?"

"I traded her to a circuit-riding preacher for a can of beans and a new hammer."

"Oh?"

"That's right. Next time I saw that preacher, he tried to return her. Said he was tired of wondering when his next bruise was coming. I gave him back his beans and hammer and sent the horse out to pasture."

"Really?"

"Oui." He paused to give his message full effect. "You, Mademoiselle Trahan, remind me very much of Stella. Just like that circuit-riding preacher, I wonder where my next bruise is coming from whenever you're around."

For a moment, she seemed to be waiting for the rest of the story. Then she nodded as though understanding dawned. "Merci."

What in the world? He shook his head, then gave her a sideways glance. "Excuse me?"

"That Stella must have been one smart horse. She ended up getting her way after all." The woman had the audacity to grin. "I appreciate the comparison."

Cleo watched with smug satisfaction, then remorse, as the big man's handsome face turned several shades of scarlet. Of course she knew he hadn't meant to compliment her by comparing her to some ornery horse he used to own.

She should be ashamed for teasing him. If only she didn't find it so easy to spark his ire—and so much fun. Unfortunately, her behavior had done nothing to gain his cooperation in her plan.

Her plan.

Staring up into Theophile Breaux's eyes, she almost forgot her plan. *Time to make amends.*

"Monsieur Breaux, I'm terribly sorry." She rose and ducked under his watchful gaze and walked toward the window. A sweet orange cat lounged on the woodpile. She watched it swat at a butterfly and miss. "I know I've caused you much distress."

"Distress?" He repeated the word. "Now what makes you think that?"

She waved away his question with a lift of her hand. "No need to spare my feelings. I realize I tend to cause, well, disasters when I'm around you."

He said nothing, and she dared not turn to gauge his expression. Instead, she watched the cat yawn and settle in for a nap atop the woodpile, then felt for the letter in her pocket.

"I'm sorry about causing you to hurt your foot today and for all the other bruises I've inflicted." She turned around slowly. "None was intentional."

The carpenter stood in the shadows, arms crossed over his chest. His face showed no sign of emotion. "Never thought they were."

"I should get to the reason why I came here."

His lips quirked into a wry smile. "There's a reason?"

Cleo thought a moment before plunging into an explanation of her plan. "The sooner my uncle sees how well I can teach the children, the sooner he will realize he doesn't need to hire a teacher from that fancy college in New Orleans."

When Theophile offered no response, Cleo closed the distance between them to press on with her explanation. "Or maybe he will be so impressed with my abilities that he will send *me* to the college. Either way, I need your help."

He peered down at her with a look of amusement. "Why me? Surely there are other men you can torture, eh?"

"I'm going to ignore that comment, Monsieur Breaux." She took a deep breath of dusty air, then tried not to cough. "The time is limited, and I really need you to get busy finishing the schoolhouse before this happens." She pulled the letter out of her pocket and waved it under the carpenter's nose. "It came today."

Theophile took a step back and shook his head. "Wait a minute. What are you talking about?"

Unfolding the letter, she thrust it in his direction. "Here, read it for yourself."

He waved away the paper and turned to reach for the sledgehammer. "I'm too busy to be trifled with, Mademoiselle Trahan. Allons. Go home to your aunt and uncle."

Cleo trotted behind him as he strode into the fresh air. As he stepped off the porch, she followed, fairly running to keep up with his long, hobbled strides.

"Wait. You don't understand. You're the only one who can help me!" she called, yet he kept walking.

Finally, she lunged forward to grasp the carpenter by the elbow. To her surprise, he whirled around, causing her to run into him. Stunned, she reeled back and let go of the letter. It fluttered to the ground, where Theophile retrieved it.

"Here, now go home." He tried to place the letter in her hand, but she refused to take it.

"Just read the letter," she said as she tested her balance and straightened her apron. "Then maybe you'll understand why I need your help."

He carried the letter as if it might burn him, barely touching the edges of the paper with his thumb and forefinger as he held it at arm's length.

The flush of scarlet anger caused earlier now reappeared on his face. His expression bore something besides anger. Was it embarrassment? Cleo studied the carpenter closely.

Eyes downcast, he placed the letter in her hand. Without a word, he tossed the sledgehammer atop the woodpile. Thankfully the orange cat had already lit out for parts unknown, for Theophile certainly hadn't so much as cast a glance in that direction before he made his throw.

"What?" she called as he strode away. "What did I do this time?"

Again she raced to catch up. "It's this letter, isn't it?"

He slowed his uneven pace, but not by much. "What is it you want from me?" he asked over his shoulder as he headed for the thicket.

"I came to ask you to speed up the repairs on the cabin so I can begin teaching sooner, that's all. I want a chance to show Uncle Joe that I can do the job." She took a deep breath and darted to cut him off, coming to a halt on the path between him and the bayou. "This letter says the new teacher will be here by the end of summer. See?"

She stuck the letter under his nose and pointed to the line telling her uncle when the teacher would arrive. The carpenter stared in the direction of her finger, but curiously, his eyes did not seem to be reading, nor did he look to comprehend the information the page contained.

"Oh, no," she whispered as realization dawned. "You can't read."

Chapter 12

I'm so sorry!" the girl called as Theo made tracks toward the bayou and the road home. "Please forgive me" followed him on the breeze.

Forgive? Forgetting was more his concern, for he never wanted to think on the events of this day again.

Never had he been so humiliated. Leave it to the Trahan girl to hit him right where it hurt, and he wasn't thinking of his sore foot. What *was* it about that woman? If she wasn't inflicting bruises on his body, she was paining his heart.

In this case, she had no idea what she'd done. If only he'd managed to hide his lack of education. Always before he'd been able to bluff his way through any situation where reading was required. Why, he'd sat at Joe Trahan's kitchen table any number of times and looked at the scribbles and lines Joe put on the page, never letting on he couldn't decipher them.

He'd always tucked the pages into his pocket and taken them home for his brother Alphonse to read, and then he'd come back to the Trahan place the next morning armed with the information contained on the pages. If Joe's snoopy little niece hadn't barged into his life, his secret would still be safe.

Now the whole town of Latagnier would know that Theophile Breaux was illiterate. Oh, he knew plenty of pretty words, and his mama made sure he used them correctly. He just couldn't make any sense of them on a page. Worse, when he opened Mama's Bible, the words made as much sense as the scratching the chickens made in the dirt.

It wasn't that he didn't want to read. He did. Unfortunately, there had been no time for book learning.

The eldest of the bunch, he'd always been called on to help Papa with the trapping or the trotlines, so schooling had been sparse through the years. Finally, when he grew two heads taller than the other students and stuck out like a sore thumb in the classroom, he gave it up altogether.

Sometimes in church he prayed that the Lord would help him make sense of the garbled letters and numbers that made up scripture and hymns. Other times he decided he was destined to go through life with other folks reading it to him.

Never, though, had he envisioned anyone besides Alphonse knowing his shortcoming. He'd always been a quick study, fast to learn and memorize and faster still to pretend he could decipher the words on paper. Papa never knew, or he'd be disappointed for sure, being as he'd nearly gone to college. The fact that the Trahan girl had been the one to figure it out stung.

"Please don't go!" the object of his thoughts called. "Come back!"

He debated for a half second before picking up his pace, grimacing with every step. A moment later, he entered the thicket. If he was lucky, she'd run into difficulties with that skirt and apron of hers and be unable to pass through the narrow path.

A tap on his back answered the question of his luck—not that he truly believed such a thing existed. It just seemed easier to blame luck, or the lack of it, than the Lord for his current situation.

Theo cast a glance behind him and was greeted by Clothilde's smiling face. She had a lot more stamina than he expected, especially for a girl of her small size wearing a pretty spring frock. Of course, he could outrun her if he wanted, even with the handicap of an injured foot, but somehow he knew he'd never get rid of her that way.

Better to face his nemesis here and now than to wonder when she would find him. From what he knew of Clothilde Trahan, she *would* find him.

Nova Scotia was beginning to sound awfully tempting right now. He imagined for a moment arriving in Canada only to find the Trahan woman had beat him there.

"Just listen."

"Please stop for a moment, Monsieur Breaux."

"Listen."

"All right," he said as much to her as to the gentle but insistent voice in his mind.

Theo stopped and turned to face her. She lagged only a few steps behind, a vision in blue, with the hated paper still crumpled in her hand.

"Say it," he demanded, pointing to the letter. "Go ahead. Laugh at me for not being able to read. I know you must find it highly amusing."

He affected a menacing stance, hands on hips and the worst grimace he could conjure up. After a moment, he noticed it had no effect on the girl. She stood very near, looking up with eyes shimmering with tears. To make matters worse, her bottom lip trembled.

Something inside crumbled.

His grimace melted, and he jammed his fists into his pants pockets. Looking away, he pretended to study the spiked leaves of a nearby palmetto.

It took every bit of gumption he had not to take her into his arms and soothe her strife. Instead, he reminded himself that this woman was dangerous. Not only did she know his secret, but she also held the key to a heart he'd locked up for its own protection.

Did he want to end up like his papa? Did he truly believe that seeing those brown eyes look up at him every morning and feeling those lips kiss him every night were worth putting away his traveling shoes and taking up the plow?

For a horrible moment, Theo actually considered that the answer to both questions might be yes. Then good sense prevailed, and he shook off the crazy thought with a wave of his hand.

"I *said* I would stop, and I *did*. Speak your piece so I can get on home."

What to say? Cleo bit her lip to keep it from trembling. She waited for something brilliant to come to mind, some word or phrase that would soothe the ruffled feelings of the carpenter. Instead, she could only think of how she might feel in the same circumstances.

"Well now, looks like I've done the impossible," Theophile said. "I've silenced the most talkative woman in Latagnier." He bowed from the waist in an imitation of courtly manners. "I'm so pleased to have been of service." With that, he turned and stalked away.

"*Arête!* Do you always run away like a coward?"

Did I just say that out loud?

The carpenter froze. Time seemed suspended. Even the birds ceased their chirping.

Cleo felt the letter crumple as her fingers squeezed her hand into a fist. She hurriedly stuffed the ruined paper into her apron pocket. Telling Uncle Joe she'd snooped and read the contents of his letter was the least of her worries at this point.

Theophile Breaux still stood with his back to her. Cleo carefully picked her way through the narrow path until she reached him. There was no going around him—the width of the path would not allow it—and turning back would brand her as much of a coward as he.

Her heart sank when she saw his shoulders slump.

The carpenter was *not* a coward. How awful of her to think that, much less make the accusation aloud. Someone who tried so hard to cover up something embarrassing could only be thought of as courageous for making such an effort. That he would leave rather than continue a discussion on his inability to read seemed understandable.

What was wrong with her? She always said or did the wrong thing when she found herself in his presence.

Cleo reached out with a trembling hand to touch his sleeve. "I'm terribly, terribly sorry. I shouldn't have—"

"Shouldn't have what?" Jerking his arm away, he turned to face her. Despite the flash of fire in his eyes, his face appeared calm. "Shouldn't have told the truth? I suppose to you I *am* a coward, running away instead of staying here at this cabin and listening to you laugh at me."

She blinked back tears. "I never laughed at you."

The carpenter seemed to consider her statement for a moment before looking away. "I'll have the schoolhouse finished as quick as I can, and then I'll be gone." He swung his gaze back to meet hers. "Call it running or just getting away, but I intend to be on the first train out of town after this job is done."

Before she could respond, he turned and walked away. He'd gone a few yards down the path when he stopped abruptly and faced her once more.

"I'd be obliged if you'd not mention this to anyone. I'll be gone soon enough."

Gone. No more visits with the carpenter and no more casual suppers or coffees with her uncle. No more fussing and debating and apologizing for causing him to fall through the roof or step through a rotten porch board. No more teasing. No more pine needles in her hair or close encounters with overlarge cottonmouths.

No more Theophile Breaux.

She looked up into his face and felt her heart skid to a stop. Before she could think better of it, she spoke the words that were on her heart.

"Monsieur Breaux, I don't want you to leave Latagnier."

Her statement seemed to take him by surprise as much as it did her. For a second he looked to be fumbling with his words. She, on the other hand, began wishing with all her might that she could reel hers back in.

"I don't see as how you have a say in the matter," he finally stated. *"Sa te regard pas."*

"Maybe I *am* making it concern me. What do you think about that?"

Cleo couldn't believe her own brazenness. Why, if this were any man other than Theophile Breaux, she might consider their exchange to be flirting.

"I try not to think about you at all, Mademoiselle Trahan."

He said it, but something in his demeanor gave Cleo serious doubts about whether he actually meant it.

Whirling around to make the short walk home, she wondered if she'd made a mistake. No matter what Theophile Breaux thought, he was stuck with her—at least until the schoolhouse was complete.

After that, only *le bon Dieu* knew for sure.

"I'll be back tomorrow to see how the renovations are progressing, Monsieur Breaux."

"Is that a promise or a threat, cher?" came his quick reply.

She stopped and suppressed a smile. "What did you call me?" she asked without turning around.

When he failed to respond, she headed for home. This time she wore a smile.

Chapter 13

Knee deep in the thicket with an aching foot, Theo tried to make sense of what he had just heard. The prettiest girl in Latagnier stood right there in front of him, calling him a coward one minute and asking him to stick around the next.

She seemed to think better of the words as soon as she spoke them, for she pressed past him and fled. But she left without taking the statement back, a sign she *did* mean what she said.

Then there was the business of calling her cher. That endearment hadn't come out of his mouth in regard to a woman in years.

He should have gone after her. He could have caught her in no time. She wasn't any bigger than a minute and wore those silly skirts that would more than slow her down.

But if he had, what would he have said? That he didn't want to leave her, either? That he'd stay?

While the first thought was true, the second was impossible. He and the Lord had a deal, and Clothilde Trahan was *not* a part of it.

He would miss her. That much was certain. But stay here in Latagnier, give up his plan to head for Nova Scotia? How could he do that for a mere slip of a girl?

He'd spend the rest of his life wondering if she was worth it. *"No, you won't."*

Ignoring the insistent voice, Theo watched the Trahan woman's back until she disappeared up the path. When he could no longer see blue skirts and dark hair, Theo turned and headed back to the cabin. The schoolhouse, he corrected. He'd have to start thinking of the place as a school. It was sure going to be one in short order.

That would make Mademoiselle Trahan very happy.

Once she saw his handiwork, she would forget all about thinking he ought to stick around. What did she have in mind for him anyway? Courting? That hardly seemed possible.

He'd fallen hard that night across the supper table, but since then he'd had no trouble keeping his distance. At least *he'd* managed to stay away.

She's the one who keeps ending up underfoot.

A thought dawned, and he stopped to savor it. Clothilde Trahan didn't want him to leave Latagnier, and she couldn't keep away from the schoolhouse.

What did those two things add up to?

Theo ducked under a low-hanging pine branch, then shook his head.

Nothing that made any sense. Logic told him the Trahan girl didn't have a brain in her head when it came to men, but his heart told him otherwise. Something in her words today showed her feelings—he just knew it.

Something that said she cared.

He headed back to the site with this thought still chasing him. Picking up the hammer to pound nails reminded him of the expression on her face when he'd been caught off guard while demolishing the wall. As he looked around, he realized just about everything at the schoolhouse reminded him of Clothilde Trahan.

He sighed. The whole idea of taking up with Joe Trahan's niece just seemed too far-fetched. What would a smart girl like her want with a dumb carpenter like him?

"Ask her."

"Now that's the craziest thing I've heard in a long time," he said under his breath. "Crazier than thinking a girl like her would be interested in a man like me."

Still, he walked home with a spring in his step, or at least as much of a spring as he could manage with only one good foot. His sunny disposition carried him all the way to bedtime, when he finally lay his head down on his pillow and closed his eyes.

There, in the darkness, he generally met his Savior one last time before falling asleep. Tonight, however, thoughts of the day intruded.

Allowing the events of the afternoon to unfold once more in his mind, Theo recounted each word, every exchange of conversation between himself and Joe's niece.

As he fell into the blackness of sleep, he realized one important thing: Either he made it his business to court Clothilde Trahan, or he made it his business to leave her alone. Dangling between the two extremes like a puppet on a string would only lead to disaster.

~

He awoke knowing he had to make a decision. Taking his time would be best, he decided, as something of this importance could not be rushed. He bade his mama and papa good-bye and headed off to the schoolhouse to see how much one man could get done in a day.

Along the way, his path somehow veered off, and he ended up on Joe Trahan's doorstep. Flo welcomed him in and poured his coffee, dealing him his fair share of eggs and bacon without asking if he wanted any. To his surprise, Clothilde joined them.

"Bonjour, Monsieur Breaux," she said as she breezed in, looking as if she'd taken all morning to get that pretty. Today she wore pink. It matched the color in her cheeks.

If he had his way, she'd never wear any other color.

Her braid lay coiled on the back of her head. Theo's fingers itched to set it free, to let the braid fall and release the blue-black strands altogether.

Would her hair fall in curls, or did she have straight, thick strands? He'd never seen it down around her shoulders, nor would a proper lady be seen that way. Still, whichever she possessed, he knew it would feel like silk in his hands.

"Monsieur Breaux," Flo said. *"Quoi y'a?"*

"Wrong? Nothing's wrong." When he realized the other three inhabitants of the kitchen were staring at him, he cast about for something to say. "Bonjour, Mademoiselle Clothilde," he finally said over the rim of his coffee cup as he watched her settle onto the seat across from him. "Comment ça va?"

"Very well, thank you, but please call me Cleo. Everyone else does."

"Cleo." Yes, he liked the sound of that. Clothilde was too sizable and formal for such a tiny thing. "All right, but only if you call me Theo."

"We rhyme." When his confusion showed, she shrugged. "Theo and Cleo. We rhyme."

"Yes," he said slowly. "I guess we do."

She nibbled at the corner of a piece of dry toast, then dabbed at her mouth with a napkin. "I'm surprised to see you here this morning." She paused to offer a radiant smile. "In light of our conversation yesterday, I mean."

Theo cleared his throat and gave Joe a sideways glance. He seemed to be taking in their exchange with interest. Thankfully, if he had any thoughts on the matter, he held his peace.

Their conversation yesterday? What in the world was she up to?

Time to change the topic fast. Theo cast about for another item to discuss—something that didn't involve Clothilde Trahan, at least not directly.

"So, Joe, you got anything new to show me this morning?"

Joe seemed to think on the question a moment. "No," he said. "Nothing new this morning."

What? Joe Trahan with no new scribblings to show him? Nothing he'd figured since yesterday? Not likely. Theo met Cleo's direct gaze. Had she mentioned to her uncle that his carpenter couldn't read?

She gave him an innocent look, then reached for the sugar bowl. Dousing her coffee with several spoonfuls, she began to stir the black liquid in leisurely circles.

Her smile should have been a warning. Innocence like hers was dangerous. "Uncle Joe, Theo and I have a confession to make."

Theo nearly dropped his fork. "We do?"

Joe seemed to take particular interest in Cleo's statement. He pushed his spectacles onto his nose and peered at her, then turned his attention to Theo. "Oh?"

Cleo set a folded piece of paper on the table, then pushed it toward Joe. "This came yesterday."

"Is that right?" he asked. "Why am I just now getting it today? I thought I had all of the mail already. It looks like it's been read." He paused. "And fought over."

Cleo turned her substantial charm on her uncle. "Now that part's mostly my fault. You see, I was anxious and—"

"And so you snooped."

She nodded as Joe picked up the slightly crumpled sheet of paper and began to read. The mere act of watching someone else read generally gave Theo a range of mixed feelings. This morning, however, he only had one: dread.

"Well now," Joe said as his eyes scanned the page. "Isn't this interesting?" He peered over the paper to look at Theo. "What part did you play in this, son?"

Before Theo could answer, Cleo came to his rescue. "He didn't actually play an active part. His was more like a supporting role."

Joe shook his head. "Speak plain, child."

Cleo offered another radiant smile. "You see, when I read that there would be a new teacher for the school, of course I wanted to go out and see if the place would be ready for her in time." She broadened her smile. "Well, it turns out there is a slight problem with that, isn't there, Theo?"

Joe turned to Theo as if he might be able to shed some light on the subject. Theo shrugged.

"The problem," Cleo continued, "is that the schoolhouse renovations will be completed well before the teacher's arrival."

"Is that right?" Joe asked him.

When Theo nodded, Joe turned his attention back to Cleo. "So what does that have to do with a problem at the schoolhouse? I'd say that the teacher arriving to a completed classroom is what we want."

Cleo shifted in her chair and stared at Theo. Again innocence shone on her face. Again he made a note to watch out for her. Pretty things came in small packages. . .but so did dynamite.

"Do you want to answer that?" When he shook his head, she continued. "The problem is that we will have a whole block of time that will be wasted if we wait until the teacher can come from New Orleans. The classroom will sit empty, and the children will be spending their time doing other things rather than learning."

"I see your point," Flo interjected.

Joe waved away her statement with a lift of his hand. "I don't." Once again he turned to Theo. "Do you know what she's talking about?"

"Well," he said slowly, "actually, I do." He took a bite of Flo's scrambled eggs and savored them while the three Trahans watched. When he could postpone his answer no longer, he nodded toward Cleo. "You have a schoolhouse almost finished and a whole passel of children who want to learn, right?"

"Right," Joe said.

"So what Cleo here is saying is that she can take on the teacher's job until your friend from New Orleans shows up to relieve her from duty. The kids have a head start on their book learning, and Cleo stays out of trouble." He paused, ignoring the look on her face. "Well, at least she gets in less trouble, eh?"

Joe reached for his coffee mug and took a long drink of the stiff brew. Setting the cup back on the table, he turned his gaze on Flo. She smiled and nodded. A moment later, he echoed her gesture, then expanded it to a chuckle.

"I don't suppose it would hurt to have my niece teaching the children, at least until a proper teacher arrives," he said.

"Cleo, is that something you want to do?" Flo asked.

"Oui," she said. "I want this very much, Tante Flo." She reached for her uncle's hand. "I promise I'll do a good job, Uncle Joe."

"Be careful what you promise," Joe said.

Funny, he was speaking to Cleo but looking at Theo.

Theo chewed another mouthful of eggs, then swiped at his mouth with the napkin. "I'd best be off," he declared as he rose. "I've got plenty to keep me busy today."

"I'm sure you do, dear," Flo said. "Do be careful out there. You never know what's going to happen."

"Especially with my niece on the loose." Joe pushed his spectacles back down on the bridge of his nose. He winked at Cleo, then picked up the newspaper. "Maybe I'll come out there later and check on your progress."

"That'd be fine, sir." Out of the corner of his eye, Theo saw Cleo watching them. "I'd welcome the chance to show you what I've been up to. I think you'll be surprised at how much progress has been made."

"Or maybe I'll just send Clothilde. Most days she seems to end up out there anyway." Joe seemed to take no notice of his niece's cry of protest as he lowered the paper a notch and peered over the pages.

"I wish you'd rethink that," Theo said, ignoring the urge to glance at Cleo to gauge her reaction. "It's awfully dangerous what with all the work going on out there, and Mademoiselle Trahan *is* a woman after all."

Joe paused a moment, then suppressed a smile as he stared down at Theo's sore foot. "I see your point."

"Well then, I'd best be off to work." He braved a look at Cleo, who stared back with no visible sign of emotion. Beside her, Flo sipped her coffee, barely hiding a grin with her cup.

"Pleasure seeing you this morning, Theo," Flo said. "Give your mama and papa our best, will you? And tell them I'll be over tomorrow with a fresh mess of shelled peas."

He nodded. "Yes'm. I will."

Theo headed for the door as if a hive of bees were on his tail. Nothing would please him more than to see Cleo Trahan's pretty face out at the schoolhouse every day. Unfortunately, nothing would be more dangerous—to his health and to his heart.

"Buck up, man," Theo said under his breath. "That girl's poison to your plans. One false step and you'll be heading to the church instead of Canada."

"Did you say something, Theo?"

"I'm sorry. What?" He whirled around to see Cleo standing in the doorway.

Arms wrapped around her middle, a smile decorated the Trahan girl's face. She took a couple of tentative steps toward him, then leaned against the porch rail and wrapped her fingers around the post.

"Who—me, say something? No." *Not to you, anyway.*

"That's funny," she said. "I thought I heard you say something about Canada."

His breath froze in his throat. What else had she heard?

"Canada? Oui. It's nice there this time of year," he said, hoping the casualness in his response hid the truth of his feelings. "A little chilly, but nice."

She looked perplexed. *Good. Maybe she'll think I'm one of those old men who talks to himself, and she'll steer clear of me.*

"Yes, well, thank you for speaking to Uncle Joe on my behalf," she said. "I hope that now I will get a chance to show him what I can do."

"I'll do my part and get the place in shape as quick as I can."

He turned and set off down the road, wondering if she still stood on the porch, watching. As he turned toward the path leading to the schoolhouse, he glanced back to see that she did.

"Theo, boy, you are in a whole heap of trouble," he said as the Trahan place disappeared behind the thicket.

Chapter 14

Allons, you lazy thing. Get up from your nap in that hammock, and let's go fishing. You're wasting a perfectly good Sunday afternoon."

Theo lifted one eyelid to see his brother Alphonse staring down at him. If the truth were known, he'd been wide awake well before the skinny kid had begun stomping around the far end of the porch in the process of gathering his fishing gear.

"Arête."

"No, I don't believe I'll stop." Alphonse balanced the net in his hand, then swung it like a tennis racket within inches of Theo's head. "Vien ici, big brother. The big ones'll be biting this afternoon. I feel it in my bones."

"Those bones of yours are going to find themselves broken if you come near me with that net again." Leaning up on one elbow, Theo balanced himself on the wobbling hammock, then fired a nasty look at his brother. "Unlike *you*, who snored like Great-granny Delchamp's old bulldog, *I* stayed awake during the pastor's sermon this morning."

Alphonse shrugged and tossed the net over his shoulder. "You're absolutely right, Theo." He paused to gather up the net and his cane pole. "But then, I'd stay awake, too, if the girl I was sweet on sat three rows ahead of me on the right in a pretty yellow dress with a bow in her hair."

Theo fairly flew out of the hammock, causing Alphonse to make tracks to the other side of the porch, then off into the yard. "Has it ever occurred to you that I might be staying awake to hear what Pastor Broussard has to say?"

His brother seemed to consider Theo's statement for a moment. When a smile broke out on the boy's face, Theo braced himself for the smart-aleck answer he knew he was about to hear.

"Has it ever occurred to you that I might be taking a nap in church to let Pastor Broussard's message sink in deeper? I read something about that somewhere. Scientists think we learn just as much when we're asleep as when we're awake, sometimes more. Why, just last Friday night I dreamed about Joseph and the coat of many colors. Wasn't that in last week's sermon?"

Theo nodded and relaxed his stance. "I believe it was."

Alphonse took a step backward. "So what part of the sermon were you dreaming about last night when you kept calling the name of Cleo Trahan?"

Theo lit out across the porch and down the steps, taking care to favor his injured foot. He made a dive for his brother just in time to let him get away.

Alphonse ran cackling with laughter until he disappeared behind the house.

A few minutes later, Theo heard Alphonse calling to the little guys, then watched the trio head toward the bayou for an afternoon of fishing. As one last hurrah, Alphonse turned and saluted him with the cane pole.

"All hail, King Theophile!" he called. "See him pine away on the porch, wishing he could make Cleo Trahan his queen."

Stomping across the grass, Theo pretended to give chase. Alphonse broke out in a run, the younger brothers following in hot pursuit.

Theo laughed at his brother's antics. He'd have to slug him if he caught him, so allowing the kid to think he could outrun his big brother served two purposes. It got rid of Alphonse without hurting him, and it left Theo with peace and quiet.

Just in case Alphonse had a mind to return, Theo hobbled around the perimeter of the porch a few times before settling back into the hammock. He was about to close his eyes when he spied a flash of color coming up the road from the far end of the property.

Sitting up, he narrowed his eyes and tried to make out the identity of the one who walked toward the house. As the person drew nearer, he pegged her for a female—most likely one of his numerous aunts or cousins—clad in a light-colored dress.

"Figures," he said under his breath.

After all, the house was quiet, the boys were fishing, and Mama and the girls were away making visits. Why wouldn't he and Papa have their naps interrupted?

Theo groaned. *Another reason to head on down the road as soon as possible.*

A man needed his Sunday afternoon nap, or Monday morning just didn't start right. Once Monday was ruined, the rest of the week generally followed suit.

"Before you know it, a whole week's lost and all for want of a nap."

He decided to pretend deep sleep in the hopes that whichever aunt or cousin arrived on the doorstep would not disturb him. After all, no woman—Cajun or otherwise—who'd been raised right would wake up a workingman on a Sunday afternoon, leastways not in his opinion.

So he settled back and headed for dreamland, only occasionally taking a peek from beneath his eyelids to check the visitor's progress. She wore yellow and carried a package under her arm.

How nice. At least she thought to bring something.

"I hope it's a pie," he murmured as he snuggled deeper into the softness of the hammock. "One good thing about being back in Latagnier. A man can sure eat good here."

He cast one last glance at whichever aunt or cousin approached, then closed his eyes. What seemed only a moment later, he awoke with a start. The woman was within spitting distance of the house before his tired brain made the connection.

Yellow.

Cleo Trahan.

He sat up so fast, the movement made his head spin. Actually, it spun the hammock, too, landing him rear-end first on the porch floor. Theo scrambled up and landed on his sore foot.

For a minute, he gave serious consideration to heading indoors to hide or taking to the woods in the hopes she might give up and go home. But before she went home, most likely she'd run into at least one family member.

Wouldn't Papa have fun talking to her? First thing you know, his father would be spilling all sorts of information, not the least of which would be his opinion about the fact that his eldest son was well past twenty-five and still unmarried. Then he'd surely inquire as to whether Mademoiselle Trahan had a steady beau. After that, who knew what can of worms Papa would open?

Well, Theo just wouldn't let that happen.

Groaning, he hobbled off the porch. The foot that had seemed to be healing now felt worse than yesterday.

Further proof that Cleo Trahan was a menace.

Better to head her off than to take the chance that she might be spotted by one of the family. The brothers were fishing, Papa was napping, and the ladies were visiting, but around here, you never knew when a relative would pop out of the woodwork.

The last thing he needed was to have one of the family see him visiting with Cleo Trahan. He might be closer to thirty than twenty, but teasing from his family still plagued him. He had a mind not to hear more of it on the Lord's Day.

Cleo waved and picked up her pace. "Bonjour."

To compensate, Theo had to hurry along, as well—not an easy thing, considering the shooting pain in his foot. His gaze shifted from his guest to the package she carried in the crook of her arm.

"Well now. This is a surprise."

She shifted the package to her other arm and looked up at him, eyes wide. "I'd hoped to speak to you after church this morning, but you were gone before I could reach you."

"Yes, well, I tend to slip out quickly."

"I've noticed."

Her smile should have pleased him. Instead, it set his warning bells off. An awkward silence fell between them. He could stand here all day and look at her. He also needed to send her home.

Only the sound of children's laughter set him in motion. "Why don't you and I find someplace quiet and set a spell?"

"That would be lovely."

Lovely? She had no idea.

Taking her by the elbow, Theo led his visitor toward the nearest source of cover—a stand of oak trees just ahead on their left.

"The bayou is so pretty this time of year," she said as she allowed him to guide her to a secluded spot beside a crook in the bayou.

So are you, he could have added.

Theo looked both directions before choosing a little grassy place beside the water. "Here, how about you and me sit over there?" He pointed to an upended cedar log, a natural bench he and Alphonse had found just that past week.

With no sign of the fishermen and no more noise from the children, he felt almost certain they could have a measure of privacy. Now if he could just get the woman to speak her piece and go on home.

Once she settled herself on the log, the Trahan woman placed the package in her lap, then waited for him to take a seat beside her. She traced the length of the string-tied package and picked at the brown paper wrapping.

"I have a gift for you." She bit her lip and looked away. "I hope you like it."

A fish jumped with a plop, sending ripples out from the center of the black bayou water. Theo watched the circle widen and tried to think of the right way to send this sweet girl back home without accepting her gift. If he took whatever she'd brought him, he'd be beholden to her, and that just wouldn't do.

He finally braved a look down into a face that beamed with happiness. Once again, his heart sank.

How easy it would be to let himself fall in love with her. Not just be smitten, as he'd been ever since their dinner together several weeks ago, but actually be in once-in-a-lifetime love. No, he'd begun to believe that he might actually be able to spend the rest of his life with this woman.

Happily, no less.

Theo shrugged off the frightening thought with a roll of his shoulders. "How come you bring me a present, Cleo, eh?"

Cleo continued to toy with the wrappings. Finally, she smiled. "I have several reasons, actually." She paused and seemed to be considering her words. "First, I feel I owe you a debt of gratitude for all you've done."

"Aw, I haven't done anything."

She shook her head. "That's not true. Way back at the beginning, you could have told my uncle on me, and you didn't. You brought back the basket I left at the schoolhouse, even though it meant you got soaked by the storm."

He lifted a finger as if to make an important point. "I'll admit you're right about the first one, but I got a shrimp dinner out of bringing that basket to you. I'll tell you something. Your aunt's shrimp étouffée makes me want to fetch more baskets. I'd never admit it to my mama, but I hadn't thought anybody could best her in a cooking contest until now."

"Actually," she said slowly as she gave him a sideways glance, "I cooked the shrimp."

"Did you, now?"

Well, this was some news. Pretty as a newborn foal, and she could cook, too? Good thing he was sitting down. His knees were feeling a little wobbly.

Chapter 15

"I love to cook. I do it every day."

What a dumb thing to say, Cleo thought. She sounded like a foolish girl trying her hand at flirting for the first time.

Immediately ashamed, she looked away. While she could admit to cooking daily, saying she loved it was a bit of an exaggeration. She'd grown up at her aunt's side, helping to cut buttermilk biscuit dough with an iced-tea glass and learning to stir up a roux for thickening before she could spell her own name.

Cooking was, well, merely what ladies did. There was nothing remarkable about this, at least nothing worth mentioning. And yet she *had* mentioned it. Perhaps she *was* a foolish girl trying her hand at flirting.

The carpenter nodded, seemingly interested. His grin made her toes tingle. "I like to eat every day, so I guess we've got that in common."

"Right." She stretched her legs out in front of her and flexed her feet.

A soft breeze blew past, on it the scent of spring and the promise of summer. Two tiny ladybugs landed on the toe of her shoe and began to crawl in circles. She wiggled her foot, and they flew off together.

Cleo clamped her lips tight and fought the urge to offer any further attempts at conversation. Who knew what less-than-witty statement she might make next time?

The man beside her said nothing but rather seemed to be studying a single fluffy cloud as it floated past above the tree line. They sat in silence for what seemed like an eternity.

"Can you bake a pie?"

Startled, she nodded. "Sure. Why?"

He shrugged and reached over to pick a strand of wild honeysuckle off the vine. "Just wondering."

"Oh. Any particular kind you like best?"

"Nope."

So much for that discussion. Cleo drummed her fingers on the parcel in her lap and watched the bayou ripple past. Two marsh birds landed on the low-slung branch of a dogwood on the opposite bank, while a couple of fish jumped like synchronized swimmers.

Cleo sighed. Was it her imagination, or was it true that everywhere she looked today, things seemed paired off?

Sometimes it gave her pause to think what it might be like to be a part of a pair, maybe with someone big and handsome like the man seated next to her. Most days, however, she remembered that hers was a higher calling.

To be a teacher meant she would have to give up any thoughts of pairing up with any man. A married teacher didn't last long, for soon babies came along and the career was over.

Uncle Joe had already proven that getting qualified teachers in Latagnier was a difficult proposition at best. Just because this woman from New Orleans had agreed to come didn't mean she would. And if she did take the job, how long would she stay?

"Daydreaming?"

Cleo startled, and the package landed at her feet. "I'm sorry. I do that sometimes. I was thinking about being a teacher."

He nodded. "From what I can tell, you think about that a lot."

"Oui." She collected the gift and placed it in his hands. "Here. I brought you this."

At first he seemed reluctant, holding the item at arm's length as if he were trying to recognize it. "What's this for? It's not my birthday, and Christmas is a long way off."

"Open it and see." Her heart picked up its pace. What if coming here was a mistake? "Go ahead," she added. "It won't bite. I promise."

Weighing it in his hands, he turned to face her. "Well now, considering I've already braved a cottonmouth for you, I shouldn't be surprised if it did bite."

He stood and reached into his pocket for a small knife, then settled back onto the log beside her to make short work of the string. The paper fell off, revealing his gift.

Her father's well-worn copy of *Pilgrim's Progress.*

"A book?" His tone was flat, his expression one of disbelief. "You gave me a *book*. Me?"

"Not just any book. This one belonged to my father." Cleo took a deep breath and let it out slowly. "*Pilgrim's Progress* was one of his favorites, although I never did count it as one of mine. In any case, I wanted you to have it."

"Why?" Theo met her gaze, then leaned toward her. A flash of anger clouded his features. "Is this a joke?"

"A joke? No." She paused to compose her thoughts, then plunged headlong into the reason she'd invited herself to visit this afternoon. "You see, I thought that perhaps I could. . .well, that is, if you were willing, you could let me. . ."

Understanding seemed to dawn. His features twisted into a smile, but there was no joy in his eyes. "You thought I might let you teach me to read. Is that it?"

She nodded. Suddenly her brilliant idea didn't sound so brilliant after all. "You're an intelligent man, Theo. I think you'd learn quickly, even if you are a little more advanced in years than the others I'll be teaching."

"Do you, now?" He rose and turned to help her up. "Do you really think an old man like me capable of learning, Mademoiselle Teacher? After all, I'm considerably older than your average student."

"You're not old. What are you, twenty-two, twenty-three?"

Theo straightened his shoulders and looked away. "I'll be twenty-seven come June."

Her expression of surprise gave him a certain satisfaction. Maybe now she would see that. . .that what? That he was old and ignorant? That she'd do better spending her time with people her own age instead of someone nearly nine years older?

As much as this information might achieve his goal of running her off, it gave a certain sting to his pride. Theo decided to put an end to the foolishness and just state things as plainly as possible.

"I can't accept this gift." He paused as he tried to think of the nicest way possible to get rid of the book—and of her. "So now that you know this, you can go on home."

She looked more stunned than hurt. "Is there a reason?"

Other than his trampled dignity? "Merci beaucoup, Cleo," he said as he thrust the book in her direction. "But you need to go home now."

She ignored the offer of the book and touched his sleeve. "Have I offended you?"

How he longed to light into her, to scream and yell and make all sorts of noise letting her know just how she'd injured his pride. If only he hadn't been raised a gentleman.

"Pas du tout," he said instead. "If I were offended, I would state so."

Afraid. Now that came closer to how he felt. Afraid of making a fool of himself, afraid of spending time with her, and afraid he might be giving up everything he wanted for something he never knew he needed.

"So this was all just a misunderstanding." She settled back on the log and gave him an expectant look, patting the empty place beside her. "Tante Flo's not expecting me until suppertime. If you'd like, we could begin by learning the vowel sounds."

Her glee grated on his resolve. So did her enthusiasm. The urge to sit beside her on the log all afternoon, whether for learning vowels or just watching the clouds float by, hit him hard. He squeezed the book so hard he was afraid he might soon hear the pilgrim squeal in protest.

"Come sit down, Theo, and we'll get started."

He almost gave in, almost had himself convinced. Almost—but not quite.

Taking a step back, Theo felt his mind reel with the possibility of what could happen to his dreams. His gaze scanned the perimeter, searching out any means of escape.

He found none. Either he told her the truth and risked upsetting her, or he sat down beside her and risked his freedom.

Whichever way he looked at it, spending another minute with Cleo Trahan was a bad idea. Time to get rid of her.

Dumping the book into her lap, he took yet another step back. "Please just go." He spoke the words through a clenched jaw, unsure whether he'd said them plainly enough to be understood. When the first tear glistened in the corner of her eye, he knew he'd been heard.

"Stop that," he demanded. "Take your book and your tears and go home."

Without looking back, he stalked away. Anger set him on the path for home but his conscience put up a roadblock that his mind—and his feet—couldn't get past.

Theo stopped in his tracks and turned around. As much as he didn't want to admit it, he owed Cleo Trahan an apology. He also owed her an explanation, but only if she asked.

Better she accept his apology and head for Joe's place with the book in tow. Better yet if she were already on her way home.

Even though Cleo might think otherwise, she really did not want him to tell her the why of things. Worse, he really did not want to admit it.

Theo stalked down the path and pushed past the low-lying limbs and thicket, all the while daring to hope that he wouldn't find the Trahan girl still waiting for him. His hopes were dashed when he spied her standing where he'd left her.

Before he could say a word, she lifted her hand as if to silence him. "I just have one question. Answer it, and I'll go."

He walked closer, dangerously closer, until she stood so near that he could reach out and. . .no, he didn't dare think what he could do with her within arm's reach. "Just one question?"

Leaning back slightly to look up at him, she nodded.

"All right," he said slowly. "But even though I can't read, I *can* count. You only get one chance, and I'm only going to answer one question. Now speak your piece so we can both get on home."

She blinked hard, then straightened her shoulders and drew herself up to her full height—still pitifully less than his. "One question. Why? If it bothers you that you can't read, and it obviously does, then why not let me teach you? It's what I do."

Emotions swirled and seethed just beneath the surface. Wanting to say yes, needing to say no, wanting her to stay, needing her to leave. Theo's skin tingled, and he felt hot and cold at the same time. He hadn't been this miserable since he weathered the chicken pox nearly twenty years ago.

"You want to know why I won't let you teach me to read?"

She nodded, and the sun caught her hair, glinting off the blue-black strands. "Yes, that's all I want to know," she said as she thrust the brown leather volume in his direction. "Take this book and look at it, then tell me you don't want me to teach you to read what's inside of it."

Theo removed the book from her hand and set it on the log without opening it. "I'm too old for this, Cleo. I'm heading for Canada first chance I get, and nothing's going to interfere with that."

Dark brows drew together as his companion gave him a perplexed look. "I don't understand what learning to read has to do with—"

"You're right. You *don't* understand. You're young and naive, and you don't have any idea what you're doing to me. I can't spend five minutes with you and keep my conscience clear and my plans straight. Unless you can show me everything I need to know in under five minutes, teaching me to read is out of the question."

Taking two steps back, Theo stuffed his hands into his pants pockets, as much for his own protection as for hers. He would never hurt her, but at this moment, he couldn't be held to any sort of proper conduct. His fingers itched to wrap her in his arms and hold her, and the way those lips pouted, why, he could hardly stand not kissing them.

Of course, he could do neither.

"There, I answered your question," he said a mite more gently. "Now go. Please."

"Please listen."

"Go home." He barely spoke the words through his clenched jaw. Did he say them to Cleo or to himself?

If she stayed, he might have to admit he loved her. If she left, well, that would be the best thing for both of them. Then she would merely be a fond memory instead of a serious problem.

Theo caught his breath and held it. If only he could catch his feelings so easily. Cleo stepped toward him, arms outstretched, and the tightly strung wire that held his emotions in check snapped.

"Theo, I—"

Before she could complete the sentence, he took her in his arms. Just to hold her. No harm in that. Just for a second.

And then he kissed her.

Chapter 16

Cleo reeled back, her hand covering her mouth. Her first kiss, and it was awful.

Well, not exactly awful, but it was uninvited and unexpected, and it served to awaken something inside her. Never again could she wonder what her first kiss would be like.

Theo pulled her against him, her ear pressed against his chest such that she could hear his heart thumping wildly. Hers took up the pace until she felt it might burst.

So this was how love felt. She looked up into the eyes of the carpenter, expecting to find some sign that the kiss had changed him. That he felt the same.

Instead, she saw a blank stare followed in quick succession by what looked like anger and then regret—none of the tender emotions she expected. Whatever the reason he might claim for kissing her, it certainly did not seem like love.

"I shouldn't have done that," he whispered, his voice husky and deep. "Please. . .just. . .go. . .now."

She willed the tears not to fall as she pulled away from his grasp. *Just wait, Cleo. You can't cry in front of him.*

Straightening her spine, she turned and walked away with what little pride she had left. As soon as she knew he could no longer see her, she picked up her skirts and broke into a run.

With tears staining her face, she knew she couldn't go home. Instead, she headed for the only other place of solace she could think of on a Sunday afternoon besides the church—the schoolhouse. No one would look for her there.

Racing up the steps, she threw open the door, then stepped inside and slammed it shut. The place smelled like new wood and old paint, a strange but comfortable combination. Cleo leaned against the wall. Finally, the emotions proved too much. She sank to the floor and cried like a baby.

Somewhere along the way, the door must have opened, for Cleo opened her eyes to see Theo standing there. Silhouetted by the brilliant sunshine behind him, he looked like a dark and ominous shadow. *How fitting,* she thought.

"I'm so sorry."

Gone was the voice made deep and husky by emotion. In its place was the flat and cold sound of a man without feeling. Cleo could find no answer for his statement, so she remained silent.

He moved closer but only slightly so, edging to within reach of her. Setting the book beside her, he straightened and looked away.

"Arête. Please don't cry."

She didn't want to stop, didn't want to give in to what she knew came next—the forgiveness. Again she said nothing, although she did swipe at her tear-stained cheeks with the hem of her apron.

He began to pace, then stopped short. "Cleo, I don't know what happened." Shaking his head, he pounded his fist against the door. "That's not true. I *do* know what happened."

Cleo watched him as he stood looking out the window. He grimaced, then turned his attention to her.

"I'm a fool, Cleo, and I know that," he said as he crossed the distance to her and offered his hand to pull her into a standing position.

She accepted his help with caution, pulling away as soon as he released his grip. Standing so close brought the fresh memories back, first of the kiss and then of the regret she saw on his face immediately afterward.

He still wore that regret.

Cleo wrapped her hands around her waist and fixed her gaze on his eyes, fighting the urge to look away. "I'm going to give you the same advice you gave me, Theo," she somehow managed to say. "Advice I should have taken."

Regret shifted to confusion, and he shook his head. "What's that?"

"Go home."

She turned to walk away only to see that she had nowhere to go. A large desk that had been partially dismantled blocked the back door. Several long benches were stacked atop its expansive surface. The furnishings of her schoolroom, she realized.

Escaping with what little remained of her dignity seemed the only route to take. Cleo squared her shoulders and walked back into the main room, where Theo waited. He'd begun to pace again but halted when he caught sight of her.

"I'm leaving," she said. "Do follow my advice and go home." She reached down to snatch up the book and cradle it in her arm.

Theo stepped between her and freedom. "Just hear me out," he said. "I'm real bad at this, but I'd like to try and make sense of things before you run off mad."

"Mad?" She fought for control of her voice. "You think I'm mad?"

He shrugged. "Well, if I were in your place, I'd be mad as a hornet. I mean, a man takes liberties—"

"Who is taking liberties?"

Cleo looked past to see Uncle Joe and the pastor standing in the doorway. She pasted on a smile and sashayed past Theo to head toward the pair. When she reached her uncle, she gave him a quick peck on the cheek, being careful to keep her red-rimmed eyes closed until she'd safely passed him.

"No one's taking liberties, Uncle Joe," she said over her shoulder. "Theo and I were just discussing a book."

She stopped to turn and face the three men. Of the trio, the carpenter was the only one whose face wore no expression. The other two smiled as if they shared a secret.

"If you'll excuse me, I'll be taking this book back home." She gave Theo a direct look. "Wouldn't want something so special to end up in the hands of someone who didn't appreciate it."

As her feet hit the dirt and pointed toward home, she wondered why she'd bothered to save Theophile Breaux's hide. One word to Uncle Joe and the pastor about the kiss, and the carpenter would have been in trouble up to his eyeballs.

She didn't have to wonder long. The truth caught up with her before she reached the front porch of Uncle Joe's place. She didn't tell on Theo because she wanted him to kiss her again.

And again.

"Oh my," she said as she climbed the porch steps. "Well, that will never do."

"What will never do?"

Cleo looked up to see Tante Flo sitting in the parlor, her Bible open on the rosewood table before her. She leaned down to embrace her aunt, then slipped the tattered copy of *Pilgrim's Progress* back into its place on the bookshelf beside the fireplace.

Tante Flo closed the Bible and gave Cleo a sideways look. "I asked you what would never do."

She smiled. "Anything that interferes with my becoming a teacher will never do."

"I'm glad to hear it," Tante Flo said. "I've wondered a time or two what would have happened if I had put my teaching ahead of love."

Surprised, Cleo feigned a casual attitude. "And what did you decide?"

Tante Flo smiled. "I decided that when the Lord puts the right man in your path, it doesn't matter what you're giving up. It's always a better-than-even exchange."

Cleo settled onto the settee and slipped off her shoes, tucking her feet beneath her. "How did you know that Uncle Joe was the right man?"

Her aunt leaned closer and shook her head. "I didn't," she said. "In fact, I thought he was the most exasperating man I had ever met."

Now this was interesting. After two decades of marriage, Flo and her husband seemed to be more in love than ever. Cleo assumed they'd always felt this way.

"I don't believe it," she finally said. "I've never heard you say a cross word to Uncle Joe. How could you find him exasperating?"

"Well, to start, he ran off every other beau I had."

Cleo giggled. "He did? How?"

"By planting himself in my kitchen every morning and sharing coffee with my papa. Before long, Papa didn't want any other man around except your uncle

Joe. Said they were all beneath me or some such nonsense, but I always knew Joe was giving my daddy an earful and turning him against anybody but himself."

"That's pretty underhanded, Tante Flo. I'm surprised at Uncle Joe."

"Oh, Cleo, nothing should surprise you when it comes to love." She paused to run her finger over the cracked spine of the Bible. "See, he made friends with the papa, but he was really there to see the daughter." She paused and winked. "Much like our Monsieur Breaux, I believe."

"What are you talking about? You and I both know he comes here to talk to Uncle Joe about the schoolhouse project. How else would he get the updates and the changes in plans? It's much more convenient for him to come by on his way to the schoolhouse than for Uncle Joe to go all the way out there later in the day."

As she protested, her mind reeled back to the kiss and its aftermath, the sound of his heart racing against her ear, and the feel of his arms around her. Color flooded her cheeks, and the room suddenly felt a bit too warm.

Tante Flo rose and brushed past Cleo to stand at the window. A moment later she settled beside her on the settee and took Cleo's hand in hers.

"He's kissed you, hasn't he?"

Chapter 17

Cleo stuttered and sputtered and finally made an excuse not to answer her aunt. She'd never lie—she couldn't—for her aunt knew her too well. Racing to her room, she poured fresh water in the basin and washed her face. As she toweled her heated cheeks dry, she studied her face for signs she'd changed.

Nothing out of the ordinary greeted her. Same plain face, same drab brown eyes, same hair—dark as bayou water and just as unruly.

Falling onto her bed, she stared up at the ceiling. Whatever got into her this afternoon, it would just have to get out. She had no time for love and certainly not for loving such an ornery creature as Theophile Breaux.

It was bad enough he'd kissed her, but to regret it afterward? Well, that just wouldn't do. She had half a mind to search him out and tell him so.

She rose. Yes, that's just what she'd do. She would find the fellow and give him what for. How dare he play with her affections? Surely he knew what sort of emotions he would stir up when he held her. Surely he, who was much older than she as it turned out, would know very well the results of emotions left to run free.

"Oh, Cleo, if you aren't the most dramatic thing in Latagnier, I don't know who is," she whispered as she fell against the mattress once more.

"You all right in there?" she heard Tante Flo call.

"Yes, ma'am," she responded quickly. "Just having a Sunday afternoon nap."

"Well, get up right now and come help me see to supper. Sunday afternoon's gone and evening's coming." Her footsteps stopped at the closed door. "Your uncle's going to come home hungry and wonder what happened to his dinner. And unless I miss my guess, he'll have the pastor with him, too."

"Yes, ma'am," she repeated as she rose and walked to the basin to give her face another quick scrubbing. Tante Flo might have suspected a kiss, but she'd stand and scrub all day if she had to in order to keep Uncle Joe from knowing.

She needn't have worried. Uncle Joe seemed too preoccupied with discussing the finer points of planed wood with the pastor to notice any change in his niece. Listening to snatches of conversation, her ears took special notice whenever the name of the carpenter was mentioned.

A few times, the men included her in the conversation, asking her opinion about books and other items of interest to the new teacher. Uncle Joe even mentioned the teachers' college, hinting that he thought an education of that sort to be good for a woman in some cases.

Cleo went to bed, praying the Lord would cause Uncle Joe to believe she was one of those cases. Of course, as she closed her eyes and embraced the fog of sleep, it wasn't Uncle Joe and a possible education at the teachers' college that filled her mind.

It was Theophile Breaux.

Irritating, presumptuous, handsome, stubborn Theophile Breaux.

"Go away," she whispered to his memory.

The Theo in her dreams didn't listen any more than the real Theo had. As she gave way to the blackness of sleep, she remembered the kiss.

And in her dreams, he kissed her again.

And this time it wasn't awful at all.

When she awoke, she tried to remember every detail of the dream. Then as she headed to the kitchen to help her aunt make breakfast, she tried to forget it.

Uncle Joe spied Theo coming across the clearing before she did. "Set another place, Flo," he said with a chuckle. "Here comes our regular morning visitor."

Tante Flo sent a smile toward Cleo, then reached into the cupboard for another plate and coffee mug. A moment later, silverware clanked against the tabletop.

"Reminds me of someone I once knew," Tante Flo said.

"Does it, now?" Uncle Joe chuckled. "Was he a handsome fellow, this man?"

"Why yes, he was." Her aunt paused from setting the table to give her uncle a kiss on his balding head. "In fact, he still is."

To be in love like these two. Would she ever know that kind of happiness? To banish the thought, Cleo busied herself with the pancake batter until she found her hands were fumbling terribly and allowing shells to fall into the mixture.

"Go fetch us some more eggs, child," her aunt said. "I'm afraid what we got here won't be enough at this rate."

She cast a glance out the window, then back at Tante Flo. To fetch eggs meant to walk right past Theo Breaux. Surely her aunt knew that.

So Tante Flo was matchmaking?

"It won't work," she whispered as she leaned toward her aunt.

Just before the screen door closed, Cleo heard her aunt say, "It might."

She picked up her pace and kept her gaze focused on the ground. If she didn't look him in the eyes, perhaps he'd walk past and go on inside. Surely he'd come to see Uncle Joe and not her, anyway.

Stepping a little faster, she braved a glance up at his face. Unlike yesterday, he wore a look of relief.

At what? *Probably at the fact that I'm not sitting inside waiting on him.*

"Bonjour," she said as she passed him.

"Might what?" Theo motioned toward the screen door. "What was your aunt talking about?"

Cleo shook her head and returned her concentration to the ground beneath her swiftly moving feet. "Nothing!" she called.

"Cleo, wait. Arête."

"No time, Theo." She reached for the latch on the chicken coop with trembling hands. Why did she let that man affect her?

When she returned from the henhouse, she deposited the egg basket on the sideboard, then fled the kitchen to begin her chores. Sweeping came first, so she found the broom and began in the parlor, the farthest point from the kitchen she could find.

"Cleo!" Uncle Joe called. "Could you fetch my spectacles, cher?"

"Oui."

She set the broom aside to retrieve her uncle's glasses from the table beside the settee. Stepping inside the kitchen, she saw both men pause from their conversation to look up at her. While her uncle regarded her with a warm smile, his guest showed no emotion.

"Merci beaucoup, cher," Uncle Joe said. "Now would you warm up this coffee a bit? I've done so much jawing with this young man here that I've let mine get cold." He turned to face Theo. "You need Cleo to warm you up, too?"

The carpenter looked like he'd swallowed a bug. "No," he sputtered.

Cleo brought the coffeepot to the table and filled Uncle Joe's cup, watching the steam rise off the liquid and feeling the heat rise from her cheeks. Surely Uncle Joe hadn't intended to say *that.* She glanced at his face to see that her uncle was trying not to laugh.

Well, of all the nerve.

She straightened her spine and set the pot between them on the dish towel. "If you don't need anything else, I'll get back to my chores."

Uncle Joe prodded Theo. "You need her for anything?"

Their gazes collided. For a long moment, Cleo could do nothing but stare into the carpenter's dark eyes. Then he looked away and offered her uncle a smile.

"Can't think of anything. Now what were you saying about that beam over the old parlor?"

"Well then, I'll just go back to what I was doing." She spoke to Uncle Joe, but her gaze was firmly fixed on Theophile Breaux. How dare he dismiss her as if he hadn't kissed her just yesterday?

"That's real fine, Cleo," Uncle Joe said.

The carpenter, however, said nothing.

Cleo turned on her heels and stomped away. "Humph," she muttered as she turned and headed down the hall.

"What was that?" Uncle Joe called.

"Nothing."

Cleo went back to her sweeping with renewed vigor. Part of her felt relieved that the carpenter pretended nothing had transpired between them. Another part of her felt righteous indignation at his blatant disregard for the feelings he'd caused to surface.

"What are you complaining about?" She reached to pull the settee away from the wall. "You got what you wanted. A teacher can't fall in love, so this is all for the better."

This thought sustained her until Uncle Joe once more called her to come into the kitchen. This time when she stepped inside the room, she noticed her uncle was alone. Theo must have left quietly, or perhaps her rather intense sweeping and moving of furniture had been noisier than she thought.

"Did you call me, Uncle Joe?"

"I did." He indicated the chair beside him, the spot Theo had recently vacated. "Sit down a minute, will you?"

Cleo complied, trying not to notice the chair still felt warm. Obviously the carpenter hadn't made his departure very long ago. She looked past her uncle to the window to see if she could spot him.

"He went the other way."

Turning her gaze on her uncle, she shook her head. "What are you talking about?"

"Theo. He went the other way."

She shrugged. "Didn't ask."

Uncle Joe smiled. "Didn't have to." He pushed his spectacles up on his forehead and regarded her with a serious look. "Cleo, I want you to know that your aunt and I have felt the Lord blessed us with a daughter of our own when you came to live with us. From the day you came through the door, you've had my heart. Did you know that?"

Had she? Cleo blinked back a tear. "Thank you for telling me this."

Uncle Joe covered her hand with his, then entwined his fingers with hers. "Flo and I love you, and we want what's best. Do you believe that?"

"Yes, sir."

"Then I hope you'll understand and forgive those times when I want to coddle you and treat you like a child. In my mind, I know you're a grown woman, but in my heart, you're still that curly-headed three-year-old who used to fall asleep on my shoulder in that big old rocking chair in the parlor."

The image of her uncle gathering her into his arms to rock her to sleep rose in her mind. She smiled.

"That's why it's so hard to say this."

Cleo's attention snapped back to Uncle Joe. "Say what?"

He looked away and fidgeted with the edge of the table. "Well, like I said, you're a grown woman." His gaze swung back to meet hers. "You still intend to make a teacher of yourself?"

Concern etched her thoughts. Had he changed his mind about allowing her to take on the teaching position at the Latagnier school?

"Yes." She bit her lip to keep from saying more.

"Then I think you ought to be trained proper." He shifted positions and tightened his grip on her hand. "Once your replacement arrives at the end of the summer, I'd like to send you off to get that fancy education you've talked about."

"At the teachers' college?"

She flung herself at her uncle and wrapped her arms around his neck. "Oh, thank you, Uncle Joe. Thank you, thank you."

"Well, looks like you gave her the news."

Cleo looked up to see the carpenter standing in the door. He pulled on the screen door and stepped inside, crossing the kitchen in a few long strides to deposit a broken piece of wood on the table.

Cleo stepped away from her uncle and wrapped her arms around her middle. What was *he* doing back?

"I see you found the ax handle. I'll get that changed out this afternoon." Uncle Joe rose to slap the carpenter on the back. "Well, Theo, what do you think of my niece going off to New Orleans and becoming a real teacher?"

Chapter 18

What *did* Theo think of Cleo Trahan going off to New Orleans and becoming a teacher?

Funny, he'd been asking himself that ever since yesterday when he kissed her. Never a day in his life had he ever expected he'd want to be kissing a schoolteacher.

Yet there she stood, the future teacher of the Latagnier school, and all he could think of was kissing her. The very idea made him break out in a sweat.

He wiped his forehead with the back of his hand and forced a grin. "Well, sir, I think that sounds like a fine idea."

But did he?

In a word, no.

A better idea would be to have her stay here, teach the youngsters for a few years, and then. . .what? If he had no designs on her, what did he care whether she went off to that fancy college?

Yet he did care. He cared more than he ever intended to let on, he decided as he listened to Joe rattle on about the school in New Orleans. He cared more about courting her than hearing about the teaching certificate she'd earn.

He'd never admit that to her or anyone else except the Lord, of course. He couldn't.

If he were to say anything about his feelings for that pretty girl, two things would happen. First, he'd probably end up getting hitched to her and never leaving Latagnier. Second, she'd never use the brains God gave her to shape the young folks of the parish.

If either of those things happened, it would be a crying shame. But the idea of courting Clothilde Trahan did have its merits.

Maybe he'd think on it just a bit.

He turned his gaze on Cleo and saw the happiness on her face as she discussed the teachers' college with her uncle. How could he keep her from what the Lord obviously meant her to do?

What in the world was I thinking? I'm a lot of things, but until now I didn't think one of them was selfish. And to get in the way of a girl's bright future was just plain selfish.

He made a promise right then and there that he'd give Cleo Trahan the only gift he could give her, the gift of her freedom. He of all people knew how precious that gift was.

And he alone would know how hard it was to give.

"Joe, excuse me, but I'm going to head out to the schoolhouse. I know your niece is anxious to get started on her teaching, and I'm itching to hit the road. The quicker I get things finished, the sooner both of us will be happy."

With that, he beat a path out of the kitchen and across the clearing toward the building site. Rather than head directly there, he took a winding path that led him past the bayou. To settle his thinking, he decided.

Without actually thinking, however, he ended up right back at the spot he'd been yesterday. The spot where he'd kissed Cleo.

Settling himself on the log, Theo rested his elbows on his knees and cradled his chin in his hands. He was in quite a fix this time. Maybe there was a way around this, a way where no one would have to give up anything.

Only the Lord knew how he could have his freedom and Cleo Trahan, too. And what of Cleo? Could he bear to take her dreams away from her by asking for her hand in marriage?

He hadn't managed to think of anything else but her ever since he had laid his lips against hers. She fit against him like the Lord had made them together, then broke the mold. And when they kissed, well, the fireworks display he'd watched one year in New York Harbor didn't hold a candle to the sparks going off inside his head.

"Lord, c'est moi, Theo Breaux. I know You and I don't speak out loud much, but I sure would be obliged if You would make it clear and plain what You want me to do about Cleo."

He waited expectantly, just like the Bible said to do. Any moment the Lord would speak, and then he'd know how to handle the situation. A couple of birds landed on the sweet gum tree across the bayou, and he studied them intently while he waited.

Nothing.

Silence.

"Well, Lord? Are You coming up with anything? I'm plain out of ideas."

Leaning forward, he reached for a stick and began to trace circles in the soft earth. Still nothing from God.

"Lord, are You listening? I need an answer, and I need it now. I've got work to do."

"If only He responded on our time."

Theo whirled around to see Pastor Broussard coming toward him. He dropped the stick and rose to shake the preacher's hand.

"Don't let me disturb you, son," he said. "I was heading for the Trahan place to meet up with Joe and saw you sitting here. I couldn't help but hear your petition to the Lord."

He shrugged. "Well, you might have heard, but I'm not so sure He did."

The pastor chuckled. "It often seems that way, doesn't it? I assure you that

His lack of an immediate response doesn't mean He is ignoring you, Theo."

"I know that in my head, but right now my heart's not too keen on the idea." Theo let his shoulders slump. "Truth is, I've got a problem that just about seems to be more than even the Lord can solve."

The pastor's gray brows rose. "My, my, you must have quite a problem if it's worse than spending forty years wandering in the desert unable to find your homeland or sleeping all night in a den of lions." He gave Theo a concerned look. "It doesn't look like Pharaoh's chariots have you backed up to a sea you can't cross."

"No, sir," Theo said.

"And I can't be certain, but I don't believe you've been swallowed by a whale or turned to a pillar of salt lately."

"Can't say as I have."

Rev. Broussard touched Theo's sleeve. "Then what's so terrible that it's worse than all these calamities?"

Theo took a deep breath and let it out slowly. "Love, sir," he finally said.

"I see." His brows gathered. "Well, you've got me there."

Theo chuckled despite feeling lower than a snake's belly. "You don't know the half of it, Reverend."

"I don't suppose I do," he said, "but I'd be glad to sit a spell with you and listen to your tale of woe. Who knows? I might have a word or two of advice. I *am* a happily married man. Have been for the last thirty-two years."

"What about Joe Trahan? Isn't he expecting you?"

"I reckon Joe'll understand if I'm delayed a bit." He sat on the log and patted the place next to him. "Join me, won't you?"

Theo nodded and settled beside the pastor. "I'd appreciate it if you wouldn't mention to Joe that you spent time with me. I wouldn't want him getting the idea that—"

"That you're mooning over his niece?" He must have looked surprised, for the pastor laughed out loud. "Theo, you're the last one to realize you're crazy in love with her. Some of us figured that out a long time ago."

"Well, I wish someone would have let me in on the secret." Theo picked up a pebble and tossed it toward the bayou. "I would've lit out of here while I still had a right mind."

The pastor laughed again. "Son, the moment we men take up with the womenfolk, we forfeit any right mind we ever had." He sobered quickly. "But having said that, I will tell you that I love my wife like a silly fool even after all these years, and I wouldn't have it any other way."

"I want that. . .someday."

Rev. Broussard nodded. "Who do you figure is in control here, you or God?"

"God, of course," Theo said.

"Then what are you doing telling Him when you're going to do something?

Isn't the issue of timing His concern, not yours?"

"Yes, but He and I have a deal."

The pastor gave Theo a sideways look. "Is that so? What sort of deal?"

"I travel now, and I settle down to a family and responsibilities later."

"Well now, that's quite a nice deal you've worked out with the Lord. Makes me wonder what would have happened if I'd thought to negotiate rather than blindly let Him lead me."

"He *is* leading me. I'm just setting up my life and all those plans for later. You know, after I've seen the world."

Rev. Broussard stood and dusted off the back of his trousers. "Son, have you ever considered the fact that *later* might have already arrived?"

"Maybe so, Reverend, but I'm not the only one who stands to lose here."

"Oh?"

"That's right." He pointed toward the Trahan place. "You know Cleo's got as much to lose as me. More, actually. If she were to marry, there goes her teaching career."

"And you think that's enough to cause her to give up the life God intended for her?"

Theo shrugged. "Depends. What does God want for her? I figure He didn't make her smart like she is just so she can hitch up with a bumpkin like me."

"That's your logic talking, Theo." The pastor laid his hand on Theo's shoulder. "What does your heart say? And more importantly, what does God say?"

"Well now, that's the trouble I was in when you wandered up, Reverend. God's not saying anything, not a word. As for my heart, it's telling me I ought to set her up right with a nice place to teach, then tell her good-bye and head for the hills. Canada, actually."

"Is that all your heart is telling you?"

What good would it do to lie to a preacher? Not that he was much of a liar anyway. His mama and papa raised him better than that. No, most times it was the truth that got him in trouble and not some fabrication.

"No, sir, it's telling me I'd like to have one more kiss before I go. More if it were proper, which it isn't." If the preacher seemed surprised, he didn't let on. "I'd appreciate it if you'd keep this to yourself, especially that last part."

Chapter 19

Cleo clutched the broom's handle tightly as she moved the porch rocker and reached to sweep behind it. What was wrong with her this morning?

She should be the happiest girl in Latagnier. Why, then, did she feel as though she'd just heard the worst news of her life?

Uncle Joe had given in. She was going to college to become a teacher. In no time, she'd have a teaching certificate in her hand, and she would be officially able to impart all her knowledge to eager students.

This was her dream, her fervent prayer. Now that the Lord had granted it, why was she so tempted to go to Him and tell Him she'd changed her mind?

After all, Theo Breaux thought it was a good idea, too.

She struck the business end of the broom against the wall to dislodge a spot of dirt, then swept it off the edge of the porch. Watching it land in the bed of Easter lilies, she remembered the carpenter's glee at her uncle's news.

He was downright happy.

The thought irked her and worked irritation into her bones. Couldn't the man have at least indicated he might miss her? After all, there was less than three months left before the fall term.

Three months.

If only Tante Flo were here to talk to. In anticipation of the Easter celebration, coming up in just over a week on April 3, her aunt and some of the other church ladies were busy quilting a new altarpiece. She'd likely spend the whole afternoon at the church.

Of course, Cleo knew she could join them, but sitting with a bunch of married ladies while fretting about a man and her future didn't sound like her idea of a pleasant afternoon.

Not that she'd likely enjoy any activity today.

She swiped at a pebble that had somehow found its way onto the porch, sending it flying into the same bed of lilies. How she'd like to give Theo Breaux a swipe with this broom. Maybe it would knock some sense into him.

A man didn't just kiss a girl, then act like it was a good idea that she leave town. Well, at least not an honorable man.

"My, but this floor does shine."

Cleo jumped and dropped the broom. Rev. Broussard stood on the porch steps, hat in hand.

"Forgive me, dear. I thought you heard me."

Placing her hand over her racing heart, she retrieved the broom. "No, sir, I didn't."

The pastor smiled. "Lost in thought?"

She nodded. "Actually, yes."

"Anything I can help with?" He smiled. "I do have some measure of qualification in the area of giving advice."

Pausing, she considered whether to speak her mind with the pastor and seek his counsel. Before she could decide, she heard her uncle's heavy footsteps coming their way.

"That you, Reverend?" The screen door opened with a squeal, and Uncle Joe stepped out onto the porch. "You ready to go?"

"I am," the pastor said.

"Well, give me just a minute to collect my things, and we can be off." Uncle Joe turned to face Cleo. "Reverend and I are heading to town. I thought I might mail that letter to New Orleans." He punctuated the statement with a grin, then transferred his attention to the pastor. "Looks like I'm going to have a real live certified, college-educated teacher in the family. Come the fall, Flo and I'll be packing Cleo off to school. How do you feel about that?"

"Well now," Rev. Broussard said. He crossed the distance between them to take Cleo's hand in his. "I think that's a fine honor, Cleo. A real fine honor. We should celebrate."

"Now that *is* a good idea," Uncle Joe said. "I'm going to tell Flo we need to put on a little party for our girl. The Lord blessed us with her and made her smart, and now she's going off to college. I want all of Latagnier to know it."

Cleo mustered a smile in hopes it would match the ones the men wore. Then a thought dawned, and her smile appeared for real. "They haven't accepted me yet, you know. I think we should reserve our celebrations until then."

Uncle Joe seemed surprised at her statement. Curiously, the reverend did not.

"Of course they'll accept you, but I see your point." Uncle Joe gestured toward the house. "Yes, well, I'll go fetch my things and we can be off to town, Reverend."

The pastor nodded. "Take your time, Joe. I'll just sit a spell and visit with your niece." He settled on the swing and patted the spot beside him. "Take a break from your sweeping, won't you?"

Cleo looked at the broom handle in her hand and realized she'd forgotten she held it. Propping it against the wall, she sat beside the pastor and heaved a sigh.

"Quoi y'a? Something troubling you, child?"

"No, well, oui." She curled her fingers around the chain holding the swing, then rested her forehead against the cool metal. "I'm confused, I suppose, and that does trouble me."

"How so, if you don't mind my asking, that is?"

"Oh, I don't mind. I just don't know if I can explain it." She leaned back and listened to the chains clank against one another. "It is all so complicated. I don't know where to begin."

"I suppose this sounds like a cliché, but I always recommend a body begin at the beginning." He patted her shoulder. "Or you don't have to tell me anything. We could merely pray if that will help."

She thought a moment before shaking her head. "Actually, I think it would do me good to talk to someone who could keep my confidence."

He smiled. "Well then, you have the right man for the job. Keeping confidences is what I do best."

Cleo let out another long breath and plunged into her story. "Going to college is exciting. It's amazing to think that an orphan girl from Latagnier could end up going off to college and being a teacher." She turned her gaze to the pastor. "It's what I've always wanted."

"Well then, why the confusion? Are you afraid, or is something else bothering you?"

"Afraid? No, I don't think so. I think I'm more worried that I've been dreaming the wrong dreams."

"What an interesting way of putting things." He seemed to consider her statement. "I take it you thought you wanted to be a teacher, but now you think you're being called to some other occupation. Is that correct?"

Was it? No, not exactly, but how to explain to the reverend without embarrassing herself?

"*Occupation* isn't quite the word I was thinking of, Reverend Broussard. I guess I'm trying to say I'm not sure if I am being called to an occupation at all."

He looked perplexed. "Then what are you being called to do, child? What is there to do if not work?" Pausing, a smile grew. "Ah, I think I see the dilemma."

"You do?"

The reverend nodded. "Indeed. You thought you were to teach children. Now—and perhaps I'm setting off in a direction you didn't mean to send me—you feel as though the Lord intends you to raise children instead?"

Stunned, she diverted her gaze. She hadn't thought of things quite that way. A houseful of children to raise—and to teach.

Her mind reeled back to daydreams she'd had just days ago, images of dark-haired children with names like Ernest and Angeline. Was that what the Lord wanted of her?

Suddenly her heart lightened. Maybe God had given her the ability to teach so that she could be a better mother and not just so that she might be a better teacher. The idea was no less far-fetched than imagining herself among city folk at the college in New Orleans.

Both had their appeal. And their drawbacks.

Suddenly either one could be her future. Whichever God allowed, she knew she would be happy.

"Cleo?"

She turned her attention to the reverend, who stared at her with a quizzical look. "Yes?"

"That's a nice smile. I haven't seen it for some time. I rather like it."

She broadened her grin. "I like it, too. Thank you, Reverend Broussard."

He placed his hand over his heart and shook his head. "For what? I didn't do a thing." He paused, his face grave. "Cleo, promise me one thing."

"What's that?"

Shifting slightly, he faced her directly. "Promise me that you will wait on a clear direction from the Lord and not depend on your own understanding of what you *think* He would want for you."

Cleo nodded. "I promise. Perhaps I should pray for patience then."

The pastor chuckled. "Oh dear, now that's a dangerous petition to make to the Lord. In my experience, He always seems to grant a request for patience, by teaching it to you through experience. In other words, He tends to make you wait."

"Oh my." She joined him in his laughter. "So then, asking for patience is not a good idea. I'll just ask Him to hurry. How's that?"

Rev. Broussard affected a surprised look. "Funny, that's not the first time I've heard that prayer today."

"Oh?"

"Yes, curiously I prayed with a fellow parishioner just before I arrived here. He asked the Lord for the very same thing." The pastor smiled and looked away. "Interesting indeed."

The screen door squealed a warning as it flew open and Uncle Joe spilled out onto the porch. He wore his blue suit and his best hat, and he carried a satchel of papers under his arms. Inside that satchel, Cleo knew, was a letter to New Orleans, begging on her behalf for a spot on the fall roster at the college.

He set the satchel on the porch rail and began fumbling through the items inside. "Ah, here it is. Cleo, take a look at this list and see if I've left off any supplies you need for the schoolhouse."

As her gaze ran the length of the page, her mind ticked off the items required for the schoolroom. Each seemed to be present on the list.

"No, I can't think of anything missing," she said as she handed the paper back to her uncle. "It looks like you've thought of everything."

He nodded. "Good. Theo tells me the school will be finished soon. I want everything in place to get started as soon as we can. What with Cleo leaving in a few months, I'd like to get our children into the schoolhouse and learning their lessons as soon as possible."

"I'm not sure the children will be as excited as you, Uncle Joe," Cleo said with a chuckle.

"I have to agree with Cleo," Rev. Broussard said. "But I do think it will make for a much easier transition once the new teacher arrives if the children are already used to coming to school and tending to their lessons."

Uncle Joe replaced the list in his satchel, then closed the latch. "Theo promised a progress report today. I told him you and I would stop by on our way back from town and see what he's got to show us."

"That sounds like a fine idea," the reverend said as he fell into step beside Uncle Joe.

"That sounds like a fine idea." The same words Theo Breaux had used to describe his reaction to Cleo going off to college.

Cleo reached for the broom. What the Lord did with her situation was anyone's guess. What He intended to do with Theo Breaux was another mystery.

At least she knew the One who had the situation in hand. "You know I'd just mess it up if I tried to fix it."

Chapter 20

Theo slipped into church and listened intently as the music swelled around him. He rarely joined the faithful in their singing, choosing to mouth the words rather than ruin the harmony with his squawking.

Today, however, he added his voice to the mix, swept into the words of the song as if he'd fallen into the river just ahead of Niagara Falls.

" 'Oh, what peace we often forfeit. Oh, what needless pain we bear. All because we do not carry everything to God in prayer!' "

While the rest of the congregation went on with their singing, Theo stopped right there. He'd been walking around all week, shouldering his worries and hadn't even thought to leave them at the cross. That wasn't true. He'd thought about it; he'd been afraid of the answers he might get if he asked the questions.

Ever since he and the reverend had parted company last Tuesday, he'd been miserable. Worse, every time he took his troubles to the Lord, He said the same thing, so Theo had just quit.

"Stay. Be patient."

Stay? Be patient? Stay where? Be patient about what?

Best as he could tell, he figured it went like this: He wanted to go—soon—and yet the Lord was telling him he ought to take his time in leaving. He feared God might even be telling him he ought not go at all. Worse, he felt the strongest urge to have a talk with Clothilde Trahan about *her* need to leave Latagnier.

Of course, a logical man would know that none of these things made sense. He'd head for Canada soon, and Cleo, well, she'd be in New Orleans before fall. That's just the way life worked.

Still, he had the nagging feeling the Lord was pushing him in one direction while he stubbornly continued to try to go in another.

Knowing that what he wanted to do and what he ought to do were two different things, Theo elected to do nothing but mope all week. Well, mope and take out his frustrations on several pounds of nails and a good portion of the schoolhouse.

At this rate, he'd be finished with the work out there and ready to hit the road again come the end of April. Maybe sooner.

Rather than let that thought ruin a beautiful Palm Sunday morning, Theo focused on catching up to the rest of the parishioners.

" 'Jesus knows our every weakness. Take it to the Lord in prayer.' "

He finished the singing with the rest of the faithful, then sat down between his papa and Alphonse to listen to the preaching. Expecting a message on Jesus' ride on the donkey or some other Palm Sunday topic, he was surprised to hear Rev. Broussard begin to tell the tale of an itinerant carpenter who made his living working for the less fortunate in Canada.

As the story of songwriter Joseph Scriven unfolded, Theo listened with particular attention. Seemed as though this fellow spent his days doing odd carpentering jobs and taking little or no payment in return. When his mother fell ill back home in Ireland, Scriven wrote her the poem that eventually became the song the congregation had sung that very morning.

"Think on that, ladies and gentlemen," Rev. Broussard said. "Just as the Lord used a lowly animal to carry His Son on the day we now call Palm Sunday, so He also used a regular man to carry a message that lasts." He paused to lean over the edge of the pulpit and point out into the crowd. "How many of you regular men and women are being called today to do something, and you don't know why? Maybe you don't even want to do it, eh?"

A few murmurs circulated through the room. Beside him, Theo's papa nodded while Theo squirmed.

"Do you think that donkey knew he was carrying the King of glory? Did he know why he was supposed to plod through the city gates with that man on his back, and on his day off at that? And what about that Canadian carpenter? Do you think he knew that a poem he wrote to his ailing mama back home in Ireland was going to be sung in our little church in Latagnier today?"

Again the crowd answered softly or nodded in quiet agreement. Theo saw his mama jab his papa, then watched them share a smile.

"So the next time you think you know what God wants you to do, do it, even if it doesn't make any sense to you. That carpenter, he fixed things for widows and the poor. He wasn't a fancy poet. That donkey, it probably didn't have much claim to glory, either, being as though that particular species of the animal kingdom is not exactly exalted."

Rev. Broussard paused to shake his head. "Brothers and sisters, it all comes down to obedience. Promise yourself that in light of the nature of this upcoming Holy Week, you will settle yourself into a pattern of obedience. Now stand with me while we sing the last verse of that song one more time."

The next time Theo sang about taking his worries to the Lord in prayer, he barely got the words out for the lump in his throat. Knowing he wouldn't like what the Lord was telling him, somewhere midweek he'd stopped going to Him in prayer altogether.

He'd have to remedy that today. This time, he'd listen if the Lord spoke. And as much as it put grit in his craw, he'd obey.

He'd obey even if it killed him.

Funny how he felt he had more in common with the lowly donkey than with the poet-carpenter. While the carpenter knew what he was doing when he wrote that poem, that poor donkey just put one hoof in front of the other and walked all the way to Jerusalem.

Later that afternoon, while the house lay still, Theo slipped away to go back to his thinking spot—the log beside the bayou. There he met the Savior and had a good talk.

It was a one-sided conversation, to be sure, but near the end, when he'd spoken his piece and knelt waiting for a response, Theo felt the Lord's presence.

He hadn't said a word, audible or otherwise, and yet Theo knew He was there. "Sometimes just knowing You're there is enough," he whispered.

Returning home, he felt a renewed spring in his step. While he might have to do something he didn't want to do this week, he at least hadn't been asked to do it yet.

He did have something else in mind, however, something he'd like to do if the Lord and Rev. Broussard didn't disagree.

~

Easter Sunday loomed large on Cleo's calendar, circled in red and noted with a star. Now the big day stood just one day away, and she had things to do. Important things.

Over the past week, she'd learned to press past the worries of *when* the Lord would act and *how* He would act and to just be patient and *know* He would act. Of course, this didn't make the waiting any easier, so she'd thrown herself into a flurry of activities.

She'd cooked and washed and starched and ironed. Cleo had even volunteered to participate in the quilting circle.

Listening to the married ladies cackle and go on about their husbands and children turned out to be fun. Hearing the love in their voices gave Cleo hope that she would one day have what these women already possessed.

Such was her enthusiasm for keeping busy that today she'd volunteered to clean the entire sanctuary in anticipation for tomorrow's Easter services. She collected her supplies and reached for the bucket's metal handle. Making the church sparkle and shine would be her small contribution to the Lord's Day, and she eagerly anticipated being alone with Jesus in His house as she worked.

Tomorrow would dawn early, with sunrise services being held in the churchyard beside the bayou, then preaching at half past ten in the sanctuary. The entire congregation would break bread together afterward with a spectacular Easter Sunday dinner on the grounds.

Cleo smiled. Easter Sunday had been the same ever since she could remember. Only the pastor's name had changed over the years, and even then there had been only two other preachers besides Rev. Broussard to grace the pulpit.

There was something to be said for permanence and stability. Some might look at the long and uninterrupted cycle of life in the bayou country and call it boring or backward. Theo Breaux struck her as one of those folks.

Others praised the predictable daily routine as good and comfortable. Cleo wondered if she might fit better in the second category.

Perhaps when she was older, she would know for sure.

Older like Theo Breaux.

She shook off thoughts of the carpenter. Ever since she'd had her talk with the reverend, she'd placed Theo in a carefully guarded spot in her heart and left him there—at least most days.

But on random occasions, the carpenter managed to sneak out of his confinement and dance across her mind. Well, not actually dance. When thoughts of him arrived, it was more like the infantry storming through.

Nevertheless, the idea of Theo Breaux dancing did produce a chuckle. She allowed herself that single silly thought, then tucked it away with the others and headed for the church.

Funny how she'd listened to the pastor's sermon and immediately thought of herself. Now, as she passed very near to the place where the carpenter had kissed her, she thought about how Rev. Broussard's words might apply to Theo Breaux.

Here was a man who couldn't read but who had been called on to rebuild a schoolhouse so that others could learn. She knew enough of Theo's history to know he'd left home young and stayed gone until recently, when his papa broke a leg. How difficult it must be for a wandering soul to be confined.

She sighed. "Just another reason why he and I were not meant to be."

Pausing in the middle of the path, she let her feet turn her toward the bayou and the log where she had sat with Theo Breaux. To her surprise, the giant fallen tree trunk was gone.

Chapter 21

Cleo looked around to be sure she stood in the correct place. All the landmarks were there: The pine and the sweet gum trees and the honeysuckle vine were all where she remembered them to be.

As she drew nearer, she found a deep indentation in the soft, dark earth where the tree trunk had once landed. This had to be the spot, yet the tree was gone.

Pondering the conundrum all the way to the church, she set her cleaning supplies just outside the door and reached for the massive iron handle. As her fingers wrapped around the cool metal, she heard a strange scratching sound.

Cleo released her grip and followed the sound to the back of the church, where a pile of rope and a hammer sat beside a bag of nails. The scratching sound continued. It seemed to be coming from near the bayou. Pressing through the thicket, she found the source of the noise.

Theo Breaux stood hunched over a large piece of wood while another man held the lumber still. Theo's broad shoulders rolled as he worked a saw across the end of the timber. The other man, whom she recognized as Theo's brother Alphonse, looked up to see her approach but merely nodded and returned his attention to his task.

His back to her, Theo continued to work on chopping off the rough ends of the timber. As Cleo drew near, she realized what the men were doing. Her gasp of surprise seemed to echo louder than the scrape of the saw, although neither man gave notice they'd heard.

The log where just last week she'd sat with Theo now lay in the clearing in two pieces, one significantly shorter than the other. If she used her imagination, she could see the two planks nailed together to form a cross.

Abruptly the noise ceased, and Theo dropped the saw atop the pile of sawdust. Alphonse grinned and nudged his brother, then pointed toward Cleo.

Theo straightened and turned slowly. His face wore no expression, but his brother's did.

Alphonse's grin split his face, and he looked to be having a hard time keeping from breaking into laughter. "Bonjour, Mademoiselle Trahan," he called. "Comment ça va? And your family?"

"Ça va bien, merci," she responded. "Thank you for asking."

Cleo turned her attention to Theo but found no words of greeting forthcoming. He obviously had the same trouble, for he merely nodded, then went back to his work.

Alphonse said something to his brother and bounded toward her. "So what brings you out to the church today?"

"Cleaning the sanctuary."

She looked past him to where Theo now rubbed a metal file against the edge of the freshly cut wood. The dark fabric of his shirt bunched and stretched as he worked his powerful arms to move the tool across the rough timber.

Remembering the feel of those arms around her, heat flooded Cleo's cheeks. Perhaps the fact that this man was the roaming kind was a blessing. He might never completely leave her mind, but at least she wouldn't have his presence to distract her.

Not that she minded the distraction.

"Fine day, isn't it?"

"What?" She forced her attention back to Alphonse Breaux. "I'm sorry. What did you say?"

Theo's brother gave her a good-natured grin, then shook his head. A sprinkling of wood shavings fell from his dark hair. From a distance, the two men could practically be mistaken for twins. Up close, however, the younger Breaux had none of his older brother's careworn demeanor.

Where Theo's eyes had creases at the corner, Alphonse's were wide and unmarred by time and worry. His forehead held no lines, and his square jaw bore none of the perpetual stubble like his brother's.

In a word, Alphonse Breaux was the very definition of handsome. All the girls at church thought so, and he never lacked for female companionship.

Funny, but Cleo preferred to cast her gaze on the less-perfect Theo instead.

"I was commenting on the weather. Making small talk. Never mind."

"That's nice." Her gaze swept across the landscape, from the two timbers to Theo, and finally rested on Alphonse. "What are you doing?"

He shrugged. "Can't tell you. Actually, I don't think you're supposed to be out here. Theo wanted this to be a surprise."

"Oh." She cast a quick glance at Theo, who seemed to be hard at work. "Well, I promise not to tell what I've seen. Not that I know what I'm looking at."

"That's good. I'm sure Theo will appreciate that." Alphonse swiped at his forehead, then studied the back of his hand. "You know, Mademoiselle Trahan, I'm puzzled by something. Maybe you can help me with it."

Theo glanced over his shoulder, then returned to his work as if he hadn't noticed she still stood nearby. Well, two could play this game.

"What are you confused about, Alphonse?"

"Here's how I see it. I hear tell you're going to teach at the schoolhouse until fall and then you're heading for school out in New Orleans. Is that right?"

A brisk wind blew past, and she brushed a strand of hair from her eyes. "Yes, that's right."

"And Theo over there, he's chomping at the bit to get the schoolhouse finished so he can get himself up to Canada to see the first snowfall."

"That's what I hear."

Alphonse nodded and seemed to be considering his thoughts carefully. His brow creased, and he shook his head. "So if you want to head off to school and Theo wants to head off to Canada, and you are both getting what you want, what's the problem?"

Cleo shrugged. "I don't guess there is a problem."

Again Theo's brother nodded. "I see. Well, that's funny, because I don't remember when I've ever seen my brother look more miserable, and truth be told, you're not exactly smiling real big today, either."

To prove him wrong, she forced a grin. It only lasted a moment.

"You and my brother, I think you have something special. Sa fini pas. The thing that never ends."

Sa fini pas. Interesting. But then, hadn't she just had the same thought, that he might be leaving, but he'd never completely be gone?

"Forgive me, Mademoiselle Trahan, but I think you and Theo are both stubborn as mules. Neither one of you wants to admit that you've made the wrong plans."

How could someone so handsome say something so rude and get away with it? Because it was true.

"Alphonse! Vien ici. Quit your flirting and get back over here. There's work to be done."

Alphonse waved to his brother and turned to trot away. "I'm doing your job over here, and now you want me to do it over there, too?" He glanced back at Cleo and winked. "He's going to get me for that as soon as you leave. When you see me bruised and bandaged, remember I did it for you, Mademoiselle Trahan."

"Enough, Alphonse!" Theo called. "I'm sure the lady's got better things to do than to listen to you talk nonsense."

"Yes, well, I'll just get back to work myself, then," she said, but neither brother responded. They were too busy circling one another like tomcats.

~

All afternoon, Cleo listened to mysterious clangs and bangs and other assorted sounds coming from the vicinity of the Breaux brothers' work area.

At one point, Alphonse left for a spell, then returned with shovels—two of them. He winked at her when he spied her peeking out the window. She backed up quickly and pretended to busy herself with dusting, just in case he decided to come inside to say hello.

He didn't, however, and neither did Theo.

Upon finishing the dusting, Cleo decided it was time to take a short rest—just a few minutes of repose before she tackled the job of polishing the candlesticks.

Casually stepping into the afternoon sun, Cleo stretched and sat, then stood and headed for the bayou. Whatever those two were up to out there, she intended to find out.

Getting close to the bayou was the hard part, for she had to go all the way around the church and the cemetery to avoid walking through the clearing. By the time she reached her destination, her ankles had tangled with enough thorns to mark her permanently.

Once she found her way into the thicket, she had to shift positions until she could make out the work site. To do this, she had to lie flat and crawl beneath a tangle of honeysuckle vines, not a feat she could manage easily but one she thought she could accomplish all the same.

Her apron got caught several times, and more than once she had to stop and remove clods of dirt and leaves from the pockets. Finally, she untied it and tossed it aside, giving thanks that she'd taken on the job of the Trahan family laundry several years ago.

Eventually she managed to make her way across the distance to find a spot where she could sit comfortably. From her vantage point, she could make out a mass of wood and one man working on it. Both Theo and Alphonse wore dark shirts and trousers, so it was impossible to tell who did the work.

It was also impossible to tell what sort of work was being done, so she inched forward and peered through the vines. Noting a natural clearing a few feet ahead, she decided to try to make her way toward it.

As she leaned forward, she found she could not move her right ankle. From her prone position, she couldn't tell what had happened, but she felt for all the world as if something held her in its grasp. With the thickness of the vines obscuring her view, she couldn't see a thing.

The harder she pulled, the more she seemed to be stuck. Finally, she realized she had to turn around and go back the way she came. This would be the only way to free herself.

Rolling over, she sat up and began to pull the vines apart with her hands. As the dark green leaves fell away, she saw the reason for her troubles.

Theo Breaux sat on the other side of the honeysuckle vine, her apron in one hand and her foot firmly in the other.

"Looking for your apron?"

When he released her foot, she scrambled out of the thicket. Climbing to her feet, Cleo shook the leaves from her dress and hair and reached for her apron. The carpenter stepped back and held the formerly white cloth to his chest.

"Not so fast," he said. "You were spying again."

Her dignity and her apron in shreds, Cleo didn't bother to deny his claim. She held out her hand and waited for him to place the apron in it. When he did, she ran all the way back to the church, his laughter chasing her inside.

With anger and humiliation fueling her, Cleo made short order of the rest of her cleaning, then headed home. On her way, she felt the temptation to stop by the schoolhouse. After all, with Theo at the church, there was no better time to visit.

Reaching the bend in the path, she elected to go home instead. Whatever awaited at the school, it would still be there on Monday. Tante Flo would need her to help with the cooking for tomorrow, and Uncle Joe would most likely have her school supplies.

More to the point, the schoolhouse reminded her of Theo Breaux, and his was a memory she didn't want to think about right now. Maybe not ever.

Still, as she made tracks for home, something about him gave her pause. She knew how she felt about the man, but had she ever asked the Lord His opinion?

Chapter 22

The Easter Sunday sunrise was still a good hour away when Cleo and her aunt and uncle climbed into the wagon and headed to church. Tante Flo had the back packed with enough food to feed an army, and still she fretted about whether she'd made enough.

When they arrived at the church, they found a crowd had already begun to gather inside the sanctuary. Cleo noticed the sizable Breaux family carrying on boisterous conversations among themselves over on the left-hand side of the sanctuary, so she turned to head the other way. While she busied herself helping Tante Flo and the other ladies, she kept watch over the doors in case Theo Breaux were to walk in.

Rev. Broussard and his wife greeted the visitors and moved about between the groups of families until he finally climbed to the platform to stand behind the pulpit. As was his custom, Theo slipped inside just as the preacher began to speak.

"It figures," she said as she watched him disappear into a crowd of Breaux family members. This time, however, she spoke the words gently and with humor.

"What figures, dear?" Tante Flo asked.

"Nothing," she said softly, avoiding her aunt's direct gaze. "Listen, the pastor's about to speak."

"Good men and women, let me wish you all the most blessed of Easter Sundays." He paused to allow the parishioners to add their own greetings to one another. "This year our sunrise service will be a little different. A pair of our members have prepared a surprise for us that I believe you all will like very much."

He gestured toward the back exit. "If you will all follow our elders, we will make our way outside and begin our worship."

Cleo filed out with the rest of the congregation, then stood beside Tante Flo until the pastor and his wife emerged from the church. "I wonder what this is about," she whispered to her aunt.

Tante Flo shrugged. "You never can tell," she said softly. "Let's find your uncle."

They spotted Uncle Joe and made their way through the crowd to reach his side. "Do you know what this is about, Joe?" her aunt asked.

Rather than answer, Uncle Joe put his finger over his lips and pointed toward the pastor.

"Folks, I'd like us all to begin now with a song. Rather than stand out here as is our custom, we'll be heading down to the bayou. The path's been lit up, and it should be quite safe. Still, mothers may want to watch the little ones as we all walk together."

He nodded to his wife. "Berta will begin the singing, and we'll all fall in behind her."

As the elderly soprano began the first line of "Amazing Grace," the crowd joined in. Soon the group turned the corner of the church and headed across the clearing toward the bayou.

At the edge of the path, a lantern hung from a tree limb, providing just enough light to see. The same had been done at intervals, each lantern shining a circle of light that enabled the church members to walk in safety.

Cleo held tightly to her aunt's arm, noting with wonder the way the deep blue of the night sky was gradually giving way to the gray of morning. By the time she reached the bayou, the tiniest sliver of orange showed on the horizon.

In degrees, the landscape began to emerge, becoming more visible as the sun tried harder to rise. By the time the song ended, most of the church folk had gathered. Cleo looked past them to watch the bayou flow by, an endless river of black punctuated by green on both sides.

Rev. Broussard cleared his throat. "Let us pray."

As the pastor gave thanks for the day and for the Savior who died and rose for them, Cleo let her own prayers mingle with his. When the amens were said, she opened her eyes to see that the elders of the church had retrieved the lanterns.

Five men walked single file toward the bayou, passing the crowd to stop at the edge of the trees. As the men gathered together, the light from the lanterns illuminated an amazing sight.

Behind them a massive wooden cross rose almost to the treetops. "Let us sing," the pastor said.

As the congregation's voices mingled in song, Cleo's gaze scanned the crowd for signs of Theo Breaux. She found him standing apart from the gathering, leaning against the trunk of a pine tree.

Any other time she would have let the ornery man be, but this morning something drew her to him. Making her way through the friends and relatives took some doing, but Cleo managed to reach his side before the preaching began.

"It's beautiful," she said.

The orange sky glinted off his dark hair and gave his face a golden glow, while the dim light cast half his features in shadow. Rather than the frown she expected, he gave her a wry smile.

"Yes, for once I would have to agree with you, cher."

And Theo did agree. Cleo was beautiful. Too beautiful. That made forgetting her all the more difficult.

He was no saint, even though he really wanted to be. He'd seen pretty women in his time, but not one of them held a candle to this simple bayou beauty.

As the pastor settled into his stride and began regaling the crowd with the finer points of the resurrection story, Theo allowed his attention to drift from the reverend to the cross and finally to the woman who still stood at his side. The thought occurred to him that ever since he had met Cleo, he'd been plotting on how best to remember her—and how to forget her.

What the Lord had in mind when He set her in Theo's line of sight, he'd never know. Still, Theo closed his eyes and gave thanks that the Lord had set her there all the same.

If only He weren't continuing to remain silent on what to do about her. *Lord, if You wouldn't mind meeting me here on this Easter Sunday morning, I'd sure like some sign of what You're up to.*

He opened his eyes and gazed on the cross he and Alphonse had set into the ground late last night. Even though he'd cut and planed the wood himself, with his brother's help, nothing prepared him for the sight of it standing this morning.

Somewhere between the closing hymn and the benediction, Cleo slipped her hand into his. He leaned down to protest, only to have her kiss him full on the mouth.

His shock must have shown, for he could only stand mute as she gave him a smile and slipped off into the crowd. As he looked around to see if there were any witnesses to Cleo's kiss-and-run, he noted with dismay that there had been at least one: his papa.

Their gazes met, and Theo knew his goose was cooked. Once the service ended, Papa would certainly have something to say about what he'd seen. As he expected, when the congregation began to mill about, Papa hobbled toward him and poked him with his cane.

"How about you and me speaking privately, son?" He gestured toward the bayou. "Let's walk that way."

Theo followed his father away from the crowd, staying close enough to catch him should he fall. To his relief, his father had regained his agility. Unfortunately, that same agility got them to their conversation much too soon.

Papa eased himself down on a tree stump and gestured for Theo to sit, as well. When Theo complied, his father leaned forward and regarded him with a serious look.

"You want to tell me the whole story right up front, or am I going to have to ask you a bunch of questions and drag it out of you?"

Theo sighed. "I guess I ought to just start at the beginning and lay it all out."

As his father nodded, Theo began his tale. When he got to the part about asking the Lord not to let him miss out on life like his father had, he saw Papa wince. Pressing on, he finished his story, then leaned back against the pine tree and waited for his father's reaction.

When Papa leaned on his cane and stared down at Theo, he figured the time for a lecture had arrived. And then Papa laughed. Right there on Easter Sunday morning, his father had listened to Theo tell him he didn't want to end up in the same situation as he was in, and he responded by laughing.

"I'm sorry, son," Papa said. "But I think you've got it all wrong here. I didn't miss a thing."

"But you could've gone to college, made something of yourself." Theo cringed. "I'm sorry, I didn't mean to say that. . . ."

Papa waved away the statement with a swipe of his cane. "Yes, you did, but that's all right. I'd think that, too, if I didn't know better." He shrugged. "After all, what the world looks on as success isn't always all it's cracked up to be."

Theo shook his head. "I know, but don't you ever wonder what it would have been like if you'd gone to Texas and earned your diploma at the college? I mean, you'd certainly not have ended up here in Latagnier."

He nodded. "Well, you're right about that, son, which is exactly why I believe you miss the point."

"I don't understand."

"You asked me if I ever wonder what I missed by staying here. I don't, but let me tell you what I do wonder sometimes. I wonder what it would be like if I'd set off to seek my fortune and missed out on nigh on thirty years of marriage with the love of my life."

The sounds of churchgoers buzzed in the distance as Theo thought about his father's statement. "I suppose I see your point," he said. "But look at you. You're up before the sun, work your fingers until they bleed, then fall into bed at night dead tired. The next morning you do it all over again. I don't want that life. No, not me."

Papa looked away and closed his eyes. "Is that what you see when you look at me? Do you really think that's all there is to my life?"

Theo thought a minute, then shook his head. In reality, when he considered his papa, work was the last thing that came to mind. His quick wit, his endless patience, and his ability to endure without losing his love for the Lord—those were the things he thought of.

Above all these, however, Theo knew he would remember his father for the way he openly and eternally showed how much he loved his wife and children.

"No, sir. I don't suppose I do." He repeated his thoughts to his father, then shared a grin with him. "So what do you make of Cleo Trahan?"

"Other than the fact that she has excellent taste in men?"

If Theo knew how to blush, he would have done it at that moment. Instead, he shrugged. "Runs in the family, I guess."

Papa nodded. "But my guess is, you're not sure she's the one."

"Well. . ." He struggled to answer his father.

"The fact you can't agree tells me a whole lot."

Theo slapped his knees. "I'm not sure what to do, Papa. If I admit I care for her, I risk giving up my freedom. At the same time, she'd be giving up her teaching. What marriage can survive that?"

Papa rose slowly and waited for Theo to join him. "You ask what marriage can survive? Look at your mama and me. We buried two babies before they could walk and stared each other down in head-to-head disagreements more times than a gator has scales. I'm as hardheaded as a mule, and I snore louder than a brass band on Independence Day. On top of that, and I know you'll find this difficult to believe, I tend to be set in my ways and don't like to admit I'm wrong. Know anybody like that?"

Theo dusted off the seat of his pants and met his father's gaze. "No, can't say as I do." He shrugged. "You can't be comparing yourself to me. I don't snore."

The pair shared a laugh, then walked back to the gathering together. Just before they rejoined the group, Papa laid his hand on Theo's shoulder and pulled him aside.

"Son, don't make the mistake of deciding what God's will is for that girl. You worry about what He wants you to do, and He'll take care of the rest."

"Yes, sir." He took a step toward the clearing, but his father held him back.

"And, Theo, you need to realize that what you think you're missing isn't out there. It's right here." He thumped Theo on the chest. "You get your heart right with God, and He takes care of your need to find happiness anywhere else."

"As for the adventure you think you're looking for. . ." He pointed to the group of women where Cleo stood. "I'd wager a week's wages and my good leg that it's right over there."

The object of their discussion met his gaze. She offered a smile, then a discreet wave. He nodded and turned his attention to his father. "Anything else, Papa?"

Papa nodded and motioned for him to lean close. "Just one more thing."

"All right."

"You *do* snore."

Chapter 23

"It's Sunday evening!" Uncle Joe called. "Who in the world would be calling on a body on Easter Sunday? Why, we've already talked to just about everyone in the parish this morning at church."

"Hush, Joe," Tante Flo said. "That's not neighborly at all. Cleo, would you see who is at the door?"

"Oui."

Cleo rose from her spot on the settee, leaving her book open so she could easily rejoin the adventure unfolding on the pages. To her surprise, she opened the door to find Theo Breaux standing there. Dressed in his Sunday best, he'd taken the unprecedented step of slicking his unruly hair back in a style vaguely resembling the latest fashion.

"*Bonsoir*, Cleo. Is your uncle home?" He thrust a motley collection of spring flowers in her direction.

Cleo suppressed a giggle. "Why? Are those for him?"

He seemed a bit disconcerted. "No, they're for you."

"Who's there, Cleo?" Uncle Joe called.

"It's your carpenter," she said as she stepped back and ushered him inside.

He and Joe shook hands, then Theo cleared his throat. "I'd like to speak to you in private, sir."

Uncle Joe looked up at Theo over the rim of his spectacles. "Would you, now?"

The pair went into the kitchen. When Cleo tiptoed toward the closed door, her aunt stepped out to touch her shoulder. She jumped and whirled around.

"Go and read your book, child, while I put these in some water," Tante Flo said as she took the flowers from Cleo. "For once in your life, let the menfolk be."

Somehow she managed to settle back onto the settee and pick up the book. Reading, however, was out of the question, as her mind kept reeling back in time to the morning's sunrise service.

Had she really stolen a kiss during church? Why, she'd behaved no better than. . .than what? She blushed to think of the comparison she could make.

Abruptly the kitchen door flew open, and Theo emerged, followed by Uncle Joe. Without a word, the carpenter took Cleo by the hand.

"Let's go for a walk," he said as he led her toward the door.

She cast a glance over her shoulder in time to see Uncle Joe disappear down the hall. Obviously, whatever had transpired in the kitchen, her uncle was neither excited nor upset about it.

Following Theo outside, she paused to suppress a chill. When had the air grown so cold?

Before she could turn and fetch her shawl, Theo removed his suit coat and draped it over her shoulders. The heavy wool felt heavenly against her shoulders as she snuggled into its warmth.

They walked along in silence for a time, and Cleo marveled at how comfortable it felt. When Theo cleared his throat, she almost jumped.

"You're probably wondering why I showed up here tonight." He gestured toward his clothes. "Dressed like this."

Cleo met his gaze, then allowed her attention to slide lower to his neck. A vein pulsed there, and she wondered if his heart raced as fast.

"Actually, I did wonder." She paused to add the beginning of a smile. "A bit, anyway."

He guided her toward the bayou, falling in step beside her. "I'm not sure where to start, so I guess I'll just tell you right out." He shook his head. "No, I don't think I'll do it that way. I believe I'll just show you."

Grasping Cleo's hand, he picked up his pace. She nearly had to run to keep up with his long strides. By the time they reached the schoolhouse, she was out of breath.

Theo slowed his pace when he saw her distress. "I'm really sorry, Cleo," he said. "Why didn't you say something?"

She shrugged. "We're here now," she managed. "What was it you wanted to show me?"

He climbed up on the porch, then gestured for her to follow. At the door, he stepped back and pointed to the handle. "You do the honors, Cleo. It's your schoolhouse."

Cleo gave him a long look before opening the door and stepping inside. The first thing she noticed was the smell. Everything smelled fresh and clean and—and new.

Theo rushed to the windows and began raising the shades. As light flooded the room, Cleo shook her head. It was finished.

Her gaze flitted from desk to bench to chalkboard and back to Theo. Somewhere along the way, tears had begun to fall. Theo raced to her side.

"Quoi y'a, cher? What is it? Have I done something wrong?"

"Wrong? No. Pas du tout. It's—it's perfect."

She glanced around the room once more. True to his word, Theo Breaux had turned the little ramshackle building into something resembling a proper schoolhouse.

Sturdy wooden benches sat in three straight rows on the patched cypress floor, providing room enough for nearly a dozen children to sit. Three windows on each side of the room allowed a breeze to float across the little room. Cleo closed her eyes, imagining the bright faces of children eager to learn, then opened them once more to see Theo staring.

To her surprise, his eyes seemed to be watering. Or was that a tear?

"Theo, are you all right?"

Nodding, he grasped her hand and brought her fingers to touch his lips. "It's just that I'm going to miss you."

She kissed his fingers, then fell into his arms. "Are you asking me to stay?"

Pressing her ear to his chest, she could hear his heart racing. "I can't ask that of you," he said.

The words rumbled through her heart and lodged in her throat. "Can't or won't?"

He released his grip to hold her at arm's length. "I won't be the reason your dreams don't come true, Cleo."

She stared into the eyes of the orneriest man in Latagnier and gave passing thought to what life might be like without him. "Just as I refuse to be the reason yours don't come true. Tell me I'm worth giving up your traveling ways."

She knew from his expression that she'd hit a nerve. "I'm not, am I?"

His silence spoke volumes. Shrugging out of Theo's jacket, she threw it in his direction and fled for the safety of home.

"Leave me be!" she shouted when he tried to follow her. "And don't come around me until you're ready to say I'm more important to you than some trip north. I don't want to love you only to end up with a broken heart, so if you're going, go now."

When he froze in his tracks, her heart broke for real.

~

The first week of school flew by, as did the second and third. Sometime during the fourth week, Cleo got wind through one of the church ladies that Theo Breaux had left Latagnier on the evening train two weeks back. He was heading north, she'd been told. Canada was what his brother claimed.

Cleo listened to the reports, then went back to her quilting. Her tears would wait for bedtime. They always did.

Berta Broussard met her gaze and changed the subject. Before long, the ladies had moved on to jawing about the rising cost of thread in town and the prospect of a fall festival to raise money for new candlesticks in the sanctuary.

When Uncle Joe interrupted the party, Cleo was almost relieved. "I'm sorry, ladies, but Cleo is needed at the schoolhouse."

"Really?" She gathered her scissors and thimble and dropped them into her bag. "Is something wrong?"

After all, today was Saturday. No one should be at the school.

"I think you'd better see for yourself," he said. "But don't tarry."

Cleo rushed toward the school, her gaze scanning the treetops for some sign of smoke or other calamity. When she reached the clearing, relief flooded her. Whatever was wrong, at least the place hadn't gone up in flames.

In fact, the building looked the same today as she had left it after school yesterday. Easing her way up the steps, she tiptoed across the porch to push open the door.

She stepped inside and glanced around. Everything looked to be in order.

Venturing further, she noted the books still lined up on the desks and the pencils and paper neatly stacked on the shelf beneath a chart showing the consonants and vowels. A sound behind her made her jump.

She turned in time to see a tall shadow cross the floor.

"Theo?" A dozen different emotions assailed her, each giving way to the next until she'd lost any idea of how she felt about seeing the carpenter again.

He nodded. "Am I still welcome here?"

For a moment she had no answer. Slowly she nodded. "Of course," she said. "This schoolhouse belongs to everyone who lives in Latagnier."

As soon as she said the words, she longed to reel them back in. Theo Breaux no longer lived in Latagnier. Or did he?

He crossed the distance between them in long strides and came close enough to take her in his arms. Close enough, yet he just stood there, arms at his sides, staring.

"Why did you come back?"

More words she wished she hadn't said.

"Something you said. I had to see if you meant it."

"Something I said?" She'd said plenty that day, most of it not so nice.

He nodded. "You said you didn't want to be responsible for my dreams not coming true. Did you mean that?"

It was her turn to nod. Their gazes collided. The impact rocked her to her toes.

"Yes, I meant it," she whispered.

Theo took her hand in his. "Well, I had to get halfway to Canada before I figured out you were the reason my dreams weren't coming true."

"I don't understand."

Theo went down on one knee and kissed her hand. "Without you, I don't have any dreams. I can't imagine life without you in it, and I can't see spending our days anywhere but right here in Latagnier. What I'm saying is, I had to learn the hard way that here is where I belong, and you belong right by my side. *Je t'aime*—oh, how I love you, Cleo Trahan. Will you marry me?"

Words gathered in her mind but stuck in her throat. Somehow she managed to say just one: "Yes."

His expression turned serious. "You'd better think before you answer, Cleo. Setting your sights on being the future Mrs. Breaux will mean you have to give up going to that fancy teachers' college."

She smiled. "I don't give a fig about that school." Sobering a moment, she regarded Theo. "But I wonder what Uncle Joe will think."

"Uncle Joe's fine with the idea." She looked up to see her uncle standing in the door. Tante Flo was beside him. "Has she said yes yet?"

"He knew?" Cleo looked down at the carpenter in astonishment. "How did you get my uncle involved in this?"

"Remember the day I came to the house with flowers?"

She nodded.

"And the conversation in the kitchen? The one you tried to eavesdrop on?"

Again she nodded.

"I told him then that I aimed to marry up with you as soon as I came to my senses."

"Took you long enough, boy," Uncle Joe said.

"Well, Cleo, are you willing to take on an old fool like me?"

She pretended to consider the question. "How many babies do you want, Theo?"

He seemed surprised. "As many as you and the Lord will allow."

"I like this man," Tante Flo said.

"I do, too," Cleo said.

And with that, Theo rose to kiss his future bride.

Epilogue

Cleo stood in front of the parlor's rosewood-framed mirror and endured her aunt's scrutiny yet again. The wedding dress was already perfect, and still Tante Flo insisted on one more fitting, one more pin here, one more tuck there.

"Please, Tante Flo, can't we be done with it?" A knock at the door halted Cleo's protest. "I'll get that."

Her aunt stood between her and the door. "Oh no, you don't. What if it's Theo? You know he's not supposed to see you in your wedding dress before the wedding."

"That's a silly superstition designed to keep the groom from running away out of sheer terror. The wedding's tomorrow," she said, yet she allowed her aunt to trot to the front door.

Fretting with a pin, she nearly poked herself when she heard her aunt screech. "Stop right there, Theo Breaux. You cannot go in there. Your bride is in her wedding dress."

Theo's deep voice rumbled a protest. A moment later, Tante Flo returned to the parlor, flustered.

"That man is quite the charmer. I do believe he could sell ice to an Eskimo." She bustled about the room, pulling her best lace tablecloth out of the sideboard. "Here, cover yourself with this. If I let that man in here, I don't want him to be able to see your dress."

Cleo complied, then leaned toward her aunt. "Did he kiss you, too? That's how he manages to charm me."

Her aunt blushed beet red. "Of course not. Now don't be silly. And none of those kisses until tomorrow after the wedding."

Theo peered around the door. "Can I come in now?"

When Tante Flo gave her permission, the carpenter sauntered into the room. Cleo immediately claimed a contraband kiss. Then, before she would let him explain the brown paper package under his arm, she had to steal just one more.

"Someday you're going to get tired of my kisses," Theo said.

"Never," she responded as she patted the place next to her on the settee.

"What are you wearing?"

"Great-grandmother Trahan's Irish lace tablecloth. Do you like it? It's the height of fashion. Everyone wears them over their wedding dresses nowadays."

Theo looked her up and down, then smiled. "On you it looks good," he responded.

For saying just the right thing, she stole yet another kiss. This one lingered a bit longer than the others.

"If I weren't marrying you tomorrow, I'd probably need to be rushing you to the preacher tonight," he said softly. When she leaned in for yet another kiss, he shook his head. "I need to give you this present, Cleo, and if you don't stop that, I'm going to forget what I planned to say."

Smiling, she leaned away. "Go ahead and make your speech, then."

He nodded. "I'd like you to have this, Cleo. Go ahead and open it."

She accepted the package, then pulled the string to let the paper fall away. Inside she found a beautiful leather-bound Bible. Someone had written their names and the next day's date on the page reserved for family weddings.

"Theo, this is. . ." Words failed her. "Thank you."

Her groom-to-be smiled and pointed to the handwriting. "Did I do it right?"

"Do what right?" She traced the names with her index finger. "Oh, Theo, did you write this?"

"Yes," he said softly. "Alphonse showed me how. Is it right?"

"It's perfect." The image before her swirled and disappeared as tears collected in her eyes. "Simply perfect."

"I need to ask you something, Cleo. Something real important."

"What?"

He laid his hand over the Bible. "I want to be able to read this book, Cleo. It's important to me. I want to read it for myself and. . ." He paused and seemed to have difficulty continuing. "And I want to read it to our children. I want to be the head of our house and the godly papa our children deserve, and I'm going to have to call on the words in here to be able to do that. Will you teach me to read, cher?"

She cradled his chin in her hand, feeling the rough skin graze her palm. And the bride said, "I will."

Cleo Trahan's Shrimp Étouffée

4 cups butter
2 cups each chopped onions, bell peppers, and celery
1 clove garlic, chopped
2 teaspoons salt
½ teaspoon black pepper
½ teaspoon cayenne pepper
2–3 pounds peeled shrimp (small to medium)
2 tablespoons flour
2 cups water
2 cups chopped parsley
¼ cup green onions

Melt butter over medium heat, then sauté vegetables until tender, adding the garlic for the last 2 to 3 minutes of cooking time (10 to 15 total minutes). Add salt, black and red peppers, and shrimp; stir until shrimp turn pink (about 5 minutes depending on size of shrimp). In separate bowl, stir together flour and water until mixture thickens and resembles a thin gravy. Add flour mixture to shrimp and vegetables, and stir until gravy thickens to desired consistency (5 to 10 minutes), then turn heat to low and simmer uncovered for 10 minutes. Stir in parsley and green onions, reserving a small amount to use as garnish, and cook another 2 to 3 minutes. Serve over white rice, using remaining parsley and green onion as garnish. Feeds 4 to 6 hungry Cajuns.

Tante Flo's Latagnier Gateau de Sirop with Cinnamon Pecan Topping

Cake:

1 cup solid vegetable shortening
1 cup sugar
1 cup pure cane syrup
1 cup boiling water
1 egg
½ teaspoon baking powder
1 teaspoon each cinnamon, nutmeg, and salt
½ teaspoon baking soda
1½ cups flour

Topping:

½ cup light brown sugar
2½ teaspoons cinnamon
1 teaspoon nutmeg
3 tablespoons flour
3 tablespoons butter (not margarine), softened
½ cup chopped pecans (optional)

Cake:

Grease and flour 9-inch cake pan and set aside. In large mixing bowl, cream together shortening, sugar, and syrup, then add water and stir thoroughly. Beat egg and add to mixture, blending well. In separate bowl, mix baking powder, spices, baking soda, and flour, then add to cake mixture. Beat until smooth and creamy. Pour into cake pan and bake for 30 to 35 minutes in preheated 350-degree oven. Cake is done when it shrinks away from edges of pan. Remove from oven and set aside for 5 to 10 minutes while topping is prepared.

Topping:

While cake is cooling, mix together all topping ingredients. Spread onto slightly cooled cake and return to oven to bake until topping melts (10 to 12 minutes).

BAYOU FEVER

Dedication

To the amazing prayer warriors at FOTW, Seared Hearts,
and all the others who prayed this book into existence,
and to my heavenly Father, who gave me the words when I had none.
Also many thanks to Colleen, Aly, and Jan for the meals.
I owe you this book and more. God bless you all *et merci bien*!

Chapter 1

On the banks of Bayou Nouvelle near Latagnier, Louisiana, May 1929

Sweat poured off Angeline Breaux's back and dampened the dress beneath her rough cotton apron as she worked to finish the morning's wash. If only her troubles could be so easily shed. Today Papa would return from town, and he promised to cast off the burden of her care by fetching a husband.

She knew all about husbands. They expected meals on the table and young'uns in the crib, each replacing the next with a speed that would make the pollywogs in the bayou look slow.

Allowing the Lord to take His time with a match for her had worn her father's patience thin, and Theophile Breaux had sworn to take the matter into his own hands. After all, she'd made twenty years plus one, and her finger still bore no man's ring.

She would be married by fall or to the convent she would go, he declared, even though the Breaux family hadn't professed the religion of the nuns for three generations. Still, Papa had promised as much last Monday morning when he lit out for town with a dugout canoe full of skins and her eldest brother, Ernest, and she believed him.

Papa was a good man, but his ways weren't always gentle-hearted. Should he find someone willing to claim his daughter in marriage, he might be more pleased than particular, especially since he would have one less mouth to feed.

If only le bon Dieu hadn't sent away the one man who. . .

Angeline shrugged off the thought with a roll of her shoulders. Theirs had not been love, and he had certainly not been a man. Children, both of them, and so young and stupid.

If God had a plan for her, He could begin by bringing her a husband.

One thing was for sure. He needed to hurry.

"Angie?"

She looked past the thicket to where her nine-year-old sister, Amalie, stood watching. "What is it, *bebe*?" she called. "Does Mama need me?"

"No, I just wanted to watch."

Amalie picked her way through the tall grass to sit at Angeline's side. One of her dark braids had come undone, and Angeline dried her hands on her apron and repaired the mess.

Her sister looked a bit flushed, and her hair curled in damp tendrils at her temples. It might be the heat, but Angeline worried it could be the illness that had been lingering nearly a week. One day she would feel fine; the next she seemed weak. It was all so confusing and worrisome, but today she looked to be merely tired.

Scooting as close as she could to the edge of the bayou, the little girl dipped her toes into the water and began to kick. "Mama went visitin', and Mathilde told me I had to take a nap with the babies on account of I've been sick. I told her you probably needed me."

Angeline cast a glance over her shoulder at her sister. "And what did she say to that?"

"Don't know. I didn't wait to hear. I figure the washing's more fun."

Angeline chuckled. "It isn't nearly as much fun as it looks."

"You make everything fun, Angie."

"Well, I don't know about that, but I try." She paused. "So are you feeling better?"

"Sure, I'm all better." She picked at a nearby leaf and stifled a yawn. "Why don't you tell me a story?"

"You know all my stories," Angeline said. "Why don't you go ask Mathilde to tell you one?"

"I like yours better than Mathilde's, and she doesn't know the one about T-Boy the gator, and that's my favorite." She paused to rub her eyes. "Besides, you don't tell me what to do all the time, and she does. If she tells me a story, she'll make me do some chores."

An image of Mathilde, soon to be seventeen and already wanting a husband and babies of her own, came to mind. Poor Amalie probably had a list of instructions a yard long. Mathilde generally kept things orderly and employed an army of brothers and sisters to do the work when she could get away with it.

"I suppose she can be bossy, can't she?"

With a reassuring smile, Angeline went back to her washing. A few minutes later, she noticed Amalie yawning again. The pink in her cheeks had deepened.

"Maybe you'd like to take that old sheet over there and lie down to have a little nap."

Amalie frowned. "You wouldn't make me, would you?"

"I would."

"Well, I'd rather go swimming."

"That's not going to happen, Amalie." She stifled a smile at the girl's audacity. "Now march yourself over there and take your nap before I have to get even more bossy than Mathilde."

Her sister stood. "If I'm gonna have to take a nap, I might as well sleep in a bed. Thanks a lot, Angie." The little girl stormed off, leaving silence in her wake.

BAYOU FEVER

Technically, Jefferson Davis Villare was on vacation, although he could think of a half dozen places he'd rather be. Actually, he had no more choice in the matter of visiting the bayou one last time than a cat had of running from cold water.

And he'd been like a cat, running from water, specifically bayou water, ever since Mama died and left him and Pop to rattle around the big house in Latagnier. Pop was forever arriving from or racing off to an emergency call, and Jeff was left behind to tend to his studies and learn the discipline that would serve him well in his chosen career as a medical researcher.

With the bayou to the south and the country club to the north, he grew into a man with divided loyalties—true to his patrician upbringing yet with a most stubbornly irrepressible urge to return to the murky water his people had called their own for two centuries.

His people.

The thought brought an ungentlemanly snort. Not since he fled the marsh country to study first manners and then medicine had Jeff considered the Acadians *his* people. And yet the documents his father displayed behind glass in his study proclaimed it so. What would his forebears think of him now, years and miles removed from the place they loved?

No matter, he decided. As a doctor of some importance, he would no doubt please them. His own grandfather had been doctor to the bayou people, often spending hours on the water, traveling from birth to death by means of a pirogue, a little canoe given him in lieu of payment. Pop held somewhat to that tradition as well, although his own miles through the bayou were more likely to take place by road rather than the traditional Acadian conveyance.

Jeff, however, was a different man, a doctor without the urge to follow in the tradition of the past two generations. He'd decided early on that there would be no late-night calls to deliver babies or early-morning wake-ups to set broken bones. His was to be the disciplined life of a man bent over a beaker, jotting notes that would one day save the world, in the eradication first of influenza and then of other diseases. From the happy but disconcerting chaos of his childhood, order would reign.

And reign it had for too many years, but with one trip back to his boyhood home, the reasons for his exile all came tumbling back. Chief among them was a dark-eyed Cajun girl who'd captured his heart, then handed it back to him scarred and broken. Could that be her on the other side of the Nouvelle? Had she changed so little that even at this distance, with the live oaks and the cypress casting her into deep shade, he recognized her?

Jeff removed his hat and swiped at the perspiration on his brow, then cursed himself for a fool. What bayou boy in his right mind would wear his best suit into the marsh? Had he lost that much of his past?

The woman shifted and turned, oblivious to his presence as she knelt at the bank and dipped yet another piece of clothing in the water. With a shrug of her shoulders, she caused her inky hair to ripple and catch the sunlight. *Blue-black* was the term that came to mind as he stared at the tresses of the beauty in rough clothing.

By the first year away, he'd given no more than a passing glance at the belles of the bayou, preferring instead to keep company with women of the fair-haired variety. Too many memories were dredged up in the familiar, so he sought the unfamiliar.

Thinking on it now, that had to be how he came to leave Louisiana and the bayou forever. *Not forever,* a small voice nagged, *for you're ankle deep in her mud, old boy.*

Jeff tore his gaze away from the woman to stare at the mess he'd made of his new wingtips. Why hadn't he planned his wardrobe to fit his activities today? Because the last place he thought he'd end up when he left the house this afternoon was down by the Bayou Nouvelle. He'd hated the Nouvelle, hated its murky depths, hated its dark clusters of trees and the Spanish moss that dipped into her surface like the beards of old men. Most of all, he'd hated the memories.

Yet here he stood, inches away from the water and hiding from the woman whose memory had trailed him over the years. A mosquito buzzed past his ear, but he knew it was not the ones he heard that could bite. Like thoughts of Angeline Breaux, the real harm was done by the secretive, silent ones.

And yet here you are, the voice nagged. *A real man wouldn't cower in the shadows.*

Jeff shook his head to chase away the mosquito and the thought. Both still lingered just on the edge of his sight.

Angeline Breaux, however, remained in clear view.

How simple it would be to call to her, shouting her name or perhaps a few words of greeting across the black bayou water. What would be the harm in renewing an acquaintance forged years ago?

When she turned his way, Jeff lifted a hand in greeting, then quickly swiped his brow instead. Renewing his friendship with Angeline Breaux would be worse than accepting the mantle of responsibility as bayou doctor from his father.

His was a temporary return, and any contact with the dark-haired beauty might foster a need to stay. As tempting as that might seem, he knew the Lord had another plan for him, a plan that involved much bigger stakes than one displaced man's broken heart.

Chapter 2

Angeline!"

Jeff cast about for the origin of the sound and realized it was his own voice. He watched as Angeline jerked her head up, her gaze searching and finally finding his. She mouthed a word, then pressed a hand to her heart, effectively losing the garment she'd been washing in the process.

What had he done? So much for remaining silent and making an easy exit.

"*Qui c'est sa?* Is that you, Jefferson?"

None but his late grandmother and his most formal professors called him by the appellation. His father had long since banned the use of it, determining that the family forename should be cast into history along with its former owners. But from her lips, with the inflection of one born along the banks of the Nouvelle and having never left, the overblown name bore a certain charm.

The garment, a dark mass of what looked to be a pair of man's trousers, inched away, and had he not been struck dumb, Jeff might have mentioned the fact. Instead he merely nodded when she asked, "Jefferson Davis Villare, is that you?"

She stood and dried her hands on her apron. How many times had he lingered at this bank, watching her work at cleaning clothes or some other menial task when he should have been seeing to his studies? Enough so that Pop finally shipped him off to Boston to finish his education properly.

Actually that was only a part of the reason why Pop sent him off. The rest, though unrelated to the bayou itself, had everything to do with Angeline.

It had been years since he stood on this bank and watched Angeline Breaux, and yet the last time seemed just as fresh and new as if it were merely yesterday. He'd been sent away to learn, and now his education—and the Lord—would take him away permanently. Even so, he stood ankle deep in bayou mud, watching Angeline one last time. Funny how things had a way of coming full circle.

"Bonjour, Angeline," he finally managed as he inched forward through the muck. "I. . ."

He what? Nothing he cared to admit or speak aloud came to mind, so once again he chose silence. As his gaze dropped to the black water of the bayou, he saw the mass of fabric dislodge and float toward the center of the stream.

Another moment or two and the current would carry it away from Angeline's reach. He really should say something.

"I'm sorry about your papa's passing!" she called. *"Sa c'est triste."*

Jeff redirected his attention to Angeline. "Yes, it was very sad, even though I know he's home with Jesus and Mama. I guess I just expected him to live forever."

An understatement.

Pop had been his rock, the central foundation upon which his life rested. When the busy doctor refused to take to his bed last winter, pneumonia took him to his grave instead. Now Jeff remained behind, the last in a long line of Villares.

She reached to smooth back her hair, and he wondered for a moment why it hadn't been captured into a thick braid as she'd always worn it during their childhood. *Because she's no child, old boy.* At least she hadn't succumbed to the hideous fashion of lopping off all but the last bit of length to form it into a bob like the flappers back in Boston.

"So have you come back to stay?" she asked, scattering his thoughts of any place but here.

"No." He answered a bit too quickly and far too loudly. Her startled face confirmed the fact.

"Oh."

Dare he hope she looked the least bit disappointed? "I had to hurry back to school after the funeral. Closing up the house and disposing of a few of Pop's things were postponed until the end of the term."

"I see."

Jeff attempted to venture a few steps forward but felt the warm sludge pull against him.

Affecting a casual stance, he offered Angeline a smile. "Pop never learned how to get rid of anything."

"Oh no. I imagine there must be plenty to go through, then."

"You wouldn't believe the bits and pieces I've been finding in his office."

"Really?" The edge of her apron ruffled in the breeze.

"Yes, the medical books will be split between me and Doc Broussard, but there are some things like old pictures and journals that I'm at a loss as to what to do with."

An uncomfortable silence fell between them. "So what brings you this far out of town?" Angeline finally asked.

You, he almost said, but that wasn't quite right.

No, it wasn't Angeline Breaux herself who drew him to the Bayou Nouvelle but rather the memory of who he used to be when he was with her. Or maybe it was God.

"I suppose the day just seemed right for a sentimental journey," he offered instead.

~

Sentimental journey?

Angeline shook her head. If only *she* had the time to stand around staring at the water like a fool.

Mais non. With a house full of brothers and sisters to be fed, little Amalie worrying her, and her mama needing the washing done before she could even think of cooking, she had no time to—

The washing!

"Papa's trousers!"

And there they were, heading south toward the Gulf of Mexico just as surely as if she'd put them on a barge and sent them there.

What to do? The day would already end badly if her prayers were answered and Papa arrived without a prospective son-in-law. How much more of his ire would she draw by admitting she'd lost his best trousers while passing the time with Jefferson Villare?

Angeline reached for the stick she used to chase off snakes and leaned out to snag the fabric. To her relief, the end caught on the wet fabric and held tight. Bayou water ran off the legs of Papa's Sunday pants as she lifted them safely out of the current.

Now *she* wouldn't be the reason for his crossness tonight, at least not if she could convince Jefferson to go back to Latagnier and leave the bayou to those who belonged there. But just knowing Jefferson Villare had come back to Bayou Nouvelle would be enough to keep Papa rattling the rafters of their little cabin with his complaints long after her poor tired mama and the babies had gone to bed.

A glance in Jefferson's direction drew a sigh along with a touch of embarrassment at her lapse in attention. *Where have the years gone?*

"Angeline? Quoi y'a?"

"The matter?" She shrugged. *"Pas rien."*

Not the complete truth, of course, telling him nothing was wrong. Oh, but she did like hearing the Acadian words and the way the old Jefferson Villare came through in them.

When he spoke to her in the language of their childhood, the Acadian of their parents, grandparents, and others too old to remember, she could almost close her eyes and believe nothing had changed between them. That the years had not rolled by like the black water of the Nouvelle.

That he hadn't gone far beyond Bayou Nouvelle—and her.

"T'es sur de sa, ma chère?"

Ma chère? He hadn't called her by that pet name in how many years? "Yes," she said quickly. "I'm sure."

Again, she'd been less than fully truthful in her answer. *Mais non, just look at him, the city boy in his fine clothes. So handsome, so—*

Angeline recognized the source of the loud snap before she felt the stick break.

"Arête!" But the contrary trousers did not stop. Rather they headed downstream as if they knew she would give chase.

And so she did.

At first she loped along on foot, dodging beneath the low limb and sweeping skirt of a weeping willow and hurdling a palmetto as she kept pace with the trousers. Seizing a fallen sweet gum branch nearly as thick as Papa's arm, she raced ahead of her prize and waded into the water ankle deep, gathering the hem of her skirt with her free hand to keep it dry. Leaning out as far as she could, she just brushed the tip of the branch beneath the floating trousers.

"*Gete toi*, Angeline!"

"I am watching out for myself," she snapped.

As if the city boy had never seen her ankle deep in the bayou. Why, many a day the both of them had shucked their work—her, the washing or some other job Mama had assigned, and he, the schooling his papa felt to be so important—

"Angeline, come out of the water and let them go. *Sa vaut pas la peine.*"

"Yes, they *are* worth it, and Papa will have my hide if I lose them." She looked up to see Jefferson pushing through a stand of reeds and cattails to frown at her. "How many times did you laugh at me when I dropped something or another in the water and had to fetch it?"

His worried look eased and a grin began to dawn. "And how many times did you dare me to throw it so the both of us could go swimming?"

Somehow his grin irritated her. Maybe it was because he stood dry on the bank and she alone was left standing in the Bayou Nouvelle.

No, those things were just the here and now. It was the past that irked her—what could have happened and what did.

"We were silly children, but now the games are done and so are we."

A fast-moving current caught one leg of the trousers and dragged the entire soggy mess—and her—toward the middle of the bayou, hauling her under.

Chapter 3

Angeline emerged sputtering and wiped the muddy water from her eyes. When she spied the trousers drifting toward the opposite bank, she dove after them only to be jerked backward.

"Let me go!" She pummeled blindly at the thing holding her and fought to gain her footing. "I mean it!"

If a gator had her, she would go down fighting. If it were something else, like a rabid dog or a wild boar or maybe even one of those big brown bears Ernest and Papa sometimes shot, she stood a good chance of getting away if she could just keep moving. If it was one of her brothers pulling a prank, the more blows she landed the better.

"Arête. Be still!" It was Jefferson, his voice near enough to be. . .

Whirling around, she came eye to eye with him. Soaked to the skin from his chest down, he bore a nasty scratch across his left cheek, no doubt from her hand. His fancy summer suit was streaked with mud, and his bowler hat floated past as if it were giving chase to Papa's trousers.

"I have to get those pants. Just let me be." She wrenched out of his grip and started after the trousers only to have the stubborn man restrain her once more. "Are you crazy?" she shouted.

"Are you?" His voice was soft, deadly calm, and he barely moved except to gather her close to him. *"Tas toi,"* he whispered.

First he manhandled her, and then he demanded she stop talking? How dare he? And the way he held her, well, if she thought on it, it made her blush for sure.

As she watched little streams of bayou water trace a path down the side of Jefferson's neck, Angeline tried not to think of what it might look like should someone come along and catch them like this. She might be an uneducated girl and an old maid at that, but she knew improper when she saw it. Anyone passing by would think the same thing for sure.

Again.

She pressed both palms against his chest and pushed hard. He didn't budge.

"Let me go," she said, panic beginning to rise. *"S'il vous plait."* What if he meant to take by force what she'd shamefully wanted to offer all those years ago?

Her heart began to pound, and she cast a glance at the sun to see where it stood in the sky. If only she could remember how long she'd been at her work.

Surely Mama would send her sister Mathilde or brothers Julien and Martin to fetch her for lunch soon. Maybe Amalie would wander back. But what could they do?

Julien was as fast as Tante Flo's rooster and Martin could swim like a duck, but neither boy could best a man of Jefferson's size. And Mathilde, well, with her mind full of the silliness of a girl who wants to be a woman, she paid more attention to her reflection in the bayou than anything else.

Like as not, she'd miss the scene entirely if she caught sight of a honeysuckle vine that could be woven into her braid. Only little Amalie, the nine-year-old, would have the sense to do something, anything, to rescue her sister. But Amalie had probably fallen asleep even though she complained that she wouldn't.

No, she was on her own.

Angeline tried one last desperate move—reasoning with the fool. *"J'sus parti a la maison,"* she said.

"Non." His grip tightened. "You can't go home yet, ma chère. Look behind you." Little by little, he raised his free hand to point to the opposite bank, where a mama gator watched them closely while her two little ones lay sunning themselves at her side.

Angeline froze. She had seen some big gators in her time, but this one was huge. And judging from the way it followed their every move while edging its toothy snout toward the water, the beast was hungry, as well.

"She's not going to get us, understand?"

Their gazes met and Angeline nodded. "Yes."

"Okay, I plan to walk out of this bayou with all my arms and legs, and you're going with me, so hold on tight and don't say a word."

"But I—"

"Hush." He hitched her nearer and she stifled a gasp. "You might want to start praying now, ma chère. That old alligator, she's looking at me like she's in love."

Angeline buried her head against his shoulder and did as he said, silently begging le bon Dieu to get them out of this mess. Jefferson began taking slow, easy steps backward.

When she heard the loud splash that signaled the gator had tired of waiting, Angeline scrambled out of Jefferson's arms and dove toward the bank. No matter how fast that old gator could swim, she prayed Papa had taught her to swim faster.

But instead of swimming, she felt herself rise from the water, caught up in Jefferson's arms. "What are you doing?"

"No time to explain. Just hold tight."

He raced with her onto the bank and thrust her toward the bent branch of a cypress tree. Scrambling up just ahead of the gator, Jefferson fought for his grip on the branch with wet hands.

"Hurry, Jefferson! It's right behind you."

He made a swipe at the limb and missed. "Back up," he said as he reached for it again. "I'm afraid I'll pull you down."

"I'm stronger than I look."

Angeline caught hold of his wrist and held tight to the tree's gnarled trunk as she helped haul him up just seconds before the gator's claws hit the wood. A moment later, Jefferson perched beside her, his breath coming in ragged gasps, while the alligator made noisy circles beneath them.

"That was close," he said.

"Oui," she whispered. "Too close."

~

Too close indeed, both the encounter with the alligator and the encounter with this woman.

Jeff expelled a long breath and waited for his racing heart to slow. He cast a glance at his companion, flushed a pretty pink and still as wide-eyed as she'd been moments ago in the bayou. Funny, the alligator's menace paled in comparison to the trouble he could find up here in the tree.

As long as he'd known her, Jeff had never thought of Angeline Breaux as a delicate creature, but now she looked as fragile as his mother's favorite china teacup. He knew he'd have to watch her carefully for any signs of shock.

As a man, you've been doing that ever since you caught sight of her, old boy.

He shook his head and cleared the thought. *"T'es puer?"*

Jeff cringed and looked away. *Of course she's afraid, you idiot.* A check below proved the alligator had neither left nor slowed her pacing. *Think of something intelligent to say, something to take her mind off her fear.* "Remember when I dared you to kiss a frog and your papa caught you and thought you'd lost your good sense?"

They'd been fearless back then, the two of them. Only the Lord and their parents held their behavior in check. Sometimes he thought of those times, reminded of the simple innocence by the flicker of a firefly or the chirp of a cricket.

Her shoulders sagged an inch. "You told me a handsome prince would come and take me away if I did, and I figured if I had to kiss a frog to get out of the bayou, I'd do it."

The tiniest of smiles dawned, and she cast her gaze in his direction. He had caused that smile. His chest swelled despite the gravity of the situation. "That's better."

Angeline looked away. The smile faded. "You're bleeding and your suit is ruined."

Jeff swiped at his face and felt dried blood crumble beneath his fingers. At some point he'd have to treat it, but for now it seemed to be nothing more than a minor inconvenience. His suit, however, was another story entirely. He'd have to arrange for Pop's tailor to make another before he left for New York. This one was a total loss.

Another glance at Angeline told him her frock had fared no better. The white apron had muddied to a dull brown where the current had dragged her across the bayou floor, and her dress. . .well, he preferred not to look too closely at the damp and clinging frock.

When he slipped out of his jacket and placed it around her shoulders, her color deepened but she did not protest. Rather she gathered the soggy material around her and began to fret with the brass button on the right sleeve.

Beneath them the alligator seemed to be losing interest. Jeff leaned against the tree's knotty trunk and stared through the branches at the clear Louisiana sky. Under other circumstances, a man could have spent a considerable amount of time in this spot and called it relaxation.

"Jefferson?"

He cut her a sideways glance. "Yes."

"You could've stayed close and gone to the medical college at Baton Rouge, you know."

"I know."

"Why'd you up and leave? The real reason, I mean, and not what your papa told everyone about Boston being the 'best place to further your education.'" Her pensive voice caught him off guard, while her dead-on imitation of Pop made him chuckle.

Why indeed? Half a dozen plausible explanations came to mind. None was the real reason.

"I suppose it had something to do with you." There, he'd finally said it.

Their gazes locked. Her thick hair had begun to dry in soft tendrils, framing a face that could hold its own against any of the heavily painted and powdered flappers back in Boston.

A face that most likely attracted many a suitor among the boys of the bayou.

Chapter 4

He swallowed a gulp and asked the question to which he had no right to know the answer. "Is there someone special, ma chère?" He paused and cleared his throat before he could continue. "Or maybe you have a husband and three or four bebes?"

"Non," she said quickly. Was that shame that crossed her pretty features? "I never found someone who could believe I was. . ." She paused. "That is, everyone thought we had, well. . ."

His heart wrenched. He knew what everyone thought. When Pop put him on the first train north, it was all too obvious he thought the same thing.

If only something *had* happened between them. No, that was wrong, he quickly amended.

Both he and Angeline had honored the Lord and waited on Him to lead the direction of their relationship. He'd always wondered why God hadn't honored them in return, why he'd been allowed to rise above the whispered talk while Angeline was forced to stay behind and endure it.

Another unsettling thought to discard; another reason to flee the bayou and the past.

"My life is good, Jefferson," Angeline said without warning.

Why didn't he believe her?

"With another one on the way, Mama needs me more than ever. And my little brothers and sisters, they're like my own babies, all of them. Well, except for Mathilde, but she's so silly. *Elle est amorouse.*"

"Little Mathilde, boy crazy?" He shook his head. "I don't believe it."

"She's plenty old enough. Older by nearly a year than I was when you left and ready to be married off when it's her turn." The statement hung heavy between them.

"It seems like yesterday, us spending time together."

Angeline nodded with a wry smile. "But I don't recall us ever spending much time in a tree."

"Mais non," he said.

"So what is it you're going to do with yourself now that you've finished medical school and graduated with honors?"

"How did you know that?"

She upped her smile a notch. "The bayou, it's a small place, Jefferson. Everyone knows everything about everyone."

"Ah," he said with a nod. "I suppose I'd forgotten." He studied the face of his friend, then cleared his throat. "Actually, I'm going to be doing medical research."

"So you're not going to be a doctor?"

"Yes, I'll still be considered a doctor, but I won't be treating patients." When she looked confused, he felt the need to explain. "You see, I've been given an opportunity to do research, and I'm very excited about it."

"Oh?"

Jeff nodded. "Yes, I'll be working at Columbia University's College of Physicians and Surgeons in New York. I was asked to join a team of doctors who are researching a cure for influenza and the complications of pneumonia. It's very exciting."

Her expression told him it was more confusing to her than exciting. "That's nice," she said.

Once again silence fell between them. Generally Jeff found it easy to talk to the fairer sex. Where were his wit and charm now? Most likely drowned in the black water of the bayou.

"Well, now, it looks like our friend's gone." Jeff gestured toward the opposite bank, where a mother and child reunion was taking place among the alligators. "What say we take our leave, mademoiselle?"

He scrambled down and turned to help Angeline to the ground. A glance over his shoulder told him the creatures had lost interest in the taste of humans, at least for the moment. When the last one disappeared into the undergrowth, he relaxed.

"Allons, Angeline. I'll walk with you."

She looked as if she might argue, but then she nodded. He fell in step beside her, and they walked in companionable silence along the path that snaked by the bayou.

Jefferson committed each detail to memory—the warm sun on his back as his wet shirt stuck to his damp skin, the call of the mockingbird as it fled the diminutive dogwood tree, and most of all the dark-haired woman as she strolled barefoot and beautiful beside him.

"So up in New York, what will you do with yourself?" Angeline asked.

Jeff shrugged and affected a jaunty stance, pretending to tip the hat he no longer wore. "Medical research is exciting enough, and I don't have any other plans. That's what God has called me to do. And you, what's in your future?"

She seemed to consider the statement, all the while looking past him at the bayou. "*Sa fait pas rien.*"

He stopped short and grasped her by the shoulders. "It *does* matter, Angeline. Never say it doesn't." She tried to duck out of his grasp, but he wouldn't allow it. "Are you going to let wagging tongues and gossip keep you down? People *talk some*, but God alone *knows all.*"

Jeff felt her shoulders tense beneath his fingers. When her gaze collided with his, he felt the jolt deep in his gut. He scrambled to think of something, anything, to fill the desperate silence. *Help me know what to say, God.*

"You used to have such dreams." The words tumbled out, and he prayed they were from the Lord and not from his scrambled brain. "What happened?"

"That's all they were, Jefferson, dreams." She spat the words at him as if he were the cause.

"Dreams can come true," he said. "Women are doing all sorts of things now. Why, just last week in New York, I saw a woman who—"

"You have no idea what you're talking about. Look at you." She cast a disdainful glance at him. "You're the great and perfect Dr. Jefferson Villare. You've never had to do anything in your life that you didn't want to. Nobody's ever told you what to think or who to be."

Jeff opened his mouth to argue but thought better of it. "Okay," he said slowly, "what's the one thing you always wanted to do but never did?"

Her eyes narrowed. Good, he'd struck a chord. Maybe with a little more encouragement, this shrinking violet just might bloom yet.

She tilted her chin and gave him a sideways look. "You really want to know?"

The challenge surprised and delighted him. *This* was the Angeline he remembered. "Why, yes. In fact, I dare you to—"

Her kiss, laid just an inch off center of his lips, stopped him from finishing the provocation. Too soon, she took a step backward and covered her mouth with trembling fingers.

"I'm sorry, *excusez moi.* I don't know what I was thinking." With that she bolted and ran, darting so close to Bayou Nouvelle that several times Jeff felt sure he'd be carrying her out of it again.

When he caught her, he planned to tell her there was no need for apologies among old friends; that a kiss shared in secret would remain a secret. Instead, he reached her just yards from where he'd first seen her and, without comment, wrapped her in his arms, still damp and smelling of bayou water.

"You missed," he whispered as he showed her exactly how two sets of lips should match up.

The kiss might have continued indefinitely had the *click* of a shotgun against Jeff's ear not brought the proceedings to a screeching halt.

"Take your hands off my baby girl, Villare, and I *might* be convinced to let you leave this stretch o' bayou by some way other'n the undertaker."

Jeff froze and cut his gaze toward the sound. Theophile Breaux stood inches away, his angry countenance eclipsed only by the matching look of ire on his son Ernest's face. Behind them a stranger stood taking in the scene with a blank expression.

Jeff could only pray this man was the new pastor at the local church or perhaps an itinerant preacher set on a nice meal and an afternoon nap beneath the overhang of the Breauxs' front porch. Given the temperament of Villare men, the stranger could be his only hope of escape.

Angeline slipped out of Jeff's grasp, and had Ernest not enveloped her in a bear hug, she might have reached the path to her cabin in short order. Instead she stood motionless. The stranger shifted to stare at Angeline, his expression still unreadable.

"Pleased to see you again, Monsieur Breaux." Jeff forced the apprehension from his voice and attempted a pleasantry in the older man's native tongue. "Comment ça va?"

"Ain't no bidness o' yours how I is," he said, "but rather you ought to ask how steady a hand I've got these days."

To his credit, Theophile seemed not to have the slightest tremor. The barrel of the shotgun still rested against Jeff's temple, the only shaking possibly his own.

Now what, Lord?

"Doc Broussard tole me you been closin' up that big house o' your papa's over t' Latagnier an gettin' rid o' his things," Theophile said.

Jeff swallowed hard and gave thanks for what looked like the beginning of a civil conversation. "Yes, sir, that's right. I have."

He could stand here all day facing the old man, but Angeline shouldn't have to endure the humiliation. The fault for the situation was his alone.

"Then if you gots bidness in Latagnier, I don't reckon you got any bidness down here." He peered down the barrel, then shook his head. The strangest look of sadness passed over his tanned, weathered features. "Sa fini pas."

It never ends? What an odd thing to say.

"*Il n'a in bon boute*, Villare," Ernest said flatly.

Jeff smiled. "Yes, it has been a good while, Ernest," he managed to say without taking his gaze off the gun. Perhaps his former fishing buddy had finally come to his senses. "How about letting Angeline go, old friend?"

No response. His hopes for rescue plummeted.

"She had nothing to do with this. You see, she was just minding her own business when I—"

"When you mistook her for her sister Mathilde and let your heart run off wid your good sense." Theophile lowered the shotgun and stared at Jeff, then cocked his head to one side. "Now ain't that right?"

Had the Acadian lost his mind along with his good sense? He'd never even been on speaking terms with little Mathilde, much less anything resembling what he suggested. "Well, sir, I really don't know what you—"

"Theophile Breaux, what on earth have you gone and done? Put that shotgun away afore someone gets hurt, eh?"

An obviously pregnant Clothilde Breaux pushed past her husband to clasp Jeff's hand into hers. The years had been kind to the woman, and he could see much of her eldest daughter in her graceful bearing and unassuming beauty.

"Good morning, Mrs. Breaux."

"Jefferson Villare, is that you?"

When he nodded and said, "Yes, ma'am," she released his hand to drag him into a tight embrace.

A moment later she held him at arm's length and gave him an appraising look. "You're a sight for sore eyes, for sure, you. Look at you all growed up and handsome and. . ." She paused and then touched his cheek. "What happened to you?"

"Actually, I—"

"Theophile, what you gone an' done to this boy here?" She turned her attention to her husband, hands on her hips. "He look like he done been dropped by his feets into the shallow end of the bayou, then rolled over by a big ole gator. Is this how we treat Doc Villare's boy? After his papa done come doctor you for nothin' but a pot o' Angeline's gumbo an' a couple o' eggs from my layin' hen? Be ashamed."

Before Theophile could protest, Clothilde pried the shotgun from his fingers and handed the weapon to Angeline. "Scoot on up to the house with this an' put it somewhere safe, eh, bebe? You an' me, we talk about this later when the mens aren't underfoot."

When Angeline hesitated, her mother turned to Jeff. "Walk her home, would you, eh? She don't look like she could find a piece o' straw in a hay bale about now." She leaned in close and winked. "I can handle her papa, but you'd best skedaddle quick till I do."

Jeff nodded. "Oui, Madame Breaux, merci beaucoup."

"You don't got to thank me, no. You papa, he a good man, and you dear mama, a real lady if I never did saw none, Lord rest they souls. They raise you right, to go to church an' love the Lord, an' that's what a good mama and papa do, eh?"

"Yes, ma'am," he said.

"That's right. Now you know you welcome here always, eh? Say, how 'bout you come back for supper?"

Possibly the worst idea he'd heard since deciding to take a quick side trip to the bayou this morning. And yet it held a certain appeal.

"I couldn't, really."

But as he said the words, he caught Angeline's gaze and felt his resolve weaken. A few more hours with her before he took his leave permanently did sound enticing, even if it meant enduring her overprotective father and strangely menacing brother.

Clothilde nudged him and smiled. "Angeline's gone make us up a mess o' shrimps and gumbo. You still like that, don't you?"

"Yes, ma'am."

In truth, he hadn't had shrimp gumbo since he left for Boston. Even during holidays back at home, he hadn't been able to bring himself to partake. No one could make gumbo like Angeline Breaux anyway, so why bother?

"Just like you daddy a-lovin' that gumbo. Well, *je va vous voir plus tard*, young man," Clothilde said loudly to Jeff before placing his hand on Angeline's elbow and giving them both a shove. "Now scoot, the both of you."

"You won't be seeing him later, an' that's fo' sure, Clothilde Breaux," he heard Theophile say. "And take yo' hand off my girl, Villare, or you'll draw back a nub next time you try it."

"Yes, sir," he said as he quickly complied.

"Hush now, Theophile. Have you left your manners back in town, eh?" Clothilde asked. "We might be poor folk, but the good Lord still expects us to be charitable. The Villare boy's coming back for supper and that's that. Now who is this nice young man you've brought to see us today?"

Chapter 5

Angeline shouldered Papa's shotgun and lit out down the path toward home. What had she done? Losing Papa's Sunday trousers was nothing compared to what just happened. In front of God, her papa and brother, and who knows who else, she'd kissed Jefferson Breaux like the Jezebel they all thought she was.

She allowed an ironic chuckle as she tried in vain to balance the big gun and keep Jefferson's jacket hanging around her shoulders. At least she hadn't disappointed them.

If only the kiss hadn't been all she'd imagined—and more.

No, she couldn't think on it any further. Papa had brought a man home from town, and unless she missed her guess, the man was for her. Now she had to go home, get herself cleaned up, and cook a meal. To make it worse, Jefferson tagged a half step behind her.

There would be no rest for the weary—or the humiliated—today.

Angeline whirled around and put out a hand to stop her shadow. He pulled up just short of running her over. "Stop following me."

"Just following orders. I told your mother I would see you got home, and she isn't someone I'd like to cross." He shrugged and gave her that goofy smile she used to find so cute. "Besides, you've got my jacket."

Sliding the damp coat off her shoulders, she thrust it toward him. "Here, now go home," she stated as calmly as she could. "I can find my way back just fine."

"I'm sure you can, ma chère," he said as he folded the jacket over his left arm and linked his right arm with hers. "Still, I'm going to keep my word and walk you home."

It was the fastest walk Angeline ever took. By the time she'd wrenched free of Jefferson's grip and crossed the porch to close the door behind her, she was out of breath. Her apron hung limp and her skirt stuck to the backs of her legs as she leaned, eyes closed, against the heavy old cypress door.

"Lord, what am I going to do?" she whispered.

"You're going to move out of the way and let Papa and that handsome man in, Angie."

Angeline opened her eyes to see Mathilde standing at the hearth, baby Eileen on her hip and the four-year-old twins on the floor at her feet. Amalie hid behind her skirts, still looking flushed.

Before Angeline could say something back, Papa's heavy footsteps rocked the wood beneath her feet. She stepped out of the way just before the big door crashed open and Papa filled the doorway.

Eileen began to wail, and Mama slipped past Papa to grab the baby and bundle her outside. The boys toddled behind her, oblivious to the situation. When Mama called Mathilde and Amalie to follow them, Angeline found herself alone in the cabin with Papa and the stranger.

What Mathilde called handsome, Angeline preferred to call merely pleasant, at least in comparison to the city boy who'd just left. He had a kind face, this man who looked to be only a few years older than she, and a mouth that appeared capable of a broad smile. Now, however, he held his lips in a tight line, and only the slight tint of red on his cheeks hinted to Angeline that embarrassment might be the cause of his own discomfort.

For an eternity, Papa stood staring at her, taking in every inch of her wet and muddy clothing, her damp hair, and her shame. Hot tears threatened, but somehow she managed to hold them back. Outside of disappointing her heavenly Father, disappointing her earthly one was possibly the worst thing she could ever think to do.

She'd only done it once before, and the pain of that moment still stung.

"Nicolas Arceneaux," Papa finally said, "meet my eldest daughter, Angeline."

Mr. Arceneaux gave Papa a quick nod, then wiped his palm against the bib of his overalls before thrusting his hand toward Angeline. He mumbled a few words of greeting, eyes averted, and she responded as she'd been taught.

"May I offer you coffee, Monsieur Arceneaux?" she added when a sideways glance caught sight of Papa's frown.

"Fetch the pot quick, girl," Papa said. "We've business to discuss, eh, Arceneaux?"

The look that passed between them told Angeline they had already been in discussion. Unfortunately, it didn't take a city education to know what they'd talked about. As she headed for the summer kitchen, she cast a glance over her shoulder at the man who could someday be her husband and sighed.

"So what you think of my girl?" she heard Papa ask. "She all I tole you an' more, eh?"

"She is indeed, although. . . ," she heard Arceneaux say before Papa's laughter and the closing of the front door drowned out the rest of his statement.

As she passed by the open window, she slowed her steps to listen again. This time Papa's words were clear. "The man, he is nothing to her. *T'es trompe.*"

But *was* he mistaken? Angeline carried that question all the way to the summer kitchen and back onto the porch. As she set the coffee in front of the men, she looked into the eyes of Nicolas Arceneaux and heard the answer.

He is mistaken. The man—Jefferson Davis Villare—is indeed something to me.

But what? And even if she could figure it out, what could she do? How could she stop this thing Papa had already set into motion?

"She's just shy, that's all," she heard Papa say a moment before he jerked the coffeepot from her hand. "You pour youself some o' my Mathilde's good coffee, an' me and Angeline, we be right back, eh?"

Papa's hand clamped around Angeline's wrist and jerked her toward the door. Out in the yard, he brought her to an abrupt stop beside his toolshed.

"What you think you doin', baby girl?" he demanded. "That man there, he a good man what wants to make you his wife, an' you go an' throw youself on some boy what run off an' don't even give you the time of day for all these years?"

"I'm sorry, Papa."

He released her and stood back to look at her as if he were seeing her for the first time. A second later, his harsh features softened.

"My girl, she's good, an' I know it." He swept his hand toward the bayou. "But people 'round here, they don't know what I know, eh? Not a one o' them gone let they boys come 'round here after you long as they think you. . ."

Papa's words faded, and he cast a glance skyward. Angeline bit her lip as the first tear fell.

"To find you a husband, you gone have to go somewhere else, but I don't want nobody to take you off o' this bayou," he continued, his voice rough. "Angeline, this man, he promised me he'll not take you away. He got a boat an' he fishes down t' the Gulf. He need a good woman what to help him and to give him strong sons." Papa reached to take Angeline into his arms. "Le bon Dieu, He tole me this morning you was gone meet your husband today, baby girl."

Angeline buried her face in the familiar curve of Papa's shoulder. "He did?"

"Oui," he whispered as he smoothed her hair, then held her out at arm's length. "Now get yourself cleaned up an' set to cookin' the gumbo, eh?"

Angeline swiped at a tear and chose her words carefully. "Papa," she said slowly, "when God told you I would meet my husband today, did He specifically say it would be Mr. Arceneaux?"

Papa's eyes narrowed, and his face flushed bright red. "Get on in that house an' do as you're tole, Angeline Breaux. I ain't gone talk about this no more."

~

Easing into the welcoming softness of Pop's favorite chair, Jeff leaned his head against the smooth leather and tried to make sense of the morning. With all he could want in the way of things to think about and deal with spread across Pop's desk, his mind couldn't settle on any of them. Instead, his focus kept returning to Angeline Breaux.

"Busy?"

Jeff looked up to see Doc Broussard leaning against the door frame, his ancient black medical bag caught in the crook of his arm. When Jeff smiled and stood, his father's dearest friend approached to envelop Jeff in a bear hug.

"You know I'm never too busy to see you, sir," Jeff said.

To his credit, the man said nothing of Jeff's rumpled appearance and the still untreated scratch on his cheek. Instead, he dropped the well-worn satchel, settled into the chair across from Jeff, and perused the thick stacks of papers littering the desk's surface. "Made any headway in all this?"

"Does it look like it?"

Doc studied him a moment. "Actually, it looks like you've been busy with something altogether different. Dare an old man ask what that might be?"

"You could ask."

"But you're not going to tell me." He smiled. "I understand. It's just my meddling ways, you know. After all, either your papa or I delivered just about every baby born in this parish in the last thirty years—you and Miss Angeline Breaux included." He paused and feigned innocence. "Not that I'm of a mind to think you've been down to Bayou Nouvelle today."

"You heard?"

Doc's smile bloomed into a full-fledged chuckle. "Gertie Cousins had it on good authority from Teensie Landry, who heard it from Enola Joseph, that your daddy's Model A was left beside the road a skip and a jump from the Bayou Nouvelle. I believe it was Marie Boudreaux who added that it was just a quarter mile or so upriver from the Breaux property, although Ouida Simon said she thought it was more like a half mile."

Jeff leaned back again and contemplated what the wagging tongues of the parish would make of it if they knew any more details of his morning. Absently, he touched his cheek. He thanked the Lord that no one had seen his dip in the bayou or watched Angeline's endearing attempt at a kiss.

Or his more practiced response.

"Better let me take a look at that scratch," Doc said. "You got to be careful with bayou water this time of year." Again the old man feigned innocence while he made a fuss of examining Jeff's wound. "Looks like it just needs a bit of cleaning." The doctor reached into his bag. "Let me just see what I've got in here." He made quite a show of fishing around in the battered satchel. "Ah, here it is." Instead of cleaning solution, Doc Broussard produced a pair of dark trousers.

Theophile Breaux's trousers. Jeff wanted to crawl under the desk.

"The reverend recognized them right off," Doc said.

"What does Rev. Dautrive have to do with this?"

"Well, you see, Theophile never misses a Sunday service, and he and the family sit right down in front, just a few feet from the pulpit." Doc looked at him as if his answer made perfect sense, then thrust the damp trousers toward Jeff. "If you've got any plans to go out there before you leave, you might want to bring these along. Theophile probably won't miss them until Sunday morning."

"*If* I have plans?" Jeff gave him a sideways look, then balled up the trousers, tossing them into the corner. "Your sources didn't tell you I'm invited for gumbo tonight?"

All innocence once more, Doc shook his head and rose. "My sources? I don't know what you're talking about, and I don't have the time to sit and figure it out. I'm afraid we're going to have another nasty outbreak of influenza."

"Let's hope it doesn't spread like last time," Jeff said. *Like when it took my mother,* he left unsaid. "Let me know if you need help seeing patients. I'll do what I can while I'm here."

"I appreciate that, Jeff, but I pray it won't be necessary." He paused. "However, the invitation is always open to join me in my practice. I could sorely use the help."

"No." The word sprang from Jeff's lips much too quickly. "As much as I would love it, I'm afraid God has called me elsewhere."

"Well, I never make it a practice to argue with the good Lord." The old doctor regarded him. "You sure you can handle all this?"

"All what?"

"Everything. I don't know how you're going to get it all sorted through before Wednesday." He gestured toward the desk. "You got any idea what you're going to do with all that? Beyond the books and medical papers, I mean."

Jeff shrugged. "I'm still deciding. As for the house, I think it's time to sell."

"I see." If he had an opinion, his expression did not give it away. "Well, I understand there's a fortune to be made in stocks these days. Maybe you ought to go that route first before you start thinking of selling your family home. There are a whole lot of happy memories in this old place."

Jeff tapped his temple. "There are a lot of happy memories up here, too, sir."

"Yes, well, I see your point." Doc scooped up his satchel and headed for the door, stopping as he reached the threshold. "I do have it on good authority that Angeline Breaux's shrimp gumbo is the best in south Louisiana. I took a pot of Miss Angeline's gumbo in payment for delivering Clothilde's last three babies, you know. Don't know if I'll last until the fall, when the next one's set to arrive. Maybe you could ask for an extra bowl for me."

"Very funny, Doc!" Jeff called as he hurried to walk his guest to the door. "Say, you seem to know a lot. I don't suppose any of the folks you talked to today mentioned the name of the fellow Theophile Breaux brought home today."

The old man stopped short and turned to face Jeff. For a moment he looked as if he might answer, but after a few seconds he shook his head and walked away. "I believe you'll find that out soon enough!" he called.

Jeff watched Doc Broussard shuffle down the steps and disappear around the corner. His age really had begun to show. How long before the work hours wore him down like Pop? He shook off the thought along with the nagging idea of taking Doc's employment offer to the Lord for His opinion.

"You still here, Mr. Jeff?" his father's housekeeper, the formidable matron known as Mrs. Mike, called from the kitchen.

He followed the voice to the kitchen, where Mrs. Mike had just placed two steaming peach pies on the sideboard. "Yes, ma'am, I'm here," he said as he stopped short. "Why did you cook two pies?"

She mopped her brow with the corner of her apron and drew herself up to her full height. "I ain't gone send you out t' sit down at Clothilde Breaux's table without you carrying a pie t' go wit the gumbo. It wouldn't be polite, and your dear departed mama and papa would have my hide when I see them up in heaven."

Jeff shook his head. "You knew I was going out there tonight." He paused. "But Doc just left, so he couldn't have told you, and I don't think I mentioned it."

"What that got to do wit anything, Mr. Jeff?" she asked as she folded her apron back into place. "Can't an old woman bake a pie or two without all these questions?"

Jeff leaned against the cabinet. "How long does it take you to make a good pie, Mrs. Mike?"

"Well, let me see. Once I get me the peaches cut just right, I. . ." Her eyes narrowed. "Now don't you try to start with me, Mr. Jeff. You might be all growed up and a doctor like your daddy, but you always gonna be a young'un to me, you understand?"

"Yes, ma'am," Jeff said with a chuckle. "Say, I'll be needing a suit of clothes ironed before this evening. Do you mind?"

"I already done that," she said, "but if you'll fetch me Mr. Breaux's pants, I'll have them looking just as nice as new afore it's time for you t' go."

"How'd you know about. . ." He paused. "Oh, never mind."

Chapter 6

The gumbo was terrible. Angeline knew it without being told. She'd put in too much of something, or maybe not enough.

Whatever the problem, the only fix for it was to toss out the whole pot and start over again. She hoisted the pot and turned to throw it to the dogs, only to run into her mother. The gumbo sloshed and threatened to spill, but she leveled the pot in time to whirl it back around onto the stove.

Looking down, she realized she'd saved the very gumbo she meant to throw out while she'd ruined her one good dress in the process. At least she hadn't been burned by the hot roux.

"Goodness, bebe, you don't have to carry that heavy thing. Let the mens come on out an' get it." Before she could respond, her mother shoved her toward the house. "Now you go on and get yourself prettied up afore someone sees you wearin' the gumbo, eh?"

A few minutes later, Angeline stood among the wreckage of two ruined dresses. One still brown and streaked with mud from the bayou and the other wearing gumbo roux in splotches across the front.

The only dress left in the armoire was her Sunday dress, and she could hardly show herself downstairs in that on a Friday evening. Why, it would look like she was headed for church instead of. . .

Her mind caught on the thought of Sunday clothes and hung there. Papa's trousers.

"Oh no!"

~

Jeff circled the path twice before setting his feet toward the Breaux cabin, the peach pie in a tin tucked into the crook of his arm and the trousers wrapped in brown paper and tied with a string. Leave it to Mrs. Mike to think of a way to return Mr. Breaux's trousers without making a fuss. Now if he could just hand off the package to Angeline without drawing attention to the fact.

Surely the Lord would do the both of them this small favor. Neither he nor Angeline needed to face any more ire from Theophile Breaux.

Deep threads of purple and orange decorated the edges of the sky and danced across the waves on the bayou. Beneath Jeff's feet, the hard-packed terrain wore a layer of decaying leaves, each step sending up the earthy scent so peculiar to south Louisiana to tease his nose.

And the sounds—no words could do justice to the symphony of bayou creatures when they began their evening songs. It was the music of his childhood, the anthem of his youth. Soon it would be the sound of a fading memory.

Wednesday morning he would climb aboard a train headed north and trade those brilliant hues and fresh scents for a city where progress made up for beauty and symphonies were conducted only within the hallowed halls of the opera house.

And Wednesday would be here ever so soon.

What had he been thinking? An evening of stolen happiness—a lifetime of what-ifs—that's what Jeff would face if he continued with his ridiculous notion to actually sit at a table with Angeline Breaux and her father.

He squared his shoulders and picked up his pace. It would be neither, he determined. Tonight would merely serve as a good-bye to the bayou and the life he must sacrifice to do what God created him to do.

Tomorrow was Saturday, a good day to finish collecting the things he wanted sent to his apartment in New York. Sunday would be a day of worship, of course, and Monday would bring more decisions. He would call on Pop's lawyer that day to start the process of selling the big old place. Tuesday would be reserved for packing and last-minute errands, and Wednesday morning he would be on the train to New York. By Friday his well-ordered life would resume, and he would probably find himself working the weekend in the lab just to catch up with his research.

He cradled the pie and stepped over a protruding root, nearly losing his balance, the package, and the pie in the process. Yes, he decided as he righted himself, it would be good to get back to his comfortable routine—to his quiet life.

He heard the noise before he actually saw the cabin. A chorus of sounds, male and female, echoed among the trees and seemed to shake the tails of the Spanish moss. A lone fiddle played soft and low, a mere accompaniment to the true Acadian concerto—the Acadians themselves.

Rounding the corner, he stepped into the clearing. With the sun behind the wood-frame home, the front yard lay bathed partially in shadow. In places across the lawn, if one could call the expanse of green and brown a lawn, groups of men and boys stood in clusters while children ran among them.

Jeff searched the crowd for a glimpse of Angeline. He even stared hard into the lighted windows to capture a glance of her. Finally, his gaze landed on the porch and a group of older women.

Clothilde Breaux stepped away from a knot of ladies on the porch to meet him halfway. "Well, there you are, Jefferson Villare. Come on over here."

After a mind-numbing introduction to aunts, cousins, and other assorted relatives, he handed Mrs. Breaux the pie. "Mrs. Mike sends this with her compliments," he said.

"Why, thank you very much, Jefferson. Your Mrs. Mike makes the best peach pie in all of south Louisiana, she does. You tell her I'll be sending her a little something come tomorrow morning, eh?" Angeline's mother looked from the pie to the package under his arm. "What else you got there?"

He shifted the paper-wrapped trousers and searched for an answer. To his surprise, Mrs. Breaux looked past him to offer up a broad smile.

"Now look who else is here." She handed off the pie to one of the elderly ladies with a brisk word of direction in French and clasped Jeff's hand. "Jefferson, I want you to meet Nicolas Arceneaux. Proper-like, that is."

Jeff whirled around to come face-to-face with the stranger he'd seen that morning. He stuck out his hand, and the Arceneaux fellow took it in a viselike grip.

"Pleased to meet you," Jeff said.

"Likewise." The stranger smiled and squeezed harder. "I didn't think you would come back."

For a moment Jeff stood mute, sizing up what he quickly decided was to be his competition. Strange he thought of that word, and yet as he studied the strapping Acadian, he felt exactly that.

"Now why wouldn't he come back, eh?" Clothilde asked. "You two boys go on inside and make merry with the rest of the family. How about that?"

"Actually, I'd like to speak to this man a moment," the Acadian said. "If you don't mind, Mrs. Breaux."

Angeline's mother stared hard at him, then turned her gaze to Jeff. "Just a minute and not one second more, you hear?"

"Yes, ma'am." He turned to Jeff. "Why don't you and I take a little walk?"

The challenge in his words was unmistakable. "Fine," Jeff said.

He looked down at the package beneath Jeff's arm. "Do you want to leave that here?"

Jeff leveled a hard stare. "Do I need to?"

The Acadian instantly backed away and smiled. "Not unless you want to."

Jeff let the statement hang between them just long enough to see the bigger man square his shoulders. "I suppose it doesn't matter, does it?"

"We're not talking about the package anymore, are we?"

To his surprise, the Arceneaux fellow clapped him on the shoulder and began to walk toward the edge of the clearing. "Ah, you are a smart man, are you not, Dr. Villare?" He did not wait for an answer. "I know this because we first talk about that package there, but then we begin to talk about my Angeline. You know this, too."

"*Your* Angeline?" The question slipped out before Jeff could stop it.

The big man smiled. "Actually, yes."

His temper flared. How dare the big oaf assume any proprietary relationship with *his* Angeline? "Would you care to be more specific, Arceneaux?"

Instead of giving him an answer, Nicolas Arceneaux laughed. Jeff notched up his anger and took a step forward.

"There you are." Clothilde Breaux appeared at the edge of the clearing. "I have been looking all over for you."

She stared at Jefferson, then turned her attention to Nicolas. "Have you made friends with our Jefferson? He's practically like one of my own, you know. Why, his daddy and my daddy go way back. His daddy or Doc Broussard birthed every baby I had, including my Angeline."

When neither responded, Mrs. Breaux linked arms with both men and turned toward the house. "Let's us go see the family, eh?" she said as she led them across the lawn and onto the porch.

Jeff stepped over the threshold behind Clothilde and allowed himself to be drawn into the boisterous crowd of Breaux family members. When he left, he knew he would leave a little piece of his heart beneath the patched roof of this cabin beside the Nouvelle. While he stayed, he would wonder what Nicolas Arceneaux meant.

The Acadian pressed past the crowd to meet Theophile Breaux in a serious conversation. A few moments later, Clothilde joined them and seemed to lighten their moods. At least she had them smiling until she walked away.

Meanwhile, Jeff made polite conversation with a distant cousin of Clothilde's, keeping a safe distance from Theophile and Arceneaux, who now huddled in the corner, casting him furtive glances. Suddenly Angeline appeared in the room, stopping his heart and ensuring that it would be left at her feet forever.

Flushed despite the relative cool of the May evening, she wore a pretty frock of pale green dotted with yellow rosebuds. Her thick hair had been captured and pinned in a knot at the base of her neck, the severe style only serving to emphasize her beautiful face. Dare he hope this show of beauty was for him?

Jeff rose from his seat by the fire to watch her float toward him. The room tunneled and closed until only the two of them occupied its space.

He took a step toward her, then froze as her father caught her by the elbow and tugged her over to join his conversation with the stranger. Angeline spared him only the slightest backward glance of regret before turning her attention to the men.

A familiar voice called his name. With difficulty, he tore his gaze from Angeline.

"Jefferson, welcome." Ernest Breaux grasped his hand in a hearty greeting and laughed. "So you're braver than I thought, eh?"

Brave? Foolish seemed a more apt description.

He thrust the package toward Ernest. "Say, Mrs. Mike sent this to Angeline. Would you see that she gets it later?"

"Sure," he said as he tossed the bundle onto the top of the old cypress pie safe. "Now tell me what's new with you."

"I'd rather hear what's new with you, Ernest. I'm afraid my life's terribly boring."

As Ernest began to regale him with his latest adventure working his father's traps, Jeff cast covert glances at Angeline.

When she smiled, he wondered why, and when she laughed, he longed to be in on the joke. But when her hand rose to her lips, shaking fingers pressed against her mouth, something turned to lead in his stomach. The stranger, he'd said something that caused her reaction. Was it good, this surprise, or terrible? From the high color on Angeline's cheeks, Jeff could not say.

Chapter 7

Ernest once more clapped a hand on Jeff's shoulder and drew him aside. "Why the long face, my friend? The food is plentiful and the company good."

Jeff shrugged out of the smaller man's grasp. *And yet I have eyes only for. . .* The sound of laughter, Angeline's laughter, stopped him, and he had to clear his thoughts. "So when do we eat?"

"It is too long since you had the gumbo, eh? Well, you'll not eat like this for a long time, I understand," he said. "The word in town is that you'll be gone in two weeks."

"Actually, I'm expected to report for work in New York on the fifteenth, but I've got train tickets for Wednesday. I'd rather get settled before I start work."

Ernest's eyes narrowed. "Then why you nosing around my sister, eh? And I don't mean Mathilde."

He pondered several brilliant answers and gave up. *"J'aurais pas du de venire me fourer ici."*

"You're probably right. You *shouldn't* have come here, but yet here you are, eh?"

Ernest touched Jeff's sleeve and gestured toward the tight group of people gathered around Theophile and the stranger. Only Angeline seemed to ignore the conversation and allowed her gaze to flit around the room. A second later she noticed his stare and offered a shy smile before returning her attention to some anecdote Theophile was sharing.

"And little Angie," Ernest continued, "she looks to be happy you're here. Why, I haven't seen her wear that pretty dress since old man Fouchet married the youngest of the Viator girls last January. No, she didn't get herself prettied up for nothing, and I would bet my best pirogue it's not for that fellow Papa brought home."

Something like hope coiled inside Jeff, and he almost asked Ernest to repeat the statement. Instead, he shook his head. "Angeline and I are friends, Ernest, you know that."

"Some say more than friends, eh?"

So there it was again, the old rumor that he and the beautiful Angeline had allowed their passion to find action. Would it never die?

"What we have just goes beyond good sense, I guess, but it *never* went where the gossips claimed."

"Sa fini pas."

Jeff jerked his attention toward Ernest. "That's what your father said. 'The thing that never ends.' Yes," he said with a wry chuckle, "I will admit that just might be the best way to put what your sister and I share. Ah, but it is bittersweet, my friend. She was meant to stay here, and I was meant to leave. What is the point of dwelling on it?"

Ernest looked thoughtful for a moment. "Do you love her?"

"Sa fait pas rien."

"Oh, but it does matter."

"Monsieur Jefferson." Jeff felt a light touch on his sleeve and turned to stare into the wide brown eyes of Mathilde Breaux. "Perhaps you could help me with a few things in the kitchen? I find my strength is just about gone, and the gumbo pot is quite heavy to lift tonight."

She did look a bit pale, and delicate smudges of charcoal shadowed her eyes. Still, he saw mischief on her face. "Perhaps your brother might—"

"Ernest, get over here an' tell this good man about that ole three-legged gator we done saw last week!" Theophile called.

"Looks like you're elected, my friend," Ernest said as he turned his back and headed toward his father.

Jeff reluctantly allowed himself to be dragged across the room and into the starry night toward the summer kitchen. Clothilde shouted a warning to one of the little ones as they strolled past the window. "I'm going to check the gumbo for Angie, Mama!" Mathilde called. She giggled when her mother responded with a complaint about her sister's forgetfulness tonight. "I don't mind, really." She gave Jeff a wink.

Jeff took in a deep breath of damp air and let it out slowly. This evening was not going as he had planned. Perhaps he should forget about Angeline and her gumbo and take his leave. A wise man knew when to cut his losses. Isn't that what Pop always said?

He watched Mathilde lift the lid on the iron pot and reach for the long metal spoon hanging on a hook beside the stove. The aroma of gumbo wafted toward him, and he inhaled deeply. "That smells good," he said as he watched her stir the thick brown roux.

"I've been wondering something, Monsieur Jefferson," Mathilde said as she reached for a canister and added something to the mixture.

"What's that?"

"Nothing." She dipped a small spoon into the pot, then held it to her lips to blow away the steam. "Taste this to see if it's ready."

It was heavenly. Every bit as good as he remembered. Jeff nodded. "Definitely ready."

"Good. I'll tell Mama." Mathilde dropped the spoon into the wash bucket, then swayed a second before grasping the corner of the stove.

Jeff steadied her. "Are you all right?"

She turned to face him and offered a weak smile. "Of course I'm fine." She looked past him, and he followed her gaze to stare at the house. A sliver of yellow light danced across the yard, chased by the laughter and voices of the people inside. "Angie loves it here," she whispered. "This is her home."

He nodded and pushed away the sadness that went along with this truth. "Yes, it is."

"She will never leave this place, you know?"

Jeff leaned against the rough wooden wall and stared into the window, hoping to catch a glimpse of Angeline. "I know," he said softly. "I've always known that."

"This question I wanted to ask, it is difficult and personal. May I still ask?"

"Well, I don't know." He cast a glance at her and saw she was serious. "Of course."

"Do you love her?"

Jeff chuckled and continued to watch for Angeline's face at the window. "Is that all? Would it make you feel better to know you're not the first person to ask me that today?"

"It might," Mathilde said in a weak voice. "What was your answer?"

Before he could respond, Mathilde fainted.

~

The last thing Angeline expected Jefferson to carry through the door was her sister Mathilde. As the crowd parted and allowed the doctor to deposit her on the settee, Angeline drew near.

Mama pushed her away to press her palm against Mathilde's brow. "She looks a bit flushed," she said. "You think it's the heat or something else, Jefferson?"

"I'm not sure. Let me have a look at her."

Jeff knelt at Mathilde's side and cradled her hand in his as he listened to her pulse. Mathilde's eyelids fluttered open. "What happened?" she whispered.

"You had another dizzy spell, bebe." Mama directed her attention to Jefferson. "That's the second time today my girl done fell off her feets. This morning I thought she was gone fall right into the baby's bathwater."

"Why didn't you tell me none of this, Clothilde?" Theophile demanded. "A man ought to know what goes on in his own house, eh?"

"How long have you been feeling dizzy, Mathilde?" Jefferson asked.

"Just today, I suppose."

"Then maybe it's nothing, eh?" Mama asked as she gave Jefferson a hopeful look. "Our little Amalie, she down wit the fever, but she don't got the dizzies. You think they might have caught the same thing, my girls?"

"I say we call a real doctor!" Theophile shouted.

"Hush now." Mama gave Papa a look she generally reserved for the worst behaved of the little ones. "What's wrong with my bebe, Jefferson? Can you tell?"

Jeff shook his head. "Could be nothing that a good meal and a night's rest won't cure." He paused. "I don't detect a fever, but should one arise, that would definitely be a cause for concern. As for Amalie, I recommend you watch her for signs of change. I assume she's resting tonight."

Mama nodded. "She was tired, so I put her to bed early. What are you thinking? You don't think this is the bad fever, no?"

Angeline could see the panic in Mama's eyes. They both remembered the influenza epidemic of Angeline's childhood, the one that started so innocently and ended with the deaths of far too many.

"I'm thinking this is probably nothing, Mrs. Breaux, so don't worry just yet." He addressed Mathilde. "How are you feeling now?"

She struggled to sit upright. "I'm a little shaky, but I'll be fine." She batted her eyes. "Maybe it was just the company."

Theophile shook his head. "I think all she needs is some good gumbo in her. Angie, go fetch the pot. Nicolas, would you mind helping my girl? I'm afraid the pot's a mite heavy for her."

Banished, Angeline strode toward the summer kitchen not caring whether the stranger followed or not. In her current frame of mind, she could have carried two gumbo pots to Latagnier and back, much less one to the long table just inside the front door.

She stomped past Mama's Easter lilies and ducked under the low branch of the magnolia at the corner of the house. If Papa's stranger was behind her, he'd definitely glimpsed a less than ladylike side of her.

Convicted of her rudeness, she slowed her pace and cast a glance over her shoulder. To her surprise, Nicolas had kept up with her and now tagged only a step behind.

"Do you always move this fast?" he asked when their gazes met.

"I'm sorry," she said. "My mind was on other things."

"I see." He ducked his head. "I feel as though we ought to visit a bit alone, Mademoiselle Breaux. Would you mind?"

"Of course not." Angeline took a step backward and leaned against the corner of the house. Under other circumstances, she might have found him quite pleasing to the eye. Tonight, she only had eyes for a certain doctor.

"I suppose you're wondering why I'm here." He paused. "Or maybe you're not."

She cast about for something to change the direction of the conversation. "Papa speaks very highly of you. I understand you are a fisherman."

"I am." He met her gaze with eyes that seemed to study her intently. "As my father before me and his before him. It's not an easy life, but it is a good one."

"I see."

He grasped her hand with work-roughened fingers that felt like Papa's. "I know this is sudden, but—"

She broke from his touch and turned toward the kitchen. "Allons! The gumbo needs bringing inside."

"Don't be afraid," he whispered. "I know it is not me you love." Nicolas caught her elbow and whirled her around. "I saw how you looked at that city fellow."

All she could do was stare. What in the world did he intend by bringing up something such as that? "What business is that of yours?"

He shook his head. "I may be just a bayou boy, but I'm not dumb. If you keep company with that man, you're going to hurt more than just your mama and papa."

"Honestly, I don't know what you're talking about. Now can we just go back inside?"

Nicolas tightened his grip. "Tonight you will seek the Lord, eh? Le bon Dieu, He will tell you what to do about this problem you will be having."

"What problem are you talking about?" Angeline stared at the big Acadian. She looked past him to the stand of trees and thought of the bayou beyond, how it flowed at will and bowed to no man. "The only problem I have right now is you."

Chapter 8

As soon as she said the words, she wanted to reel them back in. What had gotten into her tonight? More to the point, what had gotten into her all day?

Of course, the answer to that question stood just inside the cabin door. Seeing Jefferson Villare had turned her day—and her whole world—upside down.

"Let's just bring in the gumbo and forget we had this conversation, Monsieur Arceneaux."

"Call me Nicolas, please, and I will call you Angeline, eh?" He released her to touch her chin with his thumb and guided her attention back to his. "I'll get straight to the point."

"The point?"

"Oui. I will treat you like a queen, mademoiselle. I will love you like the Lord requires a husband to love his wife."

Wife. Angeline stifled an indelicate gulp. Until this moment, the reality of her situation had only danced at the edge of her mind. With Jefferson Villare so near, how could she determine tonight to pledge her life to another?

And yet if Papa insisted on it, how could she not?

"Please let us not talk of these things tonight." She walked toward the gumbo pot and worked the spoon through the thick brown roux.

Nicolas removed the spoon from her hand and placed it on the hook. Once again, he enveloped her hand with his. "Your man, he will be gone soon and you will forget him. Then where will you be?"

The look he gave her stilled her tongue and kept her cry of denial from becoming words. She allowed her shoulders to slump. Forget Jefferson Villare? Never. Admit to that? Also never.

"I say this not to hurt you but to show you the logic of things as they are between my family and yours."

"The logic of things?" She shook her head. "What does logic have to do with anything?"

A smile brightened his face. The change, and its resulting effect, was dazzling. Angeline averted her gaze, startled.

"Ah, now you ask a question I can answer." He once again placed his thumb beneath her chin and directed her to look into his eyes. "You are a smart woman, eh? A woman who understands how things are."

"I don't know what you mean."

"Come, let's sit." He indicated the rough bench Papa and Ernest had made last winter, now nestled beneath the branches of the flowering magnolia. When she settled beside him, he rested his elbows on his knees and let out a sigh. "Your papa and my papa, they strike a deal, Angeline."

"A deal?" She batted at an errant mosquito. "What do you mean?"

"You and me, we're the deal."

Angeline stood. "I don't know what you're talking about, but I do know that Mama will come looking for both of us if we don't fetch the gumbo to the table."

Her companion gently pulled her back down beside him. "My papa, he was in a bad way, and he needed a pirogue and some skins, a little wood for the winter fire, and a little money for the summer fishing. Your papa, well, he needed. . ." His voice faded and disappeared against the chirp of the crickets.

Humiliation drove her to finish his sentence. "He needed a husband for his *vielle fille*, his old maid daughter."

Nicolas wrapped an arm around her shoulder. "No, hush now, that's not what he said." He paused. "I probably shouldn't tell you what he *did* say, though."

"Why?" She looked at him. He did have the nicest smile.

"Because I'm afraid it might go to your head." He nudged her shoulder with his. "It wouldn't do for you to think you're the most beautiful belle on the bayou."

The sentiment took her breath away. "Papa said that?"

"No," Nicolas said slowly, "I did." He straightened his shoulders and stood, then offered her a hand to pull her up beside him. He held her hand for a moment. "Your papa, he merely said you were very pretty. Now perhaps we should keep your family waiting no longer."

"My family?"

Again he offered that smile. "Oui, Angeline, they are waiting for the gumbo."

"The gumbo. Oui."

How foolish she felt as she followed Nicolas inside, carrying the smaller pot of rice while he easily bore the burden of the iron gumbo pot. After setting the rice on the table, she turned to her mother while Nicolas allowed Papa to lead him away.

Her mother leaned close. "How you like Papa's friend, bebe?"

"He's nice enough," she said.

A raised eyebrow served as her mother's response before she bustled off to supervise the setting of the table. Angeline joined her.

When Papa tugged on her arm and pulled her aside, Angeline's heart sank. Standing with him was Nicolas Arceneaux.

"Nicolas, he told me he talked to you," Papa said. When she nodded, he said, "Good, then tonight we make the announcement, eh?"

Angeline froze. "Please, Papa, no."

Papa gave Nicolas a confused look. "She don't look like you talked to her."

"I did, sir," Nicolas said. "Maybe I didn't talk plain enough."

"Then make it plain, eh?"

Please, Lord, don't let this happen. You know I don't love this man.

Nicolas reached for Angeline's hand. "Angeline Breaux, will you be my wedded wife?"

"Angie, sweetheart," her mother called, "where's the gumbo ladle?"

"The ladle?" She reached behind her to pick up a dish towel and look beneath it, anything to distract Papa and Nicolas from this conversation. "I thought we had it. Check the gumbo pot. Maybe it fell inside."

"It's not there. Did you leave it in the summer kitchen?"

"I'll go look."

Angeline slipped out the door and headed for the summer kitchen, moving across the lawn at a fast pace. The sounds of the night rang in her ears, along with the memory of her conversation with Nicolas.

Did he tell the truth? Had Papa really promised her hand in marriage to a fisherman just to keep her close to home? Even if his intentions had been good, how could Papa sell her like a prize pig to the highest bidder?

No answers came, so she turned to the Lord as she stalked toward the little kitchen. Even He seemed to be silent.

Once inside the summer kitchen, Angeline found the ladle hanging on the hook beside the stove and grabbed it. "How could we have forgotten this?" she muttered.

Because you were too busy discussing marriage.

Clutching the ladle, she stepped outside and took a deep breath. The sooner the food was served, the sooner the night would end. Better to hurry than tarry.

Of course, if she tarried, Nicolas might not have time to ask her to marry him. She shook her head. It didn't matter. If Papa intended her to wed Nicolas, all the time in the world wouldn't change his mind.

If only Jefferson weren't here to witness the announcement.

As she rushed back toward the house, she turned the corner to race up the porch and ran headlong into Jefferson Villare. The ladle fell and she nearly tumbled after it.

"Slow down there," he whispered as he helped her upright.

"I'm sorry, I wasn't watching where I was going." She took a step backward to pick up the ladle and wipe it off on the front of her skirt. "Mama will have my hide for getting this dirty."

Even in the shadows, she could see the twinkle in his eyes. Oh, but he did look handsome all dressed up in his Sunday clothes!

Don't look at him. You can't. You're about to become engaged, and he's leaving.

"I doubt that," he said in a husky voice. "You could talk your mama out of being mad every time."

Angeline chuckled despite herself and shook her head. "I think you must have me confused with someone else."

His gaze turned from amused to tender, and he reached out to touch her cheek with his hand. "I assure you that would never happen."

Without thinking, she placed her hand over his and leaned into his embrace. A moment later, he kissed her.

Unlike the kiss they shared earlier in the day, this one was sweet and soft and could have gone on forever if Mama hadn't appeared at the door.

To her credit, Mama said nothing but rather removed the ladle from Angeline's fingers and stepped back inside. She did make eye contact with Angeline as she passed by the window. There would be some serious talking between the two of them tomorrow—that much was certain.

There would also be some serious talking with the Lord tonight.

Angeline held the back of her hand against her lips and averted her gaze. Heat flamed her face, and her fingers trembled slightly.

"We shouldn't have done that," she whispered.

"And yet we just can't seem to stop."

"But we can't just keep—" Jefferson leaned closer and gave her another quick kiss, silencing her words as he enveloped her in an embrace.

"All right, everybody," Mama called, "the gumbo's ready! Set yourselves at the table and get ready for some good eatin', eh?"

"We can't ever do that again, Jefferson," she said as she leaned her head on his shoulder.

"Why?" he whispered against her ear.

"Because Papa has other plans for me."

Jefferson held her at arm's length and gave her a confused look. "What are you talking about, Angeline? What plans?"

Try as she might, she couldn't find the words to tell him her father had promised her to another man. Instead, she broke free and darted inside, unsure if her legs could carry her as far as the table.

What Jefferson did not know now, he would most likely find out by the end of the night. Papa and Nicolas had been thick as thieves most of the evening. To her mind, that meant one or both of them would be delivering the news that a wedding was afoot, even if she hadn't given Nicolas a proper answer to his proposal.

Busying herself with serving duties, she did not see Jefferson slip inside, but he must have, for she looked up to see him standing next to Mathilde. Her sister laughed at something Jefferson said, then touched his hand, and the green monster of envy hit Angeline.

As soon as she recognized the feeling for what it was, she pushed it away. Maybe the Lord meant for Jefferson to find happiness with the younger of the two Breaux women. Perhaps that was why He'd led him back to their doorstep.

If only she could muster some enthusiasm for the idea. But with the young doctor's kisses still warm on her lips, Angeline could find nothing good about encouraging such a relationship.

No, if she couldn't have Jefferson Villare, then it would be best that he just leave. Having him as a brother-in-law would be the worst possible thing.

"Go set yourself, girlie!" Papa called. "The food's gettin' cold and I'm gettin' old a-waitin'."

"Yes, Papa," she said as she forced her attention in his direction.

Fortunately, he gave no indication of having noticed that she'd been staring at Jefferson. Unfortunately, when she turned her gaze to Nicolas, who stood beside Papa, she knew for sure that *he* had.

While Mama bundled the little ones off to their own smaller table in the corner, Papa took his seat at the head of the big table and instructed Nicolas to sit on his right. Mathilde settled in the chair on his left. Jefferson was ordered to deposit himself in the spot beside her.

Somehow, when all those in attendance were seated, there was only one place left at the table for Angeline—next to Nicolas and across from Jefferson. Mathilde rested happily next to the young doctor, her silliness already apparent in the way she monopolized the conversation with him.

Angeline's gaze met Mama's, and she cringed when her mother's eyes narrowed. Should she raise a fuss about the awkward seating arrangement, Mama would say something for sure. Rather than risk yet another embarrassment, Angeline meekly slipped into the spot next to Nicolas and bowed her head while Papa prayed.

As her father offered up thanks for the meal and a blessing for those in attendance, Angeline added a silent prayer of her own. *Please, Lord, get me through this evening.*

Chapter 9

Please, Lord, get me through this evening.

Jefferson added an "amen" to the chorus, then held out his bowl for white rice and gumbo. He tried in vain to catch Angeline's attention, but she seemed inordinately interested in the elderly maiden aunt seated beside her. At least that conversation kept her from talking to the Arceneaux fellow.

The discussion also kept him, at least in part, from thinking about the kisses he'd shared with Angeline. Still, as the sweet elderly lady droned on about chickens and eggs, he drifted back to those few blissful moments on the porch when time had fallen backward and he and Angeline hadn't a care in the world.

"Are you listening, young man?"

"Oh, I'm sorry," he said as he forced his attention back to the present.

Half an hour later, he'd dropped his spoon three times, allowed a sizable shrimp and some roux to land on his trousers, and spilled rice down the front of his shirt. He finally gave up when Angeline's father caught him picking rice out of his pocket.

During the entire time, Angeline did not look at him once. Had she not been as moved by their kiss—actually, kisses—as he? Surely she had, for he'd seen the look on her face before she fled.

As long as he lived he would never forget that look.

He neatly tucked the fluffy white grains under his napkin and attempted to pay attention to a loud conversation between Ernest and the Acadian. He did all this despite the constant flow of words from Mathilde, to his right.

His mind wandered and so did his gaze. Both landed on Angeline.

Silhouetted in the lamplight, she now gave her complete attention to the fisherman as he told another story, the topic of which totally escaped Jeff. When Mathilde's elbow collided with his rib, he nearly knocked his plate of peach pie off the table. Recovering with an embarrassed grin toward the incredulous Mr. Breaux, he ignored Angeline's stare to turn his attention to her younger sister.

Even in the yellow light of the kerosene lamp, he could see her skin was pale and the dark smudges beneath her eyes had deepened. The doctor in him sounded a warning, while the man in him wanted to voice his irritation. Instead, he remained silent as she leaned toward him.

"The last thing you want Papa to know is how much you care for my sister," she whispered.

He cast a quick glance at Mr. Breaux, who was now heavily involved in a debate over water rights with the fisherman. "I don't know what you're talking about."

"You're looking like a lovesick puppy, Jefferson Villare, and everyone in this room except Papa and Angie has noticed." She punctuated the statement with an innocent smile, then dabbed at the corner of her mouth with her napkin. "Once Papa notices, I'm sure he'll speed up the wedding just to save Angie from the likes of you."

"Wedding? What wedding?" Jeff knew he'd spoken too loudly when all conversation at the table ceased.

Mathilde dropped her napkin into her lap and broadened her smile. "We were talking about Sissy Fontenot's big Christmas wedding. Jefferson here didn't realize little Sissy had gone and got married without sending him an invitation. They were practically neighbors, you know."

"Well, how about that, eh?" Mrs. Breaux chimed in. A moment later, the various members of the Breaux clan were buzzing with their memories of what must have been the wedding of the century.

The only two people not participating in the conversation were Jeff and Nicolas Arceneaux. Jeff gave the intruder a direct look, sizing up his competition, and Arceneaux seemed to do the same. Without breaking eye contact, the fisherman quirked a corner of his mouth into a smile and placed a hand on Angeline's sleeve. As she turned her attention to him, Jefferson pushed away from the table.

"Excuse me, folks, but I really must leave."

"Sit down, young man." Theophile Breaux's voice echoed in the room, bouncing off wooden walls to land squarely in Jeff's gut. "Nobody goes anywhere just yet. I got somethin' to say."

~

Angeline nearly jumped out of her chair when Papa turned his attention to her. Nicolas removed his hand from her arm and rested it around the back of her chair.

All through dinner, she'd expected Nicolas to repeat the question she hadn't answered. When he did not, she'd felt some relief. Now that relief turned to stone in her throat.

Obviously Papa and the groom were going on with the wedding plans even if the bride hadn't yet said she would attend.

"What's this about, eh?" Clothilde asked as she dropped her napkin onto the table. "You running for mayor or somethin', Theophile? 'Cause if you are, you don't have to make no speeches in this house, no. We would all vote for you, now, wouldn't we?"

Peals of laughter erupted at the comment until Papa held up his hand to bring order to the room. "Now you just go and be funny some other time and place, Cleo, why don't you? Can't a man be serious in his own home?"

Mama hid a smile behind her hand as she nodded. "Of course you can, dear.

Please don't let me interrupt. Go ahead with what you were going to say."

Papa cleared his throat and stood, placing his palms on the table. "We all had some good gumbo tonight, eh?"

When the cries of agreement from those settled around the table died down, Papa spoke again. "Well, my girl Angeline, she made that gumbo. She's a right good cook, and she helps her mama with the babies, too." He slapped Nicolas on the shoulder. "She'll make a man a good wife someday, eh?"

"Oui, Monsieur Breaux," Nicholas said as he gave her a brief but admiring look. "She will indeed."

Waves of embarrassment washed over Angeline. Surely Papa didn't intend to announce her wedding, not in front of Jefferson.

"Goodness, Papa, now you're making it sound like Angie's running for office," Mathilde said with a giggle.

"Lord, please deliver me from the females in my home," Papa muttered as he glared at Mathilde. "Now, as I was tryin' t' say—"

"Mama! Angie!" Amalie's plaintive cry interrupted her father's words. "I'm thirsty."

"I'll see to her." Angeline jumped up and raced toward the back bedroom with a cup of water, not waiting for an answer.

"Angie, tell me a story," the little girl whispered. "I want to hear the one about T-Boy the gator and his friend Redfish."

"A little later, maybe," she said. Right now she couldn't tell a story if her life depended on it. Her mind, such as it was, held only one thought, and it had nothing to do with a fictional alligator and his fishy friend.

As she held the cup to her little sister's lips, she gave thanks for the small reprieve she'd been granted. Just in case Papa decided to try again, Angeline nudged Amalie over a bit and climbed into bed beside her. If anyone came looking for her, they would find her asleep—or at least pretending to be asleep.

And while that might only delay the inevitable by a day, it might also give God time to act. What He would do was a mystery, but surely He didn't intend for her to be wed to a stranger.

~

A moment later, with Theophile Breaux distracted, Jeff made all the appropriate gestures of gratitude to Clothilde and made his escape. He got all the way to the car before he heard someone call his name. Praying he could still leave quickly, Jeff turned toward the feminine voice.

"Yes?"

Clothilde Breaux stood on the bottom step of the porch with a dark, round object in her hand. "Hold up there, Jefferson, eh?" she called as she began to cross the shadowed lawn.

His heart sank. If Mrs. Breaux insisted, he would stay all night. He couldn't possibly let the sweet woman down, but he also couldn't possibly spend another moment in the room with Angeline and the Acadian.

"Here, bebe," she said as she thrust the dark object toward him. It was the covered pie plate, and she'd put something inside—it felt heavy and sloshed a bit. "You tell Mrs. Mike that was the best pie she's ever made."

"I'll do that," he said as he leaned over to set the plate on the floor of the car.

"I sent her a little gumbo. I know how she likes the shrimps, so I put her some extra in." Clothilde touched Jeff's sleeve. "You don't have to run off, you know. Uncle Joe, he's gone play his fiddle for us in a bit."

Jeff smiled. "I appreciate the offer, but I'm tired. I think I need to get back home."

Her smile didn't quite match his. In the moonlight, she looked so much like her daughter—older and wiser, to be sure, but no less beautiful. How funny that she held her beauty and the inner peace that radiated around her, even though she'd never left the banks of the Nouvelle.

How could anyone be so happy in a place so small and stifling?

"I understand," she said. "Tell Mrs. Mike I've got her some Easter lilies ready to go."

"I will."

To his surprise, she winked. "And don't you worry about our Angie. God's got something special for her; I just know it. And you're gonna know it, too, you'll see."

"What do you mean?"

Her smile grew. "Leave Angie's papa to me and the Lord. You pray to God about your problems, and He give you the solutions, eh?"

"I will," he said, although he had no idea what she meant.

As he drove away, he glanced back and watched the cabin fade in the shadows. He wondered: Was he destined always to remember this place in that way—as a comfortable spot that had faded to black?

All the way back into town, he thought about the Acadian's smile and his hand atop Angeline's.

The way Arceneaux huddled with Mr. Breaux indicated the two were in league with each other. Could Mathilde be correct? Did Angeline's papa intend to marry her off to Nicolas Arceneaux?

By the time he parked Pop's car and trudged up the back steps, he'd almost convinced himself that nothing Angeline Breaux did mattered anymore. He would have completed the process had he not been confronted by Mrs. Mike.

"Waiting up for me?" he asked with a grin.

"I wish that were the case," she said. "But Doc's been here twice looking for you. He left you this note."

She fished a piece of paper out of her pastel-striped housecoat and handed it to Jeff. Struggling to read the doctor's handwriting, he finally deduced that he was needed at the clinic immediately. Something about having too many patients and not enough doctors.

Jeff groaned. When he'd agreed to help Doc, he hadn't actually expected he might be needed.

"Bad news?" she asked.

"I hope not." He handed her the pie tin. "Mrs. Breaux sends her thanks along with some shrimp gumbo and said for you to come see her. She's got some Easter lilies for you." He shucked off his tie. "Oh, and she said this was your best pie ever," he added as he rounded the corner toward the front foyer.

"How is Clothilde?" he heard Mrs. Mike ask.

"She's very well. Very well indeed."

"And Angeline?"

"Why don't you go on out there tomorrow and see for yourself?"

"I just might."

As Jeff took the stairs by twos, heading toward his room and a change of clothes, he could hear Mrs. Mike expounding on the virtues of the Breaux family. He strode past the bed and pulled a clean shirt out of the armoire. Thoughts of Angeline mingled with concern over the emergency that would keep him from much-needed sleep a bit longer.

When he arrived at the clinic, he saw the need for the urgency. Three families waited on the porch, and four more sat inside. Each had at least one member exhibiting signs of the dreaded influenza.

Thoughts of Angeline Breaux fled as Jeff went to meet Doc in the exam room. Three hours later, the patients continued to trickle in, and Jeff had given up any idea of sleeping that night.

Chapter 10

Angeline stood beside the shed and watched Mama work at tending her precious bed of flowers. With the little ones taking a Monday morning nap and the others playing quietly, it was the perfect time to have a heart-to-heart talk with the one person in the world besides the Lord who knew her best.

Thankfully Nicolas had left after church yesterday to return to his fishing, and Papa and Ernest were out this morning in the pirogue. For a short while, she and Mama would be left alone to talk.

Grabbing a trowel from the peg on the wall, she strolled toward Mama and dropped down beside her. Mama gave her a smile, then went back to her weeding.

"Something on your mind, bebe?" she asked without looking up from her task. "Maybe something to do with your intended, Mr. Arceneaux?"

"So Papa told you?"

"Of course he did. You don't think my Theophile can keep something like this from me, do you?" She paused. "Besides, the mama of the bride's got to make the plans, eh?"

"Bride," she said with a groan.

"Maybe you think you the only woman in love who is gonna get married, eh?"

Angeline stuck the trowel in the ground and crossed her arms over her chest. "I'm not in love, Mama. That's not the problem."

Mama stopped her work. "Then maybe you tell me what's the problem, eh?"

"Men, that's the problem." Angeline shook her head. "Why do they all have to think they are the only ones with an opinion? And why is it that when we have an opinion, no one asks us for it?"

"And yet this don't have *nothing* to do with love?"

"No, Mama," she said, "it has to do with Papa."

Her mother smiled. "Now that's a subject I know a little about. Why don't you and me go get a cool drink of water and sit over there in the shade and talk about your papa, eh?"

Angeline stood and helped her mother to her feet. Together they walked in step toward the well. While Angeline poured two dippersful of water into tin cups, Mama settled on the bench beneath the magnolia.

"I am forever grateful to your papa and brother for making me this little resting bench," she said as she accepted the cup from Angeline. "It does a body good to sit a spell when you're tired, eh?" She shook her head. "But we were talking about your papa. What is it he's done this time, bebe?"

"You know what he's done, Mama." She took a furious gulp of water. "He's gone and sold me off to the highest bidder against my will. That's what he's done."

Mama seemed to contemplate the statement a moment. "And you said this had nothing to do with love."

Angeline fairly jumped off the bench. "It doesn't! Papa never asked me if I loved Nicolas Arceneaux, and he certainly didn't ask me if I wanted to marry him."

"And if he had, what would you have said?" Angeline's silence must have spoken for her, for Mama began to smile. "You're just like me, you know? You love a man, and you love him forever. That's how it is with me and your papa."

Angeline settled back beside Mama and took her hand. "How did you know, Mama? What told you Papa was the one?"

Mama patted Angeline's hand. "Not what, bebe, but who. God—He told me your papa was the one."

"Well so far, God's not the one making decisions around here, is He?" Since Mama looked like she was about to launch into one of her lectures about God always being in control, Angeline pressed forward with her point. "See, Mama, Papa's making all the decisions. He's not even bothering to ask me."

"But do you know whether he's bothering to ask God? That's the real question, eh?" Mama sighed. "Do you know why your papa picked Nicolas Arceneaux for you?"

She nodded. "Nicolas told me Papa made a deal with his father, something about furs and other things."

"That's only a part of it, Angie."

"So you admit that Papa traded me like a pile of furs?"

"No, I admit nothing of the sort." Inside the house, the baby began to fret. Mama stood and stretched her back. "What I'm trying to tell you is that Papa picked Nicolas Arceneaux for a reason, and it has nothing to do with the fact that his papa needed some furs for the winter."

Mama tossed the remains of her water into the flower bed and returned the cup to its place at the well. Angeline followed suit, then tagged behind her mother as she trudged toward the steps. "I'll get her, Mama. You just rest here."

After the baby had been changed and returned to Mama to nurse, Angeline broached the subject of marriage once more. "Mama, will you tell me why you think Papa sold me off to the Arceneaux family?"

Mama toyed with the baby's dark hair and looked off into the distance. "The bayou, she is a beautiful thing, eh? For a man or woman of proud Acadian birth, she is our life." She looked to Angeline for confirmation.

"Oui," she said.

"And this place, this is our home. We have deep roots here, bebe. Your papa's people and mine, they come to settle this place two hundred years ago, eh?"

"Yes, Mama."

Her mother's dark eyes flashed with anger. "Then why would your papa allow his precious girl to leave her roots and her home? Why lose his bebe when there is a godly man who promises not to take her away?"

"Mama, what are you talking about?"

Mama lifted the baby to her shoulder and began rubbing circles on her little back. "I'm talking about love and marriage, Angie, same as you."

Angeline leaned against the porch post and tried to make sense of the conversation. Why would Papa think she might leave home if she wasn't married off to the likes of Nicolas Arceneaux? She never even considered the idea.

But she had considered what it would be like to marry Jefferson Villare, hadn't she?

"A penny for your thoughts, Angie."

"You and Papa have nothing to worry about, you know," she said with a sigh. "There never was anything between Jefferson and me besides a friendship. I thought you believed me."

With her free hand, Mama lifted Angeline's chin and offered a smile. "I never did doubt. I know my girl's a good girl, and I know Jefferson; he's a good boy." She paused. "But I know love when I see it, and I know Jefferson thinks he's not meant to stay. Marry up with him, and he'll take you where you'll never see home again."

"Is that what this is about? Papa thinks I'm going to marry Jefferson if he doesn't find someone else for me?" She pounded her fists on her knees. "Why can't he just let me be? I promise I'm not going anywhere. You need me here to help, and I don't care if I ever get married."

Again Mama shook her head. "That is the anger talking, bebe. Even if you don't know you love him, I do and so does your papa. God knows, too. You mark my words, though. You stand too close to the fire that young doctor's got burning inside him, and you gonna get burned."

A wail went up from inside the house. It was the twins, crying in unison. "Mama," one said. "Make Amalie wake up," the other finished.

"Oh, I hope that precious child's not sick again. I thought we had her well."

Angeline placed a hand on Mama's shoulder. "See, you need me here. I'll handle this. Likely as not, Amalie's playing possum so she doesn't have to help Mathilde take care of the babies."

But when she found her sister lying on the settee, she knew Amalie was not playing possum. The little girl was burning up with fever.

"Mama, come here, please!" Angeline shouted. "Something's wrong with Amalie."

Mama handed the baby to Angeline and knelt beside Amalie. "Oh, bebe, I'm gonna pray this isn't what I think it is." She looked up at Angeline. "Put the baby in her bed, and go fetch the doctor. I don't think we can get her to the office without Papa or the boys here. You tell him this is urgent, you hear, eh?"

"Yes, Mama."

Angeline found her way to the old pirogue Papa kept around for the children and began to paddle furiously toward town. By the time she reached the docks, her fingers were raw and her back was soaked with sweat. Tying up the boat despite the pain in her hands, she set off toward Doc Broussard's office only to find a note on the door, stating that he was out seeing patients. The message referred all emergencies to Jefferson Villare.

Angeline knew all too well how to find Jefferson's home, and she returned to her pirogue to trace the winding path of the bayou until it reached the Villare place. In her mind, she'd always thought of the big house as a mansion. When Papa would read the verse in the Bible about God's house having many mansions, she always pictured Jefferson's house. Funny how her age had changed, but her perspective had remained the same.

Even now as she trudged toward the big double front doors and the wide porch filled with white rocking chairs, she felt like the teenager she'd been the last time she walked across the threshold. She'd often wondered if their last day together, the day Doc Villare had come home to find his son and the poor Acadian girl alone in the big house, had really changed the course of two lives, or if it just seemed that way looking back.

The moment had been as innocent as they were, just two friends sharing Mrs. Mike's peach pie across the kitchen table. As far as they knew, Mrs. Mike was somewhere in the house rather than out running errands for the afternoon. Angeline had never contemplated what Doc Villare accused them of doing—at least not seriously. The end result was the same. Two reputations tarnished and a pair of good friends separated.

As long as she lived, she would always wonder whether what happened that afternoon was part of God's plan or Satan's.

Chapter 11

I'm sorry, but he's unavailable right now."

The sound of his housekeeper's voice danced at the edge of Jeff's favorite dream, the one where he and Angeline sat on the banks of the Nouvelle, dipping their toes in the warm water and frightening away any fish they thought to catch. They couldn't have been more than ten or twelve, and he, the city boy, had boasted an ability to catch fish well beyond his capacity to do so.

True to her gentle and understanding nature, Angeline suggested it would be much more fun to see who could kick water the farthest.

He won that contest; he always did.

The dream abruptly changed course, and he and Angeline were seated at the kitchen table, a peach pie and two glasses of milk between them.

Jeff shifted in Pop's chair and allowed his body to relax once more. He'd worked two days and two nights straight, with only a few hours of stolen sleep on Doc's office couch in the process. When the number of influenza cases slowed to a manageable level and the house calls began, Doc sent him home. He'd gone willingly, he was ashamed to say, but he'd promised to get some rest and return in the afternoon. In the meantime, Doc promised to send someone to fetch him if things got out of hand again.

Jeff edged down into the chair and rested his chin on his chest. Just a few more minutes of sleep, a few more minutes reliving the past, and he would make the trek upstairs to his room and a real bed for sure.

Just a few more minutes. . .

"But you don't understand," a female voice said in his dream. "It's my sister; she's sick with a fever. Papa and Ernest are gone, so Mama sent me to town to fetch a doctor."

Fever. Doctor. Those words had no place in his dream.

Shaking the cobwebs from his brain, Jeff rose and stretched his complaining muscles. Too many hours bending over an exam table and too little sleep had left him feeling twice his age. How did Pop and Doc manage to attend to an endless line of patients, day after day, week after week, with no attention to schedules or office hours?

At least the life of a research physician offered regular hours and stools that didn't cause back strain. *Yes, but what of the looks of gratitude on the faces of parents or the reward in knowing a life has been saved?*

Jeff shook off the question. Many parents would be grateful and many lives would be saved by the eradication of influenza. He should be thankful God chose him to be a part of medical research, rather than spending his time wondering if he'd misunderstood the Lord's leading.

Bright shafts of sunlight pushed through the windows and formed a pattern on the old Persian rug. Dust motes danced in the light. The clock on the mantel read a few minutes before noon.

The best he could tell, he'd been asleep in Pop's chair for nearly five hours. No wonder he was so stiff.

"I'm sorry, Dr. Villare has had a long night, and he came home to get some rest only a few hours ago."

Dr. Villare. How strange to hear the housekeeper use the name Jeff associated with his father to refer to him. Others had called him that, and it seemed natural, but it sounded out of place coming from Mrs. Mike.

And to whom was she speaking? Did Doc Broussard need his services again?

As much as he'd have liked to hide, to ignore the call to work once more, he knew he could not. He'd promised he would remain available as long as he was needed.

"Mrs. Mike?" Jeff stepped into the hall and froze when he saw Angeline Breaux standing at the open front door.

He went forward and took his friend by the hand. "Angeline, come in." To his surprise, she stood firm.

"No, thank you." She winced as she slipped her hand from his. "Actually, Mama sent me to fetch you to see to Amalie."

The mention of the young girl's name brought back an image of her wan appearance two nights ago. "What's happened?"

"Could I tell you on the way?" She curled her fingers into fists and hid her hands behind her back. "Mama's powerful worried, and I'd hate to keep her waiting."

"What's wrong?"

"I told you, Mama thinks Amalie's fever is a bad sign. She wants you to come see."

He moved a bit closer. "No, I mean what's wrong with you?"

Before she could answer, he reached for her arms and turned her small hands up so he could examine them. Both palms were raw with abrasions, and a blister ran across the length of her right thumb.

He turned to the housekeeper. "Mrs. Mike, fetch my bag, would you? It's in Pop's office, on the desk, I believe." As she scurried past, he returned his attention to Angeline. "How did this happen?"

"Really, Jefferson, sa fait pas rien."

"Yes, it matters."

He acknowledged the housekeeper's return by motioning for her to follow him into the kitchen. With difficulty, he managed to get Angeline inside the house and settled in a chair at the kitchen table.

While he bound her wounds, she told him the story of her arrival at his doorstep. "You rowed all this way, ma chère?" When she nodded, he replied, "Well, if you have no objections, we'll leave your old pirogue here and take Pop's Model A. I'll have someone bring it back before nightfall. I promise."

"A motorcar?" She looked away. "Oh, I don't know."

Jeff smiled. For the bayou people, getting around by boat had been a tradition carried down through the centuries. Bad roads and wet conditions made driving treacherous in wet weather and merely bumpy and inconvenient in dry weather. Only in rare instances was it their first choice of transportation.

"Angeline, have you ever ridden in a motorcar?"

"Once," she said softly. "When I was a little girl, Papa's uncle came to visit, and he took us for a ride."

"Oh? Did you enjoy it?"

She nodded. "Very much, at least until that motorcar hit a slick spot and nearly slid into the bayou."

"That must have been quite a ride." He grasped her elbow and turned her toward the door. "I promise I will stay out of the bayou on this trip." He paused to glance over his shoulder. "Mrs. Mike, would you bring my bag out to the car?"

After helping Angeline into the Model A, he slid behind the steering wheel and placed the bag between them. To her credit, Angeline said nothing as he pulled out of the driveway and into the sparse traffic on Jackson Street. She merely held on to the edge of the seat and sat ramrod straight, her eyes barely blinking.

"Are you all right?" he finally asked.

She nodded, a stiff nod that did nothing to convince him of the earnestness of her answer. He searched his mind for something, anything, that might cause her to feel at ease, but nothing came to mind. Of course, a few stray memories of times they'd shared did occur to him, but he doubted the wisdom of mentioning them. With his train ticket bought, the last thing he needed was to schedule another trip—this one down memory lane. After the fiasco at the Breaux house two nights ago, he'd learned his lesson.

No, this visit to check on her sister would be all business, no social call. As soon as he administered treatment to Amalie, he would be on his way, never to return to Bayou Nouvelle and Angeline Breaux.

It was the only way, really.

As they rolled along the streets of Latagnier, he noticed Angeline relax a bit. She'd released her death grip on the edge of the seat and appeared to be sitting comfortably with her hands clasped in her lap. Only the white of her knuckles gave away the depth of her fear.

"So, Angeline, tell me what's ailing your sister."

She sighed. "At first we thought it might be a touch of the croup or maybe something she ate. She was a little feverish and just didn't act like herself."

"What sort of treatment did she receive?"

"Mama put a poultice on her and I kept a cool cloth on her head." She paused. "I knew she didn't feel good for sure when she just lay there and let us mess with her. That little Amalie, she's not one to sit still."

Jeff slowed to allow a horse and buggy to cross First Avenue. "How long ago did she first exhibit these new symptoms?"

"About three days ago, maybe four."

"I remember she slept through the evening I spent out at your place. Has she been sleeping excessively?"

"She does seem to be tired a lot of the time."

"And Mathilde, has she had any more fainting episodes?"

Angeline nodded. "Just this morning she nearly dropped one of Mama's good teacups on the floor when she about passed out. If she's had other fits like that, she hasn't said."

"Is there anything you can tell me about Amalie's condition and Mathilde's?"

Only when she'd said her last words on the subject did he allow his mind to wander past the confines of the motorcar to what might lie ahead of them. Dare he consider little Amalie, and perhaps even Mathilde, might bear the signs of influenza? If so, the rest of the Breaux family would be in danger of contracting the deadly disease.

"Do you think you can fix my Amalie?"

"I think God can fix anything, Angeline. Whether He uses me to do it is another matter entirely." He met her gaze and attempted a smile. "I will do my best, though."

And I'll pray my best is good enough.

Jeff turned the car off the main road and onto the narrow lane leading toward the Breaux home. Whatever he found there, God would go before him.

"Oh, and Jefferson, I've been meaning to thank you for what you did for me the night you shared gumbo with us." She offered him a radiant smile. "Papa never knew his pants went to town and back."

They shared a laugh, and Jeff felt a perplexing stab of pain. How wonderful it would be to laugh with her more often.

Moments into the drive down the ancient thoroughfare, the road fell into shadows as the trees hung low and thick. Birds dipped and flew, teasing the old car as it lumbered past. In a matter of minutes, time had rolled backward, and except for the modern motorcar, he could have been traveling a road that looked the same a century ago.

"Jefferson, do you ever wonder why God put all of us on earth to be so different?"

Surprised, he swung his gaze to meet Angeline's stare. "Now that's an interesting thought. What do you mean?"

"Well, look at us." She smiled a wry smile. "If ever two people were more different from the beginning, I can't imagine it. I mean, you're a big-city doctor and I'm just a simple bayou girl."

Jeff shook his head. "Angeline Breaux, there is nothing simple about you."

"But don't you see? There's nothing wrong with being simple, Jefferson. In fact, I rather prefer it. It's you I'm concerned for."

"How so?" he asked as the car lurched over ruts in the little road.

Angeline grabbed for the door handle to keep from sliding forward. Her face told him she bore the bouncing about much better than she had the miles they'd driven in the city. Perhaps the nearness to home helped.

"Well, I just can't imagine being up north among strangers who talk funny and move so fast. I saw downtown New York on the news reels at the picture show once, and it looked like there were more people on that one sidewalk than we have in the whole state of Louisiana."

A pair of dogs lounged in the road, and Jeff honked the horn to scatter them into the thicket. "I hardly think New York's that big."

"It's bigger than Latagnier, and that's all I need to know." She released her grip on the door as the Model A rolled over a smoother patch of road. "I don't know why anyone would want to leave such a beautiful place."

Why indeed? And yet the beauty of the lush green landscape and the brilliant blue sky paled in comparison to the dark-haired Acadian beauty seated beside him.

For a moment, he allowed himself the luxury of imagining a life spent in the bayou country. With the exception of times like now, when mysterious fevers swept the area, his would be a life of simplicity.

He remembered the kiss he'd shared with Angeline and touched his finger to his lips. If only he could give up the life he felt called toward in order to have more of those kisses, perhaps a lifetime of them.

Unfortunately, he had a one-way train ticket to New York dated for two days hence. Come Wednesday morning, he would leave the bayou and Angeline behind.

Or would he?

Lord, is that why You kept her in my mind all these years? Could I have misunderstood Your direction for my life? Do You want me to pursue a relationship with Angeline Breaux?

Chapter 12

What a strange expression Jefferson wore! Had she said something wrong? Of course, he was leaving in two days, so maybe he didn't like what she said about staying here.

For the next few minutes, they rode along in silence. Angeline couldn't think of anything else to say, and Jefferson obviously didn't want to make conversation, either. She settled for worrying with the bandages on her hands until Jefferson finally told her to leave them alone.

Mama met them in the yard as the motorcar pulled alongside the house. Several of the little ones tagged behind her, but when the vehicle roared to a stop, they scattered to the porch.

"Thank the Lord you're here, Jefferson. My Amalie, she's sick, and my Mathilde, she's not looking so well, either, no."

Jefferson grabbed his medical bag and climbed out of the motorcar. Angeline tried several times to open the door but failed. Thankfully, Jefferson noticed her troubles and circled around to help her out.

"Thank you," she said softly as she climbed out on shaking legs. The trip might have been faster than a pirogue ride, but it certainly wasn't the way she intended to go again.

"Where are they?" he asked.

"Follow me, bebe. I put them both in the back bedroom away from the rest of the babies."

"That's a good idea," Jefferson said. "Keep them separated from everyone else. I don't want to think this could be contagious, but there's no need in subjecting the children to harm."

"Yes, that's what I thought, too. I don't want to take no chances. I made plans to send the children, all but the littlest one, to Tante Flo's for today. Flo, she don't got no little ones over there, and they always like to spend the night."

"That's good," Jefferson said. "It sounds like they will be well taken care of. Depending on what my diagnosis is, they may have to stay a few days. Will that be a problem?"

Worry creased Mama's brow, but she put on a smile. "No, of course not. Flo, she would keep them forever and a day if I let her."

"Well, I don't think it will take that long for the girls to recover. Now why don't you show me where they are so I can take a look and see what we're dealing with?"

"Of course, Jefferson. Follow me, eh?"

He stepped through the front door and followed Mama through the main room of the house and into the little bedroom at the back. Through the door, Angeline could see Mathilde sleeping soundly on one big bed, while Amalie lay wide-eyed and propped up on a mountain of pillows on the other.

Before entering the room, Jefferson put down his medical bag and held up his hand to stop Mama. "I can't let you go in there, Mrs. Breaux." His gaze rested on the bulge at her waist. "In your delicate condition, it wouldn't be safe, at least not if it's what I fear it might be."

"I hadn't thought of that." Mama rested a hand on her stomach and turned to Angeline. "You go help Jefferson, you hear? I'll wait right here outside the door, but you call me if you need something, eh?"

"We will, Mama." Angeline stood at the side of the bed and watched Jefferson bend down to sit next to Amalie. "What do you want me to do, Jefferson?"

"Hand me my bag, please." When Angeline complied, Jefferson reached for it, then turned his attention to Amalie. "Your sister says you're not feeling well. Is that the truth, or did she just come all the way to Latagnier to get me so we could have some more of that good gumbo she makes?"

"I like her gumbo, too," Amalie said with a weak smile, "but today my tummy's not feeling good."

Jefferson cast a quick glance over his shoulder at Angeline and grinned. "It's not? Well, let's see if I can fix that. Is there anything else I need to examine while I'm looking at your tummy? Maybe you need your chin hairs checked."

Amalie's smile brightened, and her fingers reached from beneath the blanket to cradle her chin. "I don't got no chin hairs. See?"

"You don't?" Jefferson reached inside his medical bag and pulled out a small instrument. "Well, let me make sure they're not growing on the inside." He placed his hand over hers and gently opened her mouth to peer inside. "You're right. There's none in here."

"I told you so." She pulled the covers up to her nose and looked up at Angeline. "He's a funny man. Are you sure he's a doctor?"

Angeline nodded. "Yes, I'm sure. Now behave and let him work."

Jefferson slipped the instrument back in the bag. "Now let's see. What else do I have in here?"

He made a big show of fishing around in the bag while Amalie slowly let go of the covers. When the little girl leaned over the side of the bed to peer into the bag, Jefferson pulled out a stethoscope and said, "Aha! Look what I've found."

Amalie's squeal of glee awoke Mathilde. "What is he doing here?" she whispered.

Angeline sat on the edge of Mathilde's bed and placed her palm on her sister's damp brow. It felt warm but not exceptionally so. "Hush, Matty. Jefferson's here to doctor the both of you. He's looking at Amalie first, then he'll look at you."

Mathilde nodded and closed her eyes. "All right," she said with what sounded like the last of her breath.

Jefferson listened to Amalie's chest, looked into her ears, and completed his examination by taking her pulse. All the while, the little girl's brown eyes watched him intently. When he'd tucked her back under the covers, he pulled out a small notebook and began to scribble.

From the door, Mama called to Jefferson. "What you find wrong with my Amalie?"

"Mama, you're not supposed to be in here," Angeline said.

She feigned innocence. "I'm not in there. I'm out here."

"Mama!"

Jefferson looked up sharply. "Please, Mrs. Breaux. You cannot allow yourself to get sick, not with other children to tend and a baby on the way."

Mama's expression turned grave. "So you think it might be. . ."

Influenza. Angeline knew Mama couldn't say the word.

"I'd rather we spoke privately after I examine Mathilde."

Angeline knew for sure that her sister was sick when she allowed the doctor to complete his exam without so much as batting an eye. For Mathilde Breaux to miss a chance at flirting, she had to be ill.

Once more, Jefferson wrote in his notebook, then folded it into his medical bag along with his supplies.

"Why don't we let these ladies get some rest?"

"Angie, will you come back and tell me a story?" Amalie asked with a yawn.

"Of course, sweetheart." Angeline straightened the little girl's covers and pushed an errant curl off her forehead. "You just close your eyes and start thinking about which one you want to hear. I'll be back as soon as I can."

Amalie nodded, snuggling deeper into the mound of pillows. Odds were, by the time Angeline returned, her sister would be sound asleep. A quick check of Mathilde told her she would also sleep soundly.

Angeline and Mama followed Jefferson back outside onto the front porch. Mama sank onto the bench by the door and rested her hands on her knees.

"So what is it, Jefferson? What's wrong with my girls, eh?"

Jefferson's gaze went from Angeline to Mama and back to Angeline. "I'm encouraged that neither girl is exhibiting all the symptoms of influenza, but I'm troubled that they do have the fever and aches. Have you noticed any coughing?"

Mama shook her head and looked to Angeline. "No," Angeline said, "I don't think so. Mathilde's fainted a few times, and Amalie does nothing but sleep."

He looked relieved. "Good. That just might mean these two will get well on their own."

"Back in 1918 when the influenza hit us so hard here, we used to give the sick ones a drink of sugar water with kerosene. It seemed to help." Mama looked up at Jefferson. "What do you think, eh?"

"I think that probably isn't necessary, Mrs. Breaux. At this point bed rest is what's going to make them better." He focused his attention on Angeline. "I'll need you to monitor the girls for signs of complications and see to their needs. Your mother or any of your siblings are not to go near them, do you understand?"

Angeline nodded.

"Mrs. Breaux, I cannot overstate the importance of isolating Mathilde and Amalie until their symptoms subside. If this is influenza—and we pray it isn't—they will pass it on to anyone else in close contact within a matter of days."

"Oh, I don't want that."

"No," he said, "you don't." Again he addressed Angeline. "They will need a typical invalid diet—broth, liquids, and the like. Can you handle that?"

"Of course."

"And if either of them develops a cough, a headache, or any other symptom that worries you, fetch me immediately." His mouth quirked into a smile. "And promise me you won't come by pirogue unless you remember to put on some gloves."

Angeline looked down at her bandaged palms and matched his smile. "I promise."

"Fine, then." He reached to take Mama's hand and shake it. "I want you to concern yourself with seeing to the needs of your healthy children and let Angeline tend to the sick ones. Will you promise me that?"

Mama seemed to contemplate the question a moment, and Angeline wondered if she might not agree. After all, Mama generally took charge of everything and everyone in the Breaux household. Delegating anything of importance didn't come easily to her.

Even as she spoke, she looked undecided. "I will do that, Jefferson, but only because I know you're a smart man, and you know what's best for the bebes."

He shouldered his bag. "I appreciate that, Mrs. Breaux. Knowing I will only have two Breaux girls to doctor eases my mind greatly."

Jefferson reached for Angeline's hand. "Walk with me to the car, would you?"

Their gazes collided. Somehow Angeline managed to nod and follow him down the porch steps.

"So you'll be taking care of my girls yourself, then?" Mama called.

When Jefferson smiled, Angeline's heart melted. "Yes, ma'am, I will."

Angeline chose her words carefully. "But I thought you were leaving on Wednesday."

His smile chased away all her worries. "So did I. I guess God had other plans," he said as he gave her a quick kiss on the cheek and made his exit.

As she watched the motorcar disappear around the bend in the road, Angeline's heart soared, then sank. Jefferson was staying. This had been her dream once, to have Jefferson Villare back in the bayou country and back in her life. Now that God had brought it within her grasp, it seemed He—or at least Papa—might be taking it away.

"Who was that who done drove off from here?"

Angeline whirled around. "Papa! I thought you and Ernest were gone for the whole day."

"Well, I'm not. I sent your brother off to finish checking the trotlines while I came home to see about my girls."

"They're sleeping. Amalie seems a bit better this afternoon, but all Mathilde wants to do is sleep." She shrugged. "It sure makes for a quiet house when those two aren't up and causing excitement."

Papa nodded. "I can just imagine. Now who was that in the motorcar?"

Leave it to Papa not to let loose of a question once he'd asked it. If she didn't tell him, Mama would. Better she do it.

Debating the amount of information she gave Papa didn't take long. There was no use aggravating him more than necessary.

"The doctor. He came to examine the girls."

There, the truth had been told. If Papa asked, she would tell him the rest. Jefferson Villare *was* a doctor, after all.

Her father gave her a sideways glance, then linked arms with her. "And what did he say? How's my Amalie and Mathilde?"

"The girls are resting," she said. "The doctor says that's best."

Papa's face turned grave. "Does he think it might be the influenza?"

"He's not sure," she replied. "We're to keep them away from the others and especially away from Mama."

He chuckled and turned her toward the house. Angeline fell in step alongside him.

"Now that's going to be a trick in itself. My Clothilde, she don't like to be told not to mess with her babies, especially when they're sick." He nudged her shoulder with his. "And my Angie, she's the same way as her mama, eh?"

"About some things, I suppose," she admitted with a grin.

"Some things like doing the right thing when her papa and mama tell her to?"

Angeline stopped in her tracks. "What are you talking about, Papa? When haven't I done the right thing?"

"Theophile Breaux, what are you doing home in the middle of the afternoon, eh?"

"You sound just like your daughter, Cleo." He turned his attention to Angeline. "I've got some good news for you, Angie, and I can't wait to tell you and your mama both."

She tried not to cringe. Papa's good news might be just that—good news—or it might be something else entirely.

"This would happen to be about Nicolas Arceneaux, would it?"

Papa smiled and patted her head. "Now don't you worry your pretty self about Monsieur Arceneaux just yet. I got it all worked out, and you're gonna be so happy."

"Happy?" Her feelings went toward the opposite emotion.

"Yes, girlie, now let's go where your mama can hear." He led her toward the porch steps. "No sense in me telling this story twice."

"Papa, please tell me you didn't go and make any promises to Nicolas. I never did answer him when he proposed, you know."

Dread turned to something worse when she saw her papa's smile fade. "It don't make no never mind whether you said yes yet. Nicolas and me, we know you're gonna be happy with him, and that's what counts, isn't it?"

"What counts is what God wants, Papa."

"I know that," Papa said as he looked past her rather than at her. A sadness washed over his tanned features. "And God, He don't break up families, no. He keeps us together for always."

"But, Papa, are you sure God wants me married off to Nicolas Arceneaux?" When he didn't answer immediately, she added, "Or is that just what you want so I can be assured of not leaving the bayou?"

Papa's startled look gave her reason to hope he might actually be considering her question. She said a little prayer that the Lord would soften his heart and make him see what was so obvious to her. Nicolas Arceneaux was not the husband for her.

"What're you talking about, eh?" Mama called. "I see you two are conspiring."

"Well, now, I'm glad you asked, Clothilde." He crossed the porch to greet Mama with a kiss. "I was just telling Angie that I had good news for the whole family. Now let me go see to my two sick ones, then I'll tell you all about it."

"But, Theo, Ernest isn't here," Mama said. "If it's that important, shouldn't we wait on him?"

Papa waved off Mama's question with a shake of his head and disappeared into the house. "He'll be here soon enough" came the answer through the open door.

Angeline settled next to Mama on the bench. "What do you think Papa's up to this time, Mama?"

Her mother shook her head. "I don't know, bebe, but I think it might have something to do with that man there."

Mama pointed toward the west, where Ernest was walking toward them across the lawn. At his side were Nicolas Arceneaux and a gray-haired man in a dark suit.

As they neared the house, she realized the identity of the elderly man. It was the local preacher, Rev. Dautrive.

Chapter 13

Jefferson lay atop the sheets and stared at the ceiling in his childhood room. A painting of the constellations fanned out from the four corners of the light fixture, a fanciful feature courtesy of his mother.

She'd been the artist in the family, a woman with a creative flair and a bent for the whimsical. Losing her had meant losing nearly everything.

Everything except Pop and his best friend, Angeline.

Now Pop was gone to spend eternity with Mom. That left only Angeline.

He rolled to his side and stared at the train ticket on the nightstand. Torn in half, part of it lay atop a stack of his favorite books, while the rest sat teetering on the edge. Blowing a hard breath sent the ticket flying, and he watched it sail across the beams of light filtering through the shutters on the western-facing side of the house. It landed at the feet of his old rocking horse, a relic of a childhood he barely remembered.

"Tomorrow I'll have to let the landlady know I won't be arriving as planned," he said to the old horse. "Wonder what she'll make of that."

He shifted back into his original position, cradling his hands behind his head. "I wonder what I should make of that, Lord."

"Why do you have to make anything of it? Stop trying to figure everything out and rest in Me."

"Rest?" Jeff let out a strained chuckle. "Who could ever get any rest here?"

"You could, if you would stop trying so hard."

Outside, the strains of the evening were coming alive, a familiar combination of crickets, night birds, and the occasional barking dog. Soon the sun would set, and the night would settle around the old house.

Mrs. Mike had left enough food for four grown men wrapped up in the kitchen, and he'd promised her he would try to eat something before bed. In a few minutes, after a bit more rest, he would get up, go downstairs, and make an attempt.

But for now, moving seemed out of the question. His old bed, with the feather mattress that seemed to mold to his form, refused to let him go.

He gave in to its embrace and thought once more of how it felt to spend time with Angeline Breaux. Yes, those moments were every bit as comfortable as this feather bed, this familiar room, this old house. Perhaps that's why he'd chosen to delay his departure.

Jeff allowed himself to believe that, all the time knowing if he dared, he would realize a deeper, more permanent reason for spending time with Angeline. Unfortunately, the Lord hadn't yet told him how he could have the one he'd always loved and the career he was called to. Until He did, Jeff was stuck waiting.

"Excuse me," he said to the ceiling. "I'm not waiting; I'm *resting*."

"No, you're not, but you could be. Stop trying to control things and turn it over to Me. You can have all that you want and more, but you've got to stop trying to make things happen by planning your whole life at once."

"But, Lord, You say in Your Word that we fail for lack of planning. What about that?"

"I also say that a man plans his steps, but the Lord knows the direction he will go."

"All right, Lord. You win."

"I always do, My son. Now rest."

With a sigh, Jeff closed his eyes and, for the first time in days, slept soundly, even though it was hours before bedtime.

~

Mama put a hand on Angeline's shoulder. "Angeline, go on in the house and see to your sisters. Let me handle the menfolk, eh?" She rose and waved toward the trio now crossing the lawn. "And tell your papa I'd like to have a word with him, would you?"

"Of course, Mama," she said as she walked inside. She met Papa and conveyed the message, scooting out of his way before he could ask any more questions.

She stepped into the bedroom and closed the door partway behind her. If anyone went looking for her, they would have to come into the room to find her, but if anything interesting was said—or if anyone called her name—she would hear.

Both of her sisters slept soundly, leaving Angeline with nothing to do but tidy up the small space. Exhausting all the possibilities for cleaning within minutes, Angeline sat on the edge of Amalie's bed and began to pray as she stroked the little girl's dark curls.

Father, You are in control, and I know that. Heal these sisters of mine, and keep whatever is ailing them from spreading to the others, especially to Mama, who needs to take care of herself and the baby coming in a few months.

As to the situation going on outside right now, I ask that You step in and do something to show what You want done. Keep Papa mindful of the fact that You have the last say on everything, and please let Your will—not Papa's will—be done in the matter of choosing a husband for me.

She almost added something about Jefferson but thought better of it. If the Creator of the universe didn't know what was best for her, no one did.

Still, she hoped He wouldn't make the same choice Papa had made for her.

"I've made my choice and that's that." Papa's voice echoed in the small room, causing Amalie to stir.

"Angie, what's wrong?" she murmured.

"Hush now, little sister," Angeline said as she smoothed Amalie's damp brow. "That's just Papa, and he's all fired up about something."

About me, I'm sure.

"Angie?" This time Mathilde spoke. "Is that handsome fisherman here again?"

Angeline looked up, startled. "Yes, actually he is, along with the preacher."

Mathilde smiled. "He's quite handsome."

"You mentioned that, Matty," she said as she rose and reached to straighten the bedcovers Mathilde had tangled. "Now get some sleep."

"I will," she whispered. "Maybe I'll dream about fishing. Or maybe I'll just dream about stealing your Nicolas for myself."

"Now that's one dream I would share with you."

Angeline chuckled. Even in the middle of her illness, Mathilde was thinking of men. Poor foolish girl with her silly imaginings. She wouldn't be so fast to fall in love if she knew what a mess of trouble it could bring.

Actually, Papa's threat of sending her to the nunnery was starting to look better than the alternative. Even if Jefferson was interested in something more than a fleeting romance, and there was no evidence he was, she would have to defy Papa and leave Mama, the babies, and the bayou to follow him. Could she do that?

"I just don't know," she said softly.

The alternative was to be the dutiful daughter and follow her papa's wishes to marry Nicolas Arceneaux. She would stay among family, for sure, and Mama would never want for her help.

"But I don't love him."

"I know you don't, bebe. That's why you're going to do just what I say."

Angeline jumped and whirled around to stare at the doorway. Mama stood just outside the room.

"How are my girls?" she asked as she peered around the door frame for a better look at Mathilde and Amalie.

"Resting comfortably," Angeline said. "Matty feels a little warm, but Amalie seems to be doing well. I don't think either of them is hungry, but Jefferson says they need to keep up their strength. At least both are drinking their water." She picked up the two empty water glasses from the nightstand and walked toward the door. "Maybe I ought to fix them bowls of chicken broth. We still have some of that chicken stock left over, don't we? I could go do that right now."

"Angie, you're a natural-born nurse if I ever did see one," Mama said.

"Well, I don't know about that," Angeline replied as she left the room and closed the door behind her. "Now what did you mean when you first came to the door? You said something about my doing exactly what you said."

Mama placed her finger to her lips to silence Angeline. Motioning to the back door, she turned and headed that way. Angeline followed, still holding the water glasses.

"Go put those in the summer kitchen and wash your hands. I'll wait right here," Mama said as she stood on the back steps.

When Angeline returned, the faint sound of male voices told her that the men were still there.

"Mama, what is Papa doing with Nicolas and the pastor?"

Rather than answer, Mama headed down the narrow path that led through the thicket and ended at the banks of the Bayou Nouvelle. With every step, Angeline's worries increased. The combination of Nicolas, Papa, and Rev. Dautrive could only mean one thing.

A wedding was afoot.

Her wedding.

Keeping silent was nearly impossible, so she shouted her thoughts to the Lord in prayer. *Please hear me, Father! Please don't let them do this to me. I don't love this man.*

A quietness settled in her heart as she heard the gentle response. *"I know, My child. But now you must wait on Me."*

Angeline halted her pace to stare up into the canopy of trees and the blue sky beyond. A single cloud, wispy like pulled cotton, teased the edges of the trees and floated slowly on the breeze.

"Then do something," she whispered.

Mama cast a glance over her shoulder. "What's that, bebe? Something wrong, and you can't walk no more?"

"No, Mama," she answered as she fell back into step behind her mother. "I can walk just fine."

It's the waiting I'm having trouble with.

Finally, Mama stopped at the edge of the bayou and settled down on a grassy spot in the shade. "Sit here, bebe," she said as she patted the place next to her. "You and me, we got some talking to do."

Dread formed in her chest, and she knew the thing she feared most would soon happen. Strange, but she knew. "It's about Papa and Nicolas, isn't it?"

Mama nodded. "The wedding, they've started planning it."

Everything inside her crumpled. Where was God? How could He allow this to happen? Couldn't He see she did not love Nicolas Arceneaux?

"Oh, Mama, how can I stop this?" she cried. "I just can't marry Nicolas. I can't. I don't love him. I'll *never* love him."

"Hush now, Angeline. This crying and worrying won't change a thing. You know you can't stop this and neither can I." She lifted Angeline's chin and looked into her eyes. "But God can."

"Yes, Mama, He can." She swiped the back of her hand across her eyes to push away the tears. "But will He?"

Mama leaned back and looked up into the sky. "I pray He will, bebe. But until He does, you and me, we've got to do some things."

Angeline sniffed. "What kind of things?"

"Now I want you to listen to everything I've got to say before you talk, you hear?"

"Yes, Mama."

"All right, the first thing you and me have to do is start planning this wedding of yours." She held up a hand to stop Angeline's protest. "Now I know what you're gonna say. You don't want no wedding, eh?"

"That's right."

"Well, just because you don't want a wedding, that doesn't mean there won't be one. Do you understand?" When Angeline nodded, Mama continued. "We can go about this thing in two ways. The first way is to do what you're doing right now."

"What do you mean?"

"I mean, you can go kicking and screaming all the way to the altar with your papa following right behind you, holding his big old shotgun and the whole town watching. Is that what you want, eh?"

An image rose in her mind. She could see the interior of the little church where the Breaux family had worshiped for three generations. In every row of seats were friends, family members, and townspeople, all dressed in their Sunday best to attend a wedding.

White bunting had been tied to the ends of the old cypress pews, and big white ribbons decorated the edges of the pastor's lectern. Her groom, dressed in a suit of dark color, awaited her arrival with his head bowed, as did Rev. Dautrive.

Such a beautiful picture it was, and then she and Papa emerged from the back of the church, and a gasp went up from the crowd. At her side stood Papa. At his side stood the big shotgun.

The crowd began to laugh. Worse, so did the pastor and her groom.

Angeline dissolved the image with a shake of her head. "Oh, Mama, that would be awful."

"It would indeed." She offered a wry smile and batted at a mosquito buzzing around her bare arm. "Now if you'll listen to your mama, there just might be a better way of going about this."

Hope dawned inside Angeline, and she sent it skyward with another prayer. Her mother was wise, especially in the way of love and marriage. Surely she could give her some way out of this mess.

"What do you have in mind, Mama?"

"Well, what I have in mind is this." She grinned and clapped her hands together in excitement. "You and me, we're gonna plan a wedding, eh?"

Chapter 14

Again Mama stopped Angeline's protest with a wave of her hand. "Now just let me finish. You were always an impatient child, Angeline. Why don't you sit on your questions and give me a minute to explain?"

"I'm sorry."

She took a deep breath and let it out slowly. "God and me, we've been talking a whole bunch about this problem of yours, and I think He wants us to just go on about our business and plan you a pretty wedding."

Angeline's heart sank. "Forgive me, Mama, but I don't see how giving in to Papa's demands and planning a wedding for Nicolas and me is going to get me out of this mess."

"First off, let's get this straight, young lady. Your papa is the head of this household, and as such, what he says goes, you hear?" When Angeline nodded, Mama continued. "So now that we got that straight, we know we can't just tell him you're not gonna marry the Arceneaux boy. That would be disobedient to Papa and to God, since He sent Papa to be in authority over you long as you live in our house, eh? Tell me you understand that much."

Why did Mama have to make so much sense? It would be so easy to protest the unfairness of the situation by refusing to cooperate. And with Jefferson Villare's kisses still warm on her lips, even after all this time, she desperately wanted to protest a marriage to someone else.

"I understand."

"Well, all right then. You asked me how this is going to help. Angie, bebe, I don't know, but I trust that le bon Dieu, He does. My prayers, they tell me I need to help plan a wedding for my Angeline, and that's what I'm gonna do. I don't know how God's gonna fix this, but I do know He will. Do you trust Him?"

Did she? How easy it was to claim trust in the Lord when things were going well! How much more difficult to profess that same trust when God seemed to be doing the exact opposite of what made sense.

"Yes, Mama, I trust Him," she said finally.

"Good," Mama said. "Then let's go visit with the menfolk. I'm sure they're wondering where we got off to."

Angeline stood and helped her mother to her feet. "You're not going to be able to do that much longer," she said.

"I know that, bebe." Mama rubbed her back, then dusted off her skirt. All at once, her face turned serious. "Before we go back and talk to the menfolk,

I need to ask you something, and I want you to tell me the honest truth. Will you do that?"

Dread returned, and Angeline swiped at the grass on her legs rather than look directly at her mother. "Of course I will. I'm always honest with you, Mama."

"Good." She paused. "I want to know *why* you don't want to marry Nicolas Arceneaux."

Angeline swung her gaze to meet her mother's. "Well, to start off, I don't even know the man. He seems nice enough and all, but I can't imagine spending the rest of my life with a stranger."

"Fair enough." Mama seemed to consider the statement for a moment. "Any other reasons? I mean, he's handsome enough, and he does come from a good family."

"Yes, that's true," she said. "But I don't care about those things."

"All right then, let me see. He's a hardworking man, that's for sure, eh? While he was here, he helped your papa and Ernest every day and worked as hard as two men. You can't fault him for being lazy, no, not at all."

"No, I don't suppose you could fault him for that." Again Angeline looked away.

"And he loves the Lord; you know that."

"Yes, I believe he does."

Mama placed a hand on Angeline's shoulder and sighed. "Then why don't you just come out and tell your mama why you don't want to marry a handsome, hardworking young man from a good family, eh?"

The truth lay just beyond her ability to speak it. Even to try would be silly. No two people were more unevenly matched than she and Jefferson Villare. How could a simple bayou girl ever have designs on a rich, city-bound doctor?

"I can't, Mama."

"I believe you can," she said softly. "You might as well tell me. The Lord already knows."

Angeline took a deep breath and let it out slowly. Mama was right. The Lord did already know. The truth be told, Mama probably knew, as well.

"I can't marry Nicolas Arceneaux because I've been in love with Jefferson Villare as long as I can remember. I'd rather spend my life as an old maid helping you than to spend it married to someone other than Jefferson."

There, she'd said it. Angeline closed her eyes and waited for the lecture she knew her mother would deliver. Instead, she got only silence. When she opened her eyes, she saw that Mama had already begun to walk toward the house.

Mustering up as much dignity as she could manage, she followed Mama back down the path and out into the clearing. As they neared the house, Angeline could hear the raised voices of the men along with their laughter.

When Mama stopped abruptly, Angeline almost ran into her. "Angie," she said softly, "guard your heart. As a woman, I understand how you feel, eh? But as your mother, I have to remind you that you've got to be obedient to the Lord, even if He says you must give up this man you love."

Angeline nodded. "I will."

"It's gonna hurt if it happens this way, but you'll just have to trust that le bon Dieu, He don't make no mistakes." She smiled. "His is the better way, even if we don't always agree."

"I know," Angeline said.

"Good." Her mother seemed to study her a moment. "Now put on your prettiest smile, and let's go talk about a wedding that might or might not happen, eh?"

They crossed the distance to the house arm in arm, each matching the pace of the other. With every step, Angeline begged the Lord to give her the strength to put her own wishes aside and follow His. By the time she reached the back steps, she almost felt as though she could accomplish this.

Inside the house, Angeline said one last prayer. *Lord, You know my faults. Please let me do this through Your strength and not try it through mine.*

"Clothilde, where you at, sweetie?" Papa called. "Come bring yourself out here and fetch Angeline with you."

"Right here, Theo." Mama emerged from the bedroom to run her fingers through her hair and check her smile in the pier glass. "Now remember what I said, Angie. You be obedient even if you don't *feel* like it, you hear?"

"Yes, Mama." Angeline followed her through the house and out onto the front porch.

When she appeared, all conversation ceased. Nicolas, who stood apart from the two older men, gazed at her with interest, while Papa and the reverend looked as if they'd been caught conspiring.

"Come on over here, Angie-girl," Papa said.

She stepped around Mama to stand at Papa's side. He gave her a hug, then held her at arm's length. "You look mighty pretty this afternoon."

"Miss Angeline, you do look like a breath of fresh air." Rev. Dautrive removed his straw hat and mopped at his bald head with a white handkerchief. "I wonder if we will have the pleasure of hearing you sing again this Sunday."

"I don't know yet, Reverend," she said. "I suppose I'll find out tomorrow at choir practice."

"My girl, she can sing, that's for sure," Papa said. "Oh, you should hear her. I'll tell you, it's like the angels done come to Bayou Nouvelle."

Mama merely nodded and settled on the little bench as if to watch the show. If only Angeline could join her and be a spectator, instead of the center of attention.

"Beauty and a voice to match."

The words came from behind her, where Nicolas Arceneaux stood leaning against the porch rail. When she turned, she saw him smile.

"That's right," Papa said. "And don't forget she can cook, too." He turned his attention to Nicolas. "Did I tell you she's right handy with the cleaning and the little ones? Why, I'd have to say there's not a thing my Angeline can't do."

"Papa, please," Angeline whispered. "You're embarrassing me."

"Now, Theo," Mama said, "you make it sound like Angie's a prize horse. Why you want to go and talk like that and make our girl feel all uncomfortable-like, eh?"

An awkward silence enveloped the porch. Rev. Dautrive cleared his throat and pretended interest in a bee buzzing around Mama's Easter lilies, while Papa simply glared at Mama. Nicolas Arceneaux, on the other hand, stared at Angeline openly. Finally, he squared his shoulders and crossed the porch to take her hand.

"I'm a plain-spoken man," he announced, "and I don't believe in a lot of fancy talk or beating around the bush. Why don't I just get to the heart of the matter for which we've all gathered?"

Angeline's gaze darted first to the left and then to the right, hoping for a distraction or possibly a place to run. She willed the baby to start crying, one of her sisters to call out for her, or even the Lord to strike down a bolt of lightning that would call a halt to the whole proceedings.

Instead, a warm wind blew past, bringing the earthy scent of the bayou onto the porch. Somewhere to the east, a dog's bark chased the breeze.

"You go right on ahead, young man," Papa said.

Nicolas cleared his throat and stared into Angeline's eyes. "You and I have already talked about this. You know what I'm about to ask, don't you, Angeline?"

Tears welled up in Angeline's eyes. Somehow she managed to nod.

"And this time I'm going to stand right here and wait until I get an answer."

Dread closed around her throat. She couldn't have said a single word aloud at that moment if her life depended on it.

Please, Lord, please don't let him ask me to marry him.

"Angeline Breaux, it would be an honor for you to be my wife. Will you marry me?"

No, Father, don't make me answer him. Make this all go away.

Papa touched her shoulder and leaned toward her. The look in his eyes told her she could not stand mute forever. "Answer him, Angeline," he urged.

Rev. Dautrive slapped his straw hat back on his head and smiled as he stuffed his handkerchief into his pants pocket. "Oh, I do declare the tension is thick enough to cut with a knife. I'm probably speaking too soon, but the church calendar fills up fast in the summer. You'd need to get this wedding planned and done three weeks from Saturday, or you'll have to wait until September."

Angeline gulped. "Three weeks?"

"Now, Angie," Papa said, "you don't have nothing to wait for, so why put off until the fall what we can get done in three weeks?" He turned to the reverend.

"I say we take that spot on the calendar, eh?"

"Theo, hold up on yourself there!" Mama called. "I think you'd better wait until the bride says yes before you book the wedding, eh?"

Nicolas lightly squeezed her hand and smiled. "Angeline?"

Do something, please, Lord.

An image of Jefferson crossed her mind and stuck there. He had stood on this very same porch only three nights ago and kissed her—twice. How could she agree to marry another when those kisses still lingered in her mind and heart? How could she say yes when her love belonged to another? How could she say no when Papa had all but sealed her fate well before now?

"Your father wants the best for you, as do I."

"Bebe, does the cat got your tongue?" Mama asked. "It's not respectful to stand there like a statue. Better you say something before Mr. Arceneaux, he gets too old to take a bride."

God, if You're going to stop this, You need to act right now.

Angeline held her breath and waited for the answer she knew would come, the words that would end this. Instead, God was silent.

Her gaze landed on Nicolas Arceneaux and held there. "Yes, Nicolas," she whispered, "I will marry you."

Papa let out a whoop loud enough to be heard a mile down the road, while Rev. Dautrive slapped Nicolas on the back and shook his hand. Mama, on the other hand, merely winked and disappeared into the house.

Angeline stood apart from the celebration and tried not to cry. Where was the Lord? Why hadn't He saved her?

Rev. Dautrive pulled a small notepad from his pocket and turned the pages. "As long as it's official, I might as well write the wedding down on the calendar." He made eye contact with Angeline. "We wouldn't want someone else to get that date, would we?"

"No," she whispered. "We wouldn't want that."

Only Nicolas seemed to detect the note of sadness that went along with her words. The look on his face told her as much.

"Now where did I put the calendar?" The reverend continued to flip the pages. "Well, here it is." Papa leaned toward him, as did Nicolas. "There, we have an opening in three weeks. I saw it just before I left the parsonage, and I believe it's on. . .uh-oh."

"What?" Papa asked.

"Well. . ." The reverend removed his handkerchief to mop his brow, then took another look at the calendar.

"What is it, Reverend?" Nicolas chimed in.

Rev. Dautrive offered a weak smile and directed his gaze to Angeline. "Did I say three weeks? Well, that can't be right. It's not three weeks at all."

"Yes, you did," she said with a nod. *Oh, Lord, thank You for this delay,* she added silently.

"Just say it, Reverend," Papa said. "If it's not three weeks, then when's the big day?"

"Are we planning a wedding day?" Mama called from inside. "Wait just a minute and I'll be right there, eh?" She emerged onto the porch with the baby on her hip. "So what day are we gonna have this wedding, Reverend?"

The preacher smiled and held his notebook in the air. "According to this calendar here, there's just one day open this month. How's a week from Saturday?"

Angeline's jaw dropped as shock coursed through her. "But today's Monday." She fought to count the days. "That's less than two weeks away."

"Twelve days." Papa's grin widened into a full-fledged smile.

Nicolas wrapped his arm around her waist and gathered her to him. "Isn't that great, Angeline? Just twelve days and we'll be husband and wife."

She looked up into his eyes, and what she saw there surprised her. Nicolas didn't seem any more excited about the prospect of a wedding than she did.

Chapter 15

"So we've got twelve days to get to know one another," Nicolas said as they strolled down the banks of the Nouvelle. "That's not a long time, is it?"

Angeline batted at a strand of Spanish moss, then ducked to walk beneath it. "No, I suppose not."

You'll need to work fast, Lord.

"I don't suppose there's really much we have to know, is there, Angeline?" He paused. "The wedding will go on one way or another."

The truth in those words hit home, and Angeline had to blink back tears. "I suppose," she said as she turned away from his gaze to collect her thoughts.

They walked on, the sounds of the bayou filling the silence that fell between them. Occasionally something would splash on the other bank, but nothing else disturbed the easy flow of the water.

"What's it like where you live, Nicolas?" she asked as she stepped around a hole in the path.

"Oh, I suppose it's much like this place, what with the bayou and all. Why?" He slowed his pace to reach for a stick and heave it toward the water.

"I don't know." She shrugged. "I suppose I was wondering what I would be facing when I left this place."

"You'll miss it, won't you?"

Angeline nodded. "Yes, but I can't stay. The house is overflowing now, and with another on the way, there's just not enough to go around. That's why Papa. . ."

"Bartered you off to a fisherman who lives just a little way down the bayou?"

Stunned, she opened her mouth to speak and found the words were missing. She stared at him in horror.

"It's all right, *ma petite*," he whispered. "I don't mean to sound so harsh. After all, you and I, we were both bartered off, eh?"

"What do you mean?"

Nicolas stared past her with a faraway look in his eyes. "You might not believe this, but you're not the only one who doesn't particularly look forward to the wedding."

Something between surprise and relief seized her. "What do you mean?"

He returned his gaze to her and offered a weak smile. "I am ashamed to say that although you are the prettiest flower that ever bloomed in this stretch of the bayou, you weren't my first choice as a bride."

"What?" His admission shocked her. At the same time, it made her feel a bit better about her feelings regarding Jefferson Villare. How could she hold this against Nicolas when she bore the same feelings in her heart? If God should choose to allow them to wed, He would enable them to handle this.

"You do not believe a man can reach my age and not lose his heart at least once, eh?"

So his was a love from the past. So much for feeling better about her current love for the young doctor.

"Whatever became of her?" Angeline asked.

"Ah, that is something I cannot think upon, for it makes me sad."

The pain in his words made Angeline wince. "I'm sorry," she whispered.

"Me, too" was his answer.

"Was she beautiful?" Why in the world did she ask that? Angeline looked at Nicolas and found him smiling. "Yes, every bit as beautiful as you. In fact, she is very much like you, only perhaps a bit more bossy." He shook his head. "But when I met her, I was not free to marry, so it wasn't to be, eh?"

"I suppose not."

Again silence fell between them. This time Angeline used the opportunity to study her groom-to-be. Tall and strong, he wore the mantle of a son of the bayou with an easy grace.

He looked to be the type of man who would work hard, then come home to heft a baby or two atop his shoulders. Angeline prayed he was this kind of man, for she couldn't bear it if he were not.

"I have a big family, Angeline. I feel like I should warn you about that. Mama and Papa can't wait to meet you, and neither can my seven brothers and sisters. They'll all love you, I know, but when we get together, it can be loud. I'm the youngest of the bunch, so there are plenty of folks around the dinner table."

"Seven?" She laughed. "My goodness, that sounds like my family."

Nicolas stopped and turned to face her. "Actually, they are very much like your family, Angeline. Your people and our people, they settled the bayou and never forgot where they came from. Their blood, it lies beneath this land."

His fierceness startled her. "Yes," she whispered. "This is true."

"You don't speak the language of the Acadians much, do you, Angeline?"

"Oh, I don't know," she said as she averted her gaze. "I don't suppose we speak it as much as the older folks do, but we do mix the Acadian with the English. Why?"

"I just wondered. . . ." He paused and seemed to be searching for the right words. "I wondered how you felt about your past, your history."

Angeline squared her shoulders. Where was this line of questioning going? Worse, what did he know about her past? Surely someone hadn't told him about the gossip.

"I'm proud of my history. The Breaux family has lived on this bayou for two hundred years. There are more Breaux headstones in the church cemetery than anyone has time to count, and my mama's family has been here even longer." She paused to study his reaction. "I also have nothing to be ashamed of in my past."

A hawk swooped low and landed on the branch of a bald cypress nearby. Angeline watched the bird and wished she could fly away so easily.

Ah, but when you returned, your troubles would still be here, wouldn't they?

He barely blinked. "I didn't mean to say that you might be."

"Then what *did* you mean?"

"Angeline, I'm sorry. I'm not good at this thing of talking in circles, and that's what I've been doing." He took her hand in his. "I'm just going to get right to the point. I'm taking you as my wife, and I want to know if you're going to live up to that responsibility."

Confusion mixed with surprise. "What are you talking about?"

His features looked pained, and he took a deep breath before he spoke. "If I'm going to stand before the Lord and make you my wife, I want to be sure you're not going to forget your upbringing and run off up north with that city fellow."

The words stung. She would never make a promise she didn't intend to keep.

She looked up into his dark eyes veiled with pain and confusion. How much did he know about her love for Jefferson?

"Nicolas," she said slowly, "when I take my marriage vows, I intend to keep them for life."

"As do I," he said as he abruptly released her hand and turned back toward the house.

~

Wednesday morning when Jefferson arrived at the Breaux home, he found Angeline sitting on the porch, her Bible spread on her lap, and the baby playing on a blanket in the shade at her feet. When he left Latagnier, he'd told himself—and Mrs. Mike—that he would merely check in on the recuperating Breaux girls. By the time he turned onto the dirt road that wound alongside the Nouvelle, he had added another purpose to his trip.

Today he would begin the process of courting Angeline Breaux.

All the way from town, he'd planned his course. With less than two weeks before he had to be in New York, he had to act swiftly. Still, he must be wise and gentle—the enormity of his task was overwhelming.

But as Pop would say, he was a Villare, and a Villare never gives up.

"Good morning!" he called as he climbed out of the Model A and snatched up his medical bag.

"Jefferson!" Angeline closed her Bible and set it on the porch step. Rising, she scooped the baby onto her hip and strolled toward him. "I didn't expect to see you today."

"So am I a nice surprise?" He tickled the baby under her fat chin and laughed when she giggled.

Angeline's troubled expression caught him off guard. "Of course," she said a bit too quickly. "It's always nice to see you here."

"And it's even nicer to be here." He shook off the feeling that something had changed between them since Monday and proceeded with the first order of business on his agenda. "So how are our patients?"

"Mathilde is much better. She's been up and around most of the morning."

"No more fainting spells or fever?"

Angeline shook her head. "The fever broke yesterday morning, and it hasn't come back. She's not as strong as she normally is, but she seems steady enough on her feet, and she's had enough energy to help with some of the household work."

"Good. And Amalie?"

"There's been no change, Jefferson. She sleeps much of the time, and she's not lost that fever yet."

"But it hasn't gone any higher, has it?"

"No, but something's just not right with Amalie. I can feel it, but I can't put my finger on it." Angeline shifted the baby to the other hip. "To tell you the truth, if you hadn't come out here today, I probably would have gone to get you tomorrow."

"Not in that pirogue?"

She smiled and glanced down at her hands, now free of bandages but still bearing the bright pink color of her wounds. "If I had to."

"Why, Angeline, I never figured you for a nurse."

Startled, she looked up abruptly. "I'm not."

"Of course you are." Jefferson gave her a smile. "A good nurse not only reports on what she can see; she also reports on what she thinks she might soon see." He swung the bag over his shoulder and turned toward the house. "It's a rare gift. Maybe you should consider nursing as a career, ma chère."

"Oh, I couldn't," she said as she fell in step beside him.

He stopped short. "Why not?"

For a moment, he wasn't sure she would answer. When she did, her words surprised him.

"Because I've got something else planned." She turned her attention to the baby, smoothing her dark hair as she walked beside him. "Something besides a career in nursing or anything else."

What could Angeline Breaux possibly have planned for the rest of her life? The whole of her existence was wrapped up in home, family, and the Bayou Nouvelle. How could any of these things add up to a future for someone like her?

The answer hit him all at once, like a bolt from the blue. "You *are* marrying the Arceneaux fellow, aren't you?"

"Angie, bebe, is that Jefferson Villare with you?"

Jeff tore his attention away from Angeline to see Clothilde Breaux rounding the corner of the house. "Yes, ma'am," he said. "It's me."

"Good morning, Jefferson," she said as she greeted him with a wave of her hand. "Did you come to see to my girls?"

"Yes, ma'am." He cast a quick glance at Angeline. *All three of them, actually.*

Clothilde reached for the baby and settled her on her hip. "Just you go on inside, then, Jefferson. Angie, go with him and help, eh?"

"Yes, Mama."

"You know my girl, she ought to have been a nurse, eh?" She patted Angeline's shoulder. "She keeps good care of her two sisters and still finds time to watch the baby so her mama can get her yard chores done. I don't know what I would do without her."

"All right, Mama," Angeline said, a flush of pink spreading across her cheeks. "Now you're starting to sound like Papa."

"Oh, hush now. I'm just telling the truth." She motioned toward the house. "Get on in there and see to the girls, eh?"

Mathilde met them on the porch with a weak smile. "I thought I heard a commotion out here."

Jeff studied Angeline's younger sister as he walked toward her. Her coloring appeared normal, with no telltale dark smudges beneath her eyes.

"How are you feeling?" he asked as he pressed his palm to her forehead and found it cool to the touch.

"Much better, thanks to you," she said. "You're a wonderful doctor, Jefferson Villare."

"You can thank the Great Physician, Mathilde. I just work for Him."

"Well, however you did it, you managed to cure me in record time." She paused. "With Angie's help, of course."

"Mathilde, come!" Clothilde called. "I need someone to watch the baby while I put these Easter lilies in pots. Jefferson'll be needing to take one back home to Mrs. Mike when he leaves, and we don't want to keep a busy doctor waiting."

The younger Breaux sister offered Jeff a parting smile and headed toward her mother. He watched her as she took the baby in her arms, satisfied that she had made a full recovery.

"Shall we go see Amalie?" When Angeline nodded, Jeff stepped inside the normally boisterous house and stopped short. "It's quiet as a tomb in here. Are the children still with your aunt?"

"Yes. Papa didn't want to take any chances, and Tante Flo didn't want to give them up so quickly. They conspired against Mama to keep the little ones over there one more night. It wasn't easy, but Papa held his ground. I understand he told her he would hide the paddles for the pirogue, too, if she tried to slip off and fetch them herself."

Jeff walked past the pier glass and caught his reflection. Angeline moved into focus in the mirror, and his breath caught. In the morning light, she looked beautiful, not like the decorated dolls in Boston or the upper-crust doctors' daughters in New York, but with a beauty that radiated from within.

Angeline Breaux was incredible. How had he missed something so obvious? What had he ever seen in any other woman?

Why did he feel like dropping his medical bag and kissing her right on the spot?

As much as he would like to do that, her admission—or rather her lack of denial—that she was to wed Arceneaux had certainly put a damper on his plans to court her. *Lord, did I misunderstand Your intentions for us?*

"Like mother, like daughter?" he asked as he forced his mind back to the conversation. "With taking the pirogue out, I mean."

"I have no idea what you're talking about," she said with a mischievous grin. The smile disappeared, and worry etched her face. "Jefferson, do you think it will be safe to bring the children back tomorrow? I would hate for one of them to come down with whatever Amalie has. I mean, if it is the influenza, well, I remember what it was like before when—"

"Hush now," he said. "Since Mathilde recovered so quickly, I can't be sure this is influenza. Even if it is, Amalie has not shown herself to have a bad case of it. From what you've said, her symptoms seem to be fever and lethargy."

"What's that?"

"Lethargy? That's the tendency to want to sleep all the time."

"Oh." She nodded. "Yes, she's definitely had the lethargy."

Her use of the word amused him; he paused to reach for the door to the back bedroom.

"So you're sure about the children coming home tomorrow, then? It's not too soon?"

"Waiting to return until tomorrow is probably best, but I don't see the need to delay them past then." He wrapped his arm around her shoulder and gave her a quick hug. "Don't worry, Angeline. I'm sure Amalie's condition will be fine by then."

He released her to see to the task at hand, that of checking what he expected to be a recuperating Amalie Breaux.

"You really think she will be all right, Jefferson?"

Oh, but he wanted to kiss away the worry on that beautiful face!

Lord, there's hope for the two of us yet, isn't there? Ignoring all caution, he touched her cheek with the back of his hand. "As I told you, I believe she will be fine."

But when he opened the door, he realized Amalie's condition was anything but fine. Even from where he stood, he could see that the little girl had taken a dangerous turn for the worse.

Chapter 16

"What's wrong?" Angeline followed Jefferson into the room. "Has something happened to Amalie?"

Jefferson's form hid the little girl as he leaned over to examine her. From the way his shoulders slumped, she knew the diagnosis was not good. Rather than answer her question, he reached for his medical bag and pulled out an instrument. As he listened to the little girl's chest, he frowned.

"What is it?"

"How long has she been like this?"

"Like what?"

When he leaned back, Amalie came into view. Her face had gone pale, and her breathing seemed shallow and choppy, as though she'd run a long way and found it hard to catch her breath. Dark hair curled in damp tendrils around her forehead, and her fingers clutched at the sheet as if she were looking to feel something that was not there. Worse, Angeline could hear the rattle in her sister's tiny chest.

"I peeked in on her after breakfast, and she was sleeping. I thought she was fine."

She drew nearer and grasped one of her sister's hands. It felt cold despite the warmth of the room.

"How long ago?" he asked as he retrieved his notebook and pencil. "An hour or two, or was it longer?"

Angeline tried to calm her racing thoughts. "I suppose it was around seven, so that would make it two hours ago. Why is she making that sound, Jefferson? It's awful."

He looked up from his writing to meet her gaze. "I won't lie to you, Angeline. Your sister's very ill. What you're hearing is fluid in her lungs."

"That's bad, isn't it?"

"If we can't arrest the process, she could drown in her own fluids."

Terror gripped her. Little Amalie couldn't possibly die!

"It hurts," her sister whispered.

"Where does it hurt?" Angeline watched as Amalie made a weak gesture to her throat and her chest. A second later, she allowed her hand to fall limp at her side. She closed her eyes.

"Amalie, can you hear me? It's Jeff. Remember me? I'm your sister Angeline's friend." He paused to shake her gently. "Wake up and look at me."

Jefferson adjusted Amalie's body to a more upright position, piling the pillows behind her. Rather than remain where he placed her, the little girl began to fight, first lashing out with clenched fists and then twisting her body out of his grasp.

"Help me, please," he said as he clutched at her tiny shoulders. "We need her to sit up."

Angeline stood there, helpless. "What do you want me to do?"

Amalie went stock-still. Her gaze roamed about the room, focusing on nothing in particular.

"Should I go get Mama or Mathilde?"

"No, not yet. I'd rather we stabilize her first. Besides, neither of them needs to be in close proximity to her. Mathilde's too weak, and your mother's with child. I don't want either of them exposed to Amalie should she prove to be contagious." He paused and gave Angeline a direct look. "For that matter, I would prefer if you'd exercise caution while you're near her. Take care to wash your hands and practice good sickroom hygiene. It will keep you healthy."

"I will."

"Good." He turned his attention back to Amalie. "Why don't you talk to her?"

Her brain went numb as Amalie went into action again, kicking and shaking her head as if she didn't recognize her visitors.

"Talk?" Angeline asked. "Do you think that will help?"

"Yes," he said as he ducked a tiny swinging fist. "I need you to calm her down so I can get her into a better position."

Angeline squeezed past Jefferson to reach for her sister. "Amalie, honey, it's Angie. Open your eyes."

When the little girl didn't respond, Angeline looked to Jefferson for guidance. "Try again," he said as he continued to wrestle with the pillows.

"Amalie! Wake up!" No response. "Amalie Patrice Breaux, if you don't wake up this instant, I'm going to go fetch Mama and Mathilde, and they're going to make you take a nap with the babies instead of swimming this afternoon. Do you hear me?"

This time her sister's eyes opened slightly. "Swimming?" she asked. "I get to go swimming?"

Angeline pasted on a smile. "Yes, honey, just as soon as Jefferson says you're feeling up to it."

"You mean it?"

Her dark eyes focused on Angeline, then she quickly shifted her attention to Jefferson. Before she could speak, she began to cough, and Jefferson covered her mouth with his handkerchief. When he pulled it away, dark rust-colored flecks decorated the white material.

"Blood?" she whispered as Jefferson nodded his agreement.

"I'm afraid she's developed pneumonia."

"I want to go swimming," Amalie said before going limp in Jefferson's arms.

Angeline worked alongside Jefferson to position her sister as if she were sitting up. When the last pillow had been put into place, she turned to him. "Is there any hope?"

"We can still save her, Angeline," he said as he reached into his bag to remove a stethoscope. "Or rather, God can save her, with our help."

She sank down on the bed and rested her hands in her lap. "How?"

"Let me examine her, and then we'll talk about what to do."

"Can I help?"

He offered a weak smile. "I could use a good nurse right now."

"Well, I don't know how good I am, but I can learn. Just tell me what to do."

As Jefferson took care to check Amalie over, Angeline followed his instructions and assisted him. She lifted her sister when asked and held her hand when she complained. Once, she even caught the little girl before she attempted to climb past Jefferson and head for the door.

That action took the last of Amalie's strength, however. By the time Jefferson finished his exam and made his notes, she was sound asleep, her slumber interrupted only by the occasional fit of ragged coughing.

Angeline fussed with the covers, adjusting them so they were smooth and straight again. Amalie would never notice the effort and would most likely mess them up again before she awoke. Still, it made her feel that she'd done something—anything—to make the little girl more comfortable.

"It's as I expected. Her condition has deteriorated into pneumonia." He lifted Amalie's wrist and took her pulse again. "Now that she's worn herself out, her vitals are returning to a more stable rate, but I'm still skeptical as to how well she will do over the rest of today."

"What do you mean?"

"I mean that this kind of condition can cause a patient to deteriorate rapidly." His gaze met hers. "You said she looked fine a couple of hours ago, right?"

"Yes."

"Well, take the amount of change you see between the state she was in after breakfast and her condition now. As her condition worsens, she will deteriorate even faster."

Angeline stifled a gasp. "You can't let that happen, Jefferson. There must be some way to make her well again."

"Actually, the only way to begin her healing is to empty the lungs of their fluid. For that, I can only recommend one course of treatment." He scribbled one last note on his pad and looked up. "Your sister needs to be in a hospital."

"A hospital?" She shook her head. "We're just poor folks, Jefferson. We can't afford a hospital."

"But the ideal conditions for treating this type of pneumonia are constant care, and the only place she can get that is in a hospital environment." He paused.

"There are plenty of people there who are skilled in this sort of illness, and they could give her excellent care."

"We just can't."

Angeline stroked her sister's forehead and fought off panic. Influenza and pneumonia took the elderly and the weak. Amalie was neither, but she had been sick for nearly a week.

She watched Amalie struggle for a breath, then held the handkerchief against her lips when she coughed. Again the cloth came away spotted with blood.

Something had to be done.

Please, Lord, don't let my little sister die. Please fix her, and quick.

"Ma chère, you have to take her to the hospital."

His tone was insistent yet gentle and sympathetic. She knew that even as he said the words, he realized the impossibility of the situation. People like them didn't take their sick to places like that. Unlike Doc Broussard, hospitals didn't take their fees in fish or furs or some other type of bayou produce.

They wanted cash money, something the Breaux family, like too many others on the bayou, had little of. No, there had to be another way.

"Papa can barely feed us all as it is, and there's another little Breaux coming in a few months. All we've got saved will go to paying medical bills once Mama's time comes." She paused to collect her emotions. "Isn't there any other way?"

His silence, combined with the look of sorrow on his face, landed a blow that nearly caused her to double over in pain. Angeline felt a sob well in her throat, and tears stung her eyes.

"You have to do something. Please don't let her die," she whispered.

"Angeline, I. . ." His voice fell away, leaving the anguish in his eyes. "I'm a researcher, not a general practitioner."

"So what's the difference?" she demanded.

"I work with data and lab personnel, not with patients." His shoulders sagged. "You need Doc here, not me. He's the family practitioner."

"You're a doctor. You graduated with honors, so you know medicine, right?" When he nodded, she continued. "And you know about influenza and pneumonia, right?"

"Right," he said softly.

"Then if you know all of this, why can't you just use what you know on my sister?"

He seemed to consider the question a moment. "There were techniques we used in school that might work. We can try and simulate the hospital treatments here," he said slowly. "But I can't guarantee. . ."

"Only the Lord can make guarantees, Jefferson. Just tell me what you need me to do."

"First we need to elevate the bed. Can you get something to put beneath the headboard that will lift it higher?"

Angeline raced to the shed and came back with two bricks, left over items from when Papa repaired the chimney last fall. While Jefferson lifted the headboard, Angeline slid the bricks into place.

"Now what?" she asked as she climbed to her feet and dusted off her hands.

"Now we work on getting her lungs clear. Follow my lead and do what I tell you, all right?"

When she nodded and moved closer, they set to work. Half an hour later, they had pushed and pounded the poor little girl's back and chest until Angeline thought her sister would never survive the treatment that was supposed to save her. To her surprise, the chest percussion, as Jefferson called it, seemed to help.

Jefferson had patiently instructed Angeline as he went through the motions of the chest percussion. As a result, the muscles in Angeline's arms and back screamed from the exertion.

At least Amalie now lay more comfortably, her breathing a little more even and her cough subdued. Exhausted from the ordeal, however, it was all Angeline could do not to crawl up next to her sleeping sister and fall into a deep sleep.

"Well done, Nurse Breaux." Jefferson tossed a smile in her direction as he put away his notebook and set his medical bag on the nightstand. "I think we just might have caught this thing in time to beat it."

"Thanks to you, Dr. Villare. You're really good at what you do, did you know that?" When he smiled, she felt bold enough to continue. "Are you sure God hasn't called you to be a. . .what did you call it?" She searched her mind for the term he had used. "A family practitioner?"

His expression of surprise startled her. "Do you think you'll be able to do this next time on your own?"

"I'll do my best," she replied.

"Good," Jefferson said as he rose. "I'm counting on my nurse now."

Angeline nodded weakly and gave him a mock salute. "Nurse Breaux reporting for duty," she said with what she hoped would be enthusiasm.

Evidently her words fooled Jefferson, for he looked relieved. He reached for her hand and helped her stand, cradling her against his shoulder when she wobbled on unsteady feet.

"Are you sure you can do this, ma chère?"

To keep her little sister out of the hospital, she would do whatever it took. She looked up and smiled. "Of course. How often should I repeat the procedure?"

"You'll know when she's in need of a treatment, but as a guess I'd say at least once every two hours for the first twenty-four hours or so. After that, you can probably get away with going three to four hours in between treatments, unless her symptoms worsen. Regardless, someone will have to be with her constantly to monitor her vitals and see that she doesn't take a turn for the worse. Her fever may go up, and that is to be expected. Let me know if it doesn't break and go away completely by tomorrow afternoon."

"I will," she said softly. "Is there anything else I need to know?"

Jeff smiled and collected her into an embrace. "Yes, that I'll be praying for your sister and for you."

Too soon he released her and made his exit. "Every two hours," she whispered as she rubbed her tired arms and watched the motorcar disappear in a cloud of dust. *Father, You and I are going to have to do this together. I know I can't manage it alone.*

Too many hours later, Angeline slumped back in the little straight-backed chair and tried to close her eyes. The morning sun now filtered through the partially closed shutters and fell in long stripes across the floor, casting the room in an odd combination of light and shadow. In the light, Angeline watched her sleeping sister. Amalie slumbered peacefully.

The night had been a long one, and her only rest had come when Ernest and Papa took over for a few hours each so she could curl up in the empty bed. Her sleep had been fitful, filled with dreams of awakening to find Amalie dead.

It had been nearly impossible to keep Mama out of the room. Finally, when Papa threatened to take her to Tante Flo's right then if she didn't remove herself from the doorway and get some sleep, she grudgingly gave in and went to bed. Mathilde had been easier to convince. Her strength had not yet returned completely, so she could do nothing but see that the washbasin stayed filled with cool water. Finally, after midnight, she'd grown weary of even that small job and pleaded exhaustion.

With each treatment, Amalie seemed to breathe easier, and sometime before daybreak her coughing had all but disappeared. Still, the fever, which had spiked dangerously high as Jefferson predicted, failed to break.

Angeline rose and stretched the kinks out of her spine. Trudging over to the washbasin, she took a clean folded towel and dampened it. The little girl's eyes opened when the towel touched her skin but soon closed again.

She looked much better this morning, and the color had begun to return to her skin. A glance at the clock on the nightstand told Angeline another hour stood between her and the time for a treatment.

Outside she heard the sound of Papa and Ernest at work on their chores, and she could smell bacon frying in the summer kitchen. Her stomach protested its emptiness, but her legs refused to carry her any farther than the empty bed. With a sigh, she placed her head on the pillow and took one last look at Amalie.

"I'll just close my eyes for a minute," she whispered. "If you need me, you call me, Amalie."

"I will, Angie," she thought she heard her sister say.

The next voice she noticed belonged to Jefferson. "Hush now, we don't want to wake her," he said.

"The poor girl, she's exhausted," she heard Papa say.

"Tried to save her on her own," Ernest added.

When she opened her eyes, none of them were there. Angeline sat up with a start and almost knocked the clock off the nightstand, reaching for it. Four hours had passed since the moment she'd placed her head on the pillow.

"Oh no, it's almost noon and I've missed her treatment!" she wailed as she threw back the blanket and climbed over to Amalie's bed.

It was empty.

Chapter 17

Jeff stood over the sleeping form of Amalie Breaux and gave thanks to God that he had obeyed the nudging in his spirit that morning. While he had meant to spend the day preparing to leave, he'd felt the strongest urge to head for the Breaux home.

He'd known he would end up there before nightfall, both on the obvious premise of checking on Amalie and the more secret one of seeing Angeline, but he hadn't realized he would be led there to save the little girl's life. How like God that He would arrange things in such a way.

When he arrived, Amalie's fever was at a dangerous level. Thanks to Angeline and the breathing treatments, the girl's lungs were clear. This alone had kept her alive until help arrived. Now that she'd received treatment to combat the infection, her vitals were already looking better. When she awakened and asked about Angeline, Jeff knew she was on the mend.

His thoughts turned from the little girl in the bed to Angeline. She'd been exhausted, too tired even to remember that he'd tried to awaken her.

"Where is she?"

Jeff whirled around to see Angeline racing down the aisle of the children's ward. "Over here!" he called.

She caught his arm and peered down at her sister, her breath coming in ragged spurts. "How is Amalie?"

"Calm down, Angeline. Your sister's resting comfortably now."

"What happened? All Ernest would tell me is that you came and took her to the hospital. I saw Papa and Mama in the waiting room, and they couldn't tell me anything, either. She almost died because of me, and I intend to have some answers."

Fear shone in her wide brown eyes, and it took all the control Jefferson had not to gather her into his arms and kiss the emotion away. Instead, he took a deep breath and let it out slowly.

"I came out to see about Amalie this morning and found her condition had worsened," he said. "Her fever had spiked too high for home treatment, so I brought her here."

Alarm seemed to turn to anger as Angeline's fingers clenched into fists. "Why didn't you wake me up?"

Amalie began to stir, so Jeff led Angeline away from the bed toward the bank of windows. "I tried, Angeline. You were exhausted." He gave her what he hoped would be a stern look. "The last thing your mother needs to worry about is another sick child, namely you. Since you elected not to heed your need for sleep, I made the decision for you."

"But how dare you bring her here to the hospital?" She lowered her voice a notch. "You know Papa can't afford this."

"It's all been taken care of."

Angeline whirled around to see Doc Broussard standing a few feet away. "That is, if you agree to the terms," he added with a wink.

"Terms?" She glanced over her shoulder at Jeff, then returned her gaze to the elderly doctor. "What terms?"

Doc smiled and linked arms with Angeline, leading her past Jeff toward Amalie. Jeff fell in step behind them.

"Well," Doc said, "you know back in 1925, the good people on the hospital board saw fit to name this children's ward after my dear departed wife, God rest her soul."

She nodded.

The old doctor chuckled. "As such, I have a little bit of pull around here." He paused to release Angeline's arm. "So in the Acadian way, I'd like to make a deal, eh? To maybe barter something in return for something else—in this case your sister's hospital bill for something much more valuable that *you* can give to *me*."

When Angeline gave him a perplexed look, he continued. "You know how much I love that shrimp gumbo of yours, don't you?"

A smile dawned on Angeline's face. "Yes, I do," she said softly.

"Then would you consider it a fair trade if I took payment in gumbo? Say one pot of gumbo for each day your sister spends in this fine establishment?" Doc offered a mock frown. "Now I would expect we make this all legal-like. You know, draw out the terms and have both parties sign them. I'm thinking one pot every other Tuesday until the debt is satisfied would do the trick. How does that suit you?"

From where he stood, Jeff could see tears collect in Angeline's eyes. "That would suit me just fine, sir," she said in a trembling voice.

Doc held out his hand to shake Angeline's. "Good, it's a deal." Abruptly he slapped his forehead. "Wait," he said. "We need a witness." He turned to Jeff. "Come on over here and witness this, would you, Dr. Villare? I wouldn't want this young lady to skip town until her debt is paid."

Jeff closed the distance between them and smiled. "I'd be delighted," he said.

As soon as the words fell from his lips, he wanted to reel them back in. How could he promise to stick around and be sure Angeline brought gumbo to Doc when he planned to be on the train to New York in eleven days?

Surely Doc knew that. Jeff cast a sideways glance at the old man and frowned. The grin on the crafty physician's face told Jeff that Doc knew exactly what he was doing.

No matter. It was all in fun anyway. Angeline would make a few pots of gumbo, and Doc would beg off the rest of the debt in some polite but subtle way. By then, he would be long gone.

"Jefferson," Angeline said, "I would like to stay with her if I may." She pointed to a pair of chairs next to the ward door. "All I need is one of those to sit in, and I'll be fine."

"Well, I don't know," Jeff said. "Generally the rules are pretty strict about visitors."

He cringed as Angeline's dark brown eyes flashed a pleading glance. "I'm not a visitor. I'm her sister."

He looked to Doc for help. "Still, I don't think it would be allowed, would it, Doc?"

She turned to Doc and touched his sleeve with her fingertips. "Jeff taught me how to do chest percussion, and he says I'm a very good nurse. I could be of help to the staff."

The old doctor smiled. "Is this true, Dr. Villare?"

Ten minutes later, after securing permission, Angeline sat in a soft chair next to Amalie's bed. "Promise me you'll stay out of the nurse's way." Doc motioned to the ward nurse, a friendly woman of middle age, with mock fear. "She's a tyrant, so mind your manners."

"I heard that, Doctor!" the nurse called.

"I'll come back to check on the two of you in the morning," Jeff said as he gave Angeline a quick embrace and followed Doc out of the ward.

Instead of waiting until morning, however, he returned to the ward with a hamper of Mrs. Mike's fried chicken and buttermilk biscuits and a tin of fresh field peas in the front seat of the Model A. Anticipation rode high in his mind as he took the stairs two at a time and emerged at the entrance to the Bessie Landry Broussard Memorial Children's Ward.

As he pushed open the big door, he heard laughter inside. What he saw astounded him. Rows of children sat in rapt attention, some in wheelchairs and some propped up in beds, as Angeline told the story of a little alligator named T-Boy and his friend the red snapper. Amalie managed a smile in his direction. The girl looked pale but seemed much improved.

Sinking to his knees behind a little girl in a wheelchair, Jeff held his finger to his lips to tell Amalie he wished to remain hidden. When the little girl nodded and smiled, Jeff turned his attention back to watch Angeline perform each of the voices and act out parts with hand motions.

He looked around at the smiling faces of children who, on every other occasion, wore their illness with stoic silence. Even the ward nurse seemed to be caught up in the tale. When the end came and the unlikely pair lived happily ever after, the storyteller received a hearty round of applause.

Jeff rose to clap the loudest. "Bravo!" he called.

Angeline placed her hand over her mouth in surprise. "Jefferson, I didn't know you were here," she said. "How much did you hear?"

"Actually, I think I missed the beginning of the story." He linked arms with Angeline. "Would you kids mind if I borrowed Miss Breaux so she could fill me in on what caused T-Boy and Redfish to go swimming in the first place?"

A chorus of giggles followed them out into the hall and chased them downstairs. When he walked with her into the evening twilight and led her to the Model A, she stopped short and pulled out of his grasp.

"Where do you think we're going?" Her frown did nothing to detract from her beauty. "I'm not leaving her, so if you think you're taking me home, you're mistaken."

Jeff opened the car door and removed the hamper with a flourish. "Relax, ma chère," he said. "I bring greetings from Mrs. Mike. Come on. I know just the place to enjoy this bounteous feast."

Her smile restored, Angeline fell in step beside him. "You're the best, Jefferson."

"No, you are. I mean, the way you told that story—it was incredible." He glanced in her direction. "As long as I've been visiting the ward, I don't think I've ever seen those kids smile."

She looked away, clearly embarrassed. "It was nothing."

"Mais non, ma chère," Jeff said. "It was definitely something." He nudged her with his elbow. "Let's go that way."

Together they took the brick walkway toward Community Park. In the center of the park, the white wooden gazebo stood like a beacon, lit by a single streetlight. The night was warm, but not oppressively so, and the breeze smelled fresh with the promise of rain. The ring around the moon confirmed the impending shower.

In a few weeks, band concerts would fill the park with happy sounds, but tonight the music came from the crickets. It was a symphony that strangely suited Jeff tonight, and as he filled his plate with Mrs. Mike's delicacies, he felt nothing but peace.

Tomorrow he would think about leaving, about his career, and about what God intended for him. Maybe he would even think about Angeline and the fact that she'd been promised to another. She hadn't actually come out and admitted it to him, but the look on her face when he'd asked her told the tale. Yes, he just might think about that tomorrow.

Tonight, though, his only worry was saving room for peach pie. At least he thought that was his only concern until Angeline surprised him with a question.

"Jefferson, have you ever thought that maybe you misunderstood what God wanted you to do with your life?" She dabbed at the corner of her mouth with a blue-checked napkin, then allowed the folded cloth to drop into her lap. "I mean, have you ever made up your mind that the Lord had something for you, only to find out He didn't want that for you at all?"

Jeff stalled for time by pretending to chew his food a bit longer than necessary. When he finally swallowed, he could tell by the look on Angeline's face that his ploy had not worked.

"Sure," he said as he expelled a long breath. "I think that happens to everyone eventually. Why do you ask?"

"No reason, I don't guess."

Her voice told him she had plenty of reasons, but logic warned him not to ask. Instead, he went back to his chicken leg, which no longer held any taste. Eventually he tossed it into the woods and leaned back on his elbows.

While they ate, the sky had faded from blue to purple and finally to black. Now tiny stars danced at the edge of the streetlight's glow.

"You're marrying Nicolas Arceneaux, aren't you?" he asked, surprising himself with his boldness.

Silence fell between them for what felt like an eternity. Finally, Angeline spoke. "Yes. In ten days."

"Do you love him?" *Where did that come from?*

"Sa fait pas rien," she whispered.

Jeff leaned forward to place his hands on her shoulders. "It *does* matter, Angeline."

"We should go," she said softly. "Amalie will be wondering where I am."

At that moment, he wanted nothing more than to hold her in his arms and tell her she could marry him instead of the big fisherman. Instead, he released her and nodded, packing up the hamper without comment.

If she wants to marry another, who am I to stop her? I've done her a favor in not pressing my case with her.

But all the way back to the hospital's front entrance, where he allowed her to slip back inside with only the blandest of parting words, he had the awful suspicion that he'd done neither of them any favors.

Chapter 18

Nine days later, Amalie went home in Jefferson's motorcar with Angeline huddled next to her. She'd barely left the little girl's side, leaving the hospital only to accompany Mrs. Mike back to the Villare house for a hot meal and a change of clothes.

Jeff continued his habit of stopping by to check on Amalie, but he never took Angeline to the park for another picnic. When Mrs. Mike started coming by in the evenings, she saw even less of Jefferson.

It was as if their evening in the park had been a good-bye dinner between friends. Everything else seemed to take place between strangers.

The third day of Amalie's stay, Mama declared the wedding must be postponed. She could not plan a marriage ceremony for one of her girls while another of them was ill, and Rev. Dautrive agreed. Eventually Mama convinced Papa, and the date of the nuptials was erased from the church calendar. The date would be rescheduled soon, Mama promised. In the meantime, all her efforts had to go toward restoring Amalie to perfect health.

Angeline smiled as she recalled the conversation, remembering the twinkle in Mama's eyes when she spoke to Papa. Poor Papa never knew what hit him when Mama went to work on changing his mind. He always thought it was his idea, and Mama always let him.

Yes, her mother was a wise woman.

Thankfully, Angeline was spared having to speak to Nicolas during this time, although Mathilde gleefully informed her that her groom-to-be had taken the news of the postponement in stride. He hadn't said much, according to her sister, but rather listened to Mama's explanation without expression.

The car pulled to a halt in front of the house, and Jefferson got out to fetch Amalie inside.

"I don't want to take a nap," Amalie said as Jefferson placed her on her bed and pulled the covers over her legs.

"What if I promise to tell you a new story about T-Boy once you take a short nap?" Angeline said. "How would that be?"

When Amalie began to argue, Angeline held up her hand. "I'm not going to change my mind. Do you want me to call Mama or Mathilde in here?"

"No," she said as she stuck out her lip to pout.

"Then to sleep with you. Besides, I need some time to think of a new story. You wouldn't want me to tell just any old tale, would you?"

"No," Amalie whispered as she settled her head on the pillows. "Can we still go swimming?"

"No swimming, little one," Jefferson said, "but what if I come see you in a few days and take you fishing? How would that be?"

"Fishing? Oh, I suppose so."

"Good, then mind your sister and get some rest."

"But I'm not tired," she said as she pulled the blanket up to her chin. Exhausted from the trip, however, Amalie easily slipped into slumber within minutes.

Jefferson took one last reading of the sleeping girl's vitals, wrote them on his tablet, and then rose. Angeline followed him outside, listening while he fended off Mama's questions.

"I'm sure she's perfectly fine," he said for the second time. "She's a little weak from all she's been through, but she's definitely on the mend."

"And I won't catch nothing from her now?"

"You'll be fine!" he called as Mama brushed past him to disappear into the room where Amalie slept.

"That's probably the last we'll see of her tonight," Angeline said. "Papa says she's driven herself to distraction worrying about Amalie and not being able to take care of her."

"What's that you say about your papa?"

Angeline looked up to see her father standing in the door. "I was just telling Jefferson how Mama's missed being able to take care of Amalie."

Rather than comment, Papa crossed the room to stand toe-to-toe with Jefferson. "I heard tell down at the post office that you're leaving tomorrow on the morning train."

The statement hit Angeline square in the heart. Jefferson had said nothing about leaving tomorrow. While she'd kept quiet about the postponement of her wedding, she'd secretly hoped that he knew and would soon step in to declare his feelings.

What she would do if he did, she hadn't decided. After all, there was the not-so-small matter of Papa and Nicolas Arceneaux.

"What's the matter, boy? Cat got your tongue?"

"No, sir." Jefferson squared his shoulders and stared down at Papa. "Actually, that's old news."

"Is it, now?" Papa crossed his arms over his chest and frowned. "Then why don't you just give us the latest report?"

"Actually, I've been so busy helping Doc, what with the influenza outbreak, that I secured permission for another month's vacation." He locked gazes with Angeline. "I leave for my research position in New York on June tenth."

June 10. The day will be here before we know it, Lord. Work fast, please.

Papa took a step back, a stricken expression on his face. "I reckon I ought to thank you for what you did for my little girl. You saved her life, and for that, her mama and me will always be in your debt."

"Actually, it was Angeline who saved her life."

Papa whirled around to face her. "What?"

"She's quite the nurse, Mr. Breaux." Jeff smiled in her direction. "If she hadn't kept the chest percussion up, your daughter would never have withstood the fever when it spiked. I just happened to show up at the right time with the car."

Papa looked at her with admiration she did not feel she deserved. "But I fell asleep," she said. "She almost died because of me."

"That's not true, Angeline," Jefferson replied. "Because of the treatments you gave her during the night, her lungs were almost clear at the time the fever hit her the hardest. One condition had nothing to do with the other. There was nothing you could have done, even if you had been awake."

Relief washed over her. "Really?"

"Really."

That one word held more comfort than Angeline thought possible. All this time, she had worried that her lapse in nursing skills, and the weak moment when she closed her eyes, had nearly cost her sister her life.

"Theo, come see your baby girl!" Mama called. "She's awake and asking for her daddy."

Papa stuck his hand out and shook Jefferson's. "I still want to thank you for what you did."

"It was my privilege, sir," Jefferson said.

Angeline watched as the two men who mattered most in her life embraced. Only God could have brought together these most unlikely of allies.

"You're welcome back here anytime, Villare," Papa said in an unsteady voice as he hurried toward the back bedroom. "There's my little girl!" Angeline heard him call as he disappeared inside and closed the door.

"I'll walk you out," Angeline said.

Together they strolled toward the motorcar. "How long before she's completely well?" she asked when they reached the vehicle.

Jefferson tossed his medical bag on the seat and turned to face her. "Could be days, could be weeks. It's in God's hands now."

"But she's going to be fine, right?"

He nodded. "Of course she is. She's got the best nurse around." Pausing, he leaned against the car door and crossed his arms over his chest. "Still, I may have to come and supervise her care. Just to be sure."

"I would welcome that, Dr. Villare."

What was wrong with her? She was practically married off to Nicolas Arceneaux, and yet here she stood out in broad daylight, flirting like a schoolgirl with Jefferson Villare.

She should stop this nonsense right now; stop believing that God just might make a way for her to have a future with the young doctor instead of the fisherman. If God put the dream in her heart, surely He would make it come true.

"Maybe we can go fishing while I'm here. We haven't done that in a long time. If Amalie's up to it, she can come along."

The statement took her aback. Fishing with Jefferson sounded fine indeed.

Angeline met his gaze and smiled. "I would like that very much, and I know my sister would, too." When he left, the smile remained.

~

"Who's ready for some fishing?"

Jefferson burst through the door with a smile on his face and a collection of cane poles in his hand. "What's the matter? Am I early?"

Amalie giggled and raced for the door. "Let's go, Angie!" she called as she ran past Jefferson to head outside.

He'd worn his fishing clothes this time instead of his usual dapper suit. Funny how the casual trousers and shirt put her in mind of the young man he had been rather than the grown man he was.

"I see she's recovering nicely," Jefferson said. "No more symptoms?"

"None. That's four days with no fever or cough." She smiled and picked up the basket holding the lunch Mama had packed for them. "And as you can see, her strength has returned."

Jefferson turned to look over his shoulder at the little girl now skipping in circles on the front lawn. "I see that," he said. "In fact, I'm wondering if they gave her too much good care over at the hospital. Maybe you should complain."

Angeline laughed and followed him out the door. As they walked toward the bayou, Amalie lit out ahead of them. By the time they reached a good spot for fishing, she had doubled back and stood in their path.

"You're slow," she said. "Come on!"

Looping the handle of the basket over a low-hanging cypress limb, Angeline settled in a shady spot beside the bayou and watched as Amalie danced in circles. "See, Angie, I'm a princess. A beautiful dancing princess."

"Yes, indeed, you are," Angeline said. "But if you're not careful, you'll tire yourself out and we'll have to go home."

She stopped twirling to put her hands on her hips. "Before I swim?"

Jefferson shook his head. "No swimming today, young lady. That would definitely be against doctor's orders."

Amalie frowned and sank down next to Angeline. "But I wanted to go swimming."

"Hush," she said. "Today you're going to fish instead."

"But fishing's no fun."

Jefferson leaned close. "That's what I thought, too, until I learned to like it. After that, I always caught the biggest fish."

Angeline laughed. "You did not. In fact, if I remember right, you could barely sit still long enough to catch any fish at all. Generally our fishing competition ended up being a kick-the-water contest instead."

"That sounds like fun," Amalie said. "How do you play kick-the-water, Dr. Jefferson?"

"Oh no, you don't," Angeline said. "Don't show her, Jefferson. She's just looking for an excuse to get wet."

She caught the twinkle in his eyes before he spoke. "Sounds like the voice of experience." He reached for the smallest cane pole and settled down beside Amalie. "Now watch this." He reached into the fishing creel, pulled out a small tin, and retrieved a red wiggler. Spearing it like a pro, he handed the pole to Amalie. "Now keep your worm in the water and see if the fish are hungry."

"All right," Amalie said as she wrapped her little hands around the end of the pole.

Jefferson nudged Angeline. "Want me to bait one for you?"

"I'll just watch for now," she said.

A few minutes later, the little girl had tired of the activity, leaving Jefferson to take over her pole. While Amalie chased a butterfly, Angeline chased memories.

~

How many times had the two of them made the trip down to the bayou, promising to bring home fish for dinner but returning with nothing but soggy clothing and an afternoon wasted on fun?

Oh, but those were the days.

"A penny for your thoughts," Jefferson said.

For a moment, she considered not answering him, then she thought better of it. "I was just thinking about how much fun we used to have here." She paused. "Before life made grown-ups of us."

"I think about that a lot." He stuck the end of the cane pole in the soft ground and leaned back on his elbows. "Thinking about you is what got me through the first year away from home."

His statement took her by surprise. Rather than respond, she tried to hide her feelings by pretending to study the dark water of the bayou as it flowed past.

"Did you ever think about me, Angeline?" Out of the corner of her eye, she saw him roll over on his side to face her, cradling his head in his hand. "I mean, did you miss me at all?"

"Miss you?" Angeline shook her head. "That's all I did," she whispered. "I missed you until I thought I would never get over it."

"Did you?" He paused. "Get over it, I mean?"

"No." Angeline met his gaze. "Every day I expected I would look up from my chores and there you would be, standing on the other side of the bayou, looking like you'd never left."

"And then one day, I was."

She nodded.

"But I was too late."

The truth of that statement stung. Had he arrived even a week before, maybe Papa wouldn't have made plans to marry her off to Nicolas Arceneaux.

No, she couldn't be sure of that. Jefferson's return to Bayou Nouvelle could have given Papa enough reason to marry her off, no matter when it happened.

"I don't think you were too late, Jefferson," she said slowly. "I prefer to think that God just had other plans for us."

"Is that what you think?"

His dark eyes bore into her soul, and she longed to tell him how she really felt, how she would leave the bayou with him tomorrow if God would only release her to do that. Instead, she held her peace and said, "Yes, it is."

"Are you set on marrying this Arceneaux fellow, then? Do you think that's what God plans for you to do?"

"I think that's what Papa plans for me to do," she said, allowing him to gather what he would from her statement. There was no sense in revealing the details of the humiliating barter deal she'd been a part of. What good would come of his knowing she'd been traded like a pile of furs to the fisherman?

Jefferson leaned toward her. "Do you love him?"

Again the truth served no purpose, so she decided to say nothing.

Abruptly Jefferson climbed to his feet and reached for her hand. Angeline allowed him to pull her up into a standing position.

"Answer me this, and I will never ask again," he said as he held her hand against his chest. "Is it Arceneaux you love, or could it be me?"

Chapter 19

Angeline looked away, focusing on her little sister, who skipped happily in circles in the distance. "Don't ask me to answer that."

"I think you just did." With that, Jefferson swept her into an embrace. "Oh, ma chère, we are a pair, aren't we?"

It felt so right to be held in his arms, but she knew it was so wrong. Amalie might notice them and misinterpret their embrace. Or worse, she could see it and understand completely.

Such were the ways of the little ones. They seemed to know things even the grown-ups missed. Perhaps Amalie already knew of her feelings for Jefferson. She certainly went out of her way to mention the man whenever she could. And when Nicolas Arceneaux's name came up, Amalie was the first to offer a frown.

Reluctantly she pulled away. "God wants me here at Bayou Nouvelle, and He wants you up north. We weren't meant to be, so what does it matter?"

Jefferson took a step toward her, then seemed to think better of it and backed away to place his hands on his hips. "Remember when you asked me if I ever thought I might have misunderstood what God had planned for my life?"

Angeline nodded.

"I could ask you the same thing." He looked past her to the bayou and the cane pole still stuck in the dirt. "Have you ever wondered that?"

Again she nodded. "Sure."

"How do you know He didn't intend us to be together?"

"I don't," she whispered.

"Then how can you dismiss the possibility?" He caught her into another embrace, and this time he added a kiss on the forehead and another, softer one on the lips. "At least you can acknowledge your feelings for me, can't you?"

No, she meant to say. It came out "Yes" instead.

"Angie. Are you and Dr. Jefferson done with your fishing?"

The sound of her sister's voice broke the moment and the embrace. Angeline stepped away and wrapped her arms around her waist.

"Maybe we're finished with the fishing," Jefferson said softly, "but we're *not* finished with this conversation." He reached past her for the picnic basket. "And I don't think God's finished with us, either."

Angeline continued to think about this statement long after the day had ended. As she went through the motions of completing her household chores and looking after Amalie and the little ones each day, she often revisited the moment on the banks of the Bayou Nouvelle. Someday soon, she would have to put the memory behind her and be a good and faithful wife to Nicolas Arceneaux, but for now she allowed thoughts of Jefferson to entertain her as she hung the freshly washed sheets on the clothesline.

These thoughts fled with the arrival of Rev. Dautrive. "Wonderful news, Angeline!" he cried as he unfolded his large frame from the motorcar.

Angeline snapped a clothespin on the end of the last wet sheet and picked up the empty basket. "Hello, Reverend!" she called.

"Who's here?" Mama said from inside the house. When she emerged on the porch, she waved. "Hello there, Reverend. What a pleasure to see you today."

The reverend tipped his hat and lumbered toward Mama. "The pleasure is mine, Clothilde. I thought I would stop by and deliver the good news to you ladies personally."

"Good news?" Mama looked toward Angeline, who shrugged.

"There's an opening on the church calendar," he said with a grin. "I can marry Angeline and the Arceneaux boy on. . ." He paused to open his notebook and flip through the pages. "Yes, here we go, June tenth."

June 10. Oh no, not the day Jefferson is set to leave. But that's just a few weeks away.

"That's fine, Reverend," Mama said, ushering him toward the porch. "I'll give Theo the good news when he gets home, and I'll send Ernest down to speak to Nicolas in the morning. Now can I offer you a glass of sweet tea?"

Angeline dropped the laundry basket and sank to her knees. *Father, if ever there was a time to show Your sovereign will, it is now. Please do something, and quick.*

~

Jeff had to do something, and quick. With June 10 looming large on the desk calendar in Pop's office, he had little time to decide what God wanted him to do. Until his return to Latagnier, he'd always been so certain of what he was to make of his life. Now the only certainty in his life was that he was uncertain about everything.

Everything except Angeline Breaux, of course. He knew exactly how he felt about her.

He loved her. That was the problem.

The doorbell shattered his thoughts. Thankful for the interruption, he rose to answer the door before Mrs. Mike could get to it.

"Good to see you, Doc. Come in." He swung the door open wide and gestured for the old man to come inside. "What a pleasant surprise. I thought you were much too busy for house calls these days."

Doc chuckled and removed his hat, depositing it and his medical bag on the credenza. "I am busy, that's true."

"How about a cup of coffee?"

"And I've got a pie fresh from the oven!" Mrs. Mike called from the kitchen.

"I'd be delighted," Doc said.

Jeff led the way to the kitchen. "Any new cases of influenza?" he asked over his shoulder.

"One," Doc said as he fell in step behind Jeff. "A young man down at the sawmill fell sick yesterday afternoon. Foreman thought it might be heat exhaustion, but one look at him and I knew that wasn't the trouble." He sank onto a chair and leaned his elbows on the table. "I sure hope he's the last one for a while, but you never know."

"At least we can be thankful the Lord didn't take a single soul this time around," Mrs. Mike said as she placed dessert plates overflowing with peach pie in front of the men. "Back in 1918 we weren't as blessed." She touched Jeff's shoulder. "God rest your dear departed mother's soul."

He nodded and attempted to swallow the lump in his throat. Finding a cure for the disease that took his mother had consumed his life. Hearing this reminder made him remember how very much he wanted to do that.

He wanted.

Jeff stifled a groan. Had he been so wrapped up in what he wanted that he had decided that's what God wanted, too?

"Amen to that, Mrs. Mike," Doc said. "You know, the one thing I don't think I'll ever get used to is losing a patient." He stabbed at the pie with his fork. "Oh, I know there's a much better place they're headed for, but it just seems like the Lord put me here to keep those folks around as long as I can and not to usher them to Jesus."

Mrs. Mike filled Doc's coffee cup with steaming chicory coffee, then poured some for Jeff. "I agree, Doc." She deposited the coffeepot on the table between them along with the sugar bowl and shrugged. "But you can't argue with the Lord's timing. Sometimes He says to stay, and sometimes He says to go."

Those words, simple and yet complex, struck Jeff right to the heart. Yes, sometimes He did.

At that moment, over pie and coffee, Jeff felt God was telling him to stay in Latagnier. He watched the housekeeper with a new respect as she left the kitchen. Who knew Mrs. Mike was such a philosopher?

"Oh my goodness, I almost forgot." Doc fished a folded paper from his vest pocket. "This is for you, Jeff. I told Amos down at the telegram office I would deliver it and save him a trip."

Jeff unfolded the telegram and read the words. It was from Columbia University.

Huge breakthrough in pneumococcus research days away. Need full team in place immediately to process data and analyze results. June 10 no longer acceptable arrival date. Come at once.

"Bad news?" Doc asked.

Stunned, Jeff dropped the paper and watched it float to the floor. Doc picked it up and read it.

"Well, well, this is *good* news." He clapped a hand on Jeff's back. "Congratulations, my boy. Looks like you're about to make history. Your father would be so proud."

"Right," he managed to say through the cotton filling his throat.

Doc pushed back from the table and regarded him with a curious stare. "You don't look so happy. Want to tell me why?"

Jeff expelled a long breath. "I wish I knew."

Doc reached for his coffee cup and took a sip. "That woman makes the best coffee." He set the cup down and gave Jeff a wry smile. "Could it be you're having second thoughts about going to New York?"

"It could be," Jeff said slowly. "Trouble is, I don't know if I'm having a problem with this because *I* want to stay or because *God* wants me to stay." He paused to pick up the telegram and scan it once more. "Until you handed me this, I thought God was telling me to stay."

"So what changed your mind?" He pointed to the paper. "This? It's just a telegram, Jeff, not a message from the Lord."

"How do you know that, Doc? What if it is a message? What if God is telling me I'm supposed to go to Columbia and work on that team? I mean, my goal has always been to do that. I owe it to my mother's memory."

Silence fell between them. Finally, Doc cleared his throat.

"So that's why you were always so all-fired bent on doing research instead of taking over your father's practice." He leaned back in his chair and studied Jeff. "I don't know why I didn't see it before now, but it sure makes sense."

Irritation sparked. "What makes sense?"

"You getting ahead of the Lord, that's what." Doc's eyes narrowed. "Here you are a trained medical doctor who ought to be practicing medicine with real people instead of looking into beakers and microscopes all day." He leaned forward. "You're wanting to even the score over your mama's death by finding a cure, aren't you? That's why you're bound and determined to head off to New York and set the world on fire, instead of staying here and saving lives."

"Am I?"

Jeff tried in vain to conjure up an argument against the ludicrous suggestion. Surely his whole life plan hadn't come from such a simplistic need for revenge over the death of his mother.

Or had it?

"Well, before you cash in that train ticket, let me give you another option." Doc smiled and rubbed his balding head. "I'm an old man, and one of these days I'm not going to be wanting to do all the doctoring I can do now. What with your pop gone and me the only doctor left in town, I've been looking to take on a partner."

He held up his hand to silence Jeff's protest.

"Now before you go saying something you might have to take back, let me just remind you that the job of doctoring the fine people of this parish was good enough for your daddy and your granddaddy, and I hear tell your great-granddaddy did a mite of doctoring of his own." He paused and gave Jeff a direct look. "That's a long line of history you're trying to break. You'd better be sure the Lord's telling you to break it."

"Yes, sir, I'll give it some serious thought."

Doc nodded and rose. "That's all I ask," he said as he disappeared into the hall.

As the door closed behind the old doctor, Jeff leaned his elbows on the table and rested his head in his hands. All he'd ever dreamed of in the way of a career in biological research now sat within his reach. He toyed with the edge of the telegram and tried to decide what to do.

God had given him the ability to learn medicine and the opportunity to do something valuable for humankind with that knowledge. On the other hand, He had also given him a shot at doing something for the people of Nouvelle parish. Without Doc, and in the absence of any new physician who might be found, they would be forced to take the long ride upstream to New Iberia for medical care.

More important, to stay would be to press his case with Angeline. Until she walked down the aisle with the fisherman, God could still intervene.

The offer to stay was tempting. But was it what God wanted?

Jeff rubbed his face with the palms of his hands. Nothing would be gained by hashing the problem over in his mind.

Seeking asylum in his favorite place, he strolled into Pop's office and sat in the big leather chair. Perhaps something in here would give him guidance in what to do about his dilemma.

Absently, he opened first one drawer and then another until a glint of gold caught his eye. His mother's wedding ring.

Jeff picked up the delicate band and weighed it in his palm. Had it always been in the desk? He couldn't remember seeing it before now, and he must have gone through the contents of these drawers a half dozen times in his quest to clear the office of Pop's things.

Jeff leaned back in the chair and clutched the ring to his chest. *Lord, is this some sort of message from You?*

Tucking the ring into his vest pocket along with his watch, Jeff headed toward the garage and the Model A. If he hurried, he might be engaged by sunset.

Chapter 20

Angeline stood along the banks of the bayou, wondering if she'd made the biggest mistake of her life. All day she'd prayed and planned, and now, with just a few minutes to go, she began to think better of the whole thing.

What did she think would come of arranging a private meeting with Nicolas Arceneaux just to see if she could really forget her feelings for Jefferson and fall in love with him? Did she actually believe it mattered what her feelings were for him?

Papa had declared she would marry that man, and Papa's word was his bond. Nothing short of the Lord would keep the wedding from happening.

And that is why she had to see Nicolas today.

Maybe God would speak to her in the quiet of her visit with Nicolas. Maybe He would gift her with the ability to love the man. Or maybe He would guide her once and for all in the way He wanted her to go. Dare she hope it would not be with Nicolas Arceneaux?

A rustling on the trail ahead told her someone was coming. Ernest appeared in the path with Nicolas a step behind.

"I don't know what you're up to, Angie, but if Papa finds out I left my work to fetch Nicolas, he'll have my hide," Ernest said.

She gave her brother a thankful smile. "He won't find out."

"I'll be just over there." Ernest pointed to Papa's workshop in the distance. "Holler if you need me, Angie."

"I will." She offered Nicolas a shy smile. "Thank you for coming to see me, Nicolas. I know it was difficult to leave your work today, and I appreciate that you did."

Nicolas gave her a perplexed look. "I will say I was a little surprised when Ernest came to fetch me this morning and said it was an emergency. I thought something bad had happened."

She shook her head. "No, and I'm sorry you were alarmed. I just needed to talk to you." Frustration caused her to pause. "Actually, that's not exactly right."

Heat flooded her cheeks. This wasn't turning out at all like she'd planned.

Angeline looked up into the eyes of the fisherman and repeated the prayer she'd been praying for the past week. *Father, if Nicolas is the man You intend for me to marry, give me the heart to love him. Guide me and allow me to be the wife he needs me to be. Most of all, if he's not the one, please let me know.*

"Angeline, I'm confused," Nicolas said. "Why am I here?"

"For this."

With that she boldly wrapped her arms around him and kissed him soundly.

~

Jeff pulled the motorcar to a halt outside the Breaux home and scanned the property to see if Angeline might be outside. When he didn't see her, he headed for the front door, only to be met by Mathilde.

"Welcome, Jefferson," she said. "What brings you here this afternoon?"

"Actually, I came to see Angeline. Is she here?"

"Dr. Jeff!" Amalie came bounding across the room and launched herself toward him, landing in his arms just as he knelt down. "I missed you."

The collision bowled him over, and he landed on his rear. His watch flew out of his pocket and hung by its chain from a vest button.

"I missed you, too," he said when he recovered and tucked the timepiece back inside. "You look like you're feeling better than ever."

"Oh, she's perfectly well," Mathilde said. "Unless you're depending on her to do her chores. Then she suddenly feels ill and can't move a muscle."

Jeff rose to a sitting position. "Is that true, Amalie?"

Amalie shook her head and leaned close. "No, but if it was, you wouldn't tell Mathilde, would you?"

"I think she already knows," Jeff whispered, giving the older Breaux sister a conspiratorial wink before he turned his attention back to Amalie. "Say, you wouldn't happen to know where Angeline is, would you?"

"I do, but I'm not supposed to tell." She lowered her voice a notch. "If Papa finds out, he'll have Ernest's hide. That's what he told Angie before he left."

Mathilde's frown told Jeff she had no idea what Amalie meant. "Are you making up stories?"

Amalie stuck out her lower lip. "No, I'm not making up stories. I was supposed to be taking a nap, except I was sitting by the window playing with Ima Jane. . . ." She turned to Jeff. "That's my doll. Anyway, I was playing with Ima Jane and I saw Ernest and Angie standing over by Papa's shed, and that's what Ernest told her before he left in Papa's old pirogue."

"So where is Angie now?" Mathilde asked.

"I told you I'm not supposed to tell."

Jeff leaned toward Amalie and lowered his voice. "If you tell me where Angie is, I'll see if I can't get Mathilde to ease up on your chores for the rest of the day. What do you say?" He looked up at Mathilde for confirmation, then returned his gaze to Amalie. "Where's your big sister?"

Amalie seemed to consider the proposition a moment. When her smile dawned bright and wide, Jeff knew he'd won.

"C'mon, I'll take you there," she said as she tugged on his hand.

Together they rose and walked out onto the porch. Amalie began to skip across the lawn until she reached the path leading to the bayou. Jeff stopped short and knelt down to get on eye level with Amalie.

"I need to speak to your sister alone. Is that all right with you?"

Slowly she nodded. "I guess so. Will you come see me before you go home?"

"Sure," he said as he patted her on the head and sent her on her way back to the house.

Jeff rose and turned to face the path that led to Angeline. "Lord, if this is meant to be, show me in a way that is clear and obvious. If it's not, make that plain, too. Either way, I'll bow to Your desires," he whispered as he stepped onto the path.

With the ring snug in his pocket, Jeff set off toward the bayou. In a few minutes he would see Angeline. What would he say?

Perhaps he should have planned this better. Shouldn't a gentleman make some sort of presentation before actually making the proposal? Times like now, when manly advice was at a premium, he missed Pop the most. Yes, Pop would have known exactly what to say.

"Will you marry me, Angeline?"

He shook his head. Too abrupt.

"Angeline, ma chère, will you marry me and make me the happiest man on earth?"

No. Too desperate.

Flowers. He should at least have flowers to present. Jeff cast about for something in bloom and found only a smattering of pink buttercups hidden beneath the fronds of a palmetto.

Gathering up a handful, he shook the dirt off the roots and straightened his vest and jacket. Tomorrow he would bring her a proper bouquet, but for now these would have to do.

Now, back to the proposal. When nothing brilliant dawned on him, he decided to depend on the Lord.

"All right, Father, I'm leaving the words up to You," he said as he pushed past a low-lying limb and stepped into the clearing.

What he saw froze the blood in his veins. He jumped back into the thicket and peered between the greenery to be sure of what he had actually seen.

Standing a few yards away was Angeline Breaux, seemingly deep in conversation with Nicolas Arceneaux. And then she kissed him.

~

Angeline pulled away from Nicolas's embrace and touched her finger to her lips.

Nothing.

She shook her head. Why did she feel nothing? When Jefferson kissed her, she felt fireworks, shooting stars, all at once.

Maybe she should try again.

Braving a glance up at Nicolas, she saw he, too, looked perplexed. He leaned against the cypress tree and folded his arms over his chest.

"Why did you do that, Angeline?"

"I had to know," she said softly.

"Know?" Nicolas shifted positions. "What did you have to know?"

Angeline sank to the ground and patted the spot beside her. "Would you sit with me a minute?"

Still wearing his confused look, Nicolas complied. Angeline cast a glance over her shoulder and caught Ernest staring in their direction. When she waved, he went back to chopping wood.

"I'm going to be honest with you, Nicolas." She took a deep breath and let it out slowly, praying God would supply her with the right words.

"You still love that doctor, and that kiss told you that you will never feel that way about me."

"Yes."

He nodded. "I understand."

"You do?" She regarded him with surprise. "How so?"

A look of sadness came over his handsome features. "Because as beautiful and kind and sweet as you are, I don't love you, either, Angeline. As I told you before, there's someone else who will always hold my heart."

Relief washed over her. "Then it's settled. We can't possibly marry."

She stood to go, and he drew her back down beside him. "It's not settled," he said. "My word is my bond, Angeline. I made a deal with your father, and I intend to keep it."

Her heart sank. "You're right," she said. "I don't know what I was thinking." She peered up at him through eyes heavy with unshed tears. "Forgive me for trying to shirk my responsibilities. I was wrong."

Nicolas covered her hand with his. "We'll make the best of this, you and I. In time we'll get used to the arrangement. Who knows, maybe even fall in love someday, eh?"

"Yes." Angeline tried to smile. "I suppose after bringing you all this way, the least I can do is ask you to supper."

"Are you cooking?"

When she nodded, he broke into a grin. "One thing I won't have to get used to is your cooking, Angeline."

He stood and offered her a hand to pull her to her feet. Angeline saw Ernest drop his ax and head toward them.

"What will we tell Papa?" she asked.

Nicolas shrugged and stepped over a bunch of buttercups someone left in the path. "We'll tell him I had an urge to visit my intended."

Intended. She tried not to cringe as she gathered the still fresh blossoms in her hand and brought them home to place in water.

Staring at the pink flowers, she realized she must *do* something. Yes, she decided, she would speak to Papa and reason with him. It had to work—it just had to.

Angeline planned her speech as she walked alongside Nicolas to the house. Tonight, after Nicolas was settled upstairs with the boys and Mama busied herself with putting the babies to sleep, she would corner Papa and try to reason with him. The prospect of speaking to her intimidating father on this subject frightened her so badly she could hardly swallow.

The evening dragged on until Angeline thought the men would never stop talking about politics, the weather, and fishing. When the time finally came and she found herself alone with Papa, however, the speech she'd practiced in her mind went out the window.

Her father sat at the kitchen table, his spectacles on the end of his nose and his Bible spread out before him. Lips moving as he read, his dark eyes scanned the twenty-fifth chapter of the Psalms while his index finger kept his place.

Instead of using rational words, she began by pleading. "Papa, please don't make me marry Nicolas. I don't love him," she blurted out.

Papa looked up at her over the top of his spectacles, then slowly took them off and placed them on the open Bible. "What did you say?"

Angeline sank down beside him and placed her hand on his knee. "Papa, Nicolas is a fine man, but I don't love him. I can't marry him."

"You can and you will, Angie." His words were hard, but the look in his eyes was soft. "Baby girl, I don't know what I'm gonna do with you."

"What do you mean? I'm a big help to Mama, and with another baby on the way, she's going to need even more things done. Why, I could take over for all her chores, even the garden, and she wouldn't have to do a thing." She paused to take a breath. "I'll earn my keep, Papa, I promise."

Papa looked away, and when his gaze returned to her, there were tears in his eyes. He placed his hand on her head and smoothed back her hair. In the lamplight, she thought she saw his lip tremble.

"Angie, you don't have to talk me into keeping you close to home. If I could, I'd keep every one of my girls right here under my roof until I go meet Jesus—my boys, too."

"Is she complaining about marrying Nicolas again?"

Angeline looked up to see Mathilde standing silhouetted in the doorway. "Really, Angie, I don't see what you have to nag about. The man's quite a catch."

Papa slammed his fist on the table. "There, you see. Your sister understands. Why don't you?"

"Because I don't love him," she said as tears began to fall in earnest. She turned to glare at Mathilde. "Please, Papa, if Mathilde thinks Nicolas is such a catch, let *her* marry him. Sell her off like a load of furs instead of me."

"Don't be ridiculous," Papa said as he jammed his spectacles back onto his face. "You're the eldest, the plans are made, and that's final. Come June tenth, you'll marry Nicolas Arceneaux, and that's final."

Angeline fled to her darkened room and flung herself on the bed. She should have known the cause was a hopeless one. Obviously, God intended for her to forget she ever knew Jefferson Villare. Well, He would just have to show her how, because she certainly had no idea how to begin.

"Angie?"

She inclined her head toward Amalie's voice. "Yes, honey."

The bedsprings protested with a loud squeak as Amalie climbed up beside her. "What's wrong?" the little girl whispered. "Are you crying?"

"I suppose a little."

Amalie snuggled next to her and wrapped her arm around her middle. "Don't cry," she said softly. "I'll give you a present if you'll stop."

"A present?" Angeline sniffed and dried her eyes on the pillowcase. "Oh, honey, you don't have to give me a present."

She felt Amalie move off the bed and then return. "I think this was supposed to be yours anyway," she said as she placed something round in Angeline's hand.

Angeline fumbled for the light. "What do you have here?"

Opening her palm, she saw a gold ring with a brilliant ruby stone in the center of a nest of diamonds. It was exquisite and definitely expensive.

"Where in the world did you get this?"

"I think it fell out of Dr. Jeff's pocket," Amalie said, her face all innocence.

"Dr. Jeff? When did you see Dr. Jeff, and why do you think this fell out of his pocket?"

Chapter 21

Jeff stood in the circle of light illuminating his childhood bedroom. All his possessions, what little he chose to take, were packed into two suitcases and waiting in the hall downstairs. It would be several hours until the daybreak train for New York arrived, but he'd been up all night packing and saw no need for sleep now.

Better to get this over with, he decided. Shutting the door on his memories, he walked down to Pop's study and took out a sheaf of writing paper from the drawer. With a heavy heart, he penned a note to Mrs. Mike telling her to close the house and leave all Pop's things as they were. Maybe someday he would return. In the meantime, she could continue to draw her pay and have use of her rooms in the house.

It was the least he could do, considering the woman's faithful service to the Villare family. Family. He let out a wry laugh. He had no family. He was it, the last of a long line of Villares, and when the train left for New York, the line would end.

Angeline had made her choice, and with that choice his time in Latagnier had ended, as well. What good was a bayou doctor with a broken heart? No, it was better to keep away from the complicated matter of doctoring real live people and go about the business of dealing only with test tubes and microscopes.

Shouldering his bags, Jeff took one last look around, then resolutely turned and walked out into the night. Tomorrow he would be so far away from the bayou that the memories could not find him.

No, that's not right. They will always give chase. Maybe someday I'll let them catch me.

~

Angeline dressed at first light and stole away from the house before anyone could miss her. Rather than risk Papa's missing one of the boats, she set out walking toward town. By the time she arrived on Jefferson's doorstep, she was exhausted.

Worse than her sore feet was her aching heart. Amalie's story of an excited Jefferson heading down the path toward the bayou kept her awake most of the night. There could be only one reason why she never saw him yesterday. He had seen her first.

Her and Nicolas.

She summoned all her strength and pushed on the buzzer. A moment later, Mrs. Mike answered the door.

"Well, well, Miss Angeline," she said with a smile. "Welcome, child. Come on in."

Angeline followed the housekeeper inside. The big house felt as quiet as a tomb. Inside her skirt pocket, the ring rested.

"I came to see Jefferson. Is he here?"

"I'm sorry," Mrs. Mike said slowly. "He left this morning."

"Left?"

Her look of pity spoke volumes. "Yes, he's off to New York and that fancy new job of his. Didn't you know?"

Angeline squared her shoulders and forced back the tears as she reached into her pocket and produced the ring. "He left this at my house. Could you see that he gets it?"

She fled before Mrs. Mike could answer. With every step she took toward home, she said a prayer that God would allow her to be the wife she should be. As she prayed, however, she also cried.

To her surprise, she returned home that afternoon to find Mathilde sitting behind Papa's shed in the same state. "What's wrong, Matty?"

Mathilde looked up, surprised. "Nothing," she said as she looked away. "Everything. Oh, it's just more than I can bear."

Angeline sank down beside her and leaned her back against the rough cypress boards of the shed. Pulling her knees to her chest, she wrapped her arms around her legs and closed her eyes. "All right, Sis. Tell me everything."

When Mathilde finished, Angeline looked up at her. "Does he feel the same way?"

"Yes," she said softly. "I'm so sorry, Angie."

Angeline patted her sister's knee. "Don't be sorry," she said with a smile. "This just might be the very thing God meant to happen."

Mathilde swiped at her tears with the back of her hand. "Do you think so?"

"Yes, I think so. Now get up and dry your eyes. We've got some work to do." She reached for her sister's hand and pulled her to a standing position. "I've got a plan, but in order for it to work, we have to tell Ernest. Are you willing to do that?"

~

June 10 dawned bright, and as the little church began to fill with people, Angeline stood in the pastor's study along with Mama and Mathilde.

A bouquet of pink roses from Tante Flo's garden lay tied with a white ribbon atop her great-grandmother Breaux's Bible. Her veil, sewn with love by Mathilde and Amalie, sat beside the Bible. Angeline lifted the flowers to smell their fragrant blossoms.

"Are you nervous, bebe?" Mama asked as she toyed with the edge of Angeline's white veil.

"Just the usual wedding day jitters." She took the veil from Mama and set it atop her head. The layers of beaded satin and tulle were so thick, she could barely see through them. "I'll be fine as soon as the ceremony is over."

"Yes, you will," Mama said. She turned to face Mathilde. "You look more nervous than your sister."

"Don't be silly, Mama," she said.

"Here, Angeline," Mama said. "Let me pin your veil in better, bebe. It's all crooked. My goodness, this thing is heavy. Why'd you use such thick fabric, eh? You are gonna stumble down the aisle, blind as a bat, with all this stuff over your face."

"It'll be fine, Mama," Angeline said.

Mama fluffed the veil back into place. "Now that's better."

"Shouldn't you go sit down, Mama?" Mathilde asked.

"That's right," Angeline added. "It's nearly time."

Mama stared at both of them for a long moment. "You two, you're not up to something funny, are you?"

It was all Angeline could do not to giggle when her gaze met Mathilde's. "No, Mama," they said in unison.

"Angie, your papa would never forgive you if you ran off on your wedding day, you know that, eh? And besides, the Lord decides who you're gonna marry, and that's that."

"I'm not running off, Mama, I promise, and I know God's in control. Relax."

"Well then, I suppose I'll go join Papa. It's almost time for the service to start." She gave Angeline a sideways glance. "Sure is strange you wanting to walk down the aisle without your papa holding your arm."

Angeline smiled and patted her mother's hand. "Mama, I told you I wanted to see you and Papa waiting down front together. Besides, don't you think Ernest can handle the job of walking his sister down the aisle?"

Mama sighed and bustled out of the small room. Mathilde closed the door and set the lock. "Are you ready?"

"As ready as I will ever be," Angeline said.

A few minutes later, Ernest knocked on the door. "Rev. Dautrive says to fetch you. It's time."

"Just a minute," Mathilde called. She whirled around to gather Angeline into an embrace. "You can't do this," she whispered. "I can't let you."

Angeline held her sister at arm's length. "Have you changed your mind?"

"No."

"Then there's nothing to talk about. Let's go."

When Angeline and Mathilde walked out together ten minutes later, Ernest whistled low. "You're a beautiful bride. Nicolas is going to be pleased."

"I just hope Papa is," Angeline said softly.

~

Jeff urged the conductor to hurry, fairly flying down the steps before they were securely on the ground at the station. The train had been delayed in Shreveport and again in New Iberia, and the result was that he'd arrived in Latagnier a full six hours later than he'd planned.

Even if he'd been on time, he was probably too late. Still, he had to try.

"Hold up there, young man!" the conductor called. "You didn't get your bags."

"I'll be back for them later!" he cried as he raced away toward the center of town and the little church where a wedding should have started ten minutes ago.

A dark Model A that looked suspiciously like Pop's pulled to the curb beside the train station. "Mr. Jeff!"

"Mrs. Mike?" He leaned into the open window. "What are you doing here?"

"You think you can come back here and me not find out? I'm getting you to the church on time—well, almost on time." She motioned for him to open the door. "Now get in and hang on."

When he complied, she handed him an envelope with his name on it. "What's this?"

"Miss Angeline brought it the day you left." She smiled. "God and I have been talking about when you planned to give it back to her."

Jeff opened the envelope to see his mother's ring. "How did she get it?"

Mrs. Mike shrugged and checked her watch. "I don't suppose you have time to ask her that right now." She pulled next to the curb in front of the church. "Now get on inside and stop that wedding."

"Yes, ma'am." Jeff gave her a mock salute and tucked the ring inside his vest pocket.

"This time make sure it stays in that pocket until you put it on her finger."

"Will do," he called as he took the brick steps two at a time and pushed hard on the church's ancient cypress front doors.

He could hear Rev. Dautrive, but the words he said were not clear. As long as he wasn't pronouncing someone man and wife, he still had time.

At the altar were the bride and groom, the preacher positioned between them. The Acadian held Angeline's hands in his.

"Wait, stop the wedding!" he said as the doors slammed behind him. "Stop, Angeline. You can't marry him. I love you, and I want to stay here in Latagnier and take Doc up on his offer of a partnership."

"Well now, this is highly irregular," the reverend said. "Jeff, do sit down and let me finish this ceremony."

"I can't do that, Reverend." His gaze sought and found Theophile Breaux. "Sir, I have loved your daughter for as long as I can remember. I had to get all the way to New York City to realize I couldn't live without her."

Theophile opened his mouth to say something, but Clothilde put a hand on his arm and shook her head.

"If you would allow me her hand in marriage, I promise you I will never take her away from Latagnier."

An eternity passed before Theophile spoke. "Nicolas Arceneaux, what say you on this?"

"I say I want this bride for my own, sir." He gathered her to his side.

"You have your answer, son." Theophile returned to his seat. "Go on, Reverend, and marry up those two."

No, Lord, please don't let this happen. You showed me I had to come back for her; now show me Your favor and allow me to marry her.

Reverend Dautrive nodded toward Theophile, then cleared his throat. "Dearly beloved, we are gathered here—"

Desperation washed over him. Right before his eyes, he was losing the love of his life. He raced toward the altar and embraced Angeline.

"Angeline, no! Don't marry him. Marry me."

"Yes, I'll marry you."

The words came from the back of the church. A gasp went up in the crowd as Jeff looked over his shoulder to see Angeline standing behind the last row of pews.

"But if you're there, then. . ." Jeff lifted the veil of the bride to reveal Mathilde standing there. Out of the corner of his eye, he saw Angeline rushing toward him. He met her halfway and collected her into his arms.

"I missed you," he whispered. "Will you really marry me?"

She snuggled her head against the crook of his neck and leaned into his embrace. "I will."

"What in the world is going on?" Theophile shouted. "What do you girls mean by switching places?" He turned to Mama. "Did you know about this?"

Mama shook her head. "No, not this time."

"I love him, Papa," Mathilde said as she linked arms with Nicolas. "And he loves me."

"I fell in love with her the first time I saw her, but I didn't know she felt the same way." Nicolas stepped forward. "I didn't want to marry her like this, but it seemed like the only way."

"But the license," Papa sputtered. "He was supposed to marry Angie, not you."

"We got one, sir," Nicolas said. "I promise it's all legal."

"And you?" Papa whirled around to stare at Jeff. "You got a license, too?"

Jeff smiled. "Not yet, but I have a ring." He produced the ring from his pocket. "If she'll marry me today, we'll get the license tomorrow, I promise."

"Can you do that?" Papa asked the preacher.

Rev. Dautrive pondered the issue a moment. "I suppose I could, but no honeymoon until it's legal, eh?"

"You can be sure of that." Papa stood once more and glared at Jeff. "Not only is the Lord watching you, but so is her papa, and you don't want to tangle with either of us, you hear?"

"Yes, sir," Jeff said as he walked up the aisle with Angeline at his side. "And I promise I won't disappoint you or Him." He leaned toward Angeline and kissed her soundly. "And I won't disappoint you either. Je t'aime, ma chère."

"I love you, too," she said as she looked past him to Mama and smiled.

Author's Note

Every Louisiana cook has his or her own recipe for gumbo. Often these recipes have no definitive measuring involved but rather go by sight, taste, and experience. While I have attempted to offer a "real" recipe, this is by no means the only way to make authentic Louisiana shrimp gumbo.

Angeline Breaux's Shrimp Gumbo

1 cup vegetable oil
1 cup flour
1–2 cups chopped onions
1 tablespoon garlic powder
1–2 teaspoons celery salt
8 cups water
1–2 pounds shrimp, peeled and headed
¼ cup chopped green onions
Salt and pepper to taste

Combine flour and oil in large pot, preferably cast iron. Cook over medium heat, stirring constantly for 20 to 30 minutes until mixture is dark brown. Add 1–2 cups chopped onions and seasonings and cook, stirring occasionally for 10 to 15 minutes until onions are soft. Add 8 cups water to mixture and blend. Simmer uncovered for 1 to 2 hours, stirring occasionally. Add shrimp and cook for an additional 15 minutes. Stir in green onions and cook for 2 to 3 minutes. Serve over rice.

BAYOU SECRETS

Dedication

To Sharen Watson, who blesses me beyond measure
and gives me and so many others words for the journey.
Wherever your travels take you, may you always find blessings there—
and an endless source of words for your own journey.

Chapter 1

New Iberia, Louisiana, Friday, April 7, 1933

Behind the cash register, absentmindedly toying with the locket at her neck stood Genevieve Lamont Gallier. Not that anyone called her by that name. Genevieve Lamont had served her well for most of her twenty years, and she saw no reason to turn from it now.

In a few minutes, the doors of the five-and-dime would be thrown open, and her workday would officially begin. Unlike the other employees who slipped in the back in time to see customers coming in the front, Gen arrived early. Those precious few moments of quiet before the store opened were what made her day bearable.

Thank You, Lord, for Your provision and mercy. May I be Your hands and feet today, and may my mouth speak only what is pleasing to You, even when my irritation gets the better of me.

She looked up at the main source of her irritation, her boss, Lester Bonfils, currently perched on a stool at the ice-cream counter. Dorothy Barnes, the soda fountain's usual operator, had wisely waited until the last moment to take her place behind the counter. Currently, the young woman was studiously cleaning soda glasses on the farthest end of the area.

While Gen watched, Lester sopped up the remains of a plate of scrambled eggs with a triangle of buttered toast, then stuffed the entire thing in his mouth. When he wiped his mouth with his shirttail, Gen looked away. The man was a good fifteen years older than she—thirty-five, at least—with a belly the size of Mother's prizewinning watermelon, yet he strutted around the five-and-dime like a banty rooster in a henhouse. In recent weeks, Gen had become Lester's favorite hen, and only the most adamant of refusals had kept the lecherous storekeeper at bay.

Lester strolled past the register, twirling his keys and sucking the last taste of his breakfast off his fingers. He caught her staring and winked. Gen refused to react. She'd learned early on that anger piqued Lester's interest just as much as a sweet smile.

Sorry, Father. Where was I? Oh yes, make me a better person today, Father. I know I've got a long way to go, but if You don't mind, could You fix me up so's You're happy with the result? Mother, she isn't much pleased with me, and Big Mama, well, she doesn't say much one way or the other. Take care of them, Lord, and watch over my precious one. I give this day to You. All I ask is that You help me through it. Oh, and if You don't mind, make it go by fast, what with today being Friday and all.

"You praying again, girl?"

Gen swung her gaze to meet Lester's stare. Rather than respond, she turned to straighten the stack of receipts beneath the counter.

"You see that clock on the wall over there?"

"Yes, sir," she said without looking up.

"What does it say?"

Gen blinked and narrowed her eyes. Seeing things at a distance had always been a problem. Mother said she ought to get some glasses, but thus far Gen had managed just fine without them. Thankfully, the hands on the store clock were black and the numbers large.

"It says nine o'clock straight up, sir."

"That it does." Lester gave the keys one last toss. "And you know what that means, Miss Lamont?"

"The store is open for business."

"That's right." He stabbed the key into the lock and gave it a turn. "Business, Miss Lamont, not prayer. This ain't a church. Well, good morning, Rev. Brunson, Mrs. Brunson," he said as he stepped back to let the parson enter.

Did I say "amen," Father? 'Cause I've already forgotten if I did, but then, I've been a mite forgetful ever since. . . Well, You know, and that's what counts. And just in case I didn't, amen.

Lunch came and went, but Gen skipped hers so she could finish work a half hour early. Lester didn't much care for the girls trading shifts and working each other's lunches, but he rarely noticed.

Her roommate, Betty, slipped into Gen's spot behind the cash register. "You be sure and tell your mama I've been praying for her."

"I will," Gen said. *Or rather, I'll try. Not that Mother's generally willing to stay in the same room with me anymore.*

Betty gave her a hug, then pressed something into Gen's palm. She opened her hand to find a folded five-dollar bill.

"Oh, honey, no," she said as she thrust the money back at Betty. "That's a fortune. I can't take this. Absolutely not."

"I don't see how you have a choice, Genevieve Lamont. I've gone and handed it to you, and I don't plan to take it back." She feigned irritation. "Now are you going to stand there and tell me you don't need that?"

Gen tried to think of a reason. Unfortunately, Betty knew too much to believe any of them. She'd seen Gen patch her two good dresses and go without lunch to put away bus money and a little bit extra to take back home to the bayou.

At least Betty didn't know the full extent of what awaited Gen back in Latagnier.

Eyes misting with tears, Gen offered a heartfelt thanks, then slipped out the door and headed back to the little room at the boardinghouse where her packed suitcase sat on the narrow bed nearest the wall. Every Friday, she dreaded getting on the bus, and every Sunday afternoon, she felt the same about returning to the city.

Was it possible to be torn between two worlds?

She trudged up the two flights of stairs to the third-floor room she now called home and threw open the door. Trying not to think, Gen changed into her traveling dress and comfortable shoes, then snatched up her bag. She counted her money—just enough to buy a bus ticket and a few things for the folks back home—and gave thanks that the Lord had seen fit to provide her with a job. So many people were out of work nowadays, and she did not take the blessing of a job lightly.

She leaned against the wall and slipped Betty's five-dollar bill into her shoe. *Thank You, Lord. And just when I thought Mother would have to do without her medicines. . .Well, Your timing is always perfect.*

At the door, she turned to cast a glance at the sparsely furnished room and sighed. Who would have believed her life had come to this? She might be a month shy of twenty-one, but in her heart she'd become an old woman.

It was the secret she carried that aged her so—leastwise that's what Big Mama claimed. That and the choices she'd made.

Actually, one choice.

Glancing at the nightstand, Gen noticed she'd forgotten her Bible. In four steps, she crossed the room to retrieve her lifeline to the Lord and placed it atop her things in the suitcase.

As she turned quickly, she caught sight of herself in the mirror. Even though the mirror was cloudy and cracked with age, there was no denying what it told her.

She stepped closer and peered at the image that blinked back. Gen didn't need glasses to know the woman in the mirror was not the same person who had stepped off the bus from Latagnier two months ago.

I don't even recognize myself.

At the bottom of the stairs, Gen stopped and touched the locket at her neck, a habit that served to remind her of who she was and what she'd left behind. A moment later, she set off down the sidewalk toward the bus station. The clock on the town square read twenty minutes after five, plenty of time to make a detour before the 5:40 bus left.

She crossed the street and veered into Mulotte's Grocery. Mother always did like lemon sours. *Maybe this time she'll accept them.*

Last time she'd offered a gift, her mother had thrown it out the upstairs window.

A little time had passed, nigh on two weeks since she'd seen her. Maybe the woman had settled her anger a bit, possibly reconsidered her decision to cut her only daughter out of her life.

Or maybe she would take her locked-up feelings to the grave. There was no telling with Mother.

Gen tossed the bag of sours into the little basket and moved farther down the aisle. A few cans of evaporated milk and a container of oatmeal with the extra bonus of a free drinking glass inside went in after them, and her money was almost spent. She got all the way to the end of the aisle and turned back up the next before she found the treat Big Mama loved so well: a package of freshly made pork cracklings. And they were on sale.

"She'll fuss, but I'm buying them anyway."

"Who will fuss?"

Turning toward the sound, Gen let the cracklings fall. The tall gentleman snagged the bag and settled it atop her other purchases. As he moved nearer, a familiar face appeared. The fellow must be one of the Breaux boys. He certainly had that look about him.

Funny. For the life of her she couldn't place which one.

"Remember me?"

Uh-oh. "Sure," she said as she pressed past him to head for the cash register. "You're a Breaux from Latagnier, right?"

"Yes, ma'am, I am." He caught up and thrust his hand toward her. "Ernest Breaux, Miss Lamont. I'm the eldest of the bunch."

The eldest. No wonder she didn't remember him by name. By the time she arrived at the little Latagnier schoolhouse on the edge of the Bayou Nouvelle, Ernest had already finished his education.

"I'm really sorry," she said as she pried her hand loose from his grip, "but I'm in a hurry. Nice to see you again."

Not that she actually saw him that clearly. Maybe she ought to take Mother's advice and get that eye examination after all.

~

Ernest tried not to let his deflated ego show. The Lamont girl seemed to look right through him. Why, he'd been something of a man about town back in Latagnier. Maybe she liked big-city men.

Well then, she would like him for sure once she knew he'd shaken off the dust of that little bayou town and made his home right here in New Iberia. Actually, he slept in a modified storeroom with two other sawmill employees, but he'd have a real place here soon enough.

Yes, he was a city man for sure.

A city man with a car. And not just any car.

No, sir. His was a 1927 Model T roadster bought used from his boss at the sawmill after the engine went bad. The black beauty set him back almost a year's worth of salary, and the engine still wasn't what it ought to be, but every time he sat behind the wheel, he had no doubt it was worth the cost. After all, what did he have to save his money for? He was footloose and fancy-free, a single man with only himself to answer to.

Well, himself and the Lord.

"Hey, Miss Lamont, wait up."

She didn't appear to hear him. Ernest trailed her outside and looked both ways before spotting her heading east with a suitcase in one hand and a small black handbag in the other. While he watched, she crossed the street and disappeared around the corner.

Catching up to her in the roadster turned out to be easy; getting her attention, now that was another matter altogether. He idled up behind her and let the engine purr as he steered the car to the curb just ahead of her.

Ernest ran a comb through his hair and replaced his cap, then prepared himself for the attention he knew he would garner once Miss Lamont saw his means of transportation. In the rearview mirror, he saw her approach.

He checked his appearance once more and tilted his cap for a rakish effect. Pretending to study his nails, Ernest bided his time.

Any minute now, Genevieve Lamont would come strolling by. All he had to do was be patient. Just another second and. . .

What in the world? The woman in question strolled past as if he were invisible.

Well, that just wouldn't do.

"Miss Lamont, excuse me." No reaction, except to possibly pick up a little speed. He tried again. "Hello, Genevieve Lamont."

This time she slowed just a bit, then hurried toward the bus station. Ernest jumped out of the roadster to set off after her on foot, reaching the bus station door just before she reached to open it.

She looked up at him with wide eyes rimmed with thick lashes. Those eyes narrowed. "*Mr.* Breaux. If you don't mind, I have a bus to catch."

"A bus? Why take the bus when that beauty is at your disposal?"

Ernest stepped away from the door to point toward his prize possession. When he turned around to gauge Miss Lamont's reaction, she was nowhere to be found.

Chapter 2

Ernest finally found the Lamont girl at the ticket counter. She stood behind an elderly couple whose only luggage was a covered basket that contained a small yapping dog. He tipped his hat, which set the dog barking even louder.

Rather than call her name and risk not being heard, Ernest strolled over and tapped her on the shoulder. "Going my way?"

Miss Lamont gasped and dropped her suitcase, sending it crashing. When the cheap cardboard hit the floor, the latch opened and a weekend's worth of clothing spilled out.

"I'm so sorry," he said as he bent to retrieve her lost garments. "I didn't mean to scare you."

A look of horror crossed her pretty features. Ernest followed the direction of her gaze. "Oh, I, well. . ." He let the lacy item drop into her bag, then quickly stuffed the rest of the items in after it. The latch safely shut once more, Ernest jammed his fists into his pockets, his face flaming.

An eternity passed, and she still stared. Ernest looked past her to the wall where the clock's big second hand ticked off a few more seconds. Finally, he grasped at the first thought crossing his brain.

"So as I was saying, would you happen to be heading back to Latagnier today, Miss Lamont?"

At first he thought she might turn around and pretend she hadn't heard the question. She sure didn't look excited about the prospect of sharing the road with him.

"Yes, I am," she finally said as she checked the latch on her bag. "Why?"

"Because. . ." Ernest paused. Why indeed? "Well, because I am, too."

Even though he could barely wait to show Papa and the others the roadster, he had intended to put off visiting the family until he'd had a chance to work on it a bit. The Acadian beauty didn't need to know that. Besides, Mama *was* always after him to spend more time at the home place, and Papa would be tickled to watch while he worked on the big engine.

He studied her while she fidgeted and frowned. It looked as though he'd be going home alone, if he went home at all.

"That's nice of you," she said. "But really, I couldn't put you out like that. It's too much trouble."

"It's no trouble at all. Shall we?"

Ernest reached for her suitcase, then attempted to link arms with Miss Lamont. Turned out the girl was faster than she looked. Somehow she managed to grab her bag and skedaddle away before he could blink twice.

Ernest watched her tromp back into the line, which had now grown by two middle-aged women, three badly behaved young'uns, and a rapscallion of a man who gave Miss Lamont a look that should have earned him a slap.

When the fellow turned around and began to say something to her, Ernest knew he must take action. After all, how could a gentleman like himself possibly allow a sweet young thing like Genevieve Lamont to board a bus where her virtue might be in peril? He reached her side in time to hear the man in question lean far too close and inquire as to whether Genevieve "had a man back home."

The look on her face sent Ernest into action. The way he figured it, he could either deck the cad or rescue the damsel in distress. He didn't have to think too long on that choice.

"Well, there you are, honey pie," Ernest said. "I was wondering where you got off to." He looked straight into the man's eyes and gave him a stare that would wither a cactus. "Excuse us, won't you?"

This time, he led her out of the bus station without protest. At the curb, she stopped short and wrestled her elbow from his grip. Ernest glanced back to see if the fellow had followed them.

It might not do to draw blood in front of such a delicate creature, but Ernest knew he could take the chap if he had to. After all, a gentleman always protected his lady.

His lady? Well, not quite, although with a little encouragement, he could probably warm to the idea. After all, she was a looker, pretty as a newborn calf and sweeter than his mama's chocolate pecan pie. She was a mite younger than him, but it wasn't like he intended to marry her—or anyone else, for that matter.

"I can take care of myself, you know."

What?

"Yes, well," Ernest said slowly, "I suppose you probably can." Out of the corner of his eye, he saw the rogue watching them through the plate-glass window. "So why don't I just leave you and that dandy in there be and head on back to Latagnier by myself? I'm sure the two of you can find plenty to talk about on that long ride."

Ernest straightened his cap and waited for her to protest. Instead, the woman had the audacity to look less than pleased at his gallantry.

That did it.

If Genevieve Lamont wanted to ride a hot, dusty bus back to Latagnier with that fellow, then she was welcome to it. After all, there were a half dozen other girls who would like to go for a ride in the roadster.

Well, one or two that he knew of, anyway.

"Miss Lamont, it's been a real pleasure." He gave his cap one more adjustment, then turned to face the irritating woman. "Give your mama my best, and tell your papa I aim to come by and see him soon. I always did intend to find out how he managed to catch three times the fish with the same worms I use."

Head held high, he turned and closed the distance to his car, then lifted his leg over and jumped inside. Before he could crank the engine, Genevieve Lamont caught his attention. In a swirl of skirts, she crossed the road and headed in his direction.

Ernest swiveled to face her, trying hard not to smile. "Change your mind?"

She arrived at the car, face flushed. Her dark eyes peered down at him, her expression surprisingly intense. "Did you know my daddy?"

"Sure." He shrugged. "My brothers and I went fishing with him and my papa off and on all through my growing-up years. Some of my best stories about the one that got away came from him." Ernest gave her a sideways look. "Why?"

Small fingers with perfectly shaped nails drummed a furious rhythm against the door. If it were anyone else touching the roadster, Ernest would have had a fit. Somehow he didn't mind quite so much when the hand in question belonged to such a pretty thing.

" 'Cause I wonder why you would bring him up now," she said. "How long have you been gone from Latagnier?"

"Guess I've been on my own near to four years and worked at the sawmill the last three of those. I try to visit regular, but I haven't seen the folks since Christmas. Been busy trying to get this motorcar running right."

"So you haven't been to Latagnier in nearly three months?"

He shook his head. "No. Why do you ask?"

"I just wondered, that's all." She looked away and seemed to be thinking hard on something. When she turned her attention back to him, she looked almost sad. "Did he ever mention me—my daddy, I mean?"

"I don't know. Guess I didn't pay much attention." He shrugged. "He and Papa did all the jawing. The boys and I just fished." A thought occurred. "You know, the last time we all went out in the pirogue, he did say something about you."

Her interest was piqued. "What did he say?"

"Well now, let me think." Ernest let that memory play out in his head before he relayed it to the Lamont woman. "Must have been nigh on a year ago. We were fishing in the Fourth of July Chamber of Commerce Fishing Rodeo over in Nouvelle. I took off from work so Papa and your daddy and I could fish together. When Mr. Lamont reeled that big old fish up, I specifically recall him saying how he sure wished his little girl was there to see what he caught."

She looked surprised. "Are you sure about that? Did he mention me by name?"

"Well, no, but do you have a sister?"

Miss Lamont shook her head. "I'm an only child."

"Then he was talking about you."

"But why?"

What a strange woman. "I don't know. It was a record setter, for sure. Maybe he hated it that you missed him winning that five-dollar prize."

"Is that all he said?"

Ernest tried to think, but the memory was fuzzy. "I believe so. He might have said more, but I couldn't say for sure."

Before he could blink, Genevieve Lamont sat beside him, the beat-up cardboard suitcase balanced on her knees. She opened the latch and pulled out a red scarf, then tied it around her hair. That accomplished, she stared straight ahead, saying nothing.

He gripped the steering wheel and tried to make sense of the woman seated beside him. It didn't take him long to figure out that not much about her made sense.

"Guess that means we're leaving now," he said.

"Guess so." She held tightly to the suitcase and continued to look through the windshield rather than at him.

"Guess so," Ernest repeated as he cranked the engine and slipped the roadster into gear.

They drove four miles in silence, then another half mile with Ernest whistling. Then he heard it; a *ping* where there should have been a purr. At the curve on Bayou Road, Ernest pulled over under the limbs of an oak tree.

As the motor fell silent, Genevieve Lamont finally turned to look at him, eyes wide. "What's wrong?"

"Probably nothing. I just don't like how she's sounding." Ernest straightened his cap and leapt out of the roadster. "You sit tight. I won't be a minute."

He lifted the hood and tinkered with a wire that looked loose. Satisfied, he slammed the hood shut and slipped behind the wheel. The roadster roared to life, and Ernest threw it into gear.

"You like to work on cars."

It was a statement rather than a question, and it took Ernest by surprise. He glanced over at Miss Lamont, who now sat with her hands in her lap and her suitcase at her feet.

"Yes."

Given the lack of conversation between them until now, Ernest figured he'd heard the last of Genevieve Lamont. After all, another half hour and they'd reach the city limits of Latagnier.

"Who taught you?"

Ernest leaned toward her, his gaze fixed on the road ahead. "Who taught me what?"

"Who taught you how to work on cars?"

"Oh." He glanced her way and caught her staring at him. "Guess I picked it up here and there. My papa's handy with things, so I grew up tinkering with this and that. When I first left home, I worked for a man who had an old tractor. He hired me to run that tractor, and I didn't get paid 'less'n I got my work done. When the tractor wouldn't go, I didn't eat. Didn't take me long to figure out how to keep that old John Deere running so my belly wouldn't be empty."

She had the nicest laugh. It struck him that they'd been in each other's company almost an hour, counting Mulotte's Grocery and the bus station, and this was the first time he'd heard it. *I wonder what makes her so sad.*

Up ahead, the familiar landmark indicating the entrance into Latagnier loomed. Ernest let off the gas and slowed the roadster a bit. No sense hurrying to get her home when she'd finally started warming up to him.

"How about you and me take a drive before I drop you at home?" He couldn't miss her stricken look. "Or I could come by later on. I bet your daddy would love to take a spin in this little beauty."

"Thank you, but no. Mother's not herself." She met his gaze, and he could have sworn her lower lip trembled a bit. "And Daddy died New Year's Day."

Ernest pressed the accelerator and gripped the wheel. "I'm sorry" was all he could come up with. How had he been gone so long from home that he'd missed hearing about Mr. Lamont's death? And what else had he missed? Maybe he should have read Mama's letters more closely instead of scanning the first line or two and then putting them away.

"Just drop me off up there," she said.

His gaze followed the direction in which she pointed. "But that's nearly a quarter mile from your house, Miss Lamont. I don't believe you need to walk that far." He eased the car into a right-hand turn and started up the long driveway to the Lamont homestead. "I'll just head on toward the house and—"

"No!"

Ernest stomped on the brake pedal and nearly sent both of them through the windshield. When the roadster's tires ground to a halt, he shifted into neutral. Before he could say anything, the Lamont woman had her suitcase and her feet on the ground.

"Thank you so much for the ride. Please give my best to your mama and papa." She set off toward the white frame house in the distance, the tail of her red scarf lifting and falling as the breeze crossed her path.

For a moment, Ernest thought of following her and insisting he deposit her on her doorstep like a gentleman should do. She wouldn't let him; that much he knew. So he backed the roadster out of the driveway and drove up a few feet, then killed the engine.

He knew the Lamont woman could not see him or the car for the thick trees. Ernest climbed out and began to follow her on foot, dodging from the cover of a stand of oaks to the privacy of the thick weeds that choked out what looked like it had once been a garden. Three mosquito bites and one encounter with a spiderweb later, he'd just about given up shadowing the girl.

Then she did the strangest thing. Rather than turn right toward the towering two-story home, she made a sharp left and headed out toward the bayou. Ernest inched forward. *Wonder where she's going.*

Another few feet and he could see her again. Unfortunately, his next step landed him knee deep in bayou mud.

As he yanked his foot out, then dug for his shoe, he decided to head home rather than keep to his task. Where the woman went was none of his business. Besides, nothing went on in Latagnier that was a secret.

If Genevieve Lamont was up to something, sooner or later he would hear about it.

Chapter 3

Genevieve rounded the corner, then stopped and listened as the motorcar's engine roared to life and then faded into silence. She knew Ernest had been following her. How could she miss him? A head taller than most bayou boys, the lanky fellow stood out like a sore thumb among the trees and brush lining the driveway.

She smiled despite her irritation. It was nice of him to be concerned. Obviously Ernest's mama had raised him to be a gentleman.

Still, it wouldn't do for him to find her here.

Before she knocked, Gen took a second to compose herself. If Big Mama had the slightest inkling that she was tired or hungry, she'd be bundled off to a hot bath, then fed gumbo until she couldn't move.

Not that either of those things wouldn't be heavenly.

"Genevieve, is that you, hon?"

Gen forced the corners of her mouth into a smile and climbed the steps to pull open the screen door. Big Mama met her, took the suitcase, and set it down. Welcoming arms enveloped Gen in a hug.

"Honey, if you're not a sight for sore eyes." She stepped back and put her hands on ample hips. "What you doin' home so early? That bus ain't s'posed to be here for another half hour."

"How is she?" Gen ducked around Big Mama and headed for the back room. "It seems like forever and a day, and I can't hardly stand it."

"Shush now, she's as fine and pretty as ever, but I'd appreciate you letting her sleep just a touch longer before you go waking her up." She touched Gen's arm. "Now answer my question, Genny-girl. How you got home so fast from town?"

Gen reached for her suitcase. "I didn't ride the bus," she said as she opened the latch and reached for the bag from Mulotte's. "I brought you something."

"Who you rode with? Was it a man?"

"Look," Gen said, "cracklings. Your favorite."

Big Mama stared at the bag in Gen's hand, then looked directly at Gen. "Don't you try and change the subject, Genny-girl. I asked you a question, and I'll have your hide if'n you don't answer me."

Setting the bag on the table, Gen shrugged. "It was nobody."

"That nobody got a name, or did his mama just name him Nobody cause she thought it was purty?"

Gen pulled one of the mismatched wooden chairs away from the table and sat down. "No," she finally said. "His name is Ernest, Ernest Breaux." She narrowed her eyes and shook her finger at Big Mama. "And don't you dare start making something of nothing. Ernest and I happened to run into each other at the corner grocery. He saw me later at the bus station and offered me a ride. He was going home anyway, so it's not like he made a special trip. I think he was keen on showing his papa his new black motorcar. It's a beauty."

Big Mama stared a moment longer, then settled across the table from Gen. "My, my, now that was a lot of words just to say you rode with the neighbors' boy."

"Well then," Gen said, "let's just start over." She paused to remove her scarf and set it on the table. "Big Mama, I rode home with Ernest Breaux. You know him. He's the neighbors' boy."

They stared across the table in silence. Gen folded the scarf into a neat triangle, all the while searching her thoughts for something else to say, something to change the conversation from the direction it was going. At this rate Big Mama would have her and Ernest married before summer—in her mind, anyway.

Before Gen could come up with another topic, Big Mama began to giggle. Her giggle turned into a laugh, and before long, Gen couldn't help but join her.

"You always was a sassy thing," Big Mama said.

"I got it from you," Gen replied.

"You did not. You got it all by yourself. Couldn't nobody tell you nothing. Still can't." Big Mama stretched out a dark, gnarled hand, and Gen grasped it. "Genny-girl, I don't know what to do with you sometimes."

Gen entwined her fingers with the larger ones belonging to the woman who helped raise her. "Just love me," she said. "That's about all anyone can do."

Once again Big Mama chuckled. "You're easy to love, hon."

"Not everyone thinks so." Gen released Big Mama's hand and sat back, curling her arms around her middle. "How is she?"

"Your mama's 'bout as well as can be expected." She paused to worry the corner of her apron. "I 'spect she won't ever get over losing your papa."

"I suppose so." Gen slipped off her right shoe and let the folded bill drop onto the table. "Look what I've got," she said.

Big Mama unfolded the bill. "Five dollars. Where'd you get that kind of money?"

"Betty. She gave it to me and wouldn't take no for an answer when I tried to give it back."

"Well now," Big Mama said, "looks like the Lord done provided for your mama's medicines with just enough left over to make two pies."

"Two pies?"

"One for us and one for you to take to that precious Betty. The Lord done smiled on us, and we ought to thank the one who sent the smile. That's the way I see it, anyway." She leaned toward Gen. "Does she know?"

Gen shook her head. "No one does."

"Then why'd she up and give you a week's salary?"

"I think she suspects." Gen slipped her foot back into her shoe. "And she's seen my locket."

"Well, whatever the reason, praise the Lord she did it, 'cause I didn't know what I was gonna tell that druggist come Monday morning." Big Mama pressed both palms on the table and stood. "I ought to be ashamed. I've had a pot of gumbo simmering up at the big house all afternoon. I bet you're starved, and here I ain't even bothered to think about feedin' you."

"Shrimp gumbo?"

Big Mama nodded. "Yes, ma'am. You still like it, don't you?"

"Well, of course I do. Why wouldn't I?"

" 'Cause you're gettin' so skinny and citified that I don't know if my old gumbo's gonna be fit for you. You don't look like you eat nothin', Genevieve Lamont. Am I gonna have to take in your dresses again? That one there's hanging on you like a feed sack."

A familiar sound chased away any statement she might make to the contrary. "Big Mama, do you hear that?"

"I do," she said. "Sounds like a car, it does."

Gen threw open the screen door and headed around the corner to where the path led toward the driveway. Just as she cleared the thicket, she saw a motorcar approaching. A black motorcar.

"Land sakes!" Big Mama called. "Is that your young man?"

"He's not my young man," she replied. "Why don't you head on up to the house and heat the rice while I see what he wants?"

Thankfully, Big Mama did not argue. She did cast a long look down the driveway before disappearing into the big house.

As the car ground to a stop a few feet away, Gen tried to think of the best way to get rid of its owner. Saying nothing on the ride home hadn't dampened the man's enthusiasm, and she doubted him to be the type to listen to argument, either. No, the best thing to do was to act neighborly, then scoot back into the house the first chance she got.

Of course, she'd have to make sure he didn't follow her. Imagine what his reaction would be to Mother and, worse, to the situation with Big Mama, and, well. . .she just wouldn't think on it.

"Welcome back" was all she could think to say, and she tried to speak the words without too much enthusiasm. "Forget something?"

"No, but you did."

The Breaux fellow climbed out of the roadster and headed in her direction. Dangling from his outstretched hand was something small and dark.

Her purse.

It must have fallen to the floor when Ernest stopped the car. How could she have forgotten it?

You were in too big a hurry to get home, that's how.

Gen released the breath she hadn't realized she'd been holding and met him halfway. My, but he was tall—and handsome, too, if a girl were to notice things like dreamy brown eyes and coal black hair.

Too bad she didn't have the time or the interest. She might have actually thought him handsome. . .and interesting. . .and maybe even nice.

All right, so he was nice.

"Thank you," she said as she grasped the purse and clutched it to her chest. "I'm sorry you had to come all the way back out here."

Ernest shrugged. "Better I return it now than explain to my whole family how a lady's handbag ended up on the floor of my car. Even though you and I know I just offered you a ride home to be neighborly, I'd never hear the end of it." He looked past her to the house. "Everything all right, Miss Lamont?"

Gen followed his gaze and thought she saw someone step away from the upstairs window. Mother's window. No telling what he saw. Mother had taken to wearing Father's pajama's all the time, and she let her waist-length hair hang loose. Poor Ernest probably thought he saw a ghost. Not that she believed in such foolishness.

"Everything's fine," she said. The smell of shrimp gumbo hung heavy in the air, and she thought she heard the screen door groan. *Please don't let Big Mama come out and invite him to supper.*

Ernest gave her a sideways look as he straightened his cap. "You sure?"

"Of course I'm sure."

He didn't look convinced. To his credit, he offered a smile. "Well then, I'll just be going on home. My best to your mama, and if it wouldn't cause her any upset, would you offer my condolences on your papa's passing?"

"Yes, I'll do that," she said. "I'm sure she would appreciate your saying so."

"How about I come get you Sunday afternoon late, and we take the ride back to New Iberia together? Say around three or four?"

Panic struck her. The last thing she wanted was to ride the bus back to New Iberia, yet spending more time with Ernest Breaux frightened her. With a little encouragement on his part, Gen might start thinking of the handsome fellow as a friend. And after friendship, then what?

"Thank you, but no," she said.

"You sure?"

"Yes, but thank you."

"Well, all right, then." Ernest nodded and turned to climb back into the black car. As he pointed the vehicle back toward the main road, he lifted his cap and smiled. "You have a good weekend, Miss Lamont, you hear?"

"Now isn't that nice, him calling you Miss Lamont and all? Shows he's been raised up proper. But then, those Breauxs, they were always good people."

Gen turned around to see Big Mama standing in the shadows behind the screen door. "How much of that did you hear?"

"All of it," she said as she opened the door. "Now come on in here and have some supper."

Though her stomach growled, Gen shook her head. "I can't stand it any longer. You go ahead and fill the bowls," she said as she headed toward Big Mama's house.

"I will, and then I'm gonna draw you a bath, too, you hear? A good hot one with some of those sweet-smellin' salts you like so much. How does that sound?"

"Like I've died and gone to heaven, Big Mama." As soon as she said the words, Gen wished she could reel them back in. Out of the corner of her eye, she saw Mother standing in the upstairs window. "Mother, I'm sorry, I didn't mean to bring up. . .that is, what I meant was just saying that it would feel good to. . ."

Before she could find the words to finish her sentence, Mother was gone.

Gen stumbled toward Big Mama's house, tears stinging her eyes. How careless of her to mention anything about death within earshot of the house. One never knew where Mother was and what she might overhear. Big Mama said that the mention of someone passing would send Mother to bed for days.

Well, she'd gone and done it, then. Likening a hot bath to a trip to heaven. "You're an idiot, Genevieve Lamont, a complete idiot."

She sat in the last rays of the April sun, wishing, hoping, praying, and thinking. When the air began to turn cool and the chill swept past, she stood and headed inside.

Unlike the kitchen at the big house, Big Mama's was small and plain. Wooden utensils lay in a wooden bowl, and a butcher block held three knives. A bent pot with a mismatched lid sat on the counter next to a stack of fresh-cut greens. Like as not, Big Mama planned on cooking up a mess of them for lunch tomorrow.

Gen ran her hand over the scarred wooden surface of the single cabinet. How many happy childhood hours had she spent playing at Big Mama's feet in this very room? Too many to count, for sure.

She sat cross-legged in the corner and tried to remember what it had been like when Henry, Big Mama's husband, was alive. Funny, while she could remember every detail of most things, she could remember nothing of her father's foreman beyond heavy footsteps on the front porch and big muddy boots left by the screen door.

Oh, but she remembered the day he didn't come home, the day Big Mama stood at the kitchen window and watched Daddy and the sheriff come up the walk. Gen had been too little to understand words like *murder* and *lynching* back then, but she understood them now.

How Big Mama carried on was a mystery, and yet from that terrible day until now, she never failed to believe the Lord had nothing but His best for her. If only Gen could give the Lord that measure of faith.

Of course, Big Mama would say she could.

But then, Big Mama hadn't walked away from God, not even when He allowed her precious Henry to be taken in the most unjust way imaginable. It had taken much less of a calamity to cause Gen to wander from the Lord. No, she'd turned her back on everything she knew to be good and right for the love of a man.

Love.

Gen chuckled bitterly. What she thought was love turned out to be anything but, and she still bore the scars to prove it.

Inside and out.

"Why didn't You stop me?" she cried into the silence. "You knew everything that would happen and all the people who would be hurt, yet You let me do it anyway."

Bitter tears burned, and she choked them back. God hadn't abandoned her. It had been she who had done the abandoning, choosing her own way over His and Alton Gallier over whatever fellow the Lord had for her.

"Well, whoever you are, I hope you found some nice girl to take my place," she whispered. "I'm not fit for you now."

A sound, soft as the mew of a kitten, caught Gen's attention, and she smiled. In spite of her rebellious choices, the Lord had shown His forgiveness and grace in the most incredible way. Only the heavenly Father could have created such a precious blessing out of such a terrible disaster.

Gen climbed up and steadied herself on the edge of the cabinet, stealing Big Mama's dish towel to wipe her eyes.

"Coming, sweetheart," she called as she headed toward the back bedroom where Ellen Grace Gallier, her four-month-old daughter, lay awake.

Chapter 4

Ernest slowed the roadster to a crawl so as not to alert the family of his arrival. As he turned the corner and came into view of the house, he began to honk the horn. Papa spilled out of the house first, followed by twelve-year-old Amalie and the eight-year-old twins, Joseph and John.

"Quoi qui se brasse la-bas?" Papa shouted.

"What's going on? Why, I'll tell you, Papa. Come and look. Vien ici."

Mama came rounding the corner, a spade in one hand and a small bucket in the other. His sister Mathilde's son, Teddy, toddled behind her, dragging a tattered blanket in one hand and a piece of sugarcane in the other.

"Why, Ernest, is that you, bebe?" Mama called as she set her gardening equipment on the corner of the porch. "What sort of thing is that you're riding in?"

Ernest set the brake and climbed out to embrace his mother, then kiss the top of her head. "It's a roadster, Mama. A 1927 Model T roadster with a convertible top and a rumble seat." He looked up at his father. "What do you think of her, Papa?"

"Well now," Papa said slowly, "she's a beauty, eh?"

"Yeah, she's a beauty!" little sister Amalie exclaimed. "Can I learn to drive her, Ernest?"

Ernest lifted his sister in the air and whirled her around, then set her down on unsteady feet. "You're twelve years old and a girl, Amalie. What on earth do you want to learn how to drive for?"

"Oh, I don't know," she said in that dreamy way she had. "There could be any number of reasons for me to learn. What if Mama was to need something in town and Papa and the boys weren't here to go fetch it?"

"Sa fait pas rien. Then she'd just do without, cher, because no girl of mine's gonna go gallivanting about in a motorcar alone." Papa ignored Amalie's frown to run his hand over the back of the seat. "Ernest, how did you manage to pay for this contraption? It must have set you back a pretty penny."

"Not as much as you'd think," Ernest said. "I got a deal on it. My boss was about to sell it for scrap metal because the body had some dings and the motor kept going out. Well, you know how you always taught me to be handy around mechanical things?"

Papa nodded.

"I found out there's not much difference in overhauling a tractor engine and repairing one of these. Here, take a look at this." He flipped the latch and opened the hood. "Isn't that something? See, here's where the problem was."

A short while later, Papa finished his examination of the roadster and was ready for a ride. He climbed inside and settled the twins on his lap while Amalie took a spot on the rumble seat. "Come on and get in, Mama."

"Mais non." She waved them away with a shake of her hand, then lifted Teddy into her arms. "If the good Lord means me to ride around in one of those things, He'll tell me Himself. You all go ahead and enjoy yourselves, and I'll go back to my Easter lilies. Besides, the babies will be awake soon."

"Allons, Mama. Amalie will stay with the bebes. Eileen and Mary are four and three. Surely this girl can pull her nose out of her book long enough to take care of them while we go for a ride," he added, ignoring Amalie's outraged cry.

"Non, merci. You all go on," she said.

Ernest set out across the yard, circling the barn and the henhouse before turning the roadster toward town. Once he got into Latagnier, he had to pull over outside the barbershop so Papa could show his buddies the motorcar.

Of course, they all wanted to look under the hood, and most asked for a ride around the town square as well. Amalie never moved from her seat in the back, but after a few circles, the twins opted to sit and wave as the car went by. Finally, as the sun sunk below the oaks, Ernest headed the car for home.

Out of the corner of his eye, he could see his father watching his every move while holding one sleeping twin on each shoulder. The thought occurred to Ernest that if Mama and Papa hadn't elected to fill their home with young'uns, they might have had some time and money for the finer things in life.

Things like a black 1927 Model T roadster with a convertible top and a rumble seat.

Then and there, Ernest vowed that he would live his life to the fullest, never making the mistake his parents had. To be sure, he didn't mind at all the benefits of coming from a large family. There was always someone to talk to or play with when he was little and always someone to help now that he was older.

The trouble came in feeding all those mouths and seeing to their health and education. Why, they nearly lost little Amalie to the fever back in '29, and just this past winter, the whole bunch of them came down with the dreaded influenza. If his brother-in-law the doctor hadn't treated the family for free, Papa would've had to take a second job just to pay the bill.

It was too much to consider, this burden a wife and children put on a man. To his way of thinking, any blessing they might bring was not worth the cost.

From this moment on, Ernest Breaux determined he would be a confirmed bachelor, never to be called Husband or Papa. No, the roles of big brother and uncle fit him just fine. That way he could enjoy the little ones, then send them back to their mamas when they went to fussing.

To his mind, a perfect arrangement.

He made one more circle around the house, then pulled up next to the porch and took one of the twins from Papa. The little fellow opened his eyes, then closed them again and snuggled against Ernest's shirt.

"Ernest, you have a way with the babies," Mama said. "You should have a houseful, you know."

He smoothed Joseph's hair and lifted him into his mother's arms. At eight, the child's legs nearly touched the ground when Mama held him, yet he slept soundly. "No babies for me. You'll have to get your grandchildren from the others."

"Oh, you'll change your mind soon enough." Mama shifted Joseph to the other shoulder. "Just you wait and see. When you meet the right girl, well, that's all it will take. *C'est tout.*"

"It's not going to happen, Mama. Even if I do meet the right girl, I'm too old to start a family," he said as he climbed out of the roadster to join the rest of the family at the supper table. "I'm nigh on to thirty and far too set in my ways to change them now."

"You're no older than your papa was when I met him." Mama strolled past Papa and patted him on the arm. "Tell your son he's not too old to have a passel of young'uns, Theo."

Rather than respond, Papa chuckled and gave Mama a kiss on the cheek. He whispered something in Mama's ear that set her bustling off to the kitchen with a blush on her cheeks.

As Ernest settled into his spot beside Papa, he cast a glance around the table. Between siblings, nieces, and nephews, the big table was full, and another had been fashioned from a piece of wood and a barrel to hold the overflow.

He'd have to make something more suitable when he got a chance. His boss down at the sawmill had told him he could have his pick of the scrap lumber if he ever wanted to build something. Maybe now was the time to take him up on his offer. Ernest could fix a decent table and some chairs that the little ones would fit in. What with his sisters Angeline and Mathilde having babies like they were going out of style, it looked as though there would be a continual need for places to seat the children.

Little Joseph climbed off his stool at the makeshift table and tugged on Ernest's shirttail. "I wanna sit with you, Ernest."

"All right," Ernest replied as he hefted the youngster onto his left knee. "But you're not gonna get my chicken leg, you hear?"

Teddy raised a wail from his place in Mama's lap. "Me, too!" he cried. "Me sit wit Unka Ernie."

Joseph's twin, John, stood and headed Ernest's way. "If Joe's gonna sit there, I'm gonna, too."

Four-year-old Eileen and her shadow, three-year-old Mary, scrambled to join the group. "Mary and me, too," she said, speaking for her sister as she always did.

Ernest looked down at the youngest Breaux. "You, too, Mary?"

The little girl nodded. She rarely spoke. She didn't have to, as Eileen rarely left her side.

"C'est tout," Papa said. "We will all sit in our own places and leave Ernest in peace to eat his dinner, eh?" He leaned toward Ernest. "You're like the Pied Piper in that nursery rhyme, son. All the little ones, they want to follow you wherever you go, eh?"

Ernest shrugged. "I hadn't noticed."

"Well, you should. Don't think it has missed the Lord's attention, even if it missed yours."

"You're as bad as Mama," he said with a grin. "And I'll tell you what I told her. You're going to have to get your grandbabies from the others. This fellow's got plans, and they don't include bottles and diapers. *Le jeu vaut pas la chandelle.*"

"Oh, you think it's not worth it? Well, we will see, won't we? You can make all the plans you want, son, but it's the heavenly Father who decides, not you, eh?" Papa waited until the twins returned to the little table, then raised his hand to silence the chatter. "Gather your hands, and let's thank le bon Dieu for this food," he said, and then he spoke a blessing over the meal.

Thankfully, the dinner conversation stayed away from the topic of babies. Instead, Papa questioned him endlessly about the mechanics of the roadster's engine and the technique of driving the vehicle.

Finally, as Mama and the girls disappeared into the kitchen, Ernest and Papa headed for the front porch. Settling into a chair beside his father in the fading twilight, Ernest closed his eyes and thanked God for placing him here. With the crickets chirping a bayou symphony, a deep contentment settled into Ernest's bones. The only thing that felt better than sitting right here was driving the roadster through New Iberia.

"How about I show you how tomorrow? You're a natural." He snapped his fingers. "I know you'd pick it up just like that."

Papa shook his head. "Mais non, son. I've too much work to be playing at driving a motorcar."

Ernest pushed back from the table and reached for his coffee cup. "Like what?"

His father ticked off a list of a half dozen chores that needed doing and three errands he planned to run in the pirogue.

"Fine." He took a sip of the strong chicory brew. "So how long you figure the chores will take? Most of the morning?"

"And probably on into the afternoon, son. Why?"

"Because it'll take two men half the time." He smiled. "And those errands you plan to do by boat? Wonder if they might be run just as easily in that roadster out front."

Papa laughed and slapped Ernest on the shoulder. "You know, boy, I believe you just might be onto something. Now if I can just get your mama to stop worrying every time I set foot in a motorcar, eh?"

"What are you menfolk talking about? Did I hear my name?"

"Oui, Cleo," Papa said as he gathered Mama onto his lap and kissed her soundly. "I was telling Ernest here how you cannot bear to be apart from me."

Mama's blush combined with her giggle took two decades off her age. "Theo, you are the worst of rascals, you hear? You were saying no such thing."

"You been eavesdropping on the menfolk, cher? If your uncle Joe were alive, he'd surely send you off to get an earful from your tante Flo." Papa turned to smile at Ernest. "Lord rest their souls, those two put up with more than a body ought to take from this one."

"You hush now, Theophile Breaux. Don't be giving the boy ideas that his mama was trouble."

Papa chuckled and wrapped his arms more tightly around Mama. "You were trouble then and you're trouble still. You're lucky that you're the kind of trouble I like." He nuzzled her neck. "And I still say you were eavesdropping."

Mama climbed out of his lap and shook her head. "It's not eavesdropping when the menfolk are talking loud enough to be heard." She pointed at Ernest. "And you, well, I don't believe you must like my shrimp étouffée much."

"But, Mama, why do you say that? You know it's my favorite."

His mother smoothed the corner of her apron and started down the porch steps. "Because if you teach your papa to drive that motorcar, there will be no étouffée for you at the supper table tomorrow night."

"Aw, Mama." Ernest rose to follow her. "That's not fair. Isn't Papa the head of this household? If he asks me to do something, are you really expecting me to go against him?"

Mama seemed to be giving his question proper thought. Finally, she squared her shoulders and looked beyond him to Papa. "Of course not, Ernest. You should always mind your papa."

Ernest gave his father a sideways look and noted the amusement on his face, then turned his attention back to Mama. Her expression was much more serious.

"Of course, I expect your papa not to ask something of you that he shouldn't. Something like teaching him to drive one of those dangerous motorcars." With that, Mama stormed away and disappeared around the side of the house.

Papa leaned over and clapped his hand on Ernest's shoulder. "Don't worry about your mama, son. She's a handful, but she knows I love her, eh? What I would do without her, I can't imagine."

Ernest leaned back against the house and closed his eyes, trying to imagine being a part of a pair like Papa and Mama. Try as he might, he couldn't picture it.

"Why you don't want to get hitched, son?"

Opening his eyes, he regarded his father. "You really want to know?"

Papa nodded.

"You see that car over there?"

Again his father nodded.

"I like driving it. And I like living in town and being footloose and fancy-free." He shrugged. "A family man, he can't be like that. He has responsibilities."

"I suppose so." His papa looked thoughtful. "You know, son, you and I are a lot alike."

The statement struck Ernest as odd. Other than their looks, he and his father were nothing alike. Where Papa was content to be a husband, father, and bayou man, Ernest had picked the life of a city fellow, no strings and no cares.

"Would you believe I nearly lost your mother for the very reason you state, eh? I thought seeing the world was what I was meant to do. I never told you this, but I got halfway to Canada before I realized that what I was looking for sat back in Joe Trahan's house beside Bayou Nouvelle."

Now this was interesting. Still, he found it impossible to see his father as a rambling man. Theo Breaux was the most loyal, home-loving man Ernest knew.

"Oui, your mama, she was going to teach school. Her uncle Joe—he and Tante Flo, they raised her, you know—well, she had him talked into sending her to that fancy teachers' college over in New Orleans. Had my papa not broke his leg, I would have been off seeing the world and some other fellow would have built your mama a schoolhouse." Papa sighed. "She like to killed me, you know?"

"What?" Ernest chuckled. "Mama? I don't believe it."

"Believe it, son. The first time I met your mama, she caused me to fall through a roof. Or maybe that was the second time. I don't recall clearly. Still, I wore more bruises during our courtship than I've managed to collect in all the years since."

They shared a laugh, then silence fell between them. A question began to plague Ernest, and it wouldn't leave him alone until he asked it out loud. "Papa," he said slowly, "if I ask you something, would you tell me the truth?"

"Oui," Papa said. "If I can, that is."

"All right." He lowered his voice in case Mama was still in the vicinity. "Do you ever regret it? Turning in your traveling shoes for. . ." He paused to consider his words. "For the yoke of a wife and a family?"

"No."

"You didn't even take time to think about it."

His father shook his head. "Don't have to. See, I had this very same conversation with my father nigh on thirty years ago. He told me the same thing I'm telling you. What one man looks on as a burden, another sees as a blessing. I'm beholden to le bon Dieu to the blessings He has given me. All of them. And the plans for adventure, well, we can make them, but the Lord, He decides."

"But the adventure you gave up—do you ever wonder what you missed?"

Papa smiled. "Your mama is all the adventure I'll ever need. All of it and then some."

The pair lapsed once more into companionable silence. Finally, Papa spoke. "You intend to work at that sawmill all your life?"

"I don't rightly know, Papa. Guess I hadn't given it much thought."

"I see." He closed his eyes. "This sure is a comfortable bench. I believe you made this one, didn't you? And that one you're sitting on, too?"

"I believe so. Why?"

"Next time you're speaking to the Father, you might want to ask Him why He gave you such a talent for making things from scrap wood. You don't seem to be using it."

Now that was an odd statement. Where did that come from? "I'll do that, Papa," Ernest said. "Now about that driving lesson tomorrow."

Papa opened one eye and grinned. "Not necessary."

"Well, that's a relief."

"I already know how to drive. Your brother-in-law the doctor taught me. In case of emergency, you know?"

"I see."

Papa closed his eyes once more, and this time his grin tilted higher. "Yes, sir, you won't have to teach me a thing, except how to start that beauty. I can take it from there."

Chapter 5

Gen watched the Saturday morning sun rise above the trees from her bedroom window. Ellen had spent most of the night in fitful sleep, and thus so had Gen. Still, as the orange glow chased away the night sky, she sat in the little straight-backed chair lost in thought.

She'd climbed out this very window a year and a half ago last week to meet up with Alton Gallier down by the crosses behind the churchyard. From there they eloped, then lit out for Texas and the oil-patch life in Port Neches, where Alton's uncle had secured him a job on the crew working the new Bessie Heights Field.

The little shanty they rented on the edge of town had seemed cozy, at least until the morning sickness came. Not too long after, the walk out back to do her morning necessities turned into a several-times-a-night trip.

By then, Alton had taken to working the night shift, so she made the walk alone, often fighting the swarms of mosquitoes and running from threats both real and imagined. Sometimes Alton was the threat.

Even now the memory of those nights made her shiver.

Had it really been just a year and a half since she left her life here in Latagnier? Some days it seemed like a lifetime ago. Gen had certainly done enough living for two lifetimes since then.

When she thought of those days, Gen couldn't help but remember the loneliness. Newly wedded bliss gave way to long hours at work for Alton and long hours alone for Gen.

She missed her family terribly, but Daddy had forbidden her to see Alton Gallier, and Mother said she'd never speak to her again if Gen married up with Alton. Gen figured neither parent wanted to hear from her, leastways not for a while.

Only after she found herself expecting Ellen did she stop to think what Mother and Daddy were going through. When her letters were returned unopened, she wrote Big Mama, who answered promptly.

By then, it was too late. Daddy had taken sick, and Mother, well, she'd taken to honoring her promise that Gen ceased to exist.

Ellen wasn't a month old when Gen tucked her pride into her back pocket and walked up the dirt road to home, only to find a funeral wreath on the front door. Daddy had passed on not three days before. When she finally found Mother, dressed in Daddy's pajamas and asleep on his side of the bed, she realized she'd lost her mother, too.

Only Big Mama greeted her warmly.

Gen's gaze wandered past the treetops to the spot where Big Mama's cabin stood hidden by the thicket. A plume of smoke told Gen that Big Mama was up and most likely brewing coffee.

She rose to gather a still-sleeping Ellen into her arms. With the baby snuggled in the crook of her arm, Gen settled once more in the chair beside the window.

"You see that smoke, Ellen? That's where God's favorite angel on earth lives."

"Look at that precious angel," Big Mama said as Gen settled at the table in the little cabin with Ellen in her lap. "I do declare, she's the spitting image of her mama at that age."

"You think so?"

"I sure do." She smiled. "Remember now, I got to see you even before your mama did. That poor thing, she was bone tired from her laborin', and your daddy, he was beside himself with worry. When you finally decided to make your appearance, Miss Rose, she could barely lift an arm to hold you, and Mr. Carl was scared he was gonna drop you."

Gen nodded. As many times as she'd been told the story of her birth, Gen never tired of hearing it.

"I took hold of you, and you looked up at me and smiled. That old doctor, he didn't believe me, but I swear that's the honest truth. It's been you and me ever since, hasn't it?"

"Sure has," she said.

Big Mama spoke the truth. Gen never tired of sitting at Big Mama's feet or, better yet, in her lap, as her mother's housekeeper did her chores or cooked the evening meal. Funny how her memories of Mother paled in comparison to thoughts of Big Mama.

Mother used to joke that Gen didn't know which of them was her mother until she got old enough to notice the difference between Mother's light skin and fair hair and Big Mama's dark African features.

Ellen peered up at Gen with wide eyes. "I wonder if she knows who I am."

"Of course she does." Big Mama set a mug of steaming coffee in front of Gen, then took her own mug and settled across from her. "A baby knows its mama."

"I didn't. Mother told me so."

She looked surprised. "Well, that's different. Your mama's health, it was delicate, you know. Still is, for that matter. I just stepped in and helped her however I could. That was nothing like this here with Ellen. Look at that child; she loves you. It's plain as day."

Gen shook her head. "She's just a baby, and her mama's not the one taking care of her."

Big Mama waved away the statement with a lift of her hand. "That's just temporary. But that baby knowing her mama, well, that's something God makes sure of. Why wouldn't He do that when a mama loves her baby as much as you do?"

Before Gen could respond, Big Mama answered her own question.

"He's a good and merciful God, that's why." She paused to shake her head. "He knew all of this would happen before you and that baby's daddy were ever born." Big Mama took a sip of coffee and sighed. "He knew everything in the past, and He knows what's gonna happen in the future."

"I suppose."

"Ain't no supposin' to it. He said it, I believe it, and that's that."

Gen considered Big Mama's simple way of thinking. If only she could have such faith. She shifted Ellen to her shoulder. "Do you ever wonder why?"

Big Mama leaned back in the chair and gave her a sideways look. "What do you mean?"

"I mean, do you ever wonder why things happen? Why God lets people do things He knows will hurt them?" Gen smoothed Ellen's dark hair, already curly and unruly even at her young age. "I guess what I'm asking is, if He loves me so much, why didn't He stop me when He saw me about to do something so. . ." Her voice betrayed her, and she bit her lip until the moment passed. "Something so hurtful."

"Well now," Big Mama said, "you done asked the question of the ages, Genny-girl. The Lord, He don't have to tell nobody why. They's a few things I'd like Him to explain, too."

"Like what happened to Henry."

She nodded her dark head, then looked past Gen. "That's part of it."

"What else?"

Big Mama shook her head. "I done said enough. Now why don't we talk about something pleasant? Like maybe that young man who carried you home from New Iberia yesterday. He looked like he might be one of the Breaux boys."

"Yes, he's a Breaux." Gen kissed Ellen on the top of her head, then smoothed her dark hair. "Ernest. The eldest. Don't you remember? I told you that already."

"I 'spect you did, now that I'm thinking on it." Big Mama's eyes narrowed. "That boy sweet on you?"

"Sweet? No. Why, I hardly know him."

"It don't take much knowin' to set a fellow to chasin' a pretty girl." She reached for the teaspoon and jabbed it into the sugar bowl. "You been keeping time with him?"

"No, ma'am," she said. "I only ran into him at the corner grocery yesterday."

Teaspoon poised above her coffee cup, Big Mama tilted it to allow the sugar to sprinkle into the cup. "Then how came he to offer to tote you home?"

"He was being a gentleman, I suppose." She pushed back from the table and stood. "Why all the questions, Big Mama? He's not interested in me, and I'm not interested in him, so that's that. Besides, you and I both know I'm a married woman."

"I do know that, and I pray ever night for the Lord to either bring Alton Gallier back to walking with Him or take him home to glory." She shrugged. "Either way's all right with me."

Gen didn't dare think about which of those choices she would prefer. Her opinions of Alton Gallier were still colored by feelings she had barely begun to learn to live with.

Or in her husband's case, live without.

Ellen stirred and began to make whimpering sounds. Gen lulled her back to sleep by settling into the old rocker by the fireplace.

"So he just up and asked you to ride in that fancy car 'cause he happened to see you at the corner grocery?" She frowned. "Do I look like I just fell off the turnip truck? There's more to that story than that."

"All right." Gen lowered her voice. "There was a rough character in line ahead of me at the bus station. Mr. Breaux happened to see that he was making familiar conversation with me, and he rescued me from the situation." She paused. "Did you know he used to go fishing with Daddy?"

"That I did. He and his brothers used to head out with Mr. Carl and Mr. Theo Breaux. Me and your mama would pack them a mess of food in a pail, and they'd fish until suppertime." Big Mama rose to clear the table. "You know his mama always brings us an Easter lily from her garden come spring, and the pecan pies she makes, well, I do declare I'd love to be a fly on her kitchen wall so's I could see what she puts in her pecan pie that makes it so good."

Gen shook her head. "Why don't you just ask her?"

The moment she said the words, she wanted to reel them back in. Giving Big Mama an excuse to visit the Breaux place would be a recipe for disaster, not for pecan pie.

"Or maybe I could find out for you." She paused to try to pass an innocent look by Big Mama. "You never know when I'll see Ernest Breaux again."

"Well, that's right," Big Mama said. "You just don't ever know."

Chapter 6

"You going to let that young man tote you back to town?"

Gen straightened her back and stabbed at the ground with her hoe. Rather than endure silent hours in Mother's home, she'd elected to spend Saturday afternoon trying to make the beginnings of a garden from a patch of weeds on the south side of the house.

Daddy swore this section of the property bore the biggest tomatoes in Latagnier, but so far she'd found nothing left of the prized vines. Before she caught the bus back to town tomorrow afternoon, she was determined to at least uncover what was left of her father's handiwork.

"I asked you a question, Genny-girl. Now don't you go thinkin' just 'cause you're all growed up and a mama now that you can ignore your Big Mama."

Big Mama wore an apron embroidered with apples over her Sunday-go-to-meeting dress. Gen smiled.

"Why are you all dressed up on a Saturday afternoon?"

"Ellen, she's down for her nap, and your mama's sleepin', too. I aim to go a-visitin'," she said with her I-dare-you-to-argue look.

Visiting? Oh no.

Unless she missed her guess, there were probably two or three pecan pies cooling in the kitchen. As sure as she stood there, Gen knew Big Mama would make a beeline for the Breaux place with one of them as soon as she tore off her apron and slipped into her church shoes.

Gen knocked the dirt off the knees of Daddy's overalls and shook her head. "Big Mama, please don't."

"Don't what?" Her sassy look turned sweet and innocent as she rested her hands on her ample hips. "Can't a body be neighborly anymore?"

"Not when it's just a poor excuse for meddling."

Big Mama had the decency to look offended. "Well, I don't know where you think I'm headed, but I've got a mess of fish all fried up and a pot of red beans dished out and ready to go next door."

"Next door?"

"Yes'm. The Widow LeBlanc's been feeling a mite poorly lately." She paused. "And on top of that, I thought if I brought her some vittles, she just might share that squash casserole recipe she brought to church last time they had dinner on the grounds. If I don't get it soon, she's gonna head off to Mississippi to live with her daughter, and I'll never know what she puts in it."

"The Widow LeBlanc?" Gen looked past Big Mama to the brilliant blue sky and tufts of white cotton-ball clouds. Even seen slightly blurry because of her poor distance vision, it was beautiful.

"Who did you think I was headin' t' see?" She smiled. "Oh, you thought your Big Mama was goin' t' meddle in your love life?"

She shrugged. "I hardly know the man. It's not even a friendship."

Big Mama put on her sternest expression. "Well, as long as you're a married woman, there ain't gonna be no other man in your life. The good Lord, He will be what your man can't—or won't. The Bible, it says so. I done read that t' you many times."

"Yes, ma'am," she said as she yanked the hoe out of the dirt. "And I'm perfectly happy with the Lord as my husband."

Indeed she was. True, the situation wasn't what she'd expected when she had hightailed it out of Latagnier to elope with Alton Gallier, but things could be worse.

Big Mama whirled around and headed back to the kitchen, only to return a few minutes later with a plate wrapped in a dish towel and a black iron pot dangling from the crook of her arm. "I won't be long," she said as she adjusted the dish towel.

"I'll stay close and listen for Ellen and Mother."

"All right, then," she said, although she made no move to leave. Finally, she shook her head. "You didn't answer me."

"I didn't? What did you ask?"

"I asked you if that Breaux feller was coming tomorrow to carry you back to town in that motorcar of his."

"No," she said. "I'll be catching the bus at three o'clock like always."

Big Mama frowned. "You mean to tell me that rascal didn't even offer to fetch you?"

"Yes, ma'am," she said. "He asked. I told him no, thank you."

The older woman studied her for a moment, then nodded. "Smart girl. Men like that, they are pretty on the eyes and hard on the heart. You done got enough trouble without taking up with the likes of him."

Gen chuckled and went back to work, stopping only when thirst drove her inside for some of Big Mama's sweet tea. A few minutes after two, Ellen's cry echoed across the yard, and Gen raced inside to fetch the baby from her crib.

She tiptoed past Mother's closed door, tempted for the briefest moment to stop and listen for sounds of life inside. What Mother did all day behind that door puzzled Gen, and she wondered if her solitude was because Gen was home.

When Big Mama returned, she would ask. Maybe Mother only hid from her and not from the rest of the world.

After a feeding and a diaper change, Ellen was content to lie on a freshly starched blanket on the grass. As Gen struggled with the weeds and clumps of hard dirt, she watched her little girl.

Someday Ellen would be all grown up. What would she tell Ellen about her papa?

Out of the corner of her eye, a flash of white caught her attention. She looked up to see Mother standing half hidden in the shadows of her open bedroom window. Dressed in a pair of Daddy's pajamas with her hair captured in a thick braid that hung over her right shoulder, Gen's once-beautiful mother looked more like one of those ghosts from the scary tales the bayou boys told.

"Mother, why don't you come down here and sit a spell?"

Rather than respond, her mother slipped back into the shadows, leaving darkness where she once stood.

"Genny-girl, come quick."

Gen whirled around to see Big Mama hustling up the drive, waving something white. As she neared, Gen could make out a piece of paper in Big Mama's hand. The look on her face told Gen that Big Mama had returned from the Widow LeBlanc's house with more than just a recipe for squash casserole.

Ellen had begun to fuss again, so she scooped the baby into her arms. "What is it?"

"That fool mailman, he done dropped off a letter to the Widow LeBlanc that ought to have been delivered here. A letter for you."

"For me?"

"That's right."

Gen traded Ellen for the letter, then studied the envelope. There was no return address, but since the postmark read Beaumont, Texas, it could only be from one person.

Her husband.

Big Mama expelled a long breath and shook her head. "Open it, Genevieve. That letter's not gonna open itself."

Gen sank onto the grass and held the letter to her chest. "I don't want to."

"Then I will," Big Mama said. She handed Ellen to Gen, took the envelope, and tore it open. A letter folded in half and written longhand fluttered to the ground. Gen reached to hand it back to Big Mama, then kissed the top of Ellen's head.

As her gaze scanned the page, Big Mama's eyes widened. "Land o' Goshen," she said when she finished. "I swan, I don't believe what I just read."

Gen clutched Ellen so tightly the baby wailed a complaint. "What is it?" she asked as she soothed the infant.

Big Mama settled on the grass beside her, obviously ignoring the fact that her best dress would need a good cleaning when she stood. "Genny-girl, I don't know how to tell you this. It ain't from Alton, but it sure is about him."

A half dozen thoughts danced across her mind. He might be in jail, or in the hospital, or maybe he'd filled another woman's head with empty promises and run off with her.

"Just read it."

Nodding, Big Mama cleared her throat and began to read. Words like *accident* and *job site* and *fatal* combined with phrases like *our most sincere condolences* and *with deepest sympathy* to send a buzz through her ears and a jolt though her heart. A final sentence said something about insurance and how a representative would contact the widow shortly.

The widow.

Gen had barely begun to get used to being a wife when she became a mother. Now she would have to learn how to be a widow.

She waited to feel something. Sadness, anger, loss—anything. She felt nothing. It was as if a door had slammed shut somewhere off in the distance, and she'd been told about it but hadn't actually heard the sound.

And then the exhaustion arrived. Wave upon wave hit her, crumpling her into a ball. She lay on the blanket and tucked Ellen beside her, then stared up at the brilliant blue sky. All the clouds had danced away except one. It hung directly above her.

In that moment, she knew the day she had been dreading, the day Alton Gallier blew back into her life, would never come. The Lord would indeed be her husband now, and little Ellen's papa, too.

Tired.

So tired.

Ellen closed her eyes, and Gen followed suit. Ashamed at her relief, she felt tears sting her eyes. "I'm sorry I wished him dead, Big Mama. That was just awful of me."

"Hush now," Big Mama said. "You loved that boy best as you could, and you'd have kept on loving him had he been the husband and father the Lord called him to be."

"But I never wanted it to be like this. I only. . ."

Words fell away and left her speechless.

"Oh, honey." Big Mama wrapped her strong arms around Gen and Ellen. "You don't have to be afraid of Alton Gallier no more, that's for sure."

Somehow Gen managed to nod.

"And come the day that insurance check arrives, your Alton, he will have done one last good thing for his wife and daughter."

Gen lifted her head. "What do you mean?"

"Look here." Big Mama pointed to the last line of the letter. "See, the company, they're paying a death benefit. It won't make us rich, but it sure will add to what you're making at the five-and-dime."

Gen checked the figure twice, closed her eyes, and offered up a prayer of thanks. Three hundred dollars was a fortune, much more than she could make in six months at the five-and-dime. It wouldn't last forever, but with that nest egg in the bank to cover Mama's medicines and emergencies, she could find a little relief. It would go far in paying for Daddy's funeral expenses, too.

Maybe in a short while, she could think of working fewer hours or even finding a job closer to home. Not that there were many jobs to be had. The country had been through years of hard times, and she knew she should be thankful she had any work at all. Still, leaving Ellen became harder each time she did it, and eventually she knew she would just flat have to stop.

"Lord, hasten that day," she whispered.

~

That evening on the bus ride into the city, she fell into a deep sleep. Awaking as the bus pulled into New Iberia, Gen realized she hadn't slept so well since Ellen's birth—or before, actually.

Back in the boardinghouse, she dropped her suitcase and climbed into bed. The next thing she realized, it was Monday morning, and Betty stood over her.

"Awake at last," she said. "I was beginning to get worried about you."

Gen bolted upright and shook her head. She'd been in the middle of the strangest dream. Mother was driving a motorcar that looked strangely like Ernest Breaux's. Her father rode beside Mother with Gen and Ellen in the rumble seat. Running behind them, trying furiously to catch up, was Alton Gallier.

He'd almost reached the car when Betty shook her awake, and the sensation of having her arm grabbed had made her think Alton caught her. She looked up at Betty, and the strangest thing happened.

She began to cry.

Five minutes and two handkerchiefs later, Gen managed to relate the dream to Betty, carefully leaving out any reference to the identities of Ellen or Alton. The less Betty knew about her life, the better. It was shameful enough that she'd defied her parents to run off with a man like Alton, and even more shameful that she'd given birth to a daughter she wasn't raising.

No, better to keep her secrets and let Betty think what she would rather than know the truth.

Her roommate sat very still at the end of the bed. She seemed to be deep in thought. Finally, she gave Gen a direct look. "Something big happened this weekend, didn't it?"

Gen blew her nose and nodded.

"Anything you care to tell me about? I'm a good listener, you know. And what I'm told I keep to myself."

This much was true. She knew Betty to be a good friend and a godly woman. She'd seen firsthand at the five-and-dime how her friend hated gossip.

Oh no, the five-and-dime. She dropped the handkerchief and threw back the covers. "Oh, Betty, what time is it?"

Betty placed her hand on Gen's shoulder. "Hold on there, kid. There's no need to hurry. I already went down to the five-and-dime and told Lester you weren't feeling yourself." She gave Gen a stern look. "You're not, are you?"

Gen shook her head. "No, I guess I'm not. I've never slept this much or cried this hard, not even when my daddy died. I guess I just bottled it all up inside until that awful dream made it all let loose."

"Looks like you needed to let it loose," Betty said. "A body can't hold that kind of stuff in forever. I do believe the Lord fetches people home in His time, but some days I wish He might be a little slower with the fetching. Why, I don't know what I'd do if I lost my papa. And I think about Dorothy and raising that baby after her husband was killed."

As soon as the words fell from Betty's lips, Gen's tears began to flow again. This time it took more than five minutes and a sizable corner of the bedsheet to dry her eyes. She blew her nose twice, then fell back onto her pillow, exhausted. As her eyes closed, she waited for sleep to return.

"Oh no, you don't." Betty yanked off the covers and stood with her hands on her hips. "If I let you go back to sleep, I might never wake you up." She shrugged. "And what good's a roommate who does nothing but sleep?"

Gen reluctantly sat back up. Head aching from the intensity of her crying, she reeled a bit before steeling her backbone to remain upright.

"I'm afraid I'm not going to be good for much today," she said.

"That's not true." Betty offered her a hand, and she took it, rising to stand on unsteady feet. Before Gen could protest, Betty yanked the sheets off Gen's bed, then did the same with her own. "While I go run these down to the Washateria, you make coffee."

By the time Betty returned, Gen had washed her face and combed her hair. She removed the coffeepot from the little electric burner and poured two cups. With the sheets and blankets stripped from their beds, the room looked bare and depressing. Gen felt tears press against her eyelids.

"Oh no, you don't." Betty sipped at the strong black brew. "No more tears until the sheets are dry."

Gen giggled, although her good humor didn't quite reach her heart.

"You don't have to say a thing if you don't want to." Betty nodded toward the open window. "How about we take this coffee out on the terrace?"

The "terrace" was actually an oversized ledge reached by climbing through the westward-facing window and just big enough for the two of them. On pleasant days, the pair often ended the day here.

Somehow it seemed appropriate to begin one in the familiar place. Especially since things seemed so horribly unfamiliar.

She was a widow.

How awful that she couldn't grieve the loss of her husband as any normal wife would. The truth be known, she'd lost Alton Gallier long before he actually departed this life.

"Warm enough?"

Betty settled beside her and stretched out her legs, then covered them with her winter coat. The air felt fresh with the slightest bite of north wind. Gen huddled close to Betty and sipped at the steaming coffee.

They sat in silence for a bit. Finally, Gen set her coffee cup on the ledge and turned to face Betty. Her friend offered a smile.

"You don't have to say a word, you know."

"I know." Gen slid beneath the warmth of Betty's coat. "But I think I need to tell you."

"All right," Betty said.

Gen took a deep breath and let it out slowly. As she touched her fingers to the locket at her neck, the simple heart that held a lock of Ellen's dark hair, she closed her eyes.

"My husband," she said slowly, "is dead. I'm not even twenty-one years old, and I'm a widow."

"Oh, honey," Betty said.

"You don't know the half of it." Gen paused. "He's dead and I'm glad." Tears overtook her. "That's not true," she managed. "I do care, but I'm glad I don't have to be afraid of him anymore. Is that horribly selfish?"

"Oh, Genevieve, no! It isn't horribly selfish." Betty shook her head. "Remember when we met?"

Gen nodded. "At the bus station?"

"That's right. You were fresh off the bus from Latagnier, and I'd just arrived from Crowley. Your bus was early and mine was late, or we'd never have met. If that's not God's timing, I don't know what is."

She attempted a smile. Finding a friend like Betty in a city the size of New Iberia had definitely been a blessing.

"You know, honey, the Lord, He sets the lonely in families." She shrugged. "Since neither of us has anyone in New Iberia, I figure the Lord knew we would need each other."

"I guess He did," Gen said. "And you're right. I could use someone to talk to."

Betty smiled. "Want another cup of coffee first?"

"Sure," Gen said. And when Betty returned, two steaming mugs of coffee in her hands, Gen told her the story of her misguided marriage to Alton Gallier.

The part about Ellen, she decided to keep to herself, at least for now. Some secrets were harder to tell.

Chapter 7

Monday, April 17

Ernest shook off the cold and parked the roadster across the street from the corner grocery. In the ten days since he'd left Latagnier, he'd been waiting for an "accidental" meeting with Genevieve Lamont. So far, the lovely lady hadn't made a single appearance at Mulotte's, and he had no other idea where to find her.

Leaning back in the seat, Ernest adjusted his cap and set to waiting. After a while, he blew on his hands, then stuffed his fists into the pockets of his winter coat.

If only the weather hadn't turned chilly. But that was spring in Louisiana. One day the skies were blue and the weather warm, and the next gray and cold. At least he'd timed his trip home to coincide with good weather.

Home. Ernest smiled. He'd had a good time in spite of himself back at the old place. With Mama and Papa and all the family in close quarters, he'd never expected to come back to his solitary room in New Iberia and miss the fun.

Why, even enduring the hour-long, white-knuckle Sunday afternoon ride with Papa at the wheel of the roadster seemed pleasant when remembered this afternoon.

He shivered. "Must be the cold turning me sentimental."

A flash of pink caught his attention, and he swiped at the foggy glass to clear the view. Sure enough, a young woman about Genevieve Lamont's size strolled past, dangling a handbag from her wrist. He would recognize that handbag anywhere. Why, if that wasn't the very purse Miss Lamont left on the floor of his roadster, he would eat his hat.

Ernest strained to see the bag's owner. Bundled in a coat with a flowered scarf covering her hair and part of her face, he couldn't be sure it was Miss Lamont.

Still, he felt certain that was her purse.

For a moment he debated climbing out into the cold. As the woman neared the corner, he realized he'd either have to chase her down or lose sight of her. Compromising, he threw the car into gear and blended into traffic, rounding the corner just behind her. Easing the roadster to the curb, he leaned over to open the door.

"Miss Lamont?"

The woman jumped back, clutched her handbag to her chest, and whirled around to face him. It wasn't Miss Lamont.

"Sorry, ma'am," he said as he slammed the door and peeled away from the curb.

The ride back to his place took only a few minutes, but it seemed much longer. All the while he negotiated turns and steered around holes in the road, his mind was racing. What if he never saw Genevieve Lamont again? What if he'd said or done something that made her not want to see him again?

"That's ridiculous," he said as he climbed out of the roadster. The other issue, the issue of whether he might have offended her in some way, still concerned him. He sidestepped a puddle on the path to his door and shook his head. "You're just going to have to ask her yourself."

"Ask who?"

Ernest glanced over his shoulder to see his roommate, Phil Barker, coming up the walk behind him. "Just talking to myself," he said as he threw open the door and stepped inside.

Phil brushed past him to drop his coat and hat on the cot that served as his bed. His smile told Ernest he was about to comment.

"Got any coffee made?" Ernest asked quickly, hoping to head off a conversation he didn't intend to have.

"There's a little left in the pot from this morning, but I can't guarantee how it'll taste now."

"Doesn't matter as long as it's warm," Ernest said. "I hate cold weather. It's April, for pity's sake."

"I've got a feeling the cold wouldn't bother you so much if you weren't pining away for a certain girl." Phil shook off his shoes and settled atop the blanket-covered mattress. "Why don't you tell old Phil all about her?"

Ernest poured the last of the thick black coffee into the first mug he could find, then took a healthy swig. True to his friend's warning, the coffee was more warm than tasty.

"Not much to tell, actually," he said. "And I'm not exactly pining away for her."

Phil rolled over onto his stomach and rested his chin in his hands. "All right, then. What would you call it? You take the same drive at the same time every day; then you come back here to mope until bedtime. What gives?"

Nodding, Ernest set the mug beside the coffeepot. "I wish I knew. I mean, all I did was give her a ride to Latagnier. We barely spoke, and what little she said indicated she had little interest in striking up a friendship with me."

"Aha!" Phil jumped to his feet and clapped Ernest on the shoulder. "That's it."

"That's what?"

Phil smiled. "It's like this. What do you usually do when a girl shows interest in you?"

Ernest settled at the table and removed his pocket change. "Is this a trick question?" He dropped three nickels and four pennies into the peanut butter jar labeled RENT that sat on the table.

"No. See, she's not interested in you; therefore, you are very interested in her. All you have to do is spend more time with her, be properly charming until she falls for you, and voilà, you're cured, and she's out of your system." Phil clapped his hands, then reached for the one remaining mug on the shelf. "What is it like to live with someone so incredibly brilliant?"

"I wouldn't know." Ernest tossed his cap onto the table and shed his coat, then rose to trudge toward his bed. "I've spent the better part of a week trying to track her down, and she's nowhere to be found. So if you're so smart, you'd come up with a way to find her. After all, I can't get her out of my system if I don't know where she is."

Phil snapped his fingers. "Say, I think I have an idea."

Ernest stopped and whirled around to frown at his roommate. "Not another idea, please."

"No, this is a good one, I promise." He paused. "New Iberia is a big city. It stands to reason she'd be hard to find here. But back in Latagnier, now that is someplace you'd know exactly where she would be, right?"

"Right," Ernest said slowly. "You know, Phil, I think I just might be about to figure out what it's like to live with someone incredibly brilliant."

"Well, of course. So what are you going to do?"

"Do?" Ernest shrugged. "I'm busier than a one-legged man in a football-kicking contest down at the sawmill, and my boss said I can come in on my days off to work on a couple of projects I've been thinking of starting."

"What sort of projects?"

Ernest sank onto the sagging springs of his bed and tried to ignore their protest. "The boss said I could have the leftover lumber to make a few things with."

"You know, my friend, you are on the wrong end of the lumber business. I've never seen a man with such a talent for making things from wood." Phil pointed to the small chest sitting on the dresser they shared. "I can't believe you made that from discards you found in the trash bin."

The little oak box had been Ernest's "spare time" project, a little something to fill his empty hours. He had to admit as he studied it that it had turned out quite nicely.

"Now back to this girl. I don't believe you told me her name."

Ernest returned his attention to Phil. "No, I don't believe I did."

"And you don't intend to, do you?" Phil waved away the question. "Forget I asked. I'll find out soon enough. Anyway, back to my original question of what you plan to do about her."

Good question. Too bad he had no answer.

Stretching, Ernest slipped off his shoes and let each drop with a *thud*. Finally, he cast a glance over at Phil. Unfortunately, when his roommate bit into a topic, he tended to chew it until there was nothing left. He decided to give Phil an answer in hopes of ending the subject.

"You know, Phil, except for my trip home next weekend for my sister's birthday, I don't have any time off from work until the Fourth of July. Odds are, I won't remember her name next time I see her."

"Think so?"

Ernest knew he wouldn't forget her name or anything else about Genevieve Lamont, but there was no way he would admit it.

Friday, May 5

Gen folded a napkin from the soda fountain around all but seven dollars of her monthly salary and stuffed it into an envelope along with a note for Big Mama. Tomorrow morning, she would mail the money and the letter on the way to work. *If only I'd remembered my extra stamps. I could buy more at the post office, but with the sparse funds I have for the month, it would be foolish to spend the extra money just to have the letter mailed today.*

Funny, three hundred dollars had seemed like a fortune when the check arrived. Now that April had slid past and May had arrived, the money had already begun to dwindle.

Taxes and Mother's medicines had taken a toll on the balance, leaving Gen to worry that at this rate there would be nothing left by the time Ellen started school. Of course, Big Mama reminded her that worrying didn't do a bit of good. She always backed the statement up with a favorite Bible verse; then she sweetened the discussion with a slice of pie.

Gen smiled. Big Mama was a blessing, all right, and without her she'd be in quite a pickle. How a mama could work and take care of a baby was beyond her, although she knew of at least one girl at the five-and-dime who did. She'd taken to mentioning Dorothy in her prayers every night, and last payday she'd managed to slip a fifty-cent piece into Dorothy's pay envelope when she wasn't looking.

Fifty cents wasn't much, but given the amount of Gen's disposable income, it was practically the widow's mite. It had been fun to watch the girl open her paycheck and find the extra coin. She'd even played dumb when Dorothy asked about the true owner of the money.

What a blessing to be able to bless. The thought certainly brightened the dark times.

Today, however, nothing seemed to pierce the gloom. In the bottom of her purse was a letter from her landlord indicating the rent would go up substantially at the first of August. Where the extra funds would come from, she had no idea. Big Mama made the money Gen sent her stretch as far as she could. Rather than cut back there, Gen would just have to learn to live on less.

She cast a glance over at Dorothy, who had just finished placing a cherry atop a youngster's root beer float. *Lord, please allow someone else to bless her. It looks like my days of helping are over.*

A customer set a basket of items on the counter, distracting Gen. After she finished the transaction, she looked over to see Dorothy waving in her direction. Gen closed the cash register and headed toward the soda fountain.

Dorothy smiled. "I wanted to let you know I won't be coming back after today."

"Oh?"

The girl giggled and leaned toward Gen. "I'm getting married," she said softly. "Can you believe it?"

"Congratulations." Gen tried not to let her shock at the news color her excitement. "But I didn't know you were seeing anyone."

Dorothy shrugged. "It's the strangest thing. After Bobby's daddy died, I didn't think I would ever find happiness with another man. Then when I wasn't looking, the Lord surprised me with Ben." She paused. "Looks like Bobby and I finally have our family complete. Oh, Genevieve, I'm so happy."

"Well, that's wonderful, Dorothy."

She nodded. "I wanted to let you know first, because without you, Ben and I never would have met."

"I don't understand."

"The extra money in my pay envelope—it took me awhile, but eventually I figured out it was from you." She smiled. "I thought it was quite a coincidence that you were always the last one to leave on payday."

"I suppose I'm not very good at that cloak-and-dagger stuff."

Dorothy touched Gen's arm. "You don't know how much I appreciated your donations. It made all the difference, and that's why I'm telling you."

"I'm glad I could help, but I don't see how I had anything to do with your engagement."

Her friend's eyes sparkled. "Well, it's the funniest thing. After the first few weeks of getting that extra money in my pay envelope, I began to pray about what to buy with it. One day it hit me. Donate it. Well, that Sunday a man who supports missionary work in South America came to speak at church, and he told us all about this orphanage in Ecuador and the work the missionaries did there. I thought about little Bobby and how even though he didn't have a daddy, he did have a mama and how that was more than those little orphans had."

Gen nodded. This she knew firsthand to be true.

"When Ben wrote a note thanking me for my donation, I sent him a letter back, and that was how it all started. He came back to speak to us at church two weeks ago, and wouldn't you know it, he proposed to me right there in church last Sunday morning." She paused to shake her head. "Right there from the pulpit.

Can you believe it? Oh, Genevieve, the first thing I did when I got home that night was to pray for you."

"For me?" Gen shook her head. "Why?"

"Because I feel like it's time for you to be the one who is blessed. It's your turn for happiness. I just know it."

Several responses begged to be spoken, but instead Gen chose to thank Dorothy and skitter back to the cash register. As she set back to work, she couldn't help hoping that maybe Dorothy's prayer for her might be heard and the wish granted.

By the time Gen stepped out of the five-and-dime into the brisk evening air, her black mood had lifted a bit. She thought about Dorothy and tried to imagine what it might feel like to be loved by a godly man. For all his positive traits—and Alton Gallier did have a few—no one ever would have mistaken him for a godly man.

This fault had seemed a minor one, something that would change once the marriage took place. To be sure, Alton attended church with her a time or two, and once she even caught him opening the pages of her Bible. Only later did she realize a man could sit in a church on Sunday morning and still find it permissible to hit his wife on Monday.

Gen suppressed a shudder and said a quick prayer that her husband had somehow gotten right with God before his untimely death. As much as she hated how he'd treated her, no one—not even Alton Gallier—should spend an eternity away from the Lord.

By morning, her dark mood had lifted altogether. Taking care not to wake Betty, who had the day off, Gen dressed quietly and tucked the letter to Big Mama into her handbag. At the corner, she slid the letter into the mailbox and let the lid shut with a resounding *clank*. As much as she hated being away from home and family, the one day each month when she sent money back to them made the other days worthwhile. Someday soon she would figure out a way to be with her daughter on more than just weekends. She'd petitioned the Lord on that subject too many times for Him to ignore her. In the meantime, she did her part in keeping the bills paid and food on the table.

If only she could sit at that table every night with the three women she loved more than any other in the world: Mother, Big Mama, and Ellen.

"Someday," she whispered as she whirled around and slammed directly into Ernest Breaux.

Chapter 8

Oh no.

Gen took three steps back and shook her head. "I'm terribly sorry. I. . ." Surprise caught up with her, and she ran out of words.

"It's my fault, actually," Ernest said. "I should have said something."

"Yes, well. . ." Again the words stopped. Gen felt like a fool and, most likely, looked like one, too. She smoothed her hair away from her face and tried hard to remember whether she'd taken the time to apply her usual powder and lipstick.

Probably not.

"You're up early for a Saturday morning," Ernest said.

Ignoring her better judgment, Gen focused her attention on the man standing before her. He did look quite stylish, what with his hair combed just so and his cap tilted back on his head. Why, if she didn't know better, she would think he'd dressed to go courting. A glance behind him revealed his flashy motorcar sitting at the curb. Even with her poor distance vision, there was no mistaking it.

Alton had always bragged about getting a car just like that one, something that would grab attention. Alton.

Gen's heart sank. Alton Gallier had been a handsome rogue with a pretty smile and polite manners. Why, until she married him, she never guessed what lay beneath the surface. Oh, Mother and Big Mama warned her, to be sure, but she never listened. After all, Alton had been so sweet and nice.

Just like Ernest Breaux.

Ernest gave her an expectant look and then a smile. My, but he did have a nice smile.

"Daydreaming?"

"Oh, well, I. . ." Gen frowned. Surely the man thought she was an idiot. "I'm sorry; what did you say?"

"I said, you're up early," he repeated.

Gen managed a nod. "Yes, well, I suppose I am."

Her lower lip quivered, and she bit it so hard it felt like she drew blood. Just to be sure, she swiped her hand across her mouth. *Nothing. Good. Now to escape.*

Casting a glance around, she prayed for a distraction so she could slip away unnoticed. Except for a pair of lazy hound dogs sunning themselves in front of the barbershop and an elderly woman sweeping the sidewalk in front of the church, the streets of New Iberia were deserted.

She swung her attention back to Ernest. Was she mistaken, or did he look as uncomfortable as she felt?

"Mailing letters back home?"

"Yes, actually." Gen squared her shoulders and thrust her hand in his direction. "Well, it was nice running into you." She groaned at the accidental reference to their collision. "I mean, it was nice seeing you."

Before she could make a fool of herself any further, Gen slipped past Ernest. To her dismay, he fell in step beside her.

"In a hurry?"

"I'm heading to work," she said.

"Ah." He continued to keep pace with her, slowing his long stride to match hers. "So do you work all day?"

Giving him a sideways glance, she nodded.

"Until what time?"

Gen stopped short at the corner across from the church, and Ernest followed suit. "You ask a lot of questions. Did you realize that?"

Ernest looked perplexed. "I do?"

Again she nodded.

"Should I apologize?"

He looked so contrite that she couldn't give him the sharp answer she intended. The truth was, Ernest Breaux seemed like a genuinely nice man.

But then, so had Alton Gallier.

"No," she said. "There's no need to apologize. Just stop, all right?"

She headed for the corner and turned to cross the street. The elderly woman had stopped her sweeping to watch, and Gen offered her a quick smile. She nodded and grasped her broom to return to work.

"Wait!" Ernest called as Gen reached the other side. "I'd like to see you again."

"Why?"

The question was out before she realized she had said it aloud. Not only had she said it; she'd actually shouted it across the street. Color flooded her cheeks as heat filled her face.

One more reason not to take up again with a man. She was no good at it.

~

Why indeed.

Ernest pondered the question for a full minute, all the while expecting Miss Lamont to scurry back to that place where she'd been hiding all week. To his surprise, she remained rooted to the spot, no doubt enjoying his discomfort.

"Well now, Miss Genevieve, that is a good question. Why *would* I want to see you again?"

He scratched his head and pretended to consider it. Actually, the only trouble he had with answering was how much to say and what to say first, but he'd never tell her that. Before he could sort out his thoughts and give her a brilliant answer, she had the audacity to turn around and walk away.

"Never mind," she said with a wave of her hand. "I'm sure I will see you around. Good-bye, Mr. Breaux."

For a split second he thought of following her, of using his considerable charm to woo her into continuing their conversation. He certainly had no trouble making small talk with the ladies. Then his brain caught up with his pride, and he stopped. Better to approach this situation with care—and a little planning.

Why, he wouldn't hack at just any old oak tree in order to get lumber for a chair or cut down the closest pecan tree to find wood for a table. No, he would choose the best trees, take time to study them, and then treat them with care.

The same would go for Genevieve Lamont. Taking the time to approach her carefully would be his plan. He would study her and figure out just the right way to get to know her.

For, like a piece of fine furniture, she obviously had great value.

Ernest smiled at the comparison. The woman in question probably would not appreciate being compared to a nicely crafted table or chair. Still, he could think of no greater compliment.

Maybe Papa was right. Deep down he was probably made to be a furniture maker. Unfortunately, he had bills to pay, and as satisfying as it would be to chuck all his responsibilities and play with wood and chisel all day, he couldn't put gasoline in the roadster with an empty wallet.

These days, having a job at all was a blessing. How could he think of walking away to pursue a dream, especially one with so little chance of succeeding?

Ernest shook his head and captured his wits. If he didn't hurry, he would lose sight of the lovely Miss Genevieve. He thought of jumping in the roadster to catch up to her but decided to do the job on foot. Besides, he could hardly be discreet in something so snazzy.

He adjusted his cap and headed off. Up ahead he saw the object of his thoughts disappear into the five-and-dime. She'd said she was up early for work, so it was possible this was where she worked.

Or she could be doing a little shopping first.

Checking his watch, he realized the store had not yet opened. Unless she was employed there, it was highly unlikely Genevieve Lamont would be allowed inside.

"Work it is," Ernest said as he doubled back to climb inside the roadster. He paused to crank the engine, then eased the car away from the curb. As he turned to drive past the five-and-dime, he tried to look casual while peering into the windows in hopes of seeing Genevieve.

No sight of her greeted him, but that didn't matter. "At least I know how to find her."

Ernest smiled at the turn of events that had led him to meet up with the lovely lady that morning. After working a double shift, he'd arrived home with the sunrise. Although the temptation to fall into bed was strong, he'd forced himself to change clothes and head for the mailbox with his little sister's birthday letter. With the slow speed of bayou mail, Amalie might miss receiving her letter if he put off mailing it until Monday.

"Thank you, Amalie," he said under his breath as he made the turn at the end of the block and headed back home. "Oh, and thank You, Lord." He paused to allow a mama dog and two puppies to cross the road. "And as long as You are thinking of me, God, would You do just one more thing? Would You grant me some patience where Miss Lamont is concerned? I'm thinking I just might need all I can muster to keep from bothering her until she sees what a great catch I am."

Catch? Ernest guided the roadster to the curb in front of his place, then shut off the engine, suppressing a shudder. Since when had his interest in the pretty girl from Latagnier moved from a possible date to something else?

All the more reason to keep in close contact with the Lord. After all, He wouldn't let Ernest make the mistake of falling in love with a woman he barely knew.

He wouldn't, would He?

Chapter 9

Wednesday, May 10

Ernest had used about all the patience he could stand. He paced the sidewalk in front of the five-and-dime, nearly wearing a rut in the concrete before he finally decided to save on shoe leather and go inside. A second before his hand touched the polished brass doorknob, he said a quick prayer that the Lord would smile on him as he tried his best to spend time with Miss Lamont.

Once inside, he cast about for the object of his pacing. Rather than find her, he saw an oversized man with a head full of greasy hair and a belly that rivaled Papa's prize sow. The fellow frowned before rising from his perch at the soda fountain to greet Ernest.

"Something I can help you with?" He pulled a toothpick out of his shirt pocket and began to work it between his front teeth. "I'm Lester Bonfils, the manager around here."

"No, thank you," Ernest said. "I'm just looking right now."

The man looked him up and down, then gave a snort before turning to climb back on his stool.

"I see you've met Lester."

Ernest whirled around to see a pretty, dark-haired woman who looked to be about his age, standing beside a toothpaste display. "Yes, I did."

"He runs things around here, or at least we let him think he does." She smiled. "I'm Betty. Let me know if there's anything I can help you with."

Ernest looked past Betty to where a vision in pink caught his eye. There she stood, Genevieve Lamont, making change for the mayor's wife. As she finished the transaction and closed the cash drawer, her gaze collided with his.

"Something wrong, sir?"

He returned his attention to Betty, who stared at him with a perplexed look. "No, nothing," he said. "But I think I've found what I was looking for."

Rather than go directly up to Miss Lamont, Ernest took a roundabout path that led him through several aisles. By the time he reached the front of the store, he'd accumulated two packages of baking soda, a box of saltine crackers, and a pair of black shoelaces for his church shoes. As he dumped the items on the counter, he pasted a casual look onto his face and studied the ceiling.

"Ernest?"

He lowered his gaze to meet hers. "Genevieve Lamont. What in the world are you doing here?"

The pink of her cheeks and lips matched the color of her spring dress. "I work here."

She paused and seemed to be trying to collect herself. Or at least that's what Ernest hoped as he struggled to slow his racing pulse.

"Well now, how about that?" he managed.

An awkward silence fell between them. Finally, Genevieve reached for the package of shoelaces and began to punch in the price on the cash register. At the rate she was going, she would be finished in no time. Soon he'd have to hand her his money, take his things, and leave the five-and-dime. He'd have no excuse for standing there and staring or making small talk.

If he could manage small talk, that is.

He should do something. Say something. Anything to stop her before she placed his last item in the bag.

"Wait."

As soon as he said it, Ernest felt like a fool. Now what? The prettiest girl in New Iberia stood right in front of him, holding a box of baking soda and, at the same time, capturing his heart.

"Yes? Did you forget something?"

"Actually, well, I. . ." He reached back to grab a tube of toothpaste off the shelf, ignoring the strange look Betty gave him. "I need toothpaste," he said with a shrug.

As quickly as he handed her the toothpaste, she rang it up and dropped it into the bag with the other items. "Anything else?"

What now? He darted his eyes to the left and then back to the right. A display of brightly colored papers and pens caught his attention. "Oh, and a birthday present for my sister."

"Do you know what she would like?"

"Hmmm," he said. "I really don't have any idea. Would you mind helping?" There, that ought to buy him some time. "Maybe just giving me an opinion of what a girl about to turn thirteen might like for her birthday," he added for good measure.

"I suppose." She gave him a tentative look, and his heart doubled its pace. "Tell me a little about your sister. What does she like to do? Does she have any favorite activities?"

"Let's see." Ernest scratched his head. "She loves to read." He paused to think, something made extremely difficult with Genevieve Lamont's dark eyes staring in his direction. "Oh, and she says she wants to be a writer someday, but I've always said she ought to go to California and act in the movies. She just can't get enough of them."

"Well, let's see. Unless you're planning to make a special day of it at the

Evangeline Theater, I'm afraid the only thing on that list is books."

"Books." He nodded. "Yes, I think that would work just fine."

Genevieve set the bag of items aside and cleared the register, then indicated for him to follow her. Two aisles over, she stopped in front of a shelf filled with books of all sorts. He picked up one by Zane Grey that looked nifty but replaced it on the shelf when he saw Genevieve's frown.

"Maybe you ought to help me with this, what with you being a pretty girl and all." Ernest felt the heat climb into his neck. Of all the things to say. "What I mean is, you're a female and she is, too."

He dared a glance in her direction and saw her lips tilt into a smile for the briefest of seconds. For all his blundering, at least he hadn't offended her.

Yet.

"What about this one? Girls seem to love the Nancy Drew series." She moved past him, and he smelled the scent of roses. "This is the third in the series, and there are the first two. There are more titles, but we're a little slow getting them."

Ernest reached for the book and weighed it in his hand. "You recommend this for teenage girls? I mean, look at her." He pointed to the girl in the blue dress on the cover. "Looks like she's snooping around."

Genevieve stifled a giggle. "She's supposed to be snooping, Ernest. This is a mystery novel."

"Well, that explains it." He reached for the other two books with the blue-dressed girl on the cover. "Might as well get all three of them. She'll probably finish these before I know it and be asking for the next one. That Amalie reads as fast as anyone I know."

"Reading is a good way to keep a young girl out of trouble." Genevieve reached past him to fill the empty spot on the shelf with another copy. "I have to admit I like them, too. Only I have to check mine out from the library."

"If Latagnier had a library, Amalie would take a pillow and blanket and live there." Ernest chuckled. "Since they don't, I guess I'll just have to keep coming in here and buying books for her."

Rather than speak, she looked away. Ernest ran out of words, and an awkward silence fell between them.

"Excuse me, Miss Lamont, but if you're finished helping this gentleman, I could use you back at your job at the cash register."

Ernest whirled around to see Lester Bonfils blocking the end of the aisle, the toothpick planted in the gap between his front teeth. "Actually, Miss Lamont was just about to help me with a Western novel." He turned back to face Genevieve and forced a serious look. "Do you have anything by Zane Grey?"

"Yes, actually, we do, Mr. Breaux. Mr. Grey's newest one is right here." Genevieve reached for the novel Ernest had just put back on the shelf and placed it atop the three Nancy Drew novels in his arms. "I wonder if you might also like his last book. Where is it? Oh, there it is." She grabbed another book off the shelf and added it to his stack, trying not to smile. "This one seems to sell well among our gentlemen customers."

"I see." He pursed his lips to keep from laughing. "While I'm at it, is there anything else you'd recommend?"

"Well, I don't know, sir. You see, Mr. Bonfils is the manager, and I think he may need me to go back up to the register."

Ernest cast a glance over his shoulder to look at Lester. "I don't know if you realize this, but Miss Lamont here is very knowledgeable about books. If she can't spend a few more minutes helping me with my reading material, then I'm afraid I'll have to put these back on the shelf and return when she has more time."

His statement seemed to have no effect on the portly manager, so Ernest tried another strategy. "Or maybe you could help me. I've been looking for a nice book on flower arranging. I wonder if you have something like that. I do love a nice arrangement of flowers when I come home from a hard day."

Lester's face registered a blank look. "Flower arranging? I leave that to the ladies."

"Then until I can find a lady who's not too busy to advise me, I will just have to take my business elsewhere."

Before Ernest could make good on his threat, Lester Bonfils was gone. "See that you get yourself back to the register soon as you're done, Miss Lamont," he said as he disappeared around a display of Alka-Seltzer.

"Yes, sir," Genevieve called. "Right away, Mr. Bonfils."

He gave Genevieve a penitent look. "Did I get you in trouble?"

"Trouble?" She shrugged. "Now about that book on flower arranging."

"Oh. That. See, actually, I'm not much for arranging flowers. Actually, I'm not much for flowers at all." He shook his head. "That's not true. I mean, I like flowers, but I don't really find much need to. . ." Ernest gave up. "I'm rambling, aren't I?"

Big brown eyes continued to peer up at him, her expression giving away nothing of her thoughts. "Yes, actually, you are."

He looked away, out of words. To his surprise, he felt Genevieve touch his arm.

"I should get back to work."

"I could find more to buy." Ernest juggled his books and tucked them into a stack under his arm. He gestured toward the Alka-Seltzer display. "What about those? After all this reading I just might need something for indigestion."

Genevieve's grin broadened. "You're funny."

"Miss Lamont? Could you come here?"

Lester Bonfils stood beside the soda fountain, one hand on his hip and a frown on his face. Ernest watched as Genevieve scurried over and endured a crisp instruction to man the counter rather than return to the cash register. As a final insult, Lester caught Ernest's gaze, seemingly daring him to complain.

A few choice words came to mind, but Ernest swallowed them along with his pride. A job was a precious thing, and he wouldn't dare do or say anything to cause Genevieve to lose hers. The Bonfils fellow must have known this, because he walked away from the soda fountain, chuckling.

Ernest checked the clock above the fountain. It read a quarter to one. He was set to work the night shift at the sawmill, so he had nowhere to go until ten. Of course, he'd need to find time to get some sleep before then, but he had all afternoon for that.

With a grin, he headed for the cash register to pay for his purchases. The young lady behind the counter, what was her name? She'd introduced herself when he first walked into the five-and-dime, but he'd paid little attention.

Barbara? No, maybe it was Brenda. As he neared the register, he saw that her name tag read BETTY.

Yes, that was it. Betty.

Out of the corner of his eye, Ernest thought he saw Genevieve watching him; but when he turned to check, she'd looked away.

"My, but you must be quite a reader."

Setting the books on the counter, Ernest reached for his wallet. "I suppose it would seem that way, Betty, but I'm here buying birthday gifts." He cast a glance over his shoulder to find Genevieve casually cleaning a soda glass.

"Birthday gifts, huh?" Betty chuckled. "My guess is you had more on your mind than birthdays when you walked in here."

Ernest felt the heat rise in his neck. Without comment, he peeled off the cash and handed it to Betty. He'd almost made it out the door when he had a thought.

He sure was thirsty.

Adjusting his cap, Ernest sized up his options. He could head for home and slake his thirst with a cold drink of water, or he could walk down the street to Mulotte's Grocery and buy a bottle of cola. He could even take a table at the new hamburger joint around the corner where there was a large choice of beverages.

Or he could belly up to the soda fountain and have something right now.

It didn't take him long to decide which option appealed the most. Within seconds, he'd claimed the nearest stool to Genevieve Lamont and ordered a soda water with vanilla and a cherry.

"I can't visit with you anymore, you know." She looked around the perimeter of the store, then returned her gaze to Ernest. "I can't afford to lose this job, and Mr. Bonfils is looking for any excuse to fire me."

"Well, first off, the man must be out of his mind to want to banish such a lovely lady from the premises. And second. . ." He paused to take a long draw of soda water. "I'm a working man myself, and I know how precious a paycheck can be. You have my word that I won't interfere with your making a living."

Relief flooded her face. "Thank you."

"Don't mention it." Ernest faked an impatient look as he finished the last sip of water in the glass. "Now where's my refill?"

"You're teasing me, aren't you?"

"Miss Lamont, I am a thirsty man with a book to read." He selected one of the Zane Grey novels and cracked it open to the first chapter. "So fetch my soda. I've got outlaws to catch."

"Yes, sir," she said as she stifled a giggle.

Genevieve seemed amused when he ordered his third drink and concerned when he asked for a fourth. By the fifth soda water, his stomach had begun to complain, and so had Lester Bonfils. Trouble with Mr. Bonfils's complaints was that Ernest was a paying customer and there wasn't a thing that could be done about it.

By the time six o'clock rolled around, Ernest had finished his sixth soda water and nearly completed the Zane Grey novel. He'd also decided that Genevieve Lamont worked far too hard and was due an evening off.

Perhaps an evening with him.

They could have supper at the little burger joint, then head to the Evangeline Theater to see what was playing. If he had her home by nine thirty, he could still make it to work on time.

True, he'd work tonight without sleep, but the time spent with Genevieve Lamont would be worth it.

He almost missed his chance to tell her that. As he gathered his books, she slipped out the front door. Ernest caught up with her on the sidewalk.

"Where are you going?" he called, adjusting his stack of books to keep from decorating the sidewalk with them.

At first she seemed not to hear, but a moment later she stopped and turned around to face him. The good humor she had displayed in the five-and-dime was gone.

Chapter 10

Are you following me?"

"What?" Ernest stopped short when Genevieve repeated the question. "Following? No, I was. . ." He shook his head. "I can't tell a lie. Yes, I was following you. But I had a good reason."

Genevieve's expression told him she had doubts. She said nothing, however.

"Yes, see, I just wanted to ask you. . ." His tongue stuck on the roof of his mouth, and his voice disappeared. A moment later, he cleared his throat and tried again. "What do you say to a movie tonight?"

There, he'd said it. Before he could feel relieved that he'd managed the invitation, terror took over. She hadn't answered.

Instead, she stood stock-still, looking like she'd just swallowed a bug. Unless he missed his guess, she'd just heard the worst question of her life.

Ernest was about to apologize for the intrusion and head for home to lick his wounds when the most amazing thing happened. She smiled.

Then she said, "Not tonight."

His hopes plummeted. "Oh" was all he could manage.

She looked up at him and blinked hard. Was that the beginning of a smile he saw?

"What about tomorrow night?"

Considering the ache in his gut, tomorrow was probably the better choice. Still, he felt more than a little disappointment at the wait. He parted company with her after agreeing to meet on the steps of the five-and-dime at half past six.

But not before he tried and failed to convince Gen to let him walk her home.

Later, as he lay facedown on his bed, he asked his roommate, Phil, if he thought it strange that a woman wouldn't reveal where she lived to a gentleman.

"Depends," Phil said. "She could be hiding something, but as a rule I'd have to say she's probably just the cautious type."

Ernest rolled over on his back, then groaned when his stomach complained. "Maybe," he said, "but her people have known my people for a hundred years. More, actually. I know where she lives in Latagnier, and what I don't know about her, I could find out from my mother or one of my sisters. Why would it matter that I know where she lives in New Iberia?"

Phil gave Ernest a look. "Why indeed," he said slowly.

Ernest rolled up on his elbows, then forced himself into a sitting position.

Thankfully his stomach seemed to like sitting better than lying down. "What does that mean?"

"Nothing."

"Go on and say it."

"All right." Phil shrugged. "It's just that the way you've been carrying on lately, well, a body'd think you were about to fall hard for that girl. And you know the next step after a man falls. He starts hearing wedding bells."

Ernest laughed again. "Oh, that's a good one, my friend. Me married?"

"Don't sound so confident. Better men than you have taken that road. I hear some of them actually enjoy married life. Just a rumor, of course."

"Never, Phil," Ernest said. "You forget that I'm the oldest of a dozen children. Mama and Papa gave up all they had to raise young'uns. I don't plan to make that kind of sacrifice—leastwise not while I'm young enough to appreciate the finer things in life. I'm a woodworker, Phil, and someday I intend to have a nice furniture shop, maybe a little place where a man can buy a table and chairs or a bench that lasts. No, sir, I intend to make baby cribs—not families."

Phil said nothing.

"You don't believe me, do you?"

"It doesn't matter whether I believe you or not. You're falling for that girl from the five-and-dime, and you seem to be the only one who hasn't figured that out."

"Am not."

But was he? His aching gut would protest the statement. Why else would a sane, rational man down six soda waters in one afternoon when he ought to be home catching up on his sleep? It sure wasn't because the book was so good, although he had to admit Mr. Grey could tell a whopper of a tale.

No, he'd sat on that hard stool drinking cherry vanilla soda waters one after the other because he couldn't bring himself to leave the five-and-dime. Rather than be away from Genevieve Lamont, he'd chosen to sit in her presence and make a fool of himself.

Was that love?

He'd never know, because he refused to fall in love.

True, Genevieve was a nice girl; and true again, he did enjoy her company. And tomorrow night, well, it really wasn't a date. Actually, it was more like two neighbors from Latagnier meeting to pass a good time.

Well, whatever it was, Ernest certainly didn't know Genevieve well enough to figure out how to classify her. So maybe tomorrow night would be just a getting-to-know-you visit.

Yes, that was it.

For the first time since he'd ordered the afternoon's sodas, he felt better. Not that his gut had stopped complaining, for it hadn't, but he actually had the beginnings of a plan.

Ernest would spend some time with Genevieve, maybe have a laugh or two, then that would be the end of it. Surely whatever interest he felt would fade once he had a clearer picture of the mysterious Miss Lamont.

~

"Genevieve, I don't remember when I've seen you so nervous, hon." Betty stepped away from the window to touch Gen's sleeve. "Why, you look like you're about to jump out of your skin."

Gen loosened her scarf and set her handbag beside the door. "I guess I am a little out of sorts."

Betty gestured toward the window. "Coffee on the terrace?"

"Sure," Gen said. "But let me change first."

She slipped out of her working clothes and into a simple housedress that Big Mama had fashioned out of rose-printed potato sacks. As she closed the wardrobe, she caught sight of herself in the mirror. Or rather, she saw a stranger staring back.

Gen touched the rough cotton fabric, then allowed her hands to fall at her sides, resting against hips a bit more padded since Ellen's birth. Loose tendrils of dark hair fell at her temples, resisting capture into the bun at the back of her neck.

Gen leaned in to look into that woman's eyes. Despite her age, the person in the mirror looked old. Not old in the sense that many years had passed, but old in that she had lived many years in a short time.

Where had the silly girl with the head full of dreams gone?

The woman-child who believed anything was possible had realized the downside of that truth. When anything became possible, anything could happen. And sometimes, what happened wasn't what you expected.

"Gen, honey. You all right?"

"I'm fine." Gen smoothed the loose curls back into her bun and reached for a pair of bobby pins to keep them in place. "I'll be there in a sec."

"Don't take too long. The coffee's getting cold."

A trip down the hall to the only bathroom in the building kept Gen from sipping coffee that was steaming hot, but the temperature of the dark brew didn't matter. It was the warmth of friendship that counted right then.

And she really needed a friend. In short order, she finished her coffee and the story about the afternoon's visit with Ernest Breaux. Finally, she admitted she'd agreed to a movie date with him.

A cool breeze blew across Gen as she curled her legs beneath her and waited for Betty's response. What her roommate would make of the situation was anyone's guess, but Gen had the highest respect for her opinion.

Betty chuckled. "I wondered if he would stay all afternoon. I mean, it couldn't have been much after twelve thirty when the man walked into the store, and there he still sat with a half-empty soda and that book when I went home at three."

"Well, he tried to follow me home at six, so you do the math."

"That's a long time to sit in one place." Betty sipped at the remains of her coffee. "I don't have to think too hard to come up with a reason why a man would do that. What about you?"

Gen avoided her friend's direct gaze. "I suppose it's possible the book was exceptionally good and he liked the soda waters."

"I suppose." Betty rose and climbed inside to return with the coffeepot. She filled their mugs, then set the pot beside her. "Is he a nice man? Does he come from good people?"

Gen thought of his behavior at the bus station and his concern over her riding the bus. "Yes, he appears to be very nice. A real gentleman, actually, from a good family."

"He's a bit older than you, isn't he?"

"Let me think." She tried to guess his age compared to his siblings. "A few years, seven or eight at the most, I would suppose, but I know he's not yet thirty. Now *that* would be old."

Betty made a face. "It won't seem so old when you're as close to it as I am." She paused and seemed to be deep in thought. "You know, hon, it seems to me that you're afraid of something."

"Afraid?"

Nodding, Betty stared past Gen. "You have a movie date with a nice man, a gentleman, who isn't too old or too young and whose family you know and like, right?"

She blew on the steaming coffee, then took a sip. "Right."

"So what's wrong with that?" Betty rested her elbows on her knees. "I mean, sure, you've been through it, what with marrying that fellow, then having your heart broken and all, but are you going to spend the rest of your life being afraid to go out and try again?"

Gen considered the question for half a second before she dismissed it. Rising, she scooped up her mug and headed inside to wash it in the tiny sink.

"Come on, hon, don't run off." Betty followed her inside and set her coffee cup beside Gen's in the sink. She touched Gen's sleeve and shook her head. "The Lord doesn't make us to fear anyone or anything but Him."

"I know that." But did she? Hadn't she spent a good part of the last year in fear?

Betty nudged her with her elbow. "So take what you know and put it into practice."

"That's easy for you to say." Gen set the mugs to dry on the drain board, then leaned against the counter. "You really don't think going out on a date is awful?" She paused. "I mean, considering."

Her roommate shrugged. "Considering what?"

"My secrets, Betty. I've got more than my share, wouldn't you say?"

"How much does this fellow know about your past?"

Gen paused to think. "About as much as the rest of Latagnier knows, I suppose. I was raised there, then left home after I finished school. I doubt Mother bragged about my running off with Alton, and I know for a fact that my father never said a word about it."

"So it's likely your date doesn't know he's taking a widow to the movies."

"That's right." Gen wrapped her arms around her middle. "I'm confused, Betty. He's nice, and I think I could really enjoy spending time with him. On the other hand, I've felt this way before."

"With Alton?"

Gen nodded. "And it's not just me that I have to be worried about. The Lord gave me. . ." She bit down on the last of her statement and looked away. As much as she longed to confide in Betty, to tell her about the precious baby girl she missed every moment she was away from her, Gen couldn't say a word. Not yet. Some secrets were too precious.

"That's what you're afraid of, isn't it? That this man will turn out the same way, and you'll be back in a place where God never meant you to be."

How simple the trouble sounded when Betty summed it up. And how terribly complicated it was.

"Yes."

Betty seemed to ponder the point a moment. "Were you thinking of marrying this one, too?"

"No," Gen said. "Of course not."

Betty gave Gen a satisfied smile. "In that case, I say go out and have a good time. Allow yourself that much, hon. You deserve a little fun, what with the way you work so hard." She paused. "But would you do one thing for me first?"

"Of course," Gen said. "What's that?"

"Pray about the date, and ask the Lord to guide you in the matter. If He doesn't want this, you shouldn't, either. Ask Him and see what He says."

That night as Gen lay awake, she took Betty's advice. Rather than receive an answer from the Lord on her predicament, she was met with silence.

Finally, she gave up and closed her eyes. As she drifted somewhere between sleep and dreams, she felt a stirring of hope. If silence was all that greeted her, maybe the Lord was trying to tell her she'd made the wrong choice.

"Father," she whispered into her pillow, "between You and me, I don't know if I will ever be finished with that old life, even if You did take Alton home. I'm not going to expect an answer tonight, but if You want me to get on with my life like Betty said I should, would You mind sending me a message real plainlike?"

Chapter 11

Thursday, May 11

Six o'clock straight up. Fifteen minutes to go, and her nerves were already jittery. The five-and-dime's doors swung open. Gen fought the urge to run inside and hide, to somehow make herself invisible until time passed and Ernest Breaux gave up and went home.

She never should have borrowed this dress from Betty. Green was absolutely not a good color for her. Why, as she looked at her reflection in the window of the five-and-dime, there was no mistaking the fact that she looked like a stick of celery.

And why in the world had she chosen to bring that old white sweater? She removed the sweater and tied it around her shoulders, then smoothed her hair back into place.

My, but she needed a trim. Or maybe she shouldn't have worn her hair down. Just wait until she saw Betty tonight. Listening to her about the dress and her hair had been the wrong thing to do.

She took a deep breath and let it out slowly. Searching for something to calm herself, Gen began to repeat the prayer she'd begun last night. " 'And they that know thy name will put their trust in thee: for thou, Lord, hast not forsaken them that seek thee,' " she whispered, claiming the promise from Psalm 9 as her own.

Funny how she'd held on to that verse since she was a little girl, only to forget all about it when Alton Gallier came into her life. But then, she'd forgotten about a lot of things she'd once held on to when Alton came along.

"It is finished."

The words were as clear as if someone had whispered them in her ear. Gen looked to the right and the left. Other than the usual busyness of the New Iberia evening, no one stood near enough to speak.

"It is finished."

She jumped. While she regularly carried on lengthy conversations with the heavenly Father, not once had she had an actual reply—at least not one she could practically hear. She slipped around the side of the building and leaned against the brick wall.

"Lord," she whispered, "is that You?"

"Let it be finished."

"It, Lord?"

"The past. It is finished."

Gen shook her head, then began to giggle. Well, there it was. Her answer. The God of all the universe had taken the time to speak directly to her. She continued to giggle even as the tears flowed.

All at once her body felt light, and it seemed as though years of living fell away. She felt like a child, a little girl finally allowed to go out and play after a long, cold winter indoors.

Wiping her eyes with the corner of her handkerchief, Gen gathered her wits and took a deep breath. Letting it out slowly, she headed toward the front of the five-and-dime.

"I didn't think you were coming."

Ernest Breaux smiled down at her from the top step. "I'm terribly sorry," she said as she carefully tucked her handkerchief into her skirt pocket.

He met her on the sidewalk and let out a low whistle. "You look beautiful. I don't believe I've ever seen such a pretty shade of green on a lady."

Gen blushed, a strange feeling for a widowed mother. "Thank you," she said. "You look nice, too."

As soon as she said the words, she felt the heat flame hotter in her cheeks. He did look nice—awfully nice, actually—and he smelled nice, too.

But to tell him so? And on a first date? What an idiot he must think her to be.

~

She must think I'm an idiot.

Ernest stifled a groan at the stupid comment he'd made. Of course she looked nice. Actually, she looked more than nice. Couldn't he have commented on something besides her looks? True, she was the prettiest girl in New Iberia, but surely she already knew that.

And while her looks had first caught his attention, her sweet spirit, contagious laughter, and genuine personality were what kept him interested.

He looked down at her, and his breath caught. Was that a tear he saw in the corner of her eye?

"Are you all right?"

She considered the question a moment longer than he liked, but when she answered, she smiled first. "Yes, I'm fine," she said. "Why?"

Now what to say? That she looked like she'd been crying? Oh no. Ernest had too many sisters not to know better than that.

"No reason," he said as he offered her his hand. "Shall we?"

At first he thought she might say no, or worse, that she might say nothing at all and just hightail it out of there. Instead, she looked at his hand as if it had grown a second thumb.

Then she smiled.

It wasn't a real smile, actually. Not one of those broad grins that a body can't help but make. No, this was more like something she did because she knew she was supposed to.

Ernest expelled a long breath and looked away. "You sure you want to be here tonight? With me, I mean."

He swung his gaze back to collide with Genevieve's. This time the smile seemed genuine.

"I'm afraid you caught me," she said as she studied her hands.

Ernest's heart sank. It looked as though the evening would be over before it got started. "Oh," he managed. "How's that?"

Once again she met his stare. "I'm nervous, Ernest. I haven't gone out with a boy. . ." Her voice faltered, and she cleared her throat. "I mean, a man," she continued, "in so long I'm not sure I remember how."

"You?" He could tell his question startled her. "I mean, a girl as pretty and smart as you must have a whole lot of fellows moonstruck. Why, I'd be willing to bet you're putting me on."

"I'm serious, Ernest. I'm afraid I might not be very good company for you this evening." She shook her head. "I just don't know what I'm doing here."

He took two steps back and stuffed his fists into his pockets. "Well now, that's a mite disappointing. But I think I can help you with that."

She gave him a confused look. "I don't understand."

"Well, Miss Lamont, it's like this." He gestured to the step where she stood. "You're at the five-and-dime, and I'm over here on the sidewalk." When she nodded, he continued, pointing north. "Over yonder is the movie theater. You ever been to one of those? Big building with lots of pretty lights."

"Yes, I'm familiar with them." Her lips turned up in a slight grin. "I've actually been a time or two."

"Good, then I don't have to explain how to sit in the seat and watch the movie, and you won't get upset when the lights go out." Ernest rocked back on his heels. "Now, Miss Lamont, have you ever had candy? It's that sweet stuff they sell behind the counter in those movie theaters you've been to."

The grin inched up and almost became a smile. "Yes, I've had candy, Mr. Breaux, although I'm partial to watching movies without the interruption of having to chew."

"Excellent." He took a step forward and put on a perplexed look. "There's just one more thing. How proud were you of that streak you had going?"

"Streak?"

Ernest nodded. "All that time without a date. Will it bother you terribly to end that streak? Because I believe you're about to."

Her smile became a giggle and then a full-sized laugh. "You know," she said as she met Ernest on the sidewalk, "I don't believe it will bother me at all."

"Then I will repeat my original question." Ernest again offered Genevieve his hand. "Shall we?"

This time she accepted his offer, and when Genevieve touched him, he felt as though he could conquer the world.

Strolling through New Iberia, making small talk about the weather and the folks back in Latagnier, felt even better. By the time he'd bought two tickets for *Me and My Pal*, the new Laurel and Hardy film, and settled four rows back from the screen, the feeling had grown to the point where he couldn't stop smiling if he tried.

Good thing they'd chosen a comedy.

Not that he watched a bit of the movie. No, he was too busy sneaking glances at Genevieve, who seemed to be enjoying herself despite sitting so close to the screen that she had to lean back and look up.

Once or twice he considered snaking his arm around the back of Genevieve's seat, but he decided against it. With their friendship so new and tender, Ernest dared not do anything so familiar.

No, this lady was skittish as a newborn colt. She probably had good reason, although Ernest doubted it had been as long as Genevieve led him to believe since she'd had a date.

That was impossible to believe. There weren't that many stupid men in Iberia Parish; surely one of the smart ones had seen what Ernest saw when he looked at Genevieve.

He glanced back at the screen in time to see Mr. Hardy take a fall, then joined Genevieve in laughter. "Does it bother you to sit so close?" he whispered when the laughter died.

She cast a worried glance in his direction. "No," she said as she reached for her purse, "but we can move if you'd like."

"No, I'm fine." He offered a weak smile to go along with the wishful thinking. His head was beginning to throb because of the closeness of the screen. Not that he would ever let Genevieve know.

Too soon the movie ended, and Ernest found himself ushering his date through the lobby toward the glass doors and the street beyond. Without warning, Genevieve stopped and turned around.

"What's wrong?" he asked as he tagged a half step behind her.

She came to a halt in front of the candy counter. "One of those, please," he heard her say.

Before Ernest could react, Genevieve had requested two candy bars and handed over her dime. Whirling around to face him, she offered him a big smile and a Milky Way bar. He sputtered a word of thanks.

What an interesting woman.

"Shall we?" she asked.

Ernest tucked the candy into his shirt pocket. "Lead the way, m'lady," he said as he offered a mock bow.

They settled across the street from the theater on a park bench. While the last of the moviegoers filed out beneath the lighted marquee, Ernest enjoyed the best candy bar he'd had in years.

And he didn't even like candy.

But somehow sitting next to Genevieve while she obviously enjoyed hers made all the difference. Ernest heaved a long sigh and looked past the theater to the stars, nearly hidden by the brilliance of a thousand lights.

"It's a beautiful night," Genevieve said.

Ernest nodded, turning his attention from the stars to the lovely lady at his side. "Yes," he said softly, "beautiful indeed."

If she caught the compliment, she gave no indication. Rather, she continued to nibble on her candy until she'd finished nearly half of it. With care, she rewrapped the candy and placed it in her purse. A second later, she rose.

"I should be leaving," she said.

"Are you sure?"

Genevieve nodded and grasped her purse to her chest. "Yes," she said. "I've got to work tomorrow."

So did Ernest, but showing up at the sawmill was the last thing on his mind. He climbed to his feet and tossed the candy wrapper in the trash bin.

"Then let's get you home before you turn into a pumpkin, Cinderella." He paused. "Which way do we go?"

"What do you mean?" Genevieve froze, then pointed to the south. "The five-and-dime is that way."

He nodded. "Well, of course it is, but a gentleman wouldn't allow a lady to walk home alone. I'd feel much better if I could see you to your door."

"No."

Even though shadows hid part of her face, Ernest could see that Genevieve meant business. "Have it your way," he said as he offered her his arm. "But I don't like it one bit."

"Thank you," she said.

As they neared the five-and-dime, Ernest found his steps were a bit slower even as his heart raced. Just like yesterday at the soda counter, he didn't want their time together to end.

They arrived at the five-and-dime, now dark and empty. Ernest knew a gentleman would say a quick good-bye and make a hasty exit. At this moment, he had no interest in doing either. So without braving a look in Genevieve's direction, he plopped down on the third step and made himself at home.

An uncomfortable silence fell between them as Genevieve clutched her purse to her chest. Ernest searched his foggy brain for a topic they could chew on a bit. Ah, yes, Latagnier. Talking about the bayou could eat up an unlimited amount of time.

"So," he said casually, "have you been home lately?"

"To Latagnier?" Genevieve shook her head, then fumbled with the clasp on her purse. Home was the one place she longed to be, and talking about it just hurt her heart. "No, not in a few weeks," she said as she cast about for a change of topic.

"You sound like you miss it."

Her startled gaze must have surprised him. "I do?"

"Well, sort of," he said. "But then, I understand, what with losing your papa and your mama being there by herself. Must be difficult."

"Yes, it is." She affected a casual pose. "I suppose you must miss home, too, what with the little ones changing so fast. It must seem like forever when you're away."

He gave her a strange look. "Actually, I do miss some of the things at home, but crying babies isn't one of them. Of course, now that the girls are older, it's not so bad."

If he'd waited on her for conversation, he would have had a long wait. Thankfully he interpreted her dumbstruck expression as a need for more information.

"You see, Eileen was barely toddling and Mary was a newborn when I took off for greener—and quieter—pastures," he said. "Now that they're three and four, I'm getting used to them; but I'll tell you, if I never hear another crying baby, it will be too soon."

"You don't like babies?" Gen tried to keep any sign of emotion from her voice. Whether she succeeded or not, she couldn't say. Her heart was pounding too hard to hear.

"Oh, sure, I love babies, as long as they don't live at my house or cry when I'm trying to think." He shrugged. "Anyway, I'm heading home tomorrow for my sister's birthday party. I'd be honored to meet you after work and take you with me."

Amid the turmoil in her heart, she struggled to follow his change of topic. She was having a hard enough time accepting the fact that the man she'd become fond of had an aversion to babies.

"Home?" she muttered. "To Latagnier?"

"Yes," he said, clearly puzzled, "to Latagnier."

Gen shook her head. "I'm sorry, but that's not possible."

Ernest patted the step beside him. "All right, then, why don't you just sit a spell before we part company?" He grinned. "I promise I won't bite."

Gen realized she could either join him on the step or head home. There was danger in both, but allowing him to follow her seemed a bit riskier than sitting beside him until she could convince him to leave.

So without comment, she perched on the bottom step and tucked the hem of her dress around her ankles. The air had become brisk, with a slight breeze. Gen removed the sweater from her shoulders and put it on. If she couldn't be comfortable, at least she wouldn't be cold.

"Where were we? Ah, yes, we were talking about Latagnier." He peered down at her intently. "I've noticed you don't use the Acadian language."

"No," she said slowly. "I don't suppose I do."

"Do you speak it?" He paused. "At all, I mean?"

"I used to," Gen said slowly. "Daddy thought it important that I learn the language of the people. He and I spoke to one another almost exclusively in Acadian French."

"What about your mother? Does she?"

"I suppose she still remembers it, although it used to be quite a game of mine to try and get her to speak or comment in it. Daddy insisted she could understand us, but I never could get her to prove him right. She didn't much like to hear it."

"Wonder why," Ernest said.

Gen shrugged. "My father said it was because people thought the Acadians were backward. If you didn't speak English, you were somehow less, oh, I don't know."

Ernest nodded. "I know a lot of folks feel that way. Me personally, I don't, but then, I also don't use the language much here in New Iberia. Now if I'm at home in Latagnier, that's a whole other story."

"It's hard for me to hear it, even though I hear it all the time at the store." She looked away. "Reminds me too much of Daddy, I guess."

As she spoke her father's name, tears burned her eyes; tears for Daddy, for Mother, and for Ellen, but also for herself and the way she'd let both her earthly father and her heavenly Father down.

Determined not to let Ernest Breaux see her cry, Gen looked away and pretended to study something across the street. In truth, she could see nothing but a big blurry patch of grass where she knew the park should be. Someday, maybe, she'd swallow her pride and get those eyeglasses she ought to have.

But she would have to think of mundane things like eyeglasses later. For now, it was all she could do not to let the tears spill.

Ernest scooted down to sit beside her. Without a word, he took her hand in his.

How long they sat in silence, fingers entwined, Gen couldn't say. Finally, she gathered her wits and her purse and rose.

"Thank you for tonight," she said. "I had a good time."

"I'm glad to hear it." Ernest stretched his long legs, then stood. "Now about that trip to Latagnier this weekend."

The thought of seeing her precious Ellen tempted her, but she'd been offered rare overtime hours tomorrow, and with their funds dwindling at an alarming rate and the taxes on the home place coming due, she had to accept the extra work. Still, her heart broke as she forced herself to turn down Ernest's offer.

"Well then," he said slowly, "if you change your mind, let me know."

"Sure," she said, although she doubted any such thing would happen.

"All right, then. Oh, and before I forget, thank you for the candy. I can honestly say that was the best Milky Way bar a girl's ever bought for me." He grinned. " 'Course, it's the only Milky Way bar a girl's ever bought for me."

"Oh, hush." Gen gave Ernest a playful shove, and he caught her wrist with his hand.

Time suspended between silly play and serious emotions. Gen looked up into Ernest's eyes. The moment her gaze collided with his, he released his grip.

"I'm asking one more time if I can see you home, Genevieve," he said, his voice husky.

She paused to give the idea some thought. "Not this time, Ernest," she finally said. "Maybe some other time, but not tonight."

Ernest stared at her a moment longer, then gave her a curt nod. "I'm a man of my word," he said, "so I'm going to turn my back to the street and let you head on home." He captured her hand in a firm grip, then shook it and let it go. "Good night, Genevieve Lamont."

"Good night, Ernest Breaux," she said as she took a step back.

He began to turn away from the street, then stopped and glanced over his shoulder. "I made you a promise; now I want one from you in return."

"What's that?"

"How loud can you scream?"

She shrugged. "I don't know. I guess I'm not all that loud. Why?"

"Can you whistle?"

"I was raised on a farm," she said with a grin. "Of course I can."

"Show me," he said.

Gen let out her best whistle, the one she'd learned at her daddy's knee. Ernest looked suitably impressed.

So did the elderly man who lived above the five-and-dime. "You kids hush that racket down there!" the old man called. "Don't you know it's nigh on ten o'clock?"

"Sorry, Mr. Prejean," Gen called. "We were just leaving."

"See that you make it snappy. A body needs to sleep, you know." The old man completed his response by slamming his window shut. Still, Gen could see him peering through half-open curtains.

"Well now," Ernest said, "that was quite good."

"Thank you." She gave him a sideways look. "As Mr. Prejean said, it's nigh on ten o'clock. I should be going."

"Wait, you owe me a promise." Before she could comment, he held up his hand to silence her. "I only ask that if you're in trouble on the way home, you whistle. I'll come running. Would you promise me that?"

"I whistle, and you come running?" Gen grinned. "Now how could I say no to that?"

They shook on the bargain, and then Gen set off toward the boardinghouse.

More than once, she stopped to make sure Ernest kept his promise. Each time she found him standing with his back to her.

As she turned the corner and Ernest Breaux disappeared from sight, it was all she could do not to whistle.

Chapter 12

Saturday, May 13

Ernest lay on his back on the banks of Bayou Nouvelle, the warm sunshine making him feel as lazy as Papa's old hound dog. Not that he'd actually found the time to be lazy. Since he arrived, he'd been busy repairing benches and bracing tables, fixing the porch swing, and making a nice pile of wood shavings while carving new legs for Mama's rocker.

If he didn't know better, he'd think Papa left those jobs undone on purpose so he could praise Ernest when he completed them. Ernest had certainly heard enough comments about his carpentering skills to last a lifetime.

Yet he never got tired of the work.

What if Papa was right? What if the Lord did intend him to be a woodworker and not a sawmill employee?

Lord, if You intend it, You're going to have to show me how to manage it.

Through half-closed eyes, he watched Joseph and John splash in the shallows a few feet away. Each held a cane pole Ernest had fashioned to fit them, and they played at catching trophy-sized fish. Neither seemed to notice the lack of a line or hook.

Or for that matter, the lack of fish. There were none in this part of the bayou. The water was far too black to support the freshwater fish that thrived elsewhere.

"Mama's baking us a cake," John said as he pretended to cast toward the far side of the bayou.

Joseph might be younger than his twin by a full five minutes, but he lost nothing in a contest for attention. "Is not." He pointed his pole in the opposite direction and went through the motions of casting his imaginary line. "She's baking the cake for Amalie. We only get to have some on account of it's her birthday today and not ours."

"That's right, and don't you forget it." Amalie strolled toward them with a smile.

Ernest propped himself up on his elbows and watched his sister approach. Long hair hung over one shoulder in a tight braid, and her apron looked starched and spotless, a sure sign she'd been hiding somewhere reading rather than helping Mama with the chores.

At the age of thirteen as of a quarter to ten this morning, she wore her beauty as if she had no idea of it. Slender as a reed and nearly as tall as Ernest, she seemed at one moment a child and the next a woman.

This fact made Ernest want to show her off and hide her away all at the same time. Papa mentioned last night that the bayou boys were beginning to line up on the doorstep to vie for her attention. In a few years she'd be married off like Angeline and Mathilde. Then where would he be?

Most likely fashioning another crib for the endless stream of babies the old home place had entertained over the years.

Amalie settled beside him and smoothed her skirts around her ankles. The action reminded him of Genevieve and their conversation on the steps of the five-and-dime Thursday night. At the thought of the lovely Miss Lamont, he began to whistle.

Ernest also began to wonder if Genevieve had changed her mind about traveling to Latagnier this weekend. Maybe tomorrow after church he'd stop by her mama's place just to see if she was there.

His sister's chattering caught his notice. Ernest forced his mind back to Amalie. "What's that, cher?"

"I said that it's about time a girl got some attention around here, what with all these boys running around." Amalie shook her head. "Except for Eileen and Mary, even the babies are boys. Just last Sunday at church, the pastor's wife looked at Angeline and declared she would have another boy." She fisted her hands and hit her knees. "Another boy. Can you believe it?"

"I suppose," he said, "although I honestly don't see what the trouble is with boys. Someday you'll appreciate male attention, and it will be Papa or your brothers who say c'est tout. Enough."

As soon as he said the words, he wished he could reel them back in. No sense in stirring that pot until the stew was ready.

"Non, merci. I don't have time for that nonsense," she said with a wave of her hand. "Someday I'm going to write fabulous books that are turned into incredible movies that I will star in myself."

Ernest chuckled. "Now that's a lofty dream."

"Well, it might be, but God gave that dream to me, and the Bible says there's nothing God can't do. Until He changes His mind about my destiny, I'm not changing mine." She shrugged. "Anyway, just promise me that you will give Mama and Papa lots of granddaughters. Do you hear me? Girls, Ernest. This family needs more women."

Amalie turned that last statement into the height of drama. She even pretended to swoon.

Whistling turned to laughter. "Mais non, but you do say outrageous things, cher. What makes you think I plan to give Mama and Papa any grandbabies?"

"I'm young, but I'm not that young," she said, giving him a sideways glance. "I hear things."

He turned his face to the sun and closed his eyes. This should be good. Much of what Amalie claimed to hear turned out to be the fruit of her active imagination.

"Oh?" Ernest said as the sun's warmth continued to lull him into laziness. "Like what?"

"Like you've been spending time with Genevieve Lamont. Like you're sweet on her."

Ernest sat bolt upright and opened his eyes, blinding himself in the process. "Who told you that?" he asked as he tried to blink the world back into focus.

"Like I said, I hear things." She reached for a blade of grass and studied it. "People talk, Ernest, and most times they figure a girl with a book in her hand isn't listening."

The topic of Genevieve needed to be handled with care, this much Ernest knew. If his sister got wind of the fact that he truly had given some thought to developing a more serious relationship with Miss Lamont, Amalie would never let him hear the end of it.

The one thing that girl loved more than a good book or movie was a good family drama. And of course, he and his siblings were generally the stars of the story.

He gave his sister a sideways glance and decided humor was the only way to handle her.

"I'm sorry, what did you say? I wasn't listening."

She gave Ernest a playful shove, then looked toward the bayou. John and Joseph had left their poles on the bank and were now chasing turtles. "You boys get back on dry land, you hear? Mama's going to be calling us all to supper soon."

John obeyed immediately, while Joseph tarried. "Do as your sister says, Joseph," Ernest called. "And don't make me come in after you."

Well, that was obviously an invitation to disobey if ever Joseph heard one. He giggled, then disappeared under the water. A second later he rose from the murky stream, his hair wet and black as a seal and rivulets of water running off his outstretched hands.

"Look, Ernest, I'm a big old fish. I betcha won't come and catch me."

"Look at me, Ernest!" John called as he dove in after his twin. "I'm a fish, too. A big old fat fish with smelly scales and things on the side of my face that go like this." He emerged from the water with his hands beside his ears in a rough imitation of gills.

"Boys," Amalie said with a groan.

"That's right, Amalie. You'd do better to stick to your books and your movies." Ernest chuckled and climbed to his feet. "You'd better go on home and tell Mama her boys turned into bayou fishes." He paused to wink at the twins. "Even the oldest."

"Oh no," she said. "Ernest, you're not getting in the water with them, are you?"

"There was a time, Mademoiselle Amalie, when you loved nothing better than a swim in the bayou. What happened?"

She looked at him with disdain. "I grew up."

"Well, not me." Ernest kicked off his shoes and began to roll his pant legs up. Before he could prepare himself to wade in the shallows, Joseph had climbed on his back. John grabbed him around the waist, and together the three of them fell into the water.

Ernest came up sputtering, his brothers swimming in circles around him like the fish they claimed to be.

Amalie stood at the bank, keeping a healthy distance between herself and the reach of their splashes. "Oh, I'll be telling Mama, all right," she said. "I'm telling her that what I just saw proves my theory that there are too many men around here. They get together and their brains shrink up to nothing."

"Oh, please don't do that. Here, you can come swimming with us." Ernest pretended to chase her. "Come on back, birthday girl. Don't you want to have a birthday swim with us?"

Ernest watched Amalie hightail it down the path leading away from the bayou. In short order, she'd reach home, and depending on which one she saw first, she'd rat him out either to Mama or to Papa. By the time the three of them arrived on the front porch, there would be a less-than-happy set of parents waiting for them.

He knew it as well as he knew his name. Yet something made him linger just a bit longer in the black water.

It might have been the fun he had teasing his brothers and pretending to chase them in the shallows. It could have been the way he loved letting the twins climb on his back while he swam laps beneath the weeping willow. Or maybe it was the fact that he hadn't laughed so hard since his date with Genevieve on Thursday night.

Laughing was good for him, he decided. And so was playing with the twins.

Then he spied Mama heading down the path toward them. "Ernest Theophile Alfred Breaux, is that you I see acting the fool as wet as a duck in the bayou?"

Ernest knelt down and grabbed the twins, positioning them in front of him. "Quick, boys, hide me. I think Mama's gonna take the belt to me for getting wet so close to supper. Don't tell her where I am."

"Boys, where's your brother?" Mama called.

A giggling Joseph and John pointed behind them. "Right here, Mama," they said in unison.

"Thanks a lot, you turncoats. One question from Mama and you're squawking like a jaybird." Ernest stood and hefted a squealing boy onto each shoulder.

"They made me, Mama. I didn't want to get wet."

"We did not," echoed two similar yet distinct childish voices.

"Put them down, Ernest Breaux." Mama stood with her hands on her hips, obviously trying to keep a straight face. "Joseph and John, I sent you out here to keep your brother company. Do you think you ought to be swimming when you're supposed to be watching Ernest?"

She pretended to swat their bottoms as they raced past. Each one scooted out of her reach in time for her hand to hit air, a familiar ploy with Breaux children. Mama had never actually spanked a one of them, but she'd made the attempt many times over.

With the wisdom of adulthood, Ernest was left to wonder whether Mama let them think they were getting away with something or not. Surely she would have made contact with one of them along the way if she'd intended to.

Ernest swung his arms around Mama and picked her up as he hugged her. She cried out in protest at the wet embrace, all the while giggling.

"Ernest Breaux, you are as bad as your papa," she said as she smoothed her apron and brushed away the water from her shoulders. "What am I going to do with you?"

He bowed from the waist and smiled. "Why, thank you, Mama. You've paid me a high compliment."

"Oh, hush," she said as she turned toward the house. "You are just the end, son. Now come on back home and get into dry clothes. Supper's almost on the table, and I want everything to be special for Amalie."

"You're special, Mama. Don't you know that?"

Ernest caught her and swung her into his arms. Once again she squealed in protest. Finally, he let her down.

"If you do that one more time, I am going to whack the tar out of you, Ernest," she said. "Just because you've been taller than me since you turned ten, that doesn't mean I ought to be thrown about like a rag doll; yet every time you get a chance, you do just that. You got some problem that you don't understand that I like my feet on the ground, son?"

Ernest wrapped his arm around her waist and gave her a gentle hug. "I'm sorry, Mama," he said. "According to Amalie, my problem is that I'm a man."

Papa's laughter boomed. "Well now, I don't see how being a man is a problem."

Ernest looked up to see his father and brothers sitting on the porch. Amalie stood in the doorway. "Ask Amalie, Papa. She'll explain it where even a man can understand."

"Oh, hush, son," Mama said. "Don't you go causing a fuss on your sister's birthday." She pointed to the staircase beside Papa, the one that led from the porch to the upstairs portion of the house where Ernest and his brothers slept. "Head on upstairs and change into something dry. I would like to have all of you at the supper table on time tonight."

"Yes, ma'am," he said as he gave Amalie a wink, then climbed the stairs. Ten minutes later he wore dry clothes and had his hair slicked back away from his face the way Mama liked it. Mama didn't take any more kindly to hats in the house than she did to shaggy hair, so he left his cap upstairs atop his suitcase.

As he descended the stairs, Amalie's birthday present tucked in the crook of his arm, he smiled. Thanks to Genevieve Lamont, his sister would be pleased with his gift.

The fact that Amalie had heard talk of their friendship troubled Ernest. Why the bayou women had nothing better to do than speculate on his love life perplexed him.

After all, there was nothing to talk about.

"There's my oldest bebe!" Mama called as he walked in.

He kissed the top of Mama's head, then set his gift on the table with the others. "Mama, when are you going to stop calling me your baby? I am pushing thirty, you know."

"You're twenty-eight, Ernest," his sister Angeline said. "Don't rush thirty. I'm too close to you in age."

Ernest gave his heavily pregnant sister a kiss on the cheek, then allowed her toddling son to climb into his outstretched arms. "I can't help that time marches on, Angeline. Why, before you know it, this bruiser's going to have children of his own."

He tickled his nephew's chubby belly, then tossed him into the air and caught him. All the while, the little boy giggled, arms flailing. When Ernest handed him back to his father, he whirled around to find that a line of nephews and brothers had formed, each vying for his attention.

"Oh no, you don't," he said to the assembled group. "If I start this with all of you, we will never get supper."

"That's right," Amalie said as she took her place of honor at the table. "And whoever isn't washed up for supper when Papa sits down doesn't get any birthday cake."

Little Joseph peered up at Ernest, his hair still wet and slicked back from his swim. "Is that right, Ernest?"

He pretended to give the matter great thought. "Oui," he said. "That's the truth. You all better hurry outside to wash before Papa decides he wants to stand up and amble over to the table."

Papa stretched his long legs and yawned. "I am a mite tired from working the traps this afternoon. I believe my belly's complaining, too. That supper of yours almost ready, Mama?"

"It is," Mama called. "Just go ahead and set yourself at the table, Papa."

With that, the room cleared of all bodies under the age of twelve. Mama and Papa exchanged a chuckle.

"I declare, Ernest," his sister Mathilde said as she placed the gumbo pot at the center of the long table. "You are the Pied Piper of babies and little children. They all love you."

"That's right," her husband, Nicolas Arceneaux, said. "When do you intend to settle down and have a few of your own?"

"A few?" Papa said with a snort. "I told him long ago he ought to have a houseful. Babies keep a body young and a household happy."

Angeline patted her belly. "I don't know about keeping you young, Papa. Today I feel as old as the hills."

Mama shook her head as she wiped her hands on her apron. "This, too, shall pass. You just wait until your babies are this size." She gestured toward Ernest. "Then you'll appreciate them. Why, just look at those table legs. See this." She placed her hands on the table and gave it a shove. "It used to rock so bad we had to put folded paper under there. But Ernest, he built me all new legs for it. Now it sits just fine. Merci beaucoup, son."

Ernest shrugged. "It was nothing, Mama."

Papa nudged Ernest. "Maybe nothing to you, but a man who knows good work like me, well, I say it was something. You give any more thought to turning that talent of yours into a business, eh?"

"No, honestly I haven't, Papa." He sighed. "But I have been doing a little puttering around in the wood shop at work after hours. I've got some plans for a dining room set out in the car. If you'd like, I can show them to you after the party."

He smiled. "I'd like that a lot, son. Oh, and while we're out there, what say you and me take a drive, eh?"

"I'd love to, Papa," Ernest said.

"Good." Papa rose and clapped a hand on Ernest's shoulder. "I did enjoy driving your motorcar the last time you were here."

Chapter 13

Dinner came and went, and Ernest ate more gumbo than he thought possible. The first bowl disappeared well before the growling in his belly ceased, and the second didn't fill the empty spot he still felt. Finally, after consuming his third bowl, he decided he'd had enough.

While Mathilde brewed coffee and Mama cut slices of cake, Amalie began to open her gifts. As she reached for Ernest's package, he turned to watch.

He'd wrapped the gift himself, using the materials he had on hand: glue, string, and the Sunday edition of the newspaper. It took her a little longer than he expected to unwrap the gift, but when she'd finally loosened the paper, she let out a squeal of delight.

"Oh, Ernest, it's Nancy Drew!" Amalie climbed over Eileen and Mary, who were playing with the gift's torn wrappings, to give Ernest a hug. "I love these books. How did you know?"

He shrugged. "A little bird told me."

Amalie gave him a sideways look and leaned close to whisper in his ear. "A little bird or a girl named Genevieve?"

"I'm going to ignore that."

Thankfully Amalie was too busy to comment further. An hour later, the party had moved outside, as had the noise. Those children whose mothers hadn't sent them to bed were taking the rare opportunity to whoop it up and run about in the dark.

To Ernest's thinking, it looked like fun. He felt sorely tempted to join them rather than sit with the adults and sip coffee and talk about politics and the weather.

Ernest leaned back from the table and pushed his plate away. As always, Mama's cake was delicious. He glanced over to tell her so when he caught her staring.

"What?" he asked. "You look like something's bothering you."

She shook her head, then paused to nod. "I'd like to talk to you, bebe," she whispered.

"Sure." Ernest rose. "If you all will excuse us, I'm going to take a walk with my best girl." He offered his mother his hand. "Mama, shall we?"

A few minutes later, the pair had traversed the lawn and, to the dismay of the children, turned to walk alone down the path heading toward the bayou. Ernest slowed his stride to keep pace with his mother, all the while inhaling the fresh night air.

"It don't smell like this in the city, does it?" Mama asked.

Ernest held up a low branch so that Mama could walk beneath it. "No, Mama."

"But I didn't bring you out here to talk about that." She stopped beneath a circle of moonlight and crossed her arms over her chest. "You are my firstborn, Ernest, the bebe I prayed for before I ever met your papa. Did I ever tell you that when I would daydream, I would imagine a family with a boy and a girl? And that boy, I would name him Ernest."

"No, I didn't know that."

"It just seems like I've always known about you." She paused. "I'm rambling, aren't I?"

Ernest wrapped his arm around her waist and looked down on Mama with a smile. "You're doing fine."

Mama nodded. "Well then, that's all well and good, but I need to get to the point. I'm just gonna tell it to you straight."

"That'd be fine by me." He gestured to the bench he'd made some ten years ago, now used as a thinking spot for Papa. "Allons. Why don't we sit down?"

"You go on and sit. That way I can look you in the eye." After Ernest complied, Mama regarded him with a steady gaze. "There's been talk, son. They say you've taken up with Genevieve Lamont. I'm asking you if it's so."

"They?"

Her look dared him to try to deflect the question. "Don't ask me who's been talking; just tell me if it's the truth."

Ernest chewed on a couple of possible answers. Ultimately he went for the simplest and most truthful. "Not yet."

Mama settled beside him. "What do you mean by that?"

What did he mean? He sighed. "I suppose I'm saying that I've gone on one date, Mama. I like her, and maybe she likes me. Maybe she doesn't. I don't know."

He paused and hoped Mama would take her turn at talking so he wouldn't have to continue. Unfortunately, she didn't.

"She's real nice." Another pause, this one to consider just how to make his next point. "And she's pretty, Mama, real pretty. But you know what else?"

"Qui c'est sa?"

He leaned against the back of the bench and stared up into the night sky. "She makes me laugh. And more than that, when I think about her two or three days later, it still puts a smile on my face."

Mama took his hand in hers and squeezed. "Oh, son, that sounds serious."

Ernest shrugged. "Pas du tout. Not hardly, Mama. She's just someone I enjoy spending time with."

"Maybe." Another squeeze and she released her grip. "Just promise me one thing, Ernest."

He swiveled to meet her gaze. "What's that?"

"Promise that no matter what happens, you won't judge." She looked away. "Things are not always as they appear, you know."

She looked so serious that he hated to chuckle. "Mama, I don't know what you're talking about. Why would you say something like that?"

"Just promise it, Ernest."

"Sure," he said. "I promise, although I have no idea why you would think I need to."

Mama shook her head. "Honey, all I'm saying is that I don't want you to miss out on your chance for love because you made up your mind before you knew the Lord's take on things. You hear?"

"Hold on here, Mama. No one said anything about love."

His mother smiled. "No one had to."

Sunday, May 14

The preaching was fine and so was Sunday lunch, but impatience kept tugging Ernest toward the open door and the motorcar parked outside. When he finally managed to set off down the road to New Iberia, it didn't take him long to find the roadster pointed toward the Lamont place.

Ernest slowed to make the turn onto the long dirt road leading to the house, then pulled over and stopped. In the distance, the white two-story home loomed on a high spot near the bayou. Unlike the other homes in the area, this one did not bear any of the traditional Acadian features. Rather than leave the cypress boards unpainted, Mr. Lamont had them whitewashed, and instead of building his staircase outside to bypass the tax laws, he had centered his in the middle of the house. The result was a home that looked like it belonged in the city rather than set out among the weeping willows and bald cypress.

He shaded his eyes with his hand and peered across the distance. There seemed to be no one about.

For a moment, he considered turning tail and running. Then he thought about the possibility that Genevieve Lamont might be sitting somewhere inside that white house in need of a ride back to New Iberia.

It was that thought that caused him to climb back into the roadster and crank the engine. Easing the car over the ruts, he bounced toward the big house. As he neared the clearing, he noticed a thin plume of smoke coming from the chimney of the little wood frame house just beyond the summer kitchen.

It was the overseer's place—Ernest remembered that much. He also remembered the tales that were told about the man who had lived there, a man who had been killed in a way that no one wanted to describe to children.

So, as children often do, Ernest and his friends made up stories on the schoolyard about what happened to the poor fellow. Years later when he heard the true tale, he realized he'd never have understood the idea of hating a man for the color of his skin as a child.

Even now it bore hard on him.

The roadster rolled on toward the white house on the hill, and Ernest forced his thoughts back to Genevieve. Should he call her name or possibly honk the horn to announce his arrival? Maybe he ought to climb out and go to the door like a proper gentleman.

That last option appealed the most, so he did just that. Throwing his leg over the door, he jumped out of the car and straightened his cap. Satisfied he'd done the best he could to look presentable, Ernest strode to the door and knocked twice.

No answer.

He tried again, giving the old door three solid whacks with his fist. "Miss Lamont?" he called. "You home?"

Again nothing.

Ernest stepped back and stared hard at the door, willing it to open. Once more he tried knocking. He also called Genevieve's name.

"Allons! You there, Monsieur Breaux."

Whirling around, he saw a large dark woman coming up the path, carrying a bawling infant. A mongrel dog circled them, making quite a ruckus with his barks and yips. The trio made their way toward him, a noisy symphony that made him want to get on his knees right there and thank the Lord he had neither child nor dog back home in New Iberia.

"Monsieur Breaux, I'm Big Mama," the woman called again. "Comment ça va?"

"Ça va bien," Ernest answered. The proper Acadian greetings out of the way, Ernest went straight to the point. "Mademoiselle Lamont, is she here?"

"Mais non!" the woman said, shouting to be heard over the baby and dog. "Nobody's t' home. They all gone."

She brushed past Ernest to stand between him and the door. "Hush," she shouted to the dog. The command worked, both with the mangy animal and the dark-haired baby. While the dog slunk away to lie in the shade of a magnolia, the baby stared at him, lower lip quivering.

The little one couldn't have been more than six months old and, judging from the pink clothing, had to be a girl. Big eyes the color of chicory coffee stared up at him, dark lashes wet with tears.

"What's wrong, sweetheart?" he asked, giving the wet-faced girl a smile.

She blinked hard, then looked up at the dark woman who held her. Finally, she stared back at Ernest.

Then she grinned.

"Well now, would you look at that?" the woman said. "I don't believe I've ever seen her take to a stranger like that."

Before he could comment, the child burst into tears again. Her wail pierced Ernest's eardrums and made him want to run for the roadster. Only the prospect of finding Genevieve Lamont kept him rooted in place.

"You said the Lamonts are not home," he shouted. "Can you tell me when they will return?"

" 'Fraid not," she said as she reached for the door. "Miss Genevieve, she don't live here no more, and her mama, well, that's not who you came to see, is it?"

Ernest shook his head. The woman's stare unnerved him. Why, except for the obvious, she could have been Genevieve's mother the way she acted so protective. His attention went from the woman to the baby.

What a strange combination they were, these two. The calm-faced dark woman and the bawling pale child.

"If you'll excuse me, this 'un's hungry. Next time I see Miss Genny, I'll be sure an' tell her you was here. Oh, I won't forget that, no." She reached for the knob and gave it a yank. "You take care now, you hear?"

Without further comment, she stepped inside and let the door close behind her, leaving Ernest standing on the porch alone. He took two steps back and waited, thinking the woman might reappear. After a few minutes, he realized she did not intend to.

Feeling the fool, Ernest beat a path back to the roadster and climbed inside. As he reached down to crank the engine, a flash of white in an upper window caught his attention. He sat up straight and stared.

In the top right-hand window stood a woman wearing white. Upon closer inspection, he realized it was a white dressing gown over a pair of light-colored men's pajamas. Before he could react, the woman stepped back and disappeared into the shadows.

All the way back to New Iberia, Ernest debated whether he should tell Genevieve he'd stopped by her place. In the end, he decided he'd keep that fact to himself.

Unless she asked, of course.

Chapter 14

Tuesday, May 23

In his quest to win another date with Genevieve Lamont, Ernest managed to down an average of three sodas a day for a week. Finally, on the eighth day of his campaign, she said yes. This time they would go for a drive rather than see a movie, something Ernest thought might give him time to learn more about the secretive Miss Lamont. To his surprise, Genevieve insisted on bringing a picnic dinner.

That evening, he picked up Genevieve and her hamper of food on the steps of the five-and-dime at a quarter past six. She had on the same green dress she'd worn on their last date, and it pleased him that she would remember he liked it. He was about to say so when she turned to him and smiled.

All words fled, and he became, well, speechless.

Somehow he managed to help her into the roadster, then run around to jump inside himself. He cranked the engine and turned to smile at his guest.

In this light with the sun teasing the tops of the trees, Genevieve Lamont looked absolutely stunning. There she sat, wearing not a drop of makeup and with her hair caught up in an old-fashioned coil at the nape of her neck, yet he'd never seen a woman look more beautiful.

"I hope you like chicken and potato salad. Oh, and biscuits." She pointed to the hamper at her feet. "That's what I brought." The object of his attention frowned. "What's wrong?"

"Wrong? Oh, nothing," he said quickly as he turned his attention to putting the car into gear.

As he stopped the car at the first stop sign, he saw her reach for her purse, then pull out a flowered scarf to cover her hair. "To protect it from the wind," she said as she leaned back in the seat.

Ernest nodded. A horn honked, and he jumped, then pressed the accelerator. Until he could get safely out of New Iberia, he could not afford to pay any further attention to his passenger.

The results might be disastrous.

Soon the roadster was flying down a deserted country road. With the sun at his back and Genevieve at his side, Ernest could have driven until the gas ran out, except that his stomach complained. He pulled over next to a green field beside the bayou and turned off the car.

"How's this?"

Genevieve smiled and gathered up the hamper. "Perfect," she said as she climbed out.

A few minutes later, they sat on a blanket with plates of fried chicken and potato salad. Ernest took a bite and groaned. "If you cooked this chicken, I think I'm in love."

He froze. *Oh no, did I say that out loud?*

Her shocked expression was followed by a grin. "Well then," she said as she handed him a fork, "I guess you're out with the wrong girl."

"Oh," Ernest said. "How's that?"

She giggled. "My roommate, Betty, made the chicken."

"Get the recipe," he said as he stabbed his fork into the potato salad and took a healthy bite. "Now this is good eating."

"Thanks. It's a family recipe."

He leaned toward her. "I think I like your family."

She met him halfway. "Oh really?"

They were almost nose to nose. Before he could do what his heart demanded and kiss her, he listened to his head and reached for another piece of chicken. He watched her out of the corner of his eye as he chewed. Was that relief he saw on her face or disappointment?

His pride hoped for the latter.

By the time he finished his meal, Ernest decided it was time to come clean about his visit to the Lamont place. He was about to say something when Genevieve began to speak.

"Ernest, I understand you paid Mother's housekeeper a visit."

He tried to read the expression on her face. "Yes, actually," he finally said. "I thought maybe you'd changed your mind about Latagnier. I wanted to offer a ride back to New Iberia."

"I wondered why you did that." She began to pack the empty plates. "And I also wondered why you didn't mention anything about it."

"Well, actually, I was about to." Ernest shrugged. "I know the timing seems questionable, but I promise I was going to tell you. I mean, I assume you spoke to the housekeeper."

Genevieve wrapped the last of the chicken in a towel and set it atop the plates. "Yes."

"Well, ever since then, I wondered how your mother was doing."

The color drained out of her face. "My mother?"

"Yes, I saw her standing in the window. I assumed, because she was in her nightclothes and all, that she might be ill. I couldn't hardly ask how she was doing without letting you know I was there, now, could I?" He paused. "And that baby, I wondered about her. She surely didn't belong to the housekeeper. That much was obvious."

"You saw a baby there? I wasn't told this."

Ernest nodded. "Little girl about so big." He indicated the baby's size with his hands. "Had a healthy set of lungs on her, that's for sure."

Genevieve closed the lid on the hamper and gave him a direct look. This time there was no mistaking her feelings. She was not happy.

"I don't know if you've realized this about me, but I'm a very private person."

"Yes," he said. "I've noticed. What's your point?"

"Ernest, I like you." She sighed. "Actually, I like you a lot."

He leaned toward her and reached for her hand. To his surprise, she let him wrap his fingers around hers. "I like you, too, Genevieve."

"Then will you just do one thing for me?"

"Anything."

Genevieve pulled away and stood. "Would you take me home?"

Ernest scrambled to his feet and grasped her wrist. "What's wrong? Don't you feel well?"

She shook her head, and he let her go. "I'm fine. It's just that. . . Well, never mind."

Tears glistened, and she turned her head. Reaching for the hamper, she lifted it into the car, then yanked on the door latch.

"Wait." He pulled her into an embrace. "Don't cry. Whatever I've done, I'm sorry."

She rested her forehead on his chest and, an eternity later, looked up into his eyes. "Ernest, you have no idea what you've done."

"No," he said slowly, "I don't. But I know it upset you, and that's the last thing I ever wanted to do."

Brown eyes continued to stare up at him. A gentleman would have released her to offer her his handkerchief. Instead, he kissed her.

It was a soft kiss, one of those sweet, brief meetings of the lips that held much promise and no disappointment.

Their fist kiss, and it tasted of salty tears. *Lord, please let this be the last time I make her cry.*

"Do you still want me to take you home?" he whispered into her ear.

"Yes," she said in a small voice, and then she added, "please."

Reluctant to break the embrace, he let her pull away first. When she did, he helped her into the car, then folded the blanket and tucked it behind the hamper. Finally, he climbed in and cranked the engine.

"Ernest?"

He gave her a sideways look. "Yes?"

"Would you do that one more time?"

"Do what?"

She leaned over to place her hand atop his. "Would you kiss me? Just once more."

He adjusted his cap with his free hand and pretended to consider the question. "Will you let me take you home instead of back to the five-and-dime?" he finally asked.

"No," she said softly. "Does that make a difference?"

"No, but next time we go out on a date. . ." Ernest leaned toward her, stopping inches from her lips. "I will take you home"—he moved a hairbreadth closer—"to your door." He paused. "Is that understood?"

Genevieve answered with a nearly breathless, "Yes."

Wednesday, May 24

The next morning, Ernest rose with a smile, remembering the three kisses he had bestowed on the lovely Miss Lamont. Besides the two on the picnic, he'd received one more kiss before he left her off on the steps of the five-and-dime. On top of that, they had a date for tomorrow night, this time to the movies.

His feet barely touched the ground as he arrived at work. Before he could take his position on the line, Mr. Denison's secretary came to fetch him. He was needed, it seemed, in the sawmill owner's private office.

Ernest knocked twice and was let in by the boss himself. "Come on in, son, and have a seat."

Mr. Denison gestured to a leather chair Ernest knew well. He'd repaired the arm on it just last week in his spare time. He did as he was told, then watched his boss settle on the other side of a massive desk cluttered with papers and drawings. It was all he could do not to groan aloud when he noticed the drawing on top was his, a set of plans for a dining table he'd been playing around with. He must have left it on the sawmill floor after work yesterday.

Understandable since all he'd had on his mind was his impending date with Genevieve.

"Would you like some coffee?"

"What? Oh no, thank you, Mr. Denison. I just had a cup at home."

Mr. Denison nodded. "Then I'll get right to the point." He leaned forward. "Ernest, I've been watching you. You're a right fine employee. Always early to work and never missed a day in three years. That's impressive."

Ernest said nothing.

"Yes, well, one of the fellows on the night shift brought this to my attention." He fished out the drawing and thrust it toward Ernest. "Did you do this?"

He could lie and possibly keep himself employed. Instead, he told the truth. "Yes, sir, I did. I'd like to tell you I owe you an apology for doing that on company time. It's just that the machines were down for maintenance, and the boys and I were standing around waiting. I found that piece of paper and decided to make good use of my time." He paused. "It won't happen again, I promise."

"It'd better happen again," Mr. Denison said. "Today, in fact."

Ernest shook his head. "I don't understand."

"Are you a carpenter, son? What I mean is, do you make these things or do you just draw them?"

"Both, sir," he said.

"Would you be willing to make something for me? If I paid you for it, I mean?"

"Sure," Ernest said. "I'd be glad to."

Mr. Denison grinned. "I've been trying to find the time to take my new bride shopping for a dining set. I'm afraid my bachelor apartment didn't have much more than the basics, and a dining table wasn't one of them." He shook the paper at Ernest. "Imagine how happy she will be when I tell her she can have anything she wants." He paused. "Within reason, of course."

"Of course."

He rose, and Ernest did the same. "I'll bring her back here after lunch, and the two of you can talk about what she's looking for. How's that?"

"That would be just fine." He shook hands with his boss, then walked back to the line with a grin.

That afternoon, he met the new Mrs. Denison and devised a set of drawings for a table and four chairs. By the time Ernest left work that evening, Mrs. Denison had sent word that she'd changed her mind and wanted six chairs and a longer table.

"You never know how many mouths the Lord will bless us to feed," she said by way of explanation.

After he'd escorted his wife out, Mr. Denison returned to follow Ernest out to the car, chatting with excitement. When he saw the roadster, he paused. "She looks like a million bucks, Ernest." He moved closer to inspect her. "What did you do to her?"

"Just a little work here and there."

He ran his hand over the fender and grinned. "Why, I'm almost tempted to buy her back."

"I believe you'll understand if I don't take you up on that, sir."

"Yes, I do." He paused. "About my wife's dining set. Have you given any thought to what sort of wood it ought to be made out of? I'm hoping we can find something here at the mill."

Ernest nodded. "Yes, sir, I believe we can. I noticed there's a nice pile of good-quality ash over in the south corner of the warehouse. I believe there's enough to make quite a set."

"Yes," Mr. Denison said. "I know the lot you're talking about. That's expensive stuff, son."

"I agree," he said, "and there's plenty of red oak or cypress in stock to make an acceptable set." Ernest paused. "But then, I believe you would agree that your wife deserves the best. If she were to find that she'd been given cypress or oak when there was ash to be had, she might not be as happy with her purchase."

Mr. Denison studied him a moment, then broke out in a grin. "You sure are a good judge of wood and women. I'm sure your wife is pleased with you."

Ernest wiped a speck of dust off the hood with the back of his shirtsleeve. "Thank you all the same, sir, but I don't have a wife, and I don't have any plans to acquire one."

His grin broadened. "Now isn't that always the way?"

"I don't understand."

"I didn't have plans to acquire a wife, either. Told everyone who would listen I was a confirmed bachelor. The way I had it figured, I was meant to spend my time and money on the Lord's business." Mr. Denison leaned against the roadster and shook his head. "Funny, but somewhere between bachelorhood and fatherhood I realized that sometimes the Lord has other plans, and sometimes His business starts at your own front door. You see, I married a widow with a young son. So not only am I a husband now, I'm also a father."

Ernest whistled softly.

"Yep, that's my sentiments exactly, but you know what?"

"What's that, sir?"

Mr. Denison smiled. "That little fellow's not my son by birth, but it didn't take but about five minutes with him to start feeling like he's mine all the same. Now I'd welcome a dozen just like him."

Ernest chuckled. "Then, sir, I believe you're going to need a much longer table."

Chapter 15

As soon as Ernest said his good-byes to Mr. Denison and started the roadster, he pointed it toward the five-and-dime. Wouldn't Genevieve be surprised by his news?

He had to circle the block twice before he could find a place to park, but he finally managed it. By the time he turned off the engine and bounded across the street, he could hardly contain his smile.

A check of the clock on the square told him the time was half past four. Genevieve would be at work for another thirty minutes. Should he tell her immediately or buy a soda and wait until she finished for the day? Stepping inside, he looked for Genevieve. A search of the soda counter, the cash register, and even the book aisle turned up nothing.

"You looking for Genevieve?"

Ernest glanced up to see a familiar face standing at the end of the book aisle. "You're her friend, aren't you? Barbara?"

She nodded as she walked toward him. "That's right, but I'm Betty."

"Betty. Sorry. You're the one who made that delicious chicken, right?"

"That's me." Her smile faded. "Genevieve's not here today."

"She's not?" He shook his head. "Are you sure?"

"She's sure," Lester Bonfils said as he pressed past Betty. "Go on back to the register, hon. I'll handle this customer." He narrowed his eyes and stared at Ernest. "She called in sick today, and I suggest you tell her when you see her that I keep track of these things. That's twice in a month, sir. I've a good mind to fire her if she does it again."

"Have you considered that she might actually be ill, sir?"

Lester snorted and turned to walk away. "Not for a minute," he said. "Pretty ones like that girl don't last. They find a man and take off." He stopped to glance back at Ernest. "If you're the one she's latched onto, tell her if she can't get out of bed in time for work, she doesn't need to have a job." He chuckled. "But judging from the fact you're standing here with no idea where she is, I'd say you got thrown over for another fellow. Tough luck there, buddy."

Rather than punch the man, Ernest turned and stalked out of the five-and-dime. Before he could reach the roadster, he heard someone call his name. Betty caught up with him at the curb. Rather than speak, she pressed a piece of paper into his palm, then raced back toward the five-and-dime.

He opened the slip of paper and found an address. Five minutes later, he stood in front of the room listed on the page in front of him. He had to knock twice before anyone answered, but when the door swung open, there stood Genevieve Lamont.

She looked as if she hadn't slept, and the smile on her lips didn't quite make it to her eyes. Strange, but she didn't seem surprised to see him. Rather, she stepped out into the hall and closed the door behind her.

"I thought you might show up here," she said as she studied the faded roses on the carpet. "Leave it to Betty and her big mouth."

"I was worried about you." He placed his finger beneath her chin and lifted her gaze to meet his. "What's wrong?"

~

"Wrong?"

Where to begin? She could give up her secrets and tell Ernest that she'd not slept more than an hour at a time since yesterday for worrying about her daughter. A call from Big Mama on the landlady's telephone last night informed her that Ellen was running a slight fever and had a nasty cough.

Gen knew that if Big Mama had taken the trouble of going next door to the Widow LeBlanc's house to borrow the telephone, the odds were that Ellen was much sicker than the woman had let on. Gen slept in fits and starts, forcing herself to lie down even though her instinct was to pace. When the sun rose over New Iberia, Gen was ready to head to the bus station. If only she had followed her first thought and headed home. She wouldn't be standing here trying to hide yet another secret from Ernest Breaux.

"Lester said you called in sick."

She nodded.

"But you don't look sick." He studied her a moment, then pressed his palm to her forehead. "No fever. And you're not sneezing. Actually, you just look tired. Did you have trouble sleeping last night?"

"Yes," she said softly. "I suppose you could say that."

"Any particular reason?"

Exhaustion fought with fear for supremacy, and the result was tears that first glistened, then fell. Ernest took her into his arms and held her while she cried, standing silent and asking nothing of her except whether she needed his handkerchief.

Ultimately he gave her that handkerchief, even though she insisted she was fine. When she calmed a bit, she folded the handkerchief and attempted to hand it back to him. With a grin, he refused, saying she might need it later.

Gen ducked out of his embrace and leaned against the wall, the handkerchief clutched in her fist. "I should go back inside now. Maybe take a nap."

Ernest shook his head. "I wish you wouldn't. You don't need to be alone. Not when you're upset."

She looked up at him through tired eyes. "Betty will be home later. I'll be fine until then."

"Have you eaten anything today?"

She hadn't, but he didn't need to know that. "I'm fine, really, Ernest."

"Humor me, Genevieve. I'm worried about you." He laced his fingers with hers. "What if I bring you something? I can fetch something quick from Mulotte's and be back in ten minutes."

"No, really," she said. "Don't do that. My place isn't suitable to entertain men."

He looked to be at a loss, then he snapped his fingers. "I know. We'll have another picnic."

She must have looked doubtful, because he upped the wattage of his smile. "It will be great, really. This time let me provide the food. I can't top your potato salad or Betty's chicken, but I bet I can grab a couple of sandwiches and be down at the park before you."

"Oh, I don't know." She clutched at the locket lying against her neck. "I'm afraid I wouldn't be much company."

He touched her chin with his thumb. "Sweetheart, I'm not asking you to be good company. I'm just asking you to show up. Would you do that for me? I'm worried."

What harm would it do to share a sandwich in the park with him? After all, despite the impression she gave him, Ernest Breaux had consumed her daily thoughts and nightly dreams ever since those kisses they shared.

"All right," she said slowly. "What if I meet you at the park in half an hour? Will that be all right?"

"Make it twenty minutes, and you've got a deal." Ernest shrugged. "So I'm a little impatient."

"A little?" She managed a chuckle. "What say we split the difference and make it twenty-five?"

"Deal." He shook her hand, then disappeared down the hall. "Don't be late" echoed along with his retreating footsteps.

"Twenty-five minutes," she said with a chuckle. How that man could make her smile. If only she could be sure that he would accept Ellen, she might feel better about their growing relationship.

Until she knew the answer to that question, she really couldn't get her hopes up that there would be something between them. Her first responsibility was to Ellen. To fall in love with a man who wouldn't love her daughter as his own was unacceptable.

Unfortunately, she'd heard enough comments from Ernest to make her wonder what his reaction would be.

Tears burned the corners of her eyes, and she dabbed at them with Ernest's handkerchief. Holding the starched white cloth to her nose, she inhaled the masculine scent she'd come to associate with Ernest.

"Miss Lamont?" A sharp rap at the door followed her landlady's voice. "Miss Lamont, you in there?"

Gen opened the door. "Yes, ma'am, I'm here. What's wrong?"

"There's another phone call for you," she said. "Same lady who called last night."

A few minutes later, phone in hand, Gen heard the words no mother ever wants to hear. "Your baby's bad sick," Big Mama said. "You ought to come quick. I don't rightly know what to do with her."

When Gen hung up the phone, she was trembling. Rather than answer her landlady's questions, she turned and ran from the formal parlor where the house's only phone sat. Taking the stairs two at a time, she threw open the door to her room and raced for the suitcase. Ten minutes later, she was heading toward the five-and-dime, a full suitcase in hand.

Leaving the case by the back door, she walked inside, bent on making Lester understand the enormity of the emergency. "So you see, I have a sick relative," she told him when she found him sitting at the soda fountain. "It can't be helped. I have to go to her now."

Lester dug at the gap between his front teeth with a bent toothpick, his gaze never breaking with Gen's. "So I'm to believe that you'd come in here and ask me if you can just up and leave town for a spell, then come back and have your same job when you're done tending the ailing?"

"That's right," she said. "I'd be much obliged if you'd hold my job here until I get back."

The store manager let the toothpick fall to the ground and wiped the corner of his mouth with a napkin. "And you don't know when that might be?"

She shook her head.

"No idea?"

"No, sir."

He stared at her. She refused to look away. Finally, he climbed down off the stool and tossed the napkin on the counter.

"No," he said as he walked away.

"No?" She followed him to the front of the store. "No?" she repeated. "Just like that, you're going to make me choose between a sick relative and my job?"

Lester turned so quickly she almost collided with him. "That's right," he said. "Just like that. So what's it going to be? You want to keep your job or what?"

"No, thank you, Mr. Bonfils," she said, her spine straight and her heart beating furiously. "I don't believe I want to keep this job. At least not under the conditions you state. I have a sick family member, and I'm all she has. I have no choice but to go to her." Gen blinked hard to stall the tears. "And when she gets better and I return, I will be praying that there is still work for me here."

"You always did like to pray, didn't you?" He chuckled. "Guess you don't remember what I told you about work not being a place where a body ought to be praying."

"Oh, I remember," she said. "I just don't happen to agree with you."

She turned her back on Lester Bonfils, and the tears released. If only she'd seen Betty or one of the other girls before she walked outside, but none were to be found. Gen walked alone to the bus station and bought a one-way ticket to Latagnier, then went back to her room and cleared out what she could of her meager belongings, fitting them into a pillowcase and the empty corners of her suitcase. The rest she would have to come back for someday. Or maybe she would have Betty send them. Right now that decision would have to join the other ones in a place where she could take them out and examine them later.

At this moment she could barely decide to blink or to put one foot in front of the other.

Half an hour later, the bus pulled out of New Iberia, leaving the city and, most likely, one disappointed man named Ernest Breaux behind.

It was for the best, Gen decided as she pressed her back into the bus's lumpy seat. She and Ernest didn't really belong together anyway. Too many secrets stood between them.

~

Ernest sat on the park bench, studying the splinters in his hands and wondering where he'd gone wrong. When Gen didn't show after half an hour, he went back to her place and knocked until the landlady chased him away. All he could get from her as he stood on the sidewalk was that Gen had received a call. From whom, she didn't know, but the voice belonged to a woman.

He went back and sat on the park bench, just in case he'd missed her. After a while, he went to the five-and-dime and found out from Lester that she'd been fired.

Betty was too busy to talk and probably feared for her job if she did. She sent him out to the park to wait until her shift ended and she could go back to the room to check things out for herself. Now he sat waiting and hoping, two sandwiches and a broken heart short of a good evening.

"Sorry I'm late," Betty called.

He looked up to see her heading his way. As she settled on the bench beside him, she placed an overlarge handbag at her feet.

"So what did you find out? Is Genevieve all right?"

"Well," she said, "I don't think you're going to like this."

"What?"

She looked as if she were about to cry, and Ernest's heart sank. "She's gone, isn't she?"

Betty nodded. "She took all her things and left me an envelope with next month's rent and an apology. Said she couldn't help leaving on short notice; she had no choice."

"No choice?" He could barely get the words out.

What had happened in the minutes after he left her? Had the damage, whatever it was, already been done before he arrived? That would certainly account for her tired look, but it didn't account for the phone call. At least the voice the landlady heard belonged to a woman. He told this to Betty and waited for her response.

"No, she never got a phone call before," Betty said. "At least not that I know of." She gave Ernest a direct look. "I don't mean to be nosy, but did you two get into a spat or something? I mean, this isn't like Genevieve. She needed this job too much to up and leave it, and until you came along, it was all she had."

"No, we were getting along fine." Ernest balled his fingers into fists and slammed them into his knees. "I don't have any more idea than you do."

"All I know is that my friend is gone."

And so is my heart.

Ernest rose and thanked Betty before heading back to the sawmill. His boss had given him free rein to work in the spare room next to the shipping office. If he couldn't sleep, he could work on Mrs. Denison's dining set. It might keep his hands busy, even if it did allow his mind to replay the events of the evening over and over.

Thinking about Genevieve's leaving should have driven him crazy. Instead, it gave him hope that if he could just wrap his brain around all the facts, maybe he could make sense of them.

In the hours before morning, with a stack of cut lumber behind him, he finally decided that making a plan for the future was better than worrying about the past. And his plan for the immediate future was to finish the workweek and go home to Latagnier.

If Genevieve went anywhere, it was likely she went home. He didn't know for sure where she was, but he certainly knew where to find people who just might know.

When Friday finally came, Ernest was the first one out the gate. He'd stowed clothes for the weekend in the roadster, along with a pimento cheese sandwich for supper. Without delays, he could be standing on Genevieve's front porch before dark.

He made the drive in less time than usual, owing to the fact that he drove faster and much less carefully than ever. The temptation to drive right up to the house was strong, but Ernest decided it would be much better to have the element of surprise in his favor. Whatever had rattled Genevieve into running might cause her to take off before he could speak to her.

The quarter-mile driveway was made of hard-packed dirt, evidence that rain had been scarce in these parts. He arrived on the doorstep a bit dustier for the trip, but no less determined.

After the first series of knocks, he began to think that getting someone to the door might be harder than he expected. The woman who'd greeted him last time seemed to be nowhere to be found. He backtracked to find the little cabin, this time with no smoke or anything else to indicate the presence of inhabitants.

"Hello there," he called. "Bonsoir, madame. Anyone home?"

The mangy dog shimmied out from under the house and bared his teeth. "Hey there, boy. You the only one here?"

His greeting was met with a growl and raised hackles on the animal's back. Rather than risk losing a limb to go along with his broken heart, he eased away from the house. The dog barked twice, then went to sit in front of the screen door.

Thankfully the dog didn't follow Ernest back to the main house. If it had, Ernest might have gone straight back to the car rather than risk one more knock at the door.

As before, his knocks went unanswered. Then a thought occurred. What if something had happened here? What if Genevieve were inside and in need of help?

Ernest pulled back the screen and reached for the doorknob. He'd have a story prepared when he saw her, a good reason why he planned to walk into the Lamont home uninvited.

To his surprise, the door was locked.

He took two steps back and let the screen slam shut. No one locked their doors in Latagnier. What would be the reason?

"You there. You one of the Breaux boys?"

Startled, Ernest whirled around, looking for the source of the unfamiliar female voice. No one was in sight.

"Up here."

He turned back around to face the house. Then he saw her. A woman in a set of oversized men's pajamas stood in an upstairs window.

"You the oldest of the bunch?" she called.

"Yes, ma'am," he said. "I'm Ernest. Ernest Breaux."

Chapter 16

"Thank you for seeing us this morning, Dr. Villare." Gen cuddled the blanket-wrapped baby one more time and handed her over to the doctor.

"No thanks necessary," the doctor said. "I wish you'd sent for me. I would have come out to your place rather than cause you to walk to town."

Big Mama shrugged. "It don't make me no never mind." She pointed to Gen. "Even if we had a way to send for you, this girl here wouldn't have been able to sit still and wait. Walking did her good."

That much was true. While her feet hurt, the three-mile walk had given her time to think and pray.

The doctor nodded. "I must apologize, though. I'm here alone today. My nurse is out on sick leave." He winked at Big Mama. "She's my wife, actually, and she just delivered our second son last Sunday."

"Congratulations," Gen said. "Babies are such a blessing from God, aren't they?"

Dr. Villare nodded. "I'll agree with you there. Now let's see what's ailing this little blessing."

The doctor settled Ellen on the exam table and opened the blanket. Ellen barely registered any notice of the intrusion as the doctor checked her neck and eyes. She complained a bit when he looked into her throat and much more when he took her temperature. With care, the doctor replaced the blanket around her, then cradled her in the crook of his arm.

"Her color's a bit pale, but her vitals are good. How long has she had this low-grade fever?"

"The fever's going on four days." Gen looked to Big Mama for agreement. "Starting yesterday, all she wants to do is sleep."

"What's the history of this? When did she start showing signs of illness?"

He looked at Gen, and she turned to Big Mama. If the doctor found it strange that the baby's mother couldn't give a history of the child's illness, he did not let on.

"It started with a runny nose," Big Mama said. "That must have been nigh on a week ago. Just a little inconvenience, I thought. The baby, she didn't seem to take notice of it."

Dr. Villare nodded.

"Well, when she starts to coughing, I said to myself, 'Big Mama, that little one, she's coming down with something.'"

"What did you do then?" the doctor asked as he handed a sleeping Ellen back to Gen.

"Well, I prayed, naturally, and I put some of that rub Mrs. Lamont likes for clearing her sinuses on the little one's chest. That seemed to help for a bit."

"A bit?" The doctor's eyes narrowed. "How long would you say that was?"

Big Mama seemed to be considering the question. In a moment she nodded. "I'd say that was two days. I thought she was getting better, then little Ellen, she fooled me."

"How so?"

Big Mama shrugged. "Well, she just didn't seem right. She was breathing sort of funny, like little hiccoughs." She demonstrated, then waited for the doctor to nod. "And so I picked her up out of the bed and held her up to see what was the matter. Well, sir, she just kept making those little hiccoughs."

"What did you do then?"

"I hightailed it next door to the Widow LeBlanc's house, and I called her mama here to come home. I don't mind telling you, Dr. Villare, I was scared. I thought we were gonna lose our baby girl."

The doctor turned his attention back to Ellen. A few minutes later, after examining her chest and throat once more, he replaced the blanket around Ellen.

"It seems to me that she's got a cold." He reached for a pen and began to scribble notes on a pad of paper. "I think what you heard, ma'am, was her lungs fighting for air."

"Is that serious?"

He looked up from his writing. "It could have been," he said. "But your housekeeper did the right thing. She medicated the baby's chest with ointment and kept her upright so she could breathe better."

Gen cradled her sleeping daughter against her chest. "But all she does is sleep, Doctor. This is not like her." Big Mama echoed the sentiment.

"She's tired. Her body has suffered a trauma, her first infection. All the sleeping is allowing her to heal faster. And the fever, well, that's something we can take care of with medicine." He handed Gen the paper with instructions to have it filled before she headed home. "I would like to have another look at her in a week or so, but only if you think she's taking a turn for the worse."

Gen nodded and passed the paper off to Big Mama. How she would pay for not one doctor visit but two without a job was beyond her. Not that it mattered, for she would go to the ends of the earth to keep her daughter safe and healthy.

"So she's going to be all right?" Tears, her familiar friends, burned her eyes. "My daughter's going to get well?"

The doctor placed his hand on her shoulder and gave her a comforting squeeze. "Your daughter's going to be fine." He smiled. "The first illness is always the hardest—on the parents, that is. I'm sure your husband is worried, so be sure and tell him that if he has any questions, I'd be happy to answer them."

The look that passed between Big Mama and Gen must have caught the doctor's attention. To his credit, he said nothing, but he did turn to his paper and begin scribbling with eyebrows raised.

"Her daddy's dead," Gen blurted out. "That is, I'm a widow. My husband passed on after an unfortunate accident in Texas."

He met her gaze with understanding eyes. "I'm terribly sorry, Mrs. Gallier."

She paused, unsure how to answer. "Thank you," she finally managed to mutter.

"If you don't mind, I'd like to make a few notes on this before you go. I like to keep these sorts of records in case you have to bring her back in after her next visit." He looked up sharply. "Not that I'm expecting that, mind you."

Gen managed a weak smile. As the doctor worked on his notes, she allowed her gaze to travel around the sparse exam room. The usual jars of bandages and antiseptics greeted her, along with a small photograph tucked into a silver frame on the corner of the doctor's writing desk.

It was a family gathering, a wedding, she realized. To her surprise, there were two brides, one in a gown of white and the other wearing what looked like a bridesmaid's dress.

Dr. Villare noticed her staring and handed her the photograph. "My wedding day," he said by way of explanation.

"Ah," she said as she studied the brides. Both beautiful and both slightly familiar.

"It was quite a day," he said. "Actually, it was supposed to be my wife's wedding day. I sort of crashed the party, to my father-in-law's extreme displeasure." He glanced up from his work to judge her surprise, then chuckled. "I suppose I should explain."

"Please do," Gen said.

"Well, you see, my wife's father was set on her staying put here in Latagnier, so he arranged a marriage between her and the son of a family friend."

"Do people still do that?"

The doctor smiled. "You've obviously never met her papa. He would have done anything to keep his girl close by. Anyway, he brought this fellow to Latagnier to meet my wife, then set a wedding date with the preacher."

"How did he get the man to agree to this?"

"As you can see from the picture, my wife is a beautiful woman." He set the pen on the desk. "Fortunately for me, so is her sister. To make a long story short, the marriage took place, only the groom chose another bride, my wife's sister."

"How in the world did that happen?" Big Mama asked.

"It almost didn't." The doctor shook his head. "I'd given up on her and taken off with plans to forget her. When I came to my senses, I rode the train home to find a wedding taking place. I guess you can imagine my surprise when I showed up to bust up that wedding and found out the woman wearing the wedding dress and veil was not my wife."

"Land o' Goshen," Big Mama said softly. "Did her mama and papa know about this?"

"It was a surprise to almost everyone except the bride and groom. Those two had gone and applied for their own license. My wife was in on it, of course. She stood at the back of the church and let her sister walk up the aisle dressed as her.

"It would have worked, too, except when I walked up to the altar and begged the bride to reconsider, it wasn't the bride who answered. Her papa about had a fit, but her mama talked some sense into him. He let the wedding go on as planned but with two brides. Of course, he slept with a shotgun by his side and my wife under lock and key until I came back the next day with a proper license and married her all over again and made the union legal. And that time, the wedding vows included a promise from me that I'd never take his daughter from the bayou."

"That's so romantic," Gen said.

The doctor nodded. "I suppose so," he said. "I know it's worked out fine for us. Life's good when the babies are coming and love fills the house, don't you agree?" He paused, and an uncomfortable look crossed his face. "Oh, I'm terribly sorry, Mrs. Gallier. That was very insensitive of me."

"No, really," Gen said. "It's fine. And yes, life is good with babies in the house."

This much she knew to be true. The part about love, well, that would have to remain a mystery.

Gen gave the picture another look. Her gaze stopped cold when it fell on the fellow standing to the right of the white-gowned bride.

It couldn't be.

She looked up at the doctor, then down at the photograph again. "Dr. Villare, who is this man right here?"

"The tall one? That's my wife's brother, Ernest Breaux."

~

Ernest drove away from the Lamont place more confused than ever. Although the woman at the window never introduced herself, he assumed she was Genevieve's mother. From what he could tell, she appeared sickly, although her voice sounded plenty strong when she shouted at him to leave the property. Maybe she was the reason Genevieve had left in a hurry.

When Ernest begged the woman to tell her daughter he'd been there, she disappeared into the shadows and refused to speak any further. He continued to call to her until the mangy dog came to sit at the perimeter of the clearing, giving him the distinct impression he was no longer welcome on the property.

Finally, he'd been forced to make the long walk back to his automobile, taking careful glances on occasion to be certain the animal hadn't decided to give chase. He considered heading over to the house to sleep under Mama and Papa's roof, but thought better of it.

A man could get a lot of work done with this much steam to vent. Rather than head to his apartment when the wheels of the roadster hit New Iberia, Ernest guided his car to the sawmill and parked it under the arms of a spreading oak. When the sun rose on Saturday morning, the car was still there, and Ernest had not yet decided to go home.

A chair and two table legs had been created between the late evening hours of Friday and sunrise. If he kept at this pace, he'd have the entire set made before June. That sort of schedule appealed to Ernest. A man who was too busy to think was also too busy to miss anyone.

Right now he missed Genevieve Lamont something awful.

He hadn't found much time to pray over the past months, so busy was he with work and fixing up his automobile, so he remedied that right then. *Funny,* he observed when he'd finished his prayers, *how a few minutes with the Lord makes my outlook a whole lot brighter.*

Ernest slipped into the washroom and threw cold water on his face, then wiped it off with the hem of his shirt. While his stomach complained of emptiness, his eyes longed for sleep. He looked down at the specks of sawdust and smudges of dirt covering his clothing and decided breakfast at any place decent was out of the question.

He checked his watch. A quarter to eleven. Too late for breakfast and too early for lunch anyway.

Shaking off as much of the sawdust as he could, he headed for the roadster and home. He'd get cleaned up, take a little nap, then wake up and grab a bite of late lunch before heading out to the sawmill to work on the dining set some more. Maybe tonight he'd take in a movie down at the Evangeline.

Alone, of course.

Those were his plans. Unfortunately, when he opened his eyes from his little nap, he found it was Sunday and he'd missed church.

~

Gen missed church to catch the early bus back to New Iberia, something that tugged on Gen's conscience something fierce. There was no making up lost time with the Lord, but Gen used the hot, dusty ride to spend time in the Word. The page turned to Psalm 9, and she placed her finger at the beginning of the tenth verse: "And they that know thy name will put their trust in thee: for thou, LORD, hast not forsaken them that seek thee."

Gen closed the Bible and let the warm breeze blow over her face. *Thou, Lord, hast not forsaken them that seek Thee.* Oh, how she wanted to be counted among those seekers. What penalties she and her family had paid for her choice to seek elsewhere.

"It is finished."

Gen nodded. "Yes, Father," she whispered, "it is finished, isn't it?"

In truth, everything seemed to be finished. Her job, her budding relationship with Ernest. Her well-ordered world had come undone, and nothing was certain except the love she felt for her family and her Creator.

"I know that ought to be enough, God, knowing that You have not forsaken me. I wish it was, because then I wouldn't feel so afraid."

She arrived at her rooming house in time to beat Betty home from church. One look at Gen, and Betty enveloped her in a hug, asking no questions.

"Your friend Ernest was here," she said. "He looked. . .desperate." She grasped Gen's hands. "Honey, that man is slap fool in love with you. I wish you could have seen him when Lester told him he fired you. I thought that pompous you-know-what was a goner. It speaks volumes for Ernest Breaux that he didn't deck him right on the spot."

"About Lester." Gen paused. "What do you think he would say if I went and asked for my job back?"

"The truth?"

Gen nodded.

"I think he's going to say no."

Chapter 17

Monday, May 29

"No."

Lester's growl rang in her ears. Evidently his pride still smarted from all the times she had turned him down for dates.

"Please, Mr. Bonfils," she said in a voice she could barely control. "You don't understand. I need this job."

He quirked one eyebrow and leered at her. "How *bad* do you *need* this job, Miss Lamont?"

Not that bad.

She sighed and turned to walk away. The only thing worse than begging for her job back was giving Lester Bonfils the satisfaction of seeing her cry.

"Miss Lamont?"

Gen turned and blinked to hide her tears. "Yes, sir?"

He strolled toward her, thumbs in his suspenders. The image of Big Mama's banty rooster came to mind. She fought not to giggle despite the gravity of the circumstances.

"You say you really want this job back?"

"Yes," she said as she took a step back and collided with the Alka-Seltzer display. Containers of antacid went spilling to the floor, and Gen scrambled after them.

"Get up," he said with a growl. "I want you to look me in the eye when you answer me."

Gen climbed to her feet and squared her shoulders. With prayer, she managed to make eye contact with her former employer.

"Miss Lamont, you have missed work due to illness twice in the past month yet have shown no sign of having been sick. Now, without warning, you simply do not show up a third time for work?"

When he paused, she looked away. *Please, God, let him give me my job back.*

Lester placed his hand on her shoulder and squeezed just a bit too tightly. "Miss Lamont, you've put me in a bad position with the other employees. If I let you get away with this, soon everyone will want to come and go at will." He slid his hand from her shoulder to clasp the nape of her neck. "A man can't run a business with chaos surrounding him, now, can he?"

"No, sir, I don't suppose he can."

An attempt to shrug out of his grasp made Lester grip her tighter. "And yet you're asking me to pretend none of this happened?"

It was all Gen could do to stand rooted in place when everything in her wanted to bolt and run. "You have my word, sir," she said. "It won't happen again."

"Your word?"

His fingers slid from the back of her neck down her spine to rest on the small of her back. Now he stood so close she could smell what he had for breakfast.

For that matter, she could see evidence of egg yolks on his collar.

"Yes, sir" came out sounding like a squeak.

"Did I ever give you the impression that your word was what I wanted?"

"Well, yes, sir. I mean, no, well. . ."

Her voice failed her. From the day he had hired her on at the five-and-dime, Lester Bonfils had been clear about what he wanted from Gen. If she had any questions about what that was, they disappeared when he leaned over and whispered the specifics in her ear.

This time when Gen walked out of the five-and-dime, she was absolutely certain she would never work there again, leastwise not while Lester Bonfils was in charge. She said her good-byes to the few friends she'd made, saving Betty for last.

"You've been a good friend to me, Betty," she said. "Promise me you'll keep in touch."

"I will." Betty linked arms with Gen and steered her toward the front entrance. "Now let's get you out of here."

Gen shook her head. "You stay put, Betty. I don't want you getting fired for associating with me."

Betty waved away Gen's statement with a sweep of her hand. "That old windbag? He wouldn't dare fire me."

She cast a glance behind Betty to see Lester glaring at them from the back of the store. "What makes you so sure?"

Shrugging, she pointed Gen toward the door. "I know his mother," she said with a grin. "And his wife."

"His *wife*?" She took one last look back at the five-and-dime, then pushed the door open and stepped out into the warm, late-May morning. "I didn't know he was married."

"Evidently he forgets from time to time, as well. Looks like I'm going to have to go in there and remind him. Next time he forgets, I'll have his wife reminding him instead. Or maybe I'll let his mother do it." Betty patted Gen's hand. "You don't belong here, honey. I've got a feeling you're going to be just fine. Whatever's got you tied to that little town you came from is calling you home. You need to go to it."

Gen swiped at the tears that had become her perpetual companions. "Not 'it,'" she said. "Her." At Betty's confused look, she elaborated. "My daughter, Ellen. She was six months old last week. She stays there with Mother and a family friend, and I spend whatever time I manage off with her."

"Oh, honey," Betty said softly. "So that's your secret."

All Gen could do was nod.

"Then I did the right thing in bringing this with me to work this morning." She slipped an envelope from her pocket and placed it in Gen's hand. "You put that away for now. Someday you might need it."

"What is it?"

Betty shook her head. "Let me have my secrets, too, won't you?"

"Of course" was all she could manage.

Gen parted with Betty amid many tears and promises that Betty would come to visit soon.

As Gen walked one last time from the five-and-dime to the rooming house, she thought about another promise, one that Big Mama had failed to get her to make. Now that Dr. Villare had seen Ellen, it was but a matter of time before the secret of her daughter's birth was out. While Big Mama thought it best to beat the news to Ernest and tell him herself, Gen couldn't make herself agree.

"Genevieve?"

She stumbled to a halt and looked up to see Ernest Breaux sitting on the steps outside the rooming house. She smoothed her hair back and cast an embarrassed glance at the wrinkled mess her dress had become.

"Ernest, what are you doing here?"

He rose and greeted her, at first touching her sleeve, then entwining his fingers with hers. "Where have you been?" he asked, his voice husky. "I looked for you everywhere."

Silence was all she could manage. To speak might mean to say too much, or worse, to say too little.

"I don't care where you've been. I just know I can't ever let you go again." Ernest brought her fingers to his lips and gently kissed them. "Promise me."

Another promise requested. Another promise she could not make.

"Ernest," she whispered. "Please. Don't." When she looked into his eyes, she could swear she felt her heart break. "I can't."

He released his grip, then grasped her wrist and pulled her into his embrace. "Whatever's wrong, I swear I'll fix it. Just tell me what it is."

She shook her head, then rested her cheek against his chest. "I can't," she repeated.

"No, sweetheart," he said, his voice a soft rumble. "You can. You just have to trust me first."

Trust. The same issue she had with the Lord.

"And they that know thy name will put their trust in thee: for thou, Lord, hast not forsaken them that seek thee."

Trust. Yes, someday in the Lord's own time, she knew she would have to learn to trust again. *Please, Lord, not today. Not Ernest Breaux.*

Ernest seemed content to stand on the steps and hold her, oblivious to the activity surrounding them. How long they stood that way, Gen had no idea. She let the beating of Ernest's heart lull her into a calm she had no business feeling.

Then he took her by the hand and led her away, down the steps and across the street to the park bench where they were to have last met. Settling her on the bench, he knelt in front of her and touched her chin with his thumb.

"Genevieve Lamont," he said gently, "I don't claim to be a smart man, and I'm sure not the smoothest talker there is, but I've got something to tell you, and I'm just going to say it plain. Is that all right with you?"

She nodded.

"All right, then." He paused to remove his cap. "Genevieve, I might be speaking out of turn here, but ever since I met you, I have felt like you were something special. I don't know any other way to say it. I love you, Genevieve Lamont, and it took me thinking I might not ever find you again to make me see it."

"Oh, Ernest," she said as tears constricted her throat.

She loved him, too. She'd known it far too long to deny the truth of it. Yet she could never give that love, no matter how strong, to a man who would not love Ellen, too.

Trust.

Gen felt the word settle into her spirit, massaging the fear that held her voice captive. If the Lord meant her to love Ernest Breaux, she would have to be honest with him. And she would have to trust that the Lord would guide her words.

"Ernest," she said softly, "I need to tell you something. After I finish, I don't want you to say anything. Can you do that?"

He looked confused. "I'll try," he said. "That's the best I can say."

"Fair enough."

Genevieve looked away, thankful for once that her poor vision caused the world around her to seem a swirl of colors. It made anything besides Ernest's face easier to ignore.

"I need you to pray about what you hear and then see what God's telling you to do." She forced her attention back on Ernest. "I don't want your sympathy, Ernest, just remember that."

When he nodded and grasped her hands in his, she began, "It all started when I fell for a man who promised me the world. I married him and followed him all the way to Texas, believing those promises." She paused. "Even when he hit me."

Ernest's jaw clenched, but he said nothing. His grasp of Gen's fingers loosened.

"Eventually he took off and left me a month behind on the rent and without a penny in my purse. I sold everything I had just to get bus money to come home. It was three days after New Year's when I got there. Turns out I'd just missed my father's funeral."

"Oh, sweetheart," he whispered.

"Mother took to her bed and refused to let me care for her. I wasn't welcome, and she let me know in no uncertain terms. When I'd walk in the front door, she'd head for her room, and the only clothes she would wear were Daddy's pajamas. As long as I was in the house, she'd refuse to come out. I guess you could say she didn't take kindly to my running off like I did. In the one conversation we did have, she blamed me for Daddy's death. Said I'd killed him with grief."

The tears flowed freely now, and so did the words. All the secrets, so long pent up, were fighting one another to be told.

"I finally realized I could do her more good paying the bills and seeing that she had her medications. So I headed to town to try and find work. I felt so awful telling everyone I was Miss Genevieve Lamont when the Lord and the state of Texas had declared me to be Mrs. Alton Gallier."

Ernest winced but said nothing. A moment later he released his grip and rested his hands on his knees.

"Moving to New Iberia was a temporary situation," she continued. "Just something to pay the bills until we could find another way to get by. Little did I know it would be *this* temporary."

"Genevieve?"

"Yes?"

"What happened to your. . ." He seemed to have difficulty saying the word. Finally, he managed. "To your husband? Does he know what you're doing?"

"My husband? When I ran home, he stayed in Texas. I found out not too long ago that there was an accident at the oil field. He left me a widow." She paused. "But that's not all."

Gen stared at Ernest, but he refused to meet her gaze. She looked down at his hands, which were balled into fists.

"He also left me a mother." She reached for him, but he pulled away. "I have a baby girl, Ernest. Her name is Ellen, and she was six months old last week."

Gen sat back and waited for a reaction from Ernest. While she prayed for mercy, she knew she deserved whatever was about to happen.

Ernest stared down at his feet, then swung his gaze up to meet hers. The change in his expression stunned her. He looked at her as if he no longer knew her.

"You know how I feel about children, Genevieve."

"Yes, but I thought. . ." Her words sputtered to a halt as her throat closed around them. Somehow she climbed to her feet and made her way back to her room to put the last of her things in the box Betty had set aside for the purpose.

As she worked, she kept a steady watch in the window. *Surely Ernest will be here soon. After all, he loves me. He said so.*

When the last item had been stored away and she could delay her departure no longer, Gen made her trek toward the bus station. As she passed the park bench where a short while ago she'd poured her heart out to the man she loved, she saw that man was gone.

Chapter 18

Thursday, June 1

Five months after she arrived home from her disastrous marriage to Alton Gallier, Gen awoke in her old room. The sun streamed through starched white curtains, illuminating a room with what Big Mama called the Lord's spotlight.

She sat bolt upright. Being careful not to wake her sleeping daughter, she tiptoed down the hall to start the coffeepot. To her surprise, her mother had beat her to it.

Steeling herself for the inevitable, she inched into the kitchen and waited for her mother to turn around and find her there. "Do you still like yours black, Genevieve?" her mother said instead.

Gen nodded slowly.

"All right, then." Mother cinched up Daddy's dressing gown and took herself and her coffee up the back stairs. "Be sure to wash your mug when you finish."

"Yes, ma'am." Genevieve tiptoed to the door and watched her mother disappear around the corner.

"Well, how about that?" she whispered as she returned to the stove to pour a cup of coffee. "Maybe today's going to be special."

Despite the initial excitement of actually hearing Mother speak to her, the day progressed for Gen as each one had since her return to Latagnier. After Gen fed and dressed Ellen, she took her daughter outside and laid her on a blanket to play while Gen worked to bring Daddy's garden back to life. All the while, Mother watched from the window, and Gen pretended not to know. At some point Big Mama would call them for lunch, and later, after an afternoon spent doing indoor chores, for supper. Bedtime came far too soon, as did the sunrise.

This routine continued for the better part of June. Every day, Ellen seemed to be getting stronger, and soon she would be pulling up and trying to sit on her own. At least that was Big Mama's prediction.

As for Gen, she hoped her precious baby didn't grow up nearly so fast. Some nights, when she wasn't too tired, she lifted Ellen into her arms and danced a sleepy dance in the dark, pretending they were at a fancy dress ball or that they were characters out of a storybook. Most nights, however, Gen fell into bed exhausted from trying to eke a season of vegetables from the garden.

Still, in those moments between consciousness and sleep, Gen often pretended that Ernest would ride up, a valiant white knight on a prancing steed, to rescue her from this world of toil and trials.

In the daylight, her thoughts were more realistic. Logic told her what her dreams would not: It had been nearly a month with no word from Ernest Breaux. He was not coming for her.

That realization caused her to tear into the garden with renewed vigor, pulling weeds and tucking wayward strands of pole bean vines into place while the summer sun beat down on Daddy's old straw hat. She'd taken to wearing the hat a few weeks ago, and the comfort of its shady brim could not be matched.

Besides, if Mother insisted on wearing Daddy's pajamas, why couldn't she don his hat?

A movement caught her attention, and she knew it was her mother at her usual spot in the old straight-backed chair in her bedroom. Nothing out of the ordinary in this; in fact, it had become Mother's routine to awaken from her nap and go to the chair to watch.

Occasionally Gen waved, but never had her mother acknowledged her presence. She'd decided Mother was watching Ellen, who now played happily on her quilt beneath the pecan tree, and simply hadn't seen her wave. Believing this made Mother's snub more bearable.

But as Gen peered from beneath the hat's broad brim, she noticed something odd. In place of Daddy's pajamas, Mother wore a housedress of pale blue sprigged in yellow flowers.

Gen rose and dusted off her hands, then turned to face the open upstairs window. "Mother, why don't you come down and join us? Ellen's crawling everywhere, and I thought you might enjoy watching her explore."

Her mother stood very still, then disappeared into the shadows. Gen waited a moment and went back to her work. To her surprise, a few minutes later Mother stood at the edge of the garden, arms crossed. She only stayed a moment, standing warily in the shadows before beating a path back to the house. The next day, however, Mother actually sat in the chair for a few minutes before sitting on the quilt to play with Ellen.

By the last day of June, Mother not only played with Ellen, but when Big Mama carried the baby inside for a nap, Mother took up a spade and joined Gen in the garden. The pair worked in silence on opposite ends of the row until finally they met in the middle. Mother reached for a dandelion at the same time Gen did, and their fingers touched.

Rather than pull away, Mother paused, then entwined her fingers with Gen's. For a moment, neither spoke. Then Gen noticed her mother was crying.

"Oh, Mother," she whispered. "I'm so sorry."

Mother held her arms out, and Gen fell into them. "Hush now," Mother said. "It's me who should be apologizing."

"You?" Gen leaned back and wiped her eyes with the back of her hand. As soon as she did, she realized her hands were covered in dirt. Her face must be a muddy mess, not that she cared right then.

Mother nodded. "Will you forgive me for behaving so terribly?"

"Only if you will forgive me for running off and hurting you and Daddy."

"Oh, honey," Mother said softly as she smoothed Gen's hair, "it's a new day. Let's not live in the past anymore."

"Why didn't God stop me?" Gen wailed. "He knew what would happen, and He let me go and do it anyway."

Mother held Gen at arm's length and gave her a no-nonsense look that took Gen back to her girlhood. "You've got to let go of that, Genevieve. The Lord didn't make a single one of us to be perfect. He knows and so do I that I've made mistakes." She paused to look away. "Big ones." Returning her attention to Gen, she shook her head. "You can't be going about and asking God to explain Himself."

"What?"

"The Lord, He gave us free will. Now I don't like it, and I know you don't, either."

Gen shook her head. "No, I don't. It would be so much better if He would just tell me what to do and then make me do it."

"Oh, honey," Mother said. "It would be easier, that's for sure, but better? I don't think so."

"What do you mean?"

"Well, if the Lord leaves us here because we're still learning to do His will—which I believe He does—then how are we to learn obedience if we aren't given the choice to obey?"

"I never thought of it that way, Mother."

"Well, maybe you ought to." Eyes narrowed, she gave Gen a sideways look. "Have I told you lately that I'm proud of you, Genevieve?"

"Proud of me?" She could barely voice the question for the lump in her throat. "What for? I've done nothing but mess up."

Mother gathered her into her arms again. "You're a strong, brave young woman. I know I wouldn't have had the strength to carry on like you have." Her voice cracked, and tears began again. "I'm just so very proud. Je t'aime, ma fille."

"Oh, Mother, I love you, too."

By the time Big Mama called them for supper, they both were a muddy mess. Mother swiped at Gen's eyes with the corner of her apron, then used the other corner to attend to her own face.

"You ladies done lost your minds, I declare for sure," Big Mama said, hands on her hips. "Now the both of you need to get yourselves inside and get presentable."

"Yes, ma'am," Gen said as she gave Big Mama a mock salute.

"Immediately," Mother said, seemingly oblivious to the surprise on Big Mama's face.

Gen watched Mother cross the garden and disappear inside before she smiled at Big Mama. "What do you think got into her?"

"It's the power of prayer, Genny-girl. Prayer and a mother's love. Ain't nothing like it." She shook her finger at Gen. "Now go get cleaned up. You look like you been using mud pies for face paint."

That evening, all traces of mud removed, Gen came downstairs to find Big Mama and Ellen waiting. The baby sat on a blanket on the floor, happily chewing on a biscuit while Big Mama stirred something on the stove. The room smelled like heaven, and it didn't take much for Gen to muster a smile.

And then Mother walked into the room.

She wore pink, a trim housedress with white, daisy-covered buttons marching down the front and a smart pink scarf in her upswept hair. Without comment, Mother scooped Ellen up off the floor and settled with her at the table.

They ate their dinner in silence that night, but the next morning at breakfast, Mother began to talk. She chatted about the weather and the way the tomatoes were tasting so fresh, and then she paused to give Big Mama a direct look.

"I want to thank you, Emmaline, for all you've done for my family."

Big Mama ducked her head. "It wasn't nothin' you haven't done for my family, Miss Rose. Why, I don't know what I would have done without you and Mr. Carl when I lost my Henry."

"Yes, well," Mother said slowly as she reached to put her hand atop Big Mama's, "I appreciate it all the same."

Monday, July 3

Ernest closed the door to his room and fell into bed, exhausted. All his hard work at the sawmill was paying off, literally. Not only had he been made foreman of the night crew, but his furniture was the hit of New Iberia. It seemed as though the new Mrs. Denison had told just about anyone who would listen what a wonderful carpenter he was.

Phil had left to spend the holiday at his family's home in Crowley, leaving Ernest to peace and quiet—and too much time to think. While at work, he thought of Genevieve and of the secrets she had spilled that day in the park. He longed to be with her. At night before he fell asleep, he thought of the things he hadn't said to her.

If only he could have both the job and the girl.

Even if he could, there was still the problem of the child. He hadn't changed his mind about becoming a father, but he had an unsettled feeling that wouldn't let go.

With the sawmill officially closed until the fifth of July, Ernest decided to go straight to the source—to his papa—to ask him what it was like giving up so much for what seemed to be so little in return.

After a few hours of sleep and a hot bath, Ernest loaded up the roadster and headed home, intent on having a man-to-man talk with Papa. Unfortunately, he stepped out of the car and found a party going on.

"There's my boy! Come here and give your mama a kiss, Monsieur Sawmill Foreman!" Mama called.

Ernest obliged his mother with a kiss, then shook hands with his father. "I'm proud of you, son. My boy, running the night shift, eh?"

"That's right." Ernest tried to work up some enthusiasm for the topic. Papa must have noticed his lack of excitement, because he motioned for Ernest to join him on the porch.

"What is it, son? Something bothering you?"

"I reckon it is." Ernest settled onto the bench nearest the door. "I guess I'm pretty obvious."

"I guess so." Papa sat beside him and stretched his legs out. "The job, it's good?"

"Yes, sir," Ernest said. "I like this job real fine."

"And that side job making furniture, how's that going?"

"Real well." He shrugged. "Right now I'm turning away business 'cause I don't have enough time for all of it."

Papa nodded. "So work's good, and furniture making's good. What's the trouble?"

"Trouble? Well. . .where should I start?"

"At the beginning would be good."

"All right, see, the trouble actually started when I met Genevieve Lamont."

"Don't it always begin with a woman?" Papa said with a chuckle.

"Well, this one did for sure. So here's what happened." When Ernest finished, he leaned back and closed his eyes. "So what do I do, Papa?"

"Looks like you got yourself a problem, son."

"That much I know." Ernest turned to face his father. "What I don't know is how to solve that problem."

"If it were me, I believe I'd pick her a big old mess of flowers and ask her to forgive me. Might even consider begging if it came to it." Papa paused. "But you say you wonder how to solve your problem?"

Ernest nodded.

"Maybe you're not the one with the solution." He pointed skyward. "The heavenly Father, maybe He's the One you should be asking for help."

"I tried that, Papa," Ernest said.

"And what did He say?"

"Nothing I wanted to hear," Ernest said.

The truth was, all his prayers had led him to one conclusion. He was wrong about babies and families and marriage. Still, he figured there must be some wiggle room in the proclamation.

Ernest was still looking for a way out the next day when he packed his things and headed back toward town. He hadn't reached the main road before the white house on the bayou beckoned.

Maybe he'd just drive by and see if Genevieve was home. Or maybe he'd be smart and head for New Iberia while his sanity and his bachelorhood remained intact.

Chapter 19

Tuesday, July 4

With Mother feeding Ellen and Big Mama cleaning up the kitchen, Gen had nothing to do but sit and read her book while she waited for the heat of the day to pass. The garden was coming along nicely, and they'd even managed to harvest enough produce to send several bushels of vegetables to the Widow LeBlanc. In return, the woman brought over a burlap bag full of last fall's pecans, which the three of them had been taking turns shelling.

Thanks to the generosity of her former roommate, Betty, there was little need for worry. The envelope she had handed Genevieve on their last day in New Iberia had contained enough money to pay for Mother's medicines for the rest of the year.

As another cloud covered the sun, Gen put her book down and reached for the shelling tool. "Looks like it's going to rain this afternoon, Mother," Gen said.

Mother nodded, more intent on feeding Ellen than worrying about the weather. Gen tossed the empty pecan shells into a paper sack and the meat into a bowl beside her. While her fingers shelled pecans, her mind drifted back to the day she had last seen Ernest Breaux.

She often went to that park bench in her mind. Sometimes she told him the truth and pretended he accepted it, and other times she imagined she hadn't. Neither scenario did much for her, as the only real memory she had was of telling the truth and being rejected for it.

Ellen finished her lunch and strained to climb off her grandmother's lap. Lately, she crawled everywhere and loved to pull up on things. Big Mama declared she would walk early, but Mother said she would probably be late.

Personally, Gen didn't care as long as the little girl stayed healthy.

"What in the world?" Big Mama called. "Look over yonder. They's a body coming up the road."

"Well, I'll be," Mother said. "Is that who I think it is?"

"I believe so, Miss Rose. It do look like him."

"Who?" Gen picked up the spectacles in her lap and fit them on. Even though they once belonged to Daddy, they suited her just fine. Indeed there was someone coming up the road. With the glasses on, Gen could see it was a man.

As he approached, she realized that man was Ernest Breaux.

"Emmaline," Mother said, "I believe you and I have some business inside."

Big Mama came to stand beside Gen. "We do?"

Mother cleared her throat. "Yes, dear, we do."

"Oh, that's right." Big Mama tapped Gen on the arm. "Your mama and I, we got some business inside."

Gen nodded, unable to take her attention from the man now crossing the lawn. The man who she could now see carried a bouquet of buttercups in one hand.

"Land sakes, Miss Rose, looks like the boy done picked those flowers by the side of the road."

"Hush now," Mother said. "Ellen, darling, come with Grandma." When she reached for the baby, Ellen began to cry.

"Let's leave her with her mama," Big Mama said. " 'Sides, we both gonna be watching from the kitchen. It won't do to have to keep an eye on the baby, too," she said with a chuckle.

The screen door slammed behind the two women, and for a moment, all was silent. Gen tore her attention from the approaching Ernest and dug into the pecan sack. If he wanted to show up here after all this time, he sure wasn't going to catch her sitting around waiting for him.

~

Relief flooded Ernest. After all this time, it looked as though Genevieve was sitting there waiting for him. A movement at her feet caught his attention. A dark-haired girl crawled about, playing with her mother's apron strings.

He turned his attention to Genevieve, and his heart soared. As he neared the grouping of chairs, he watched her stand and scoop the baby into her arms.

"Afternoon," he said, then cringed. *What kind of idiot returns after weeks of silence to say that?*

Obviously the kind of idiot who would let her leave in the first place.

"These are for you." He thrust the flowers in her direction, then realized she couldn't take them while holding a baby. Placing them on the table beside the pecan bowl, he thrust his fists into his pockets.

Lord, this was Your idea. Now give me something to say.

"Since when do you wear eyeglasses?"

She shrugged.

All right, Lord, now what?

He looked into the eyes of the baby, and the baby looked back intently. "Hello there, little girl," he said sweetly.

To his surprise, she let out a loud wail.

"Hey now, what's this noise about?" He turned his attention to Genevieve. "What's her name?"

"Ellen," she said over the sound of the baby's cries.

"Ellen?" Ernest reached to take the little girl out of Genevieve's arms. "That's a pretty name for a pretty little girl." He whirled her around, then stopped short and did it again. By the third spin, Ernest was dizzy, and the baby was giggling.

"How did you do that?" Genevieve asked. "She's always fussy this time of day. It's her naptime."

Ernest grinned. "Mine, too, only I decided to come here instead." He set the baby on the ground, and she began crawling toward her blanket. "Will she be all right?"

Gen watched the baby settle on the blanket and begin to chew on a teething ring. "She's fine." She turned back to Ernest with an unwavering gaze. "Ernest, why are you here? And don't say that you happened to be in the neighborhood."

"Well, there went my first response." He shrugged. "I had to come here," he finally said. "I missed you."

The baby began to make cooing sounds. When Ernest glanced her way, she gave him a broad, toothless grin.

"She likes you," Gen said flatly.

"I've been told I'm a natural with babies," he said. "My brothers and sisters and all my nieces and nephews tend to gravitate to me. I don't know why."

"Yet you don't like them."

"What?" He jerked his attention back to Genevieve. "No, I never said that. I love little kids. It's the responsibility I'm not crazy about."

She sighed. "Then I repeat: Why are you here, Ernest? Because I come with responsibility, lots of it."

"Genevieve, I'm here because I couldn't stand being anywhere else." His sigh matched hers. "Because everywhere I go, I feel like you've just been there. Because I've been miserable without you."

"Yet you and I don't make a good match, do we? What with you being determined to avoid the whole family thing and me having a daughter." She glanced down at Ellen. "I'm sorry, but has anything changed in that department?"

What could he say? It hadn't. Yet. . .

"I'm working on it." That was the best he could do, and it was the truth. Surely she would recognize that much.

Genevieve nodded and reached to pick up Ellen. "That's great, Ernest," she said. "You let me know when you've got it all worked out."

With that, she turned and walked inside, leaving Ernest and the bouquet of buttercups to wilt in the July sun.

Friday, July 21

Ernest wiped his brow and stepped away from his latest masterpiece, a baby crib for the new arrival the Denisons were expecting come spring. One more stroke of the sandpaper and one more wipe of the cheesecloth, and the piece was complete.

He closed the door to the storage room and locked it, slipping the key into his shirt pocket. For the past two Fridays, Ernest had closed up shop and headed to Latagnier to see Genevieve. Each time she'd been cool—icy, actually—but today he had plans to thaw the iceberg just a bit.

"Excuse me, Mr. Breaux." Mrs. Denison stood in the hallway. "I was wondering if I might be able to see the crib."

Ernest nodded, then unlocked the door and ushered her in. She stood in the doorway in silence so long that he was certain she hated it.

"Oh, I love it," she said softly. "It's perfect."

A young man of no more than six or seven raced into the room. "Honey," she said to the boy, "look what Mr. Breaux made for us."

The boy inspected the crib and pronounced it "swell." With the same speed he used on arrival, he raced out the door.

The boss's wife looked up at Ernest with tears in her eyes. "I always wanted a beautiful crib. Thank you for making this possible." She paused. "If there's ever anything I can do for you, please let me know."

He shook his head. "Your appreciation is plenty. Besides, your husband pays me well. I've got no complaints."

She ran her hand over the polished rail, then regarded him with a strange look. "Don't you ever wish this was all you did? Making furniture, I mean?"

Ernest shrugged. "That would be something; I'll admit that for sure, but no, I don't dare wish it. That's a dream that's too big to come true."

Mrs. Denison touched his sleeve. "Mr. Breaux, I am living proof that no dream is too big if you give it to God."

"Dotty, are you in there?"

She gave Ernest a genuine smile. "Speaking of dreams coming true. In here, honey. Come and see the baby bed."

A short while later, Ernest helped to load the bed onto a truck for delivery to the Denison home. The effort made him a bit later than he intended to leave, but it was worth seeing the boss's wife so happy.

Just before the truck left, Mrs. Denison took him aside. "Mr. Breaux, if you were to have the chance to do nothing but carpentry work, would you take it?"

It didn't take him long to ponder the question and answer it. "You bet, unless the Lord told me otherwise, of course."

Her smile puzzled him, and as he drove toward Latagnier, he thought of Mrs. Denison's words.

" 'No dream is too big if you give it to God,' " he repeated. "All right, God, if that's so, then I've got a doozy for You."

When he reached the Lamont place, he felt as if a load had been removed from his shoulders. After telling the Lord all about his dreams, he'd pulled over and actually listened as God gave him a few unexpected additions to the list.

First and foremost, he had to tell Genevieve; then he planned to go see Papa and let him know he was right about love and fatherhood. He found Genevieve in the garden, wearing a straw hat, a pair of baggy overalls, and a bright red shirt. A smudge of dirt streaked her cheek, and the first thing he did was use his handkerchief to wipe it away.

As he stood there, staring into the eyes of the only woman he had ever loved, Ernest tried to think of something brilliant to say. Instead, all he could do was stare.

"Something wrong?" she asked as she pushed her silly glasses back into place.

"No." He smiled. "Actually, something is very, very right."

"Oh?"

Ernest dropped to one knee. Everything he wanted in life was right here. Now all he had to do was tell Genevieve that. She would ask about Ellen, and he needed to be prepared to answer.

He'd already asked the Lord to handle that situation when it came up. And to show him how to love a baby girl when he'd promised himself he never would.

"Genevieve Lamont, I have something to say."

"You do?" She looked suitably confused. "What's that?"

"I want you to marry me, Genevieve. I love you, and—"

"Land o' Goshen, Genny-girl, come quick." Big Mama came racing across the lawn, a limp Ellen in her arms. "Lord, please save this baby!" she cried.

The child's face was turning blue, and her eyes were wide. She looked as if she wanted to cry, but nothing could come out. The last time he had seen a baby like this, his baby sister had swallowed a bug.

Ernest took the child in his arms and, in a swift motion, pressed on her chest as he had with little Mary.

Nothing happened.

Genevieve had become hysterical, and the two older women raced about in circles.

"Quiet, all of you!" he demanded as he tried once again to press the spot beneath the baby's rib cage.

Once again, no response. Now the child's face had darkened to a dusky blue, and her eyes had rolled back in her head.

"Come on, Ellen!" he shouted. "Spit it out."

This time when he pressed the spot, out popped a slightly chewed pecan from the baby's mouth.

He quickly righted her and held her against his chest, his heart racing. Before the baby could cry, Ernest's tears began to fall. Genevieve soon joined him, climbing into his embrace to cling to him until he thought she would never let go.

Later, after his brother-in-law Jeff came by to pronounce the baby fit and fine, Ernest sat outside under the stars, staring up at the galaxy. He should go home. It had been a long day, and there was no need for Genevieve to play host to him when she had a baby to take care of.

The baby.

Tears threatened again, and he bit them back. "Thank You, Lord, for saving that precious child and for showing this thickheaded man that he's meant to be a father someday."

"Do you mean it, Ernest?" Genevieve asked as she walked quietly up to him. "Do you really believe you were meant to be a father?"

He nodded. "I'm sorry it took me so long to figure it out."

Genevieve leaned into his embrace and sighed. "I'm just glad you did."

Ernest kissed the top of her head and swiped at the embarrassing tears still falling. "Me, too, sweetheart," he said. "Me, too."

She looked up at him and smiled. "I believe you asked me a question earlier."

He affected an innocent look. "Did I?"

"You did."

"And?" He released her to drop to one knee. "Would you? Be my wife, I mean. And while I'm at it, do you think Ellen would mind becoming my little girl?"

She smiled and nodded. "Oh, yes," she said. "I will. And I can't speak for Ellen, but I'm pretty sure she'd say yes, too, if she could."

"Do you mind if we don't hold off on tying the knot until she learns to talk? I don't think I can wait that long."

Genevieve smiled. "What do you think of a springtime wedding? I'll need some time to get everything arranged, and of course I'll have to be sure Betty can take time off work. I wouldn't think of having a wedding without her. I wish I could find Dorothy. She was such a dear. I wonder if Betty might be able to track her down. Yes, you know, I'll bet she could—"

Ernest kissed her into silence, then stared into her eyes for a long moment. "What say we split the difference and set the date for January?"

Chapter 20

Sunday, December 24

"Papa!"

"Horsey again, Ellie?" Ernest scooped a giggling one-year-old Ellen into his arms and trotted around the churchyard while he waited for Genevieve to finish her gabbing with the choir ladies. In truth, he didn't mind the wait. The more time he spent with little Ellen, the more she wrapped him around her tiny finger.

For good measure, he made a circle around the spot where Genevieve's mother stood in serious conversation with Mama. As he neared the pair, he heard them comparing recipes for pecan pie.

"Since we are going to be family, I suppose I can give you the recipe, Rose," Mama said. "You know, it's just like making regular pecan pie. It's the chocolate and honey that makes the difference."

On purpose he cut a path between the ladies. " 'Scuse us," he said. "The young lady's on a horsey ride."

While Mama shook her head, Genevieve's mother called, "I declare, you'll spoil that child rotten, Ernest Breaux!"

"I fully intend to, Mrs. Lamont. And I plan to have a good time doing it."

To punctuate his statement, he made the best horse noise he knew how to, sending Ellen into stunned silence. A second later, she recovered and shouted, "Again!"

Of course, he obliged.

Twice more around the churchyard, and then he ground to a halt beside Genevieve's mother, hoisting Ellen off his shoulders and up into the air. He caught her, then spun her around and held her to his chest. Oh, how he loved this precious child.

And her mother, well, love was such a poor description of what he felt for Genevieve. Yes, it was love he held in his heart, for sure, but there was more. Something deeper.

Something that felt like forever.

How had he ever thought life was worth living without Ellen and her mother? Times had surely changed since the summer—when he'd almost lost both of them.

But the Lord had been good to forgive his stubborn pride and foolish ways.

He could now boast of a side job making furniture that paid more than his foreman's job at the sawmill. If only he could be sure the carpentry work would continue to be steady. But then, the decision was already made.

"And they that know thy name will put their trust in thee. . . ."

Out of the corner of his eye, he saw Genevieve hug the pastor's wife, a sure sign she'd finished her visiting.

"And speaking of time, it is time for this horsey ride to end, cher. Go see *Grandmère*."

Before the child could complain, he handed her to her grandmother, then made a silly face. Ellen's pout turned into a smile and then a squeal of delight when he tickled her under her chin.

She leaned toward Ernest, arms outstretched. "Papa."

"Papa has to go fetch Mama," he said. "Those church ladies must not have hungry men waiting for their Christmas Eve lunches."

"Or an impatient groom with a Christmas secret he intends to tell his bride today," Mama said.

Mrs. Lamont smiled. "Do you know how hard it was not to spill what I knew to Genevieve? Why, at least twice within my earshot, Big Mama nearly let the cat out of the bag."

"Papa," Ellen repeated, her little hands reaching.

Ernest kissed her plump cheek, then made another horse noise. "We'll play later, Ellie, after you go see the Christmas tree."

"That's right, Ellen," Mama said. "We're going to see the Christmas tree at Mama and Papa's house, and you're going to meet all your cousins and maybe even open a present or two, eh?"

Mama distracted Ellen by pointing to a bird, and as Ernest trotted toward Genevieve, he could hear the little girl trying to make chirping noises.

The breeze had a slight bite to it, indicating tonight's Christmas Eve celebration would be held in front of a roaring fire. Some Christmases on the bayou were muggy and warm, so a chilly yuletide was a blessing indeed.

He reached Genevieve in a few steps and swept her into his arms. Oh yes, there were so many blessings this Christmas.

"Well now," Genevieve said when he released her. "What was that about?"

"About?" Ernest shrugged. "Nothing." He paused. "All right, I was just thinking about how much I appreciate the Lord blessing me with you, that's all."

A pink tinge decorated her cheeks. "I think that a lot," she said.

"Is that right?" He grasped her hand in his and led her to the roadster. "How about you and I take a Christmas Eve drive while the ladies take care of Ellen?"

Genevieve cast a glance at Ellen, then looked back at Ernest. "I would like that very much," she said.

After Ernest helped her into the car, he trotted around to climb inside. The engine started smooth as silk. He sure was going to miss this car.

No, strike that.

He wouldn't miss the roadster at all, not when he'd happily gotten more than enough for her to buy a vehicle more suitable for a growing family. With what was left, he'd made another purchase.

One he now pointed the roadster toward.

Ernest cast a sideways glance at his unsuspecting fiancée and pressed down on the gas pedal. The sooner he got to where he was going, the sooner he would know whether he'd made the biggest mistake of his life.

~

"So what's this surprise you've been teasing me with all morning? I declare, I could barely concentrate on the sermon for wondering what you've got up your sleeve."

Ernest slowed the roadster to turn left off the main road. "So, any ideas on what it might be?"

"Nope."

"You sure? That mother of yours likes to talk."

"You mean Mother's in on this?"

"Sure is. Mine, too, and Papa and the boys. I didn't tell Amalie, though. She would have told you for sure."

Gen gave Ernest's arm a playful nudge. He grinned as he captured her hand in his, bringing it to his lips. "No idea at all what your Christmas surprise is?" he asked, his breath warm against the chilled flesh of her fingers.

Eyebrows raised, she yanked her hand away. "Ernest Breaux, you cad. What are you up to?"

He matched her look, then slowed to a stop. "Why don't you come out with me and see? If you dare, that is."

"If I dare? Hmmm. Maybe I should stay right here."

Ernest gave her a genuine smile. "I promise this is something you will really want to see." He turned his smile down a notch, putting on a serious look. "I have to tell you I'm a little nervous about this. It's one of those situations where I'm leaning on the Lord and not on my own understanding."

"What are you talking about?"

He pointed over his shoulder. "I can't tell you. I have to show you."

"All right." Genevieve reached for the handle, only to find Ernest had opened it before she could manage the feat. Stepping out, she looked around.

"Ernest, where are we?"

"Ah, that's the beauty of this surprise. You don't yet know where we are." He removed his driving cap in a sweeping gesture. "You think you do, but you don't really."

She regarded him with a shake of her head. "Of course I know where we are. This is the far north corner of the Widow LeBlanc's place."

"Well, that's what it seems to you." He reached into his pocket and pulled out a handkerchief. "I hope you don't mind, but I'm going to have to blindfold you."

Gen took a step back. "Oh no, you don't. I don't know what you're up to, Ernest, but I am not—"

His pitiful look stopped her protest. "Oh, all right, but remember this is Christmas Eve. If you're bad, there will be nothing but coal in your stocking tomorrow morning."

"That, my darling," he said as he whirled her around to tie the handkerchief over her eyes, "is a risk I am willing to take."

His hands grasped her shoulders as he turned her toward him. Soft lips brushed hers; then he wrapped his arm around her waist. "Hold on tight, sweetheart," he said as he lifted her easily into his arms. "Let's go find out what this Christmas secret is."

A short while later, Ernest came to an abrupt stop. Before he set her feet on the ground, he brushed another kiss across her lips.

Turning her toward him, he lifted the blindfold. She blinked hard and focused on his face.

"Before you turn around, I want to tell you something, Genevieve." He seemed to have trouble speaking. Finally, Ernest cleared his throat. "You know I wasn't always the man I should have been when it came to you and Ellen, but I need you to know that I've done my best to right that wrong."

Gen nodded. "I know that you have."

"Well, like I said, I wasn't the man I should have been, but I believe God's got a plan for us: you, me, and Ellen, that is." He shrugged. "I ought to have prepared some fancy speech, because that's what you deserve, Genevieve. I'm a plain-speaking man, and I don't know a lot of pretty words, so I'll do my best."

"All right," she said slowly.

"Merry Christmas, Genevieve," he said as he placed his hands on her shoulders and slowly turned her around. "I hope you like it. As long as you're agreeable, I'd like to set up housekeeping here with you. After the wedding," he hastily added.

"Oh, Ernest," she whispered as her gaze landed on the little house. "I don't understand. This is ours?" When he nodded, she shook her head. "But this house belongs to the Widow LeBlanc. However did you get her to part with it?"

Ernest shrugged. "You know there are no secrets among bayou people, cher. Mrs. LeBlanc's been looking for an excuse to go live with her daughter in Mississippi."

"I. . ." She walked toward the house, up the steps, and across the wide expanse of porch. "Ours?"

Again he nodded. "Yours and mine."

"But I thought we'd be living in New Iberia. What happened to your job at the sawmill? You know I won't live here without you." She grasped his arm. "A wife belongs with her husband."

"I agree completely," he said. "That's why, if you'll agree to it, I plan on quitting my job at the sawmill."

Before she could respond, he grasped her hand and led her around to the back of the house. There, situated in a clearing just the other side of the garage, stood a wooden shed.

"Go ahead, Genevieve," Ernest said. "Open the door."

She walked toward the shed alone, then doubled back to urge Ernest to accompany her. He seemed inordinately proud of whatever was behind that door, and it just seemed fitting that she should discover the contents of the shed with him at her side.

Giving the door handle a tug, she watched the wood swing open to reveal a tidy workshop. In one corner, a partially completed cradle vied for space beside a pair of matching chairs. A table stood upended with some sort of clamp attached to one leg.

On the opposite wall, shelves held neat rows of paint and tools. A wooden stool painted red waited beside what looked like a drafting table.

The place suited Ernest.

Then she rested her gaze on the object in the center of the room. A rocking chair of beautifully polished wood sat in a place of honor, a roughly tied red bow adorning one arm. Leaning beside it was a hobby horse, its head carved in exquisite detail and a thatch of what looked like real horse hair forming the mane. It, too, sported a red bow.

"Ernest," she said softly as she sank into the rocker, the horse's head in her hand. "This is magnificent."

He knelt beside her. "What's magnificent, sweetheart?"

Gen touched the dark hair of her daughter's toy, then glanced up at Ernest. "This. . .the house. . .you."

Bowing his head, Ernest rested his hand atop Gen's. "Then you're pleased?"

Gen cradled her future husband's chin in her hands, then lifted his face to meet hers. A kiss soon followed.

"Just a minute, Mr. Breaux," she said. "I believe there was something you told me long ago that I need to check on."

"What's that?"

"Remember our first date?"

He smiled. "You bought me a Milky Way bar and refused to tell me where you lived."

"And I made you promise not to peek when I walked away."

Ernest kissed her soundly, then recaptured her fingers to entwine them with his. "Yes, sweetheart, I remember. What about it?"

"Well," she said. "You told me if I was ever in trouble, I should just whistle and you would save me."

He nodded, then began to chuckle when she whistled.

"I think I'm in trouble," she said.

Ernest's puzzled look was absolutely adorable. "Why?" he asked as he tightened his grip on her hand.

"Because this crazy plan of yours is beginning to make sense."

"It is?" His smile was glorious. "You mean you're willing to take me on, even knowing we might have lean times?"

Gen nodded. "We've got each other and the Lord. What else matters?"

Ernest shrugged. "Well, I don't pretend to understand women, but I'm thinking of one thing that might matter right now."

"What's that?"

He smiled. "Your wedding dress, cher. Did you not hear me when I said I'd planned a New Year's Eve wedding?"

"You planned. . .New Year's Eve?" She shook her head. "I don't understand."

He lifted her fingers to his lips. "Don't worry, Gen. I had some help."

Chapter 21

Sunday, December 31

With the strains of Big Mama's favorite hymn playing on the old church organ, floating under the door of the pastor's small study, Gen finished her prayers and stood. One last look in the mirror that Mama had brought from home, and Gen turned toward the window and the view of the glorious cross and the bayou beyond.

"My wedding day." She spoke the words with reverence. God had given her another chance, a chance to do things His way.

The sound of a baby's giggle alerted her to Ellen's presence. She turned to see Big Mama standing in the doorway holding Ellen. Somehow Big Mama had managed to situate a bow in the midst of the baby's curls.

"Oh, I don't 'spect it to last long up there, but I figured she'd look pretty for the wedding at least."

"She's beautiful," Gen said. "And so are you, Big Mama."

Dressed in her Sunday best for the occasion, the housekeeper beamed. "I don't put this dress on for just anybody, you know."

"I know," she said as she embraced the precious woman, then reached for her daughter.

Ellen played with the buttons on Gen's dress while Big Mama fussed with her hair. A moment later, the pastor knocked. "It's time," he said.

"She be right out," Big Mama answered.

"Go with Big Mama." She gave Ellen one final cuddle before handing her off to the housekeeper. "I'll see you in a minute, baby. First I've got to go get married."

Saying the word aloud made her smile. But then, anything related to Ernest Breaux seemed to have that effect on her.

"You look like an angel," Big Mama whispered. "Baby girl, look how pretty your mama looks."

Ellen's broad smile warmed her heart. "Mommy loves you," she said as she blew a kiss to her daughter, then watched Big Mama whisk her from the room.

"And your mother loves you, too."

Gen watched her mother approach. Her upswept hair and fine silk dress made her look more like Gen's sister than her mother.

"I'm so proud of you," she said. "Your daddy would have been proud, too."

Blinking back the tears, she enveloped her mother in a hug. "He would have liked Ernest."

"Yes, he would have." She pulled away. "Let's not keep him waiting."

Another knock sounded and a tall man filled the doorway. He opened his mouth to speak, then seemed at a loss for words.

"I should get seated," her mother said.

"Oui," Theophile Breaux said. "My son's getting a bit impatient for his bride."

"I love you," her mother said as she disappeared around the corner.

Gen hurried to Ernest's father's side. "I'm ready," she said. "Thank you for agreeing to escort me down the aisle."

He managed a nod. "Thank you for marrying my son, Genevieve. His mother and I are pleased that we not only get another daughter, but we are getting a granddaughter, as well."

Epilogue

Friday, November 16, 1934

Ernest set the cheesecloth on the workbench and took two steps back. The cradle was perfect in every way, and Genevieve would love it. Even in her advanced stage of pregnancy, she was agreeable.

One of his favorite things about his wife of ten months was that she made him feel as if he could do no wrong. If only he could convince himself of that.

Times had grown lean, and it was hard not to think of how well he could be taking care of Genevieve and Ellen—and the baby due next month—if he were still working as the foreman down at the sawmill.

"And they that know thy name will put their trust in thee: for thou, Lord, hast not forsaken them that seek thee."

"I know, Lord, but I've been holding on to that promise for nigh on a year. I'm all for waiting on You, but those mouths I have to feed aren't going to be able to wait forever." He reached for the cheesecloth and gave the cradle another swipe. "Me, I don't need much, but, Lord, if You wouldn't mind, could You send a blessing to my wife and daughter?"

"Ernest Breaux?"

"Oui?"

He stepped out of his workshop to find a familiar face standing there. "Well now, Mrs. Denison. How are you?"

"Very well, thank you," she said. "But the question of the hour is, how are you?"

"Jim-dandy," Ernest said. "You were right, ma'am. There's not a dream too big when you involve God in it."

"You remembered."

"I did indeed. In fact, I wondered what happened to you. How's that baby?"

She smiled. "Perfect in every way, of course."

"Of course."

Mr. Denison stepped into the clearing and strode toward Ernest. "Now you are a sight for sore eyes. I sure do miss you down at the sawmill."

Ernest tried and failed to think of a response. Finally, he managed to ask, "How did you find me?"

Mr. Denison pointed to his wife. "Dotty remembered you were from these parts."

"I see."

"I'll get right to the point, Ernest. My wife here's got a project that just may set you over the top."

"Oh?"

"That's right," she said. "A friend of ours in Baton Rouge is opening a restaurant. When he saw your dining room set last week, he had a fit. He wants to talk to you about designing tables for his new place." Her smiled broadened. "And if he likes what you do, which I know he will, then he's going to order new furniture for his other locations." She paused for effect. "All twelve of them. Then there's the hotels he owns. Why, in no time, your work could be nationwide."

"Nationwide." Ernest rocked back on his heels. "Now isn't that something?"

He looked past his guests to see Genevieve walking toward them, Ellen toddling at her side. When Ellen caught sight of him, she picked up speed, wobbling toward him on unsteady legs.

"Papa!" she called. "Papa, Papa!"

He swept the precious blessing into his arms and kissed her soundly, then turned his attention to her mother. "Genevieve, I'd like you to meet—"

"Dorothy?"

"Genevieve?"

The women began to squeal. "What in the world?" he asked Ellen.

When the noise died down, Genevieve shook her head. "Ernest, this is my friend Dorothy from the five-and-dime."

"No, sweetheart, this is Mrs. Denison, the lady I told you about." He paused. "My boss's wife."

The woman in question giggled. "Oh, this is too much. You're both right."

Clothilde Breaux's Chocolate Pecan Pie

5 tablespoons butter
¾ cup packed brown sugar
¼ cup honey
¼ cup pure cane syrup or,
if unavailable, molasses
2 teaspoons vanilla extract
2 eggs, lightly beaten
½ cup unsweetened cocoa, sifted
2 teaspoons salt
2¼ cups chopped pecans
9-inch pie shell

Heat oven to 350 degrees. Bring butter, brown sugar, honey, and syrup to a boil, stirring constantly. Reduce heat and boil for 3 minutes, stirring constantly. Remove from heat and cool 15 to 20 minutes; then add vanilla, eggs, cocoa, and salt. Beat at medium-low speed until thoroughly blended, then fold in pecans and pour into pie shell. Bake for 45 to 55 minutes. Remove from oven, let cool slightly, and enjoy!

A Letter to Our Readers

Dear Readers:

In order that we might better contribute to your reading enjoyment, we would appreciate your taking a few minutes to respond to the following questions. When completed, please return to the following: Fiction Editor, Barbour Publishing, Inc., P.O. Box 719, Uhrichsville, OH 44683.

1. Did you enjoy reading *Louisiana Brides* by Kathleen Y'Barbo?
   - ❑ Very much—I would like to see more books like this.
   - ❑ Moderately—I would have enjoyed it more if _____

   _____

   _____

2. What influenced your decision to purchase this book? (Check those that apply.)
   - ❑ Cover ❑ Back cover copy ❑ Title ❑ Price
   - ❑ Friends ❑ Publicity ❑ Other

3. Which story was your favorite?
   - ❑ *Bayou Beginnings* ❑ *Bayou Secrets*
   - ❑ *Bayou Fever*

4. Please check your age range:
   - ❑ Under 18 ❑ 18–24 ❑ 25–34
   - ❑ 35–45 ❑ 46–55 ❑ Over 55

5. How many hours per week do you read? _____

Name _____

Occupation _____

Address _____

City _____ State _____ Zip _____

E-mail _____

If you enjoyed

Louisiana BRIDES

then read

Sugar and Grits

Southern Hospitality
Enriches Four Mississippi Romances

Mississippi Mud by DiAnn Mills
Not on the Menu by Martha Rogers
Gone Fishing by Janice Thompson
Falling for You by Kathleen Y'Barbo

Available wherever books are sold.
Or order from:
Barbour Publishing, Inc.
P.O. Box 721
Uhrichsville, Ohio 44683
www.barbourbooks.com

You may order by mail for $6.97 and add $3.00 to your order for shipping.
Prices subject to change without notice.
If outside the U.S. please call 740-922-7280 for shipping charges.

If you enjoyed

Louisiana BRIDES

then read

The Spinster Brides OF CACTUS CORNER

Four Women Make Orphans a Priority and Finally Open Doors to Romance

The Spinster and the Cowboy by Lena Nelson Dooley
The Spinster and the Lawyer by Jeri Odell
The Spinster and the Doctor by Frances Devine
The Spinster and the Tycoon by Vickie McDonough

Available wherever books are sold.
Or order from:
Barbour Publishing, Inc.
P.O. Box 721
Uhrichsville, Ohio 44683
www.barbourbooks.com

You may order by mail for $6.97 and add $3.00 to your order for shipping.
Prices subject to change without notice.
If outside the U.S. please call 740-922-7280 for shipping charges.

If you enjoyed

Louisiana BRIDES

then read

NEW HAMPSHIRE Weddings

by Rachel Hauck

Three Women's Stories of Longing for Something More

Lambert's Pride
Lambert's Code
Lambert's Peace

Available wherever books are sold.
Or order from:
Barbour Publishing, Inc.
P.O. Box 721
Uhrichsville, Ohio 44683
www.barbourbooks.com

You may order by mail for $6.97 and add $3.00 to your order for shipping.
Prices subject to change without notice.
If outside the U.S. please call 740-922-7280 for shipping charges.

If you enjoyed

Louisiana BRIDES

then read

TEXAS BRIDES

by Cathy Marie Hake

Three Gifts Lead Brothers to Romance in a New Country

To Love Mercy
To Walk Humbly
To Do Justice

Available wherever books are sold.
Or order from:
Barbour Publishing, Inc.
P.O. Box 721
Uhrichsville, Ohio 44683
www.barbourbooks.com

You may order by mail for $6.97 and add $3.00 to your order for shipping.
Prices subject to change without notice.
If outside the U.S. please call 740-922-7280 for shipping charges.

HEARTSONG
PRESENTS

If you love Christian romance...

$10.99

You'll love Heartsong Presents' inspiring and faith-filled romances by today's very best Christian authors. . .DiAnn Mills, Wanda E. Brunstetter, and Yvonne Lehman, to mention a few!

When you join Heartsong Presents, you'll enjoy four brand-new, mass market, 176-page books—two contemporary and two historical—that will build you up in your faith when you discover God's role in every relationship you read about!

Imagine. . .four new romances every four weeks—with men and women like you who long to meet the one God has chosen as the love of their lives. . .all for the low price of $10.99 postpaid.

To join, simply visit www.heartsongpresents.com or complete the coupon below and mail it to the address provided.

✂- -

YES! Sign me up for Hearts❤ng!

NEW MEMBERSHIPS WILL BE SHIPPED IMMEDIATELY!

Send no money now. We'll bill you only $10.99 postpaid with your first shipment of four books. Or for faster action, call 1-740-922-7280.

NAME _____

ADDRESS _____

CITY _____ STATE _____ ZIP _____

MAIL TO: HEARTSONG PRESENTS, P.O. Box 721, Uhrichsville, OH 44683
or sign up at WWW.HEARTSONGPRESENTS.COM